TALES OF THE TEAHOUSE RETOLD

with best wishes

Kathy 羊

Jan. 03

TALES OF THE TEAHOUSE RETOLD

Investiture of the Gods

Katherine Liang Chew

Writers Club Press
New York Lincoln Shanghai

Tales of the Teahouse Retold

Investiture of the Gods

Writers Club Press
an imprint of iUniverse, Inc.

For information address:
iUniverse, Inc.
2021 Pine Lake Road, Suite 100
Lincoln, NE 68512
www.iuniverse.com

ISBN: 0-595-25419-5 (pbk)
ISBN: 0-595-65161-5 (cloth)

Printed in the United States of America

Lovingly, to my husband Frank;

my children Francie, Kenneth, and Felix;

my grandchildren Alexa, Kathryn, and Patrick

CONTENTS

▼

Preface

This manuscript is based on my original translation from the Chinese of the book Feng Shen Yan Yi, *Investiture of the Gods*, published in China sometime during the Ming Dynasty (1368-1644). This book is of uncertain authorship. Although it has been attributed to many of the well-known scholars of the period, its actual authorship has never been verified. The tale was originally told in successive story-telling sessions as entertainment in teahouses; each day the narration would continue, but only after portions from previous days had been repeated. In rewriting the book, I have eliminated the repetition, but I have faithfully kept to the original style and ambience in retelling these tales from the teahouses.

The story is about how the Gods helped King Wu overthrow the Shang Dynasty (circa 1766-1122 BC), resulting in the founding of the Chou Dynasty (circa 1122-249 BC). The Shang Dynasty was the second earliest ruling house of China, and archeological evidence suggests these rulers were strong and cruel. The Chou Dynasty lasted 800 years and reached its zenith in the development of written history and philosophy with the writings of Confucius, Mencius, and Lao Tze, among others. These tales combine historical facts, folklore, mythology, and legends, as well as fantasy. They are tales of the time gods and men, beasts and monsters, and spirits and specters lived together on the earth and mingled with each other in peace and war.

The saga begins with King Zhou of Shang making offerings at the temple of the Snail Goddess, but he inadvertently offends her with a poem. In retribution, the Snail Goddess sends three specters to bewitch the king. These specters wreak havoc in the imperial court and disrupt the rule of the kingdom. Revolt and civil war ensue, with each side having a host of gods and other supernatural beings on its side. The chronicle ends when King Zhou of Shang kills himself in the fire, and King Wu of Chou enters the Shang capital triumphant. For their heroic deeds, many of the principals are invested as gods in heaven. The stories are filled with descriptions of the customs and daily life of the society and times. The accounts are populated with strange and magical characters whose deeds and powers are legendary and whose names resonate throughout Chinese literature.

In the matter of transliterating names, I use the new Pinyin system except in the case of Chou Dynasty, where I use the Wade system "Chou" instead of "Zhou" to avoid any confusion with "King Zhou". And I take literary license in many names, sometimes translating the "meaning", sometimes the "sound", and sometimes both. For example, the name "Huang Fei Hu" becomes "Yellow Flying Tiger;" "Nu Wa Niang Niang" becomes "Snail Goddess Nu Wa Niang Niang".

This book will be of interest to all who enjoy oriental mythology, philosophy, and literature. It is suitable for recreational reading as well as supplementary reading for students in the study of Chinese history and culture.

Introduction

This story is set in the misty, far distances of time four thousand years ago, before the Age of Bronze. It was a time of gods and men, of beasts and monsters, and of specters and spirits, all living together on this earth, and mingled with each other in peace and war.

The story tells of the forever glorious and mighty Supreme Jade Emperor of Heaven. He and he alone held the power to change man or beast into god. Those who were invested with such divine stature earned it honorably and well during their lifetimes in the world the gods called the Red Dust.

This ancient story speaks of humans the way the gods did, naming both males and females men, for theirs was the race of Man, not the race of Gods.

There were those among the race of Man who were men and yet above men, scholars of extraordinary knowledge and wisdom who cared nothing for power and wealth, and who feared not those who had it. The rules and laws of the kingdom did not bind such superior-men for such bonds were not needed. Their sense of right and wrong was as keen as the blast of the high icy winds of the mountains where they dwelt above the clouds. The world of Red Dust was far beneath them, yet ever they would heed its call and return to join combat with the forces of evil when evil threatened the good of all men.

This book tells of a king and queen, rulers of the Middle Kingdom. Pity the king, for it was he who became lost in his own power and turned tragically from his responsibility to kingdom and people. Of the queen, it can be said here that she was the king's first wife and ruled the kingdom with him. She, as the king's spouse, was duty-bound to be most virtuous, upright, intelligent and kind. By the laws of heaven and of earth, king and queen were to be as parents to their people.

Although the queen was first wife to the king, she was not the only wife. Many of the best women of the kingdom were chosen as wives of the king. They were known as concubines and were respected by all. They dwelt in palaces and imperial gardens, but in spite of the honor and respect they received, it was a grave misfortune to be chosen as a concubine. Once wedded to the king, concubines were completely isolated from both their families and the outside world. Parents knew not whether their cherished daughters sorrowed or joyed, sparkled in health or drooped in illness. To lose a daughter in this way was a great sadness and for this reason, many dukes and high officials hid the fact that they had daughters.

And there were many daughters in hiding for there were many dukes. These dukes ruled countries of their own, levying taxes, maintaining their own armies, and caring for their people, as any good rulers must. As great as was their power, they were all obligated to the king. Royal tribute was sent and any summons from the king was a command to be answered, whether it be with the duke's own presence before the king to speak of civil matters or whether it be with an army ready to join battle upon the king's order.

But business in the king's capital was mostly mundane. It began early each day at five o'clock in the dawn hours. It was then the king seated himself on his throne to receive officials, ministers, generals, counselors and masters. This daily ritual was necessary to the functioning of the kingdom and no king could neglect it.

While only high-ranking officials were permitted entry to the morning meetings, even the lowest of the king's subjects was permitted to beseech the king in matters that required his attention. For this purpose, a massive gong was set before the king's palace. One had only to strike the gong for permission to see the king. Such was never done lightly, for if the request was found unworthy, the gong beater lost the power to annoy the king further in unimportant matters by losing his head.

But perhaps we speak too long of men in setting out the beginnings of this tale, for there are specters in this story. Specters are spirits of great age, spirits of old, and time-marked animals and objects. Scoff not at the lore you have forgotten though it bides deep in your blood. In the days of our ancestors it was well known that objects were not without life. Do not your special treasures shine more brightly for your love of them? Do not those for which you have less favor dim and fade for lack of cherishing?

It was known then but now forgotten that specters were amoral. Specters knew neither morality nor immorality, and were without the sense of right and wrong that was common to both gods and men. One wish alone was theirs: that someday, the poor specter might gain the privilege of being reincarnated as human. This vulnerability allowed specters to be ordered about by the gods, for if the gods' orders were well-followed and the gods were pleased, a specter might win humanity. But amoral beings lack good judgment, and that lack could be disastrous for the whole world.

Believe these things, for they are true. They happened and they are set out here for you so that you may understand and learn. And believe also that all men who live in the Red Dust have three parts: spirit, soul, and body. Should the whole be rent asunder, the person becomes incomplete. An incomplete person cannot avoid trouble.

CHAPTER I

▼

KING ZHOU PAYS HOMAGE TO SNAIL GODDESS

The story began when Cheng Tang defeated King Jie of the Xia Dynasty, founding the Shang Dynasty. Many generations passed in peace and many kings ruled the land after the passing of Cheng Tang. After hundreds of years, the throne passed to Da Yi, who had three sons. The eldest of those was Wei Zi Qi and the second of those was Wei Zi Yan. This story is not about them. It is about the youngest son Wei Zi Shou, who was strong.

So strong was he that this story is told of him. Once he walked with his father King Da Yi in the Imperial Garden, a corner of a pavilion toppled. Third son Zi Shou reached out his arms and supported the pavilion roof with his bare strength while the column was replaced.

Witnessing this, Prime Minister Shang Rong, Grand Counselors Mei Bo and Zhao Qi and others of high rank among the ministers, spoke out saying it was a sign that the youngest son be chosen heir to the throne, for strength was needed to uphold the kingdom.

King Da Yi ruled thirty more years, but he was wise and forgot nothing. As he died, he instructed Grand Old Master Wen Zhong to crown Zi Shou king. It was done and Zi Shou became King Zhou and his great capital was the storied city, the magnificent Morning Song.

When the new king sat upon the throne, Grand Old Master Wen Zhong, most senior of officials, stood on the left side as befitted the head of all civil officials in the kingdom. His military counterpart, Prince Yellow Flying Tiger, Lord of National Security, stood on the right side of the throne.

Helping the new king in his reign was the beautiful and intelligent Queen Jiang who, as first wife, lived in the Central Palace. While Concubine Huang Shi resided in the Western Palace and Concubine Yang Shi dwelt in the Fragrant-Happiness Palace.

All the barbarians from the four corners and eight directions of the world paid homage to the Shang Dynasty and its new king. Under the new rule, as in the old, there was peace, prosperity and good harvests. All obeyed King Zhou for his rule was good and just; there was fairness in it for the people.

The land ruled by King Zhou was a mighty kingdom, so large that it required four Grand Dukes to administer it. Each grand duke commanded two hundred regional dukes and all of these pledged firm allegiance to the Shang Dynasty, as had those who ruled before them. In the Time of King Zhou, four great lords ruled as Grand Dukes and these were Jiang Huan Chu, Grand Duke of the East; E Chong Yu, Grand Duke of the South; Ji Chang, Grand Duke of the West and Chong Tiger Duke, Grand Duke of the North.

There was peace and prosperity throughout the kingdom until the Second Moon of the Spring in the Seventh Year of the Reign of King Zhou. On that day came a report that Duke Yuan Fu Tong and seventy-two of the regional dukes of the North Sea had taken arms against the dynasty in rebellion. North Sea Region was ruled by giants and monsters. Normally, Chong Tiger Duke should have been dispatched at once to put a speedy end to matters, but King Zhou hesitated. Warfare could cause great harm to the kingdom and wisdom was needed to avert danger. In particular, to fight these brute giants and monsters, military might alone would not be enough. Hoping to avert a far graver situation, King Zhou dispatched Grand Old Master Wen Zhong with an army at his command. It was King Zhou's hope that wisdom combined with strength would bring a swift peace.

It was not long thereafter that matters began to change.

*   *   *   *

King Zhou was hoping to end the morning report session early. The rebellion in the North Sea troubled him deeply and he also missed Wen Zhong sorely. He had relied so much on the Grand Old Master's advice, and many times he found himself wishing fervently for the presence of Wen Zhong to illuminate his thoughts. King Zhou sighed.

He ordered, "If there is any report, come forward and make it. If there is nothing to be discussed here, you may all return to your duties."

The words had barely been spoken when Prime Minister Shang Rong stepped before the throne and faced the king.

"Pardon me, sire," began Shang Rong in great earnestness, "but I must mention a most important matter to you. Tomorrow is the Fifteenth Day of the Third Moon of the year. I know you realize that is the date of Snail Goddess Nu Wa Niang Niang's birthday and you wish to honor her. It may be my failure, but I have heard nothing of plans to go and burn incense in her temple."

That was true indeed, King Zhou realized. There was good reason for it. He had quite forgotten the matter.

"What," asked King Zhou ritually, "has Snail Goddess Nu Wa Niang Niang done to deserve my homage?"

"The most virtuous and able Snail Goddess Nu Wa Niang Niang," began Shang Rong as he bowed his head in respect to goddess and sovereign alike, "is the daughter of the Supreme Jade Emperor of Heaven.

Her great service to us can never be forgotten. For when the notoriously ill-tempered god, Gong Gong Shi, became angered, he butted his head against Mount Bu Zhou. The power of his rage was such that the sky fell in the northwest and the earth quaked in the southeast. It was a time of terror and it was Snail Goddess Nu Wa Niang Niang who came to our aid. She forged the Five-colored stones and patched the sky where it was broken. Because these glorious stones were fashioned by the goddess herself, they have brought us good seasonal rains and winds. These have eliminated droughts and insects and since that time we have harvested crops which put all before them to shame."

"This is true," responded King Zhou. "The goddess has done tremendous good for the people."

"They have been most grateful to her, sire," said Shang Rong. "It was they who built her temple here in Morning Song so she could be worshipped in honor. I know you are a busy man with many pressing matters which require your attention. But think of your people, sire. It is for their sake that you should visit the temple and burn incense."

"So be it," said King Zhou. "Issue my edict that I will burn incense to Snail Goddess Nu Wa Niang Niang in honor of her birthday and let all be made ready."

King Zhou gave the matter little thought that day and even less as he mounted his chariot the next morning to lead the procession to the temple. It might have been better for all had he paused to reflect. It might have been even better for all had he not gone at all.

But the day was clear and golden, and the smell of incense was sweet. Banners and decorations flew from every door and window. The eight hundred members of the Palace Guard and their brave leader, Prince Yellow Flying Tiger, marched stalwartly as they led the procession through the streets of the great city. The coats of the horses gleamed as they pulled the shining chariots of the civil and military officials. All was pageantry, all was beauty, and the faces of the people smiled and their hearts were filled with pride.

It was not long before the procession arrived at the temple and King Zhou dismounted from his chariot and carefully placed his burning incense into the urns. Then he knelt, as did all his high officials, to pay respect to the goddess who was daughter of the Supreme Jade Emperor of Heaven.

All ceremonial matters attended to, King Zhou found himself somewhat curious about the temple itself. He had never examined it closely before. As he strolled through it, he was impressed by the loving work it had been given. A gentle breeze seemed to always play about so that no area was too hot, nor was it too cool. As King Zhou searched for the source of the breeze, a sudden draft blew aside the curtain which cloaked Nu Wa Niang Niang's idol from prying mortal eyes.

King Zhou should have averted his eyes in respect for the privacy of the goddess. He did not. He stared and drew in his breath with a loud gasp. Never had he seen such a woman! Her beauty put all heaven to shame and her form and figure made the moon dim and the sun fade. Zhou's eyes were dazed and now he could not tear away his gaze.

If Grand Old Master Wen Zhong had been there, he might have been quick enough of wit to whisper the warning of the old proverb: When a nation is in good condition, the omens are always good; when there is something unholy, a nation's fate declines.

But Wen Zhong was in the North Sea and the warning went unspoken.

As King Zhou's stunned eyes caressed the idol of Nu Wa Niang Niang with a mortal's gaze, his soul and spirit deserted him, torn from his body by a flood of lust.

"I am the Son of Heaven," King Zhou's tortured whisper came. "I and I alone, own the four seas, the six imperial residences, three palaces and all that inhabit these places. But I have not seen such beauty in any of these places."

Blinded by lust, King Zhou called loudly for writing instruments. Frightened attendants scurried to provide what the king demanded.

Eagerly King Zhou grasped the brush and feverishly he began to inscribe a poem on the temple's wall as Shang Rong watched in horror.

> *Behind the phoenix curtains hides great beauty,*
> *It is only the skillful fashioning of clay and gold.*
> *Framed in curves by faraway green mountains,*
> *Framed by the fluttery of a dancer's gown.*
> *It is the beauty of pear blossoms in gentle rain,*
> *It is the glory of a brilliant peony in the mist.*
> *Should it come alive,*
> *It would accompany me to my palace."*

"Oh sire, please," Shang Rong's voice was full of fear. "Nu Wa Niang Niang is an ancient goddess. Always she has been a true benefactor of our people. I am a humble person unworthy to order you in any matter. But I respectfully request that you have that poem washed off the wall before it is seen by anyone. It is blasphemy. It is disrespect and violation. If…if even the populace see it, they will believe that their king is without virtue."

"Nonsense!" King Zhou roared. "Have I not seen the face of Nu Wa? Her beauty is incredible. I praise her with my poetry. There will be no further words from you!"

Shang Rong trembled in fear and could not speak.

"I am the owner of ten thousand chariots," King Zhou spoke more softly now. "I leave this poem for all the kingdom to see. It is my legacy to them and the beauty of Nu Wa."

So saying, King Zhou swept out of the temple and mounted his chariot. The trip back was made in silence. No official, however powerful, dared to speak, so great was their fear.

*   *   *   *

It was not long thereafter that Snail Goddess Nu Wa Niang Niang returned from her visit to the Fire-Cloud Palace where she had been paying her respects to the Three Supreme Sage Kings, Fu Xi, Yan Di and the Yellow Emperor. She smiled as she descended from her Green Phoenix Chariot. Her step was light as she seated herself on her throne and her Golden Boys and Jade Maidens bowed before her and spoke to her of matters of interest between them.

As they left, Nu Wa Niang Niang's eyes fell upon King Zhou's blasphemous poem. Her scream of outrage echoed through the temple.

"How dare the depraved Zi Shou who is called King Zhou vilify me with filth! There is no pardon for this. Six hundred years ago the Shang Dynasty was founded. Today it shall end in payment for such foulness!"

It was a raging Nu Wa who summoned her servant boy Green Cloud and bade him to bring forth her chariot. Her rage did not abate as she sped earthward toward the palace. She was poised to strike death as King Zhou's two sons Yin Jiao and Yin Hong bowed before the throne to show their honor to the king their father. The glory of their futures went unseen by mortal eyes, but there was warning here to halt the vengeance of a goddess. Two fiery bolts of red light shot upward toward the throw of destruction, Nu Wa drew back her arm. Startled, Nu Wa raised a question and the response was swift. King Zhou's destiny was already set by Heaven and none dare change it. Twenty-eight more years would he rule and no less for any cause.

Nu Wa knew that she must return without revenge. But still, she vowed silently, there were things she could and would do.

Once back in her temple, Nu Wa seated herself upon her throne and summoned the servant Colorful Cloud, who placed the Golden Gourd at Nu Wa's feet. Nu Wa opened the Gourd and pointed her finger at it.

A towering white light, full fifty feet or more in height flashed upward into the air. Atop it flew the multi-hued Summoning Flag of the Specters. It shone with all the thousands of the colors of the rainbow which are forever invisible to mortal eyes. There followed immediate gusts of wind and gathering of mists that came at once from all directions. Behind the flows of mist were drawn all of the specters under heaven. In silence, they crowded the broad plaza in front of the temple.

"Dismiss all but for those three who reside in the Tomb of the Yellow Emperor," ordered Nu Wa.

Colorful Cloud obeyed swiftly.

Soon the Thousand-Year Vixen, the Nine-Headed Pheasant, and the Fat-Belly Guitar Jade Pipa entered Nu Wa's throne room. "Long life, oh powerful Niang Niang!" they cried as they knelt before her throne.

"My order to you is secret and you will listen well," Nu Wa Niang Niang intoned. "The luck Cheng Tang won six hundred years ago is dimming. I speak to you of a new mandate of heaven which sets the destiny for all. You three are to enter King Zhou's palace, where you will bewitch him. Whatever you do, do not harm anyone else. If you do my bidding, and do it well, you will be permitted to reincarnate as human beings."

No sooner had Nu Wa's words been spoken, than the three specters turned into a breeze and vanished. Words, borne on the murmur of that wind, floated in the air. The voice of the ancient vixen was heard to say: "The vixen obeys. Her charm will cut short Cheng Tang's six hundred year reign."

And somewhere in the city, the words of a poem came unbidden to the mind of a drowsing poet.

> Burning incense in the middle of the Third Moon,
> In the writing of one poem there is unexpected ruin.
> He who knew how to express his proud poetry,
> Did not expect the end of his dynasty.

*   *   *   *

But it was not poetry which occupied the mind of King Zhou as he tossed restlessly in his bed each night. Thoughts of Nu Wa Niang Niang burned within him. He could not sleep. He could not eat. It was Nu Wa Niang Niang he thought of day and night. He could no longer bear the sight of any of the women who had once delighted him. He was a starving man and they were rice of dirt and soup of dust. They did not slake his desire and he cared for nothing because of it. His miseries knew no bounds. Yet still he kept to the daily ritual of his early morning reception of his ministers. But it was obvious to all in attendance that King Zhou paid no heed to what was said and done there.

This caused Fei Zhong and You Hun to become even more bold than they had dared since the departure of the Grand Old Master. The flattery and tricks of the two Middle Counselors knew no limits. Their flowery language would have pained King Zhou in former days. But in his present state of mind, such flattery impressed him and made him prone to grant whatever favors the two requested.

After many restless nights and intolerable days, King Zhou could no longer withstand the need to communicate his troubles with those he felt would understand them. Fei Zhong and You Hun came immediately to his thoughts. He summoned them to his side after the morning session had ended.

"My friends, when I went to Nu Wa's temple to burn incense, I saw her idol quite by chance," King Zhou came swiftly to the point. "Her beauty is matchless and unforgettable. Now I can no longer stand the sight of what I have in my palaces and residences. I know that you both have my best interests at heart. What should I do?"

"Sire," soothed Fei Zhong. "Why are you troubled?"

"Aye, why indeed, oh mighty one?" agreed You Hun.

"You are the owner of ten thousand chariots," continued Fei Zhong. "You are the owner of the treasures of the four seas and your virtues rival the two Sage Kings, Yao and Shun. Why should you worry when whatever that is under the skies is yours by right? You need new and beautiful women to comfort you, to distract you from this infatuation with the image of a goddess. Tomorrow you can issue an edict to your four Grand Dukes. Tell them to order each regional duke to send a great beauty from his region for your pleasure."

"Once this is done," You Hun said with a laugh, "will you still worry about having enough beauty to select from?"

King Zhou smiled as he realized the simplicity of this solution.

"Perfect my friends. You have, in fact, spoken my own mind. I will issue that edict tomorrow."

CHAPTER 2

▼

SU HU REBELS AGAINST SHANG

Next day, during the morning assembly, King Zhou sent out his edict to his four Grand Dukes, ordering them to inform each of their two hundred regional dukes to select one hundred beauties from each region for the king's service. It did not matter whether they were high or low born, rich or poor. But they must be beautiful, and with pleasing personalities and mild temperament.

Before the Son of Heaven finished his order, someone stepped out from the left to kneel before him.

"Sire! Your faithful servant the Prime Minister Shang Rong would like to comment on your edict to the Grand Dukes.

"In your palaces are your Queen, and two concubines. In addition, there are more than one thousand young beautiful women in your service. Why all of a sudden do you desire to have even more thousands of new beauties? I am afraid your people would not stand for it.

"When a ruler takes his people's happiness and sorrow as his own, his people will do the same by taking the ruler's happiness and sorrow as theirs. By taking their daughters away from them you would create much sorrow to many families!

"Right now, there are frequent floods and droughts, and the rebellion in the North Sea is still raging on. How can you think of new, beautiful women?

"The ancient Sage King Yao and King Shun, shared their people's happiness and sorrow, guided their people with their pure virtues. Thus for them they found stars shining, precious dew falling, phoenix visiting their courts and magic mushrooms growing in the wild. Passengers on the road yielded their right-of-way to each other, and no dog needed to bark. Rain came at night and sun shone in the day. Rice plants sprouted double blooms. Yes, indeed, those were times of prosperity and peace.

"I have been Prime Minister, serving three kings of the Shang Dynasty. I cannot help but point out your folly! I do realize that I may have hurt your feelings by saying it as it is; you may punish me as you see fit. But the truth of the matter must be addressed."

King Zhou was angered that Shang Rong dared to criticize him. But on second thought, the king recalled Shang Rong had been invested by the late King Da Yi with the privilege to criticize and the immunity from punishment for such actions.

"You are right, Shang Rong. I retract my edict!" King Zhou grudgingly said after a moment of reflection.

*   *   *   *

In the summer of the eighth year of King Zhou's reign, the four Grand Dukes led their regional dukes to King Zhou's Capital City, Morning Song, to renew their pledges of allegiance and to pay their respect to King Zhou.

The four Grand Dukes were:

Jiang Huan Chu, The Grand Duke of the East in the Eastern Lu State, and the father of Queen Jiang;

E Chong Yu, The Grand Duke of the South;
Ji Chang, the Grand Duke of the West; and
Chong Tiger Duke, the Grand Duke of the North.

It seemed that all important personages had gathered at the Imperial Capital. That is, all except the Grand Old Master Wen Zhong, who was still tied down in the troubled North Sea.

*   *   *   *

It was common knowledge in the Imperial Capital that the two most powerful, but also the most unscrupulous and greedy, officials were Middle Counselors Fei Zhong and You Hun. They were King Zhou's favorites. The visiting dukes were fully aware that if ever they needed anything done on time, or simply to get anything done at all, they had better send some substantial gifts to these two rascals! In fact, everyone sent them gifts as a sort of insurance.

Among the regional dukes was Su Hu, the Duke of Ji Region who was known as a straight-forward and upright person with fiery temper. In his own region of Ji, all wrong doings were dealt with strictly according to the law of the land, no excuses were ever accepted. How would he know of such dubious matters as bribery? Thus Su Hu had incurred the deep malice of Fei Zhong and You Hun.

On New Year's Day, King Zhou came early as usual to the morning assembly to meet his officials. The Keeper of the Noon Gate reported:

"Sire. This is the year when all the dukes of the kingdom are to pay their tributes and renew their allegiance to you and the Shang Dynasty. They are gathered at the Noon Gate, sending their respects and awaiting your order."

King Zhou asked Prime Minister Shang Rong what should be done.

Shang Rong said, "Your Majesty may want to see only the four Grand Dukes to inquire about the affairs of their regions, and to praise their good work. All the regional dukes can simply send in their respects from the Noon Gate."

The four Grand Dukes, in their full morning court regalia with jade ornaments waving softly from their belts, entered the Noon Gate, walked over the Nine Dragon Bridge, and came to King Zhou's Throne-room and knelt before the king.

King Zhou said, "You have taken good care of the backward regions of the kingdom. You have done wonderfully well in educating the people, treating them with kindness and justice. You have won their respects and allegiance for Shang. We are very pleased."

Replied the Grand Duke of the East for all the Grand Dukes, "We are grateful that Your Majesty granted us these high positions and have confidence in us. We are trying to do our best. However, from time to time, we do have doubts whether we are capable of carrying out all your wishes. When we do a good job, it is only our duty. We would never dare to expect praise from you, but we do appreciate it very much."

The Son of Heaven beamed with great pleasure. He ordered Prime Minister Shang Rong and Vice Prime Minister Prince Bi Gan to entertain these four grand dukes with a banquet in the Great Happiness Hall.

The king left his Throne-room and went directly to his Informal Hall. His two favorites, Fei Zhong and You Hun, were already there waiting for him.

The king said, "The other day my edict to the dukes to send me new beauties was aborted by Prime Minister Shang Rong. What do you say if I see each of the dukes while they are here and give them my order individually?"

Fei Zhong said, "Sire. Last time Your Majesty acquiesced in Shang Rong's request, it showed the country how enlightened and virtuous you are. Now if you change your mind, I am afraid the populace would be very disappointed.

"However, I heard that Su Hu, the Duke of Ji Region has a very beautiful daughter whose beauty rivals the heavenly fairies. She could serve Your Majesty very well. Moreover, with just one woman, it will not trouble the kingdom or be noticed by the populace."

"Send for the Duke of Ji immediately!" King Zhou ordered.

Su Hu went directly to see the king.

The king said, "We heard you have a beautiful daughter; we want her to serve in our palace. You will then become a relation of the king, enjoy great wealth from the national treasury, and keep your noble position as the Duke of Ji forever. Your prosperity will be permanent, and your prestige will spread to the four seas, and envied by all under heaven."

Su Hu replied respectfully, "Sire, your humble servant is honored by your praise of his little girl. However, the fact is that his daughter is a very sickly child. Besides being rather homely, she has low intelligence and coarse manners. She has nothing worthy of Your Majesty's attention.

"Inside your palaces from the queen down to the concubines and maids, there are no less than a thousand souls. All are with matchless beauty, poise and intelligence. Are they not enough to please Your Majesty? Why then let yourself succumb to the treacherous plans of the unscrupulous small men who have nothing in their mind but to enrich themselves?"

The king laughed, "You don't know what you are saying! From the beginning of antiquity, is there a father who does not wish his daughter to marry well? When your daughter becomes one of my concubines, you will become a royal kinsman and enjoy the admiration and riches of high position. What more can one desire? Think about it. Don't be so stupid."

Su Hu felt trapped and was beside himself. In a terrible rage, he said to the king, "I know that when a king takes care of the administration of his kingdom, his people will happily pledge their allegiance to him, and the national treasury will be forever full.

"King Jie of Xia lost his mandate of heaven because he indulged in wine and women, neglecting his administration. And that was when your ancestors, who were upright and virtuous, won the hearts of the people and the mandate of Heaven, defeated the Xia, and founded the Shang Dynasty. The country has enjoyed prosperity and peace ever since.

"Instead of emulating your own ancestors, Your Majesty seems to be copying King Jie of Xia! This is a clear sign of decadence! Under you the six hundred glorious years of Shang might as well be finished!"

King Zhou exploded, "When a king summons, no one dares to delay. When a king says die, no one dares to live. Now we merely want your daughter to be a concubine, how dare you behave so ungratefully? How dare you use such rude words accusing me of terminating my dynasty! Take him out to the Noon Gate and down with his head!"

Su Hu was immediately seized by the Palace Guards.

At this very moment, Middle Counselors Fei Zhong and You Hun said to the king, "Sire. You are absolutely right to have Su Hu beheaded when he dares to speak to Your Majesty in such rude manner. However, it would not sound good when it becomes known that Su Hu is killed because he refused Your Majesty his daughter. It would give cause for your people to think that Your Majesty put more importance on beautiful women than on loyal officials.

"Why not let him go back to his Ji Region now? He will be so grateful to be alive, he will present his daughter to you willingly.

"In that event, you not only get your beauty, but your good will would be known to all under Heaven. You will kill two birds with one stone."

"All right. Let Su Hu go. He must leave the City Morning Song immediately without delay!" The king shouted.

*   *   *   *

Su Hu returned to his hostel and recounted the outrageous events. Some of his officials said, "When a ruler is not just, his ministers seek a better ruler. Now King Zhou prefers beauty to the loyalty and the ability of his officials, it is a clear signal of the coming of anarchy and doom of the reign. It is time for us to look for greener pastures, a better ruler, so that we may keep our ancestral shrine intact."

Su Hu was in a very vulnerable mood and readily agreed to their suggestion. They left the Imperial Capital, Morning Song, immediately.

When they passed by the Noon Gate, Su Hu said, "A gentleman does not do things covertly!"

He called for his writing instruments and wrote on the wall of the Noon Gate what was in his mind.

> *The Three Principles [1] have been broken by the ruler.*
> *The five relationships [2] exist no longer.*
> *I, Su Hu of Ji, will not honor*
> *The Court of Shang ever!*

*   *   *   *

King Zhou was still quite upset by Su Hu's refusal when a Guard official of Noon Gate came in with a copy of Su Hu's writing on the Noon Gate Wall.

The writing so infuriated the king, he bellowed, "Impudent traitor! I will personally lead six army divisions to annihilate him!"

The king summoned his generals and told them, "Su Hu rebels against the Shang Dynasty. No retribution is too harsh for him. Each of you lead two hundred thousand men and horses ahead, I will follow with six army divisions."

General Honest Hero thought, "Su Hu's loyalty to the court has never been questioned before. What had he done to incur the king's wrath to this degree? If King Zhou goes to Ji, it will be the end of Ji."

To the king, General Honest Hero said, "Sire, we are so sorry to hear that Su Hu has offended Your Majesty. He must be punished. However, for such a simple matter, Your Majesty need not be bothered to go there yourself. The four Grand Dukes are still in the Capital. Why not simply let them lead a regiment or two to capture Su Hu?"

The king asked, "Which of the Grand Dukes can best do the job?"

Fei Zhong said, "Ji Region belongs to the Grand Duke of the North. This would be Tiger Duke's business."

Again, General Honest Hero thought, "Tiger Duke is known to be a witless, greedy, and ruthless brute. Letting him lead this expedition will bring untold grief and harm to the populace along the way. And on top of that, what will happen to Ji Region will be unthinkable."

He said to the king, "Sire. It is true that Ji Region belongs to the Grand Duke of the North. However, Tiger Duke's prestige is not yet widely known. He may not quite qualify for such a grave campaign.

"On the other hand, the Grand Duke of the West is known throughout the nation. If you give him your Imperial Battle Axe to represent your authority, this mission will be carried out in short order."

The king pondered for a long time, then granted the suggestion.

*   *   *   *

The four Grand Dukes were still at the banquet with Prime Minister Shang Rong and Vice Prime Minister Prince Bi Gan when the king's messenger brought the king's edict to both the Grand Duke of the North and the Grand Duke of the West. The Imperial Battle Axe was given to Ji Chang, the Grand Duke of the West.

Grand Duke of the West conferred with Prime Minister Shang Rong and Vice Prime Minister Prince Bi Gan and said, "We know Su Hu is a very loyal person, has won many battles for the Shang Dynasty. And as far as we know since Su Hu arrived in the Capital, he has not been summoned by the king. Then what is this accusation of 'insulting the king, and the writings on the Noon Gate wall' about?

"Please investigate. If the crime bears out, we will certainly do as the king requested. Otherwise, we must stop the king!"

Tiger Duke interrupted, "The king's words are like silk, once out of the silkworm it can never be put back. It is an edict. How dare we not obey? If the king said Su Hu wrote on the Noon Gate wall, it must be so. Why else would the king have said so? If we doubt the king's words, all eight hundred regional dukes would follow suit. What kind of law and order would we have?"

Grand Duke of the West said, "Yes, my dear brother Tiger Duke, you are absolutely correct. However, as we all know, Su Hu is a most loyal, upright gentleman, clean of spirit, and pure of heart. He treats his people wisely with benevolence, trains his army by the law and always with justice. All these years he has not made a mistake. We don't know to whom the king listened to in this possibly trumped up charge. It is not an auspicious sign for a nation to have these kinds of happenings.

"Affairs of soldiery are bad. Routes passed by the army will be disturbed; populace will be belabored; the national treasury will be over-taxed. To start a war without just cause is not an act a ruler should entertain."

Tiger Duke said, "What you said is fine with me. But you don't seem to realize what the king wants to do, or compelled to do, given what Su Hu had done. Besides, who dares not obey the king's edict?"

"Very well, Tiger Duke," The Grand Duke of the West said. "Please lead your army and go ahead. I will follow you without delay."

Grand Duke of the West then said to Prime Minister Shang Rong and Vice Prime Minister Prince Bi Gan privately that he had to let Tiger Duke go ahead, but the Grand Duke of the West himself would go back to his own region, the Western Foothills of Mount Singing Phoenix, for a while before joining Tiger Duke.

Early the next day, Tiger Duke led his army out of the Capital City, Morning Song.

[Note: In this historical tale, the Western Foothills was a geographic name given to a region in northwest China that included both the topographic foothills and the mountainous land beyond. The region included Mount Golden Rooster, Mount Swallow, Mount Singing Phoenix, and Mount First Sun. With Phoenix City as its capital, the Western Foothills was the territorial base of the Grand Duke of the West, who founded the Chou dynasty.]

*   *   *   *

Su Hu arrived home with his entourage. He told his ministers and generals of the unfortunate events in the Capital City which led them to come home in such great hurry.

"At this very moment, no doubt King Zhou is getting ready to annihilate us. Keep your men and horses in readiness. Pile enough stones and rocks around the city walls for the use of the catapults. Check our granaries and water wells to make sure that our people will not suffer when the city is under a long siege."

*   *   *   *

Meanwhile, Tiger Duke led fifty thousand men and horses and rushed towards the Ji Region.

Cannons were booming in the sky, gongs were shaking the earth. The booming cannons sounded like Spring Thunder, earth-shaking gongs sounded like thunder clashing down from a ten thousand foot cliff. Flags were flying in the Third Spring Willow Wind, and the ribbons of the bugles were fluttering like Seven-Colored-Cloud covering the moon. The glint of the battle knives was like the silver of deep winter snow, the swords like a forest in the September frost covering the ground. Murderous atmospherics filled the air like red clouds covering the green willow shore. Like ten miles of rolling waves, a mountain of soldiers suddenly sprang out of the earth.

After many days on the road, passing through cities and villages, the forward scouts reported to Tiger Duke that they were inside the Ji Region.

Tiger Duke ordered to make camp.

In the east, the golden guns were like rush plants; in the south, flowery axes arranged in the shape of a crescent moon; in the west, broad battle knives, bridles and saddles; and in the north, bows and arrows. At the center was the headquarters for the staff of Strategic Planning. The killing air permeated forty miles into the surroundings.

Su Hu's scout reported that Tiger Duke's troops had made camp inside the Ji Region. Su Hu was incensed. Had it been the army of any other Grand Duke, there might still be a chance to explain things. But the Tiger Duke's!

Su Hu decided to meet Tiger Duke head on. He ordered his men to go out the city walls for an offensive.

The Ji army was ready. The cannon sounded, and the air of killing filled the sky. The Ji generals stood in one line at the opening of the city gate.

Su Hu bellowed to Tiger Duke's army, "Have your commanding general out here to justify his coming to Ji!"

Tiger Duke, outfitted in his Flying Phoenix helmet, golden armors, and bright red robe with a jade belt, was on his purple fat horse, his big broad knife resting on the saddle. He led his troops out of the camp. Two columns of flags and dragons and phoenix banners fluttered in the wind. Bringing up the rear was Tiger Duke's son, Chong Young Tiger.

Su Hu bent his body in salute and said, "How is the Tiger Duke? Please forgive me for not giving a full salute. I am hindered by my full armor. My duty is to guard the borders of the kingdom. Why is my good duke here to declare war on me?"

Tiger Duke said angrily, "You taunted the Son of Heaven by writing a rebellious poem on the wall of the Noon Gate. That is treason! No punishment is severe enough! You should have come out of your city on your knees. Instead, you are trying to use flowery language and arguments to confuse the issue while carrying your weapon and in full armor! Don't ever think that you can resist the Imperial order!"

Tiger Duke shouted his order to capture Su Hu. A general, riding on a green chestnut stallion, wearing a Phoenix's Wing helmet, golden armor, bright red robe with a lion-head belt, rushed toward Su Hu, shouting, "I will capture this rebel!"

On Su Hu's side, his son Su Total Loyal, shook his spear and shouted, "Wait a minute!" Total Loyal recognized that the man he was confronting was General Mei Wu.

Mei Wu said, "Su Total Loyal! You, father and son, are committing a capital crime! You know the king's army can very easily overwhelm your region and destroy your ancestral shrine!"

Total Loyal spurred his horse, aimed his spear and rushed toward Mei Wu as Mei Wu rushed toward Total Loyal with his axe.

The two generals faced each other on the battle field, amid earth-shaking drumming. Soldiers helped with their knives here and there, but who was who was difficult for the eyes to follow. Here came the axe, blocked by the spear, one round after another. Who was losing and who was winning no one could tell. After twenty rounds, back and forth, Total Loyal's spear hit Mei Wu who fell to the ground!

Su Hu and his generals joined in the fight.

Blood formed a stream, and bodies were everywhere!

Tiger Duke, and his son, Young Tiger, and his generals, were forced to retreat to ten miles beyond Su Hu's city walls.

Winning the battle, Su Hu ordered the beating of the gong to call back his pursuing troops. Su Hu sent rewards to his victorious army and said to them, "We won a big battle today. However, we expect the king would send out more men and horses for revenge. Ji is in great danger. Any suggestions?"

General Zhao Bing said, "Indeed, the war has just begun. By our defeating Tiger Duke, who represents the king, we are directly rebuking the king. The king will now send more troops, perhaps even all the

Grand Dukes with their armies. Trying to fight such a force is like eggs trying to shatter a rock. The outcome is obvious. But we have no option but to fight to the finish!

"We should take advantage of Tiger Duke's new loss. They are only ten miles away. If we plan right, we can surprise them in their camp and wipe them out! After that, we can seek a better ruler. Only then can we expect to keep our ancestral shrine intact."

Su Hu and all other generals agreed. Su Hu ordered his son Total Loyal to lead three thousand men and horses for this mission. They were to go west to the Five Hills village, and wait there to ambush Tiger Duke's retreating army. Su Hu himself would take the central position, General Chen Jizhen would take the left flank while General Zhao Bing the right flank. All were to wait for the evening cannon signal.

*   *   *   *

Thinking only of his strong army, Tiger Duke never gave second thoughts as to whether his military action was just or not. But little did he think he would encounter such strong resistance and shameful defeat. He was remorseful and very depressed.

He said to his generals, "I have been fighting for thirty years; never have I failed on any battle ground. But today, I lost my best general Mei Wu and almost all my soldiers. What now?"

A general comforted him, saying, "Don't you remember winning and losing a battle is common in a war? The Grand Duke of the West will come soon with his army. Then to annihilate Ji Region is as easy as turning your own hand. Please take it easy."

> *Tiger Duke took his army on a long campaign,*
> *Camping inside the Ji Region were his beasts and men.*
> *Fifty thousand troops killed or maimed,*
> *Left the famous warrior nothing but empty fame.*

*   *   *   *

Covertly, Su Hu and his generals led their men and horses out of the city, took their assigned positions, and waited for the evening signal.

Boom! The sky fell and the earth quaked! With great shouts Su Hu's three thousand iron troops rushed into Tiger Duke's camp.

Caught by surprise in the dark, Tiger Duke's men were so terrified that they ran here and there, completely losing their orientation. Guns and knives, spears and axes were everywhere. No one was sure who was who and what was what. One heard only the clang, clung of weapons in contact, and the moans and groans of the wounded and the dying.

Tiger Duke's men had no time to put on their armor. The officers in front were without horses while the others were barefoot on horses without saddles. Executioners were three in the east and four in the west, as wild horses rampaged south and north. The attacking generals were like ferocious tigers and the attacking soldiers were like a long dragon, chopping arms, legs, and bodies with their knives, axes, and spears. Blood and flesh flew in all directions. Men and horses collided, with no way to distinguish friend from foe. Screams from the wounded filled the air while the corpses of men and horses piled mountain high!

Caught by surprise, awakened by the shouts of his guards, Tiger Duke jumped out of his bed, put on his clothes, got on his fat horse and rushed out. In the light of the camp fire, he saw Su Hu on a green stallion, wearing golden armor, golden helmet, bright red robe with a jade belt, and carrying a Fire Dragon spear.

Su Hu shouted, "Tiger Duke, no way you can run away! Get off your fat horse for our capture!"

So saying, Su Hu lifted his spear and rushed toward Tiger Duke. Tiger Duke met Su Hu with his broad knife in fierce combat.

Suddenly Tiger Duke's son, Young Tiger, appeared with General Jin Kuai and General Huang Yuanji to help Tiger Duke. Su Hu's General, Zhao Bing, from the left and General Chen Jizhen from the right immediately joined in the fight.

Su Hu and his men had the advantage of a planned attack while Tiger Duke and his men were unprepared: in readiness and determination each of Su Hu's men was the equal of ten of Tiger Duke's.

The sky suddenly brightened as Tiger Duke's supplies caught fire and flamed up.

In no time, Tiger Duke's General, Jin Kuai, was cut down by Su Hu's General, Zhao Bing. Seeing the deteriorating situation, Tiger Duke started to run. His son, Young Tiger followed, fighting a rear-guard action.

Father and son, together, ran and ran like dogs having lost their home or fish escaping from a net. They ran and ran, not caring or knowing where.

Su Hu's men had chased Tiger Duke for about twenty miles when Su Hu ordered a beating of the gong to stop the chase and return to their city. They had won a total victory.

Tiger Duke and his son and their defeated remnant trudged on, his Generals, Huang Yuanji and Sun Zi Yu caught up with them.

Tiger Duke spoke to them from his fat horse, "Ever since I have led an army, I have never suffered such defeat. How are we to take revenge? Moreover, I think the Grand Duke of the West is disobeying the king in not sending his troops, but sitting pretty to see who may win. Oh, how I hate that fox!"

Young Tiger said to his father, "My father, don't be discouraged. Let us sit tight and rest for a few days and regroup. Meanwhile you can send a letter to Ji Chang at Western Foothills of Mount Singing Phoenix, urging him to rush his troops to help."

Tiger Duke said, "Yes, my son. We will regroup tomorrow. I am so tired right now."

Before Tiger Duke could finish his sentence, there was a sudden cannon boom and the shouts of people.

"Tiger Duke, come down from your fat horse for capture!"

Tiger Duke and his men turned and in the dim moonlight, saw a young man with a face round and fair like an open moon, whose lips were so red and beautiful you might think he painted them. His hair, tied in a pony-tail fashion on top of his head by a gold ring, held two lyre bird feathers. His forehead was covered by a gold wreath. He was wearing a bright red robe and a golden chain belt. His horse had a silver bridle.

It was Su Hu's son, Total Loyal, coming out of his ambush, shouting, "Tiger Duke! I have my father's order to capture you. Come down from your fat horse and put down your weapon!"

Tiger Duke was furious and shouted back, "You young punk! How dare you! The king's army will come soon to annihilate you. Capture this puppy!"

General Huang Yuanji rushed out with his knife straight for Total Loyal.

The two generals fought a great battle. As there was no way to tell who was winning, another of Tiger Duke's Generals, Sun Zi Yu rushed out to join the fight. Uttering a loud cry, Total Loyal speared General Sun Zi Yu to the ground.

While fencing off others, Total Loyal concentrated on Tiger Duke and knocked his breast armor plate askew. Alarmed, Tiger Duke turned his fat horse and rushed away from the fight. Young Tiger saw this, and hesitated. Just then Total Loyal speared him in his left arm. As blood oozed through his armor, he almost fell from his horse. The others rushed to his rescue and they got away.

Total Loyal would have loved to pursue. But with the moon now gone, he was afraid he might get lost in the darkness of the night. So he returned with his men to the city.

At dawn, Total Loyal reported to his father, who said, "My son had done right. But he got off too easy, that bully!"

Notes

1. The Three Principles of Social Order are Ruler-Subjects, Father-Children, and Husband-Wife.

2. The Five Cardinal Human Relationships are kindness, justice, good manners, wisdom, and honesty.

CHAPTER 3

▼

JI CHANG COMES TO SU HU'S RESCUE

Wounded in both pride and flesh, Tiger Duke and his son, Young Tiger, ran all night for their lives. When daylight came, Tiger Duke inspected his tattered army. He was saddened to see that only one out of every ten had survived, and even some of these were heavily wounded.

General Huang Yuanji said, "My Lord. Why so grim? Winning and losing a battle is such common affair in a war. Last night we lost in a sneak attack. We can rest for a few days and regroup. Meanwhile, send a messenger to the Grand Duke of the West, urging him to rush his troop to our rescue. Let him vanquish Su Hu and we will get our revenge."

Tiger Duke was silent for a long while. Then he said, "Ji Chang is holding his army, waiting to see who wins and who loses. If I ask him to help now, it would be too easy for him to get away from his crime of disobeying the King's Order!"

As he was contemplating, scout reported that a big army was approaching. Tiger Duke was so frightened his soul and spirit left his body, hanging in the air of fear!

Hurriedly he mounted his fat horse. Then he took a closer look at the approaching army. He saw between the two columns of banners a general who had a red beard, thick white eyebrows, and eyes like two golden bells with a face as black as the bottom of a kettle. The black face general wore a Nine-Cloud-Burning-Flame helmet, golden chain mail armor, bright red robe and a white jade belt. He was riding a golden-eyed beast and holding two golden axes.

With relief Tiger Duke recognized his younger brother, Black Tiger, the Duke of Cao region. What a comfort to Tiger Duke's pounding heart!

Black Tiger said, "I heard my older brother is in trouble so I have come to help. Let us go back to Ji Region. I have a plan which will set things right."

Black Tiger brought with him only three thousand flying tiger soldiers, but in the rear were twenty thousand more men and horses. Black Tiger led the joint armies and laid siege outside of the city walls of Ji.

Ji's guard flew to report to Su Hu.

Su Hu bowed his head and thought for a long moment. Softly he said, "Black Tiger is well versed in fighting skills and strategy. All our generals together will not be able to fight him."

His son Total Loyal came out to say, "My father! When flood comes, we use dikes to block it. When soldiers come, we fight to stop them! Now it is only Black Tiger, why are we so afraid?"

Su Hu said, "My son. You are a proud warrior, but you are young. Black Tiger learned many magic tricks from a strange Superiorman. From the midst of an enemy army of hundred million men, Black Tiger can get the head of the top general as easily as picking an object from his pocket. Don't underestimate him!"

Total Loyal protested, "Father, why do you boost the enemy's morale and short change our own? Let me go. If I cannot capture this black tiger, I will not return." So saying, he dashed out.

The father shouted after him, "This is your own idea, don't you regret it!"

No one could stop Total Loyal. He rushed to the enemy camp. "Guards, send my request to your lords that I want to talk to Black Tiger!"

Black Tiger was secretly delighted at the prospect and thought to himself, "I came because my bully brother is in trouble. But most of all, I want to help my very dear friend Su Hu out of this mess."

Black Tiger came out on his golden-eyed beast. He saw a pompous, conceited Total Loyal prancing around on his horse, showing off.

Black Tiger said, "My dear nephew, go ask your father to come out. I have words for him."

Total Loyal was a brash young man who did not know much of political matters or intricate human relations. He did not know that his father and Black Tiger were very good friends. He heard only what his father had said about how great and brave Black Tiger was, so how could he go back and not challenge him?

He said, "Black Tiger, your country and mine are enemies. How can my father have any friendship with you? If you put down your weapons, I may let you live. Or else it will be too late to regret!"

Black Tiger said, "Young punk, don't you dare be so disrespectful!"

So saying, he lifted up his axes and came straight for Total Loyal. Total Loyal fenced with his spear.

Who dared to stop two great generals in a dogfight? This one was like a lion, shaking his head, dashing down the mountain; that one was like a tiger, waving his tail, jumping through the air. This one fought like a god who wanted to change the face of the earth; that one fought like a giant who can easily rearrange the mountains and rivers. Back and forth, their weapons clashed no fewer than a thousand times.

Total Loyal knew strength and confidence; he could use his spear seventy-two masterful ways. He saw Black Tiger carried only two short-handled axes and would not give Black Tiger much credibility. What he did not know was when very young, Black Tiger had special instructions from a Superiorman and was given a gourd of untold magic. Black Tiger was wearing that gourd on his back now. Total Loyal fought so hard even Black Tiger was made to sweat, and he was very impressed.

Then Black Tiger lifted his axes, turned his mount and retreated. Total Loyal laughed to himself. Had he listened to his father, he would have missed this great opportunity to capture Black Tiger.

Total Loyal chased after Black Tiger. When Black Tiger ran fast, Total Loyal ran fast. When Black Tiger slowed down, so did Total Loyal. They ran and ran for a long distance.

Seeing Total Loyal was not about to give up his chase, Black Tiger finally pulled open his gourd.

A burst of black smoke spewed out, spreading like a net, blocking the sun. In the smoke a sacred eagle with an iron beak rushed toward Total Loyal with a hushed cry. Total Loyal defended with his spear. But the bird aimed instead at the eyes of his horse, making it jump and throw him off, his gold ring and the gold wreath on his head all-askew.

Total Loyal was captured and brought to Tiger Duke's camp. Tiger Duke was overjoyed. Total Loyal refused to kneel.

Tiger Duke said, "Ha, you now have your just desserts! Take him out and off with his head!"

As the guards were taking Total Loyal out, Black Tiger said, "My older brother, please take it easy. Total Loyal should definitely die. However, he and his father are both traitors, and the King has ordered to bring them to the Capital City, Morning Song, for punishment. Moreover, Su Hu has a daughter the King wants. If the Son of Heaven decided to pardon Su Hu for the sake of his daughter, where will we stand then? Won't our contributions suddenly become detractions? Besides, Ji Chang is not here yet. Why should my older brother alone take the risk? Why not lock him up now; and when we capture the whole family, we can then send them to City Morning Song and let the King do as he pleases with them."

Tiger Duke concurred and ordered a banquet to celebrate Black Tiger's victory.

✻   ✻   ✻   ✻

News of Total Loyal's capture reached Su Hu. Su Hu was saddened but not surprised.

He thought to himself, "My son did not listen to me, his capture is a matter of course. Now my son is gone, and two big armies besiege my country. My Ji Region will soon belong to someone else. Why? Why? Just because I have my daughter Daji. The muddled-headed king wants to harm my whole family and my people just because of this daughter. There is no way out! Once my Ji Region is lost, my wife and daughter will be captured and sent as prisoners to the Capital City Morning Song to be shamed in the market place. Their corpses will be exposed without burial. The populace will laugh at my witlessness! The only way out is for me to kill my daughter, wife, and myself, to keep our virtues intact."

With melancholy Su Hu carried his sword and walked to the back halls of his mansion. His daughter Daji, gently opened her cherry mouth, asked, "My Daddy, why are you carrying your sword here?"

Su Hu looked at his daughter, his own flesh and blood. How could he raise his sword on this innocent child? He said in tears, "My tormentor! Because of you, your brother is captured, our country is besieged, your parents will be killed, and our ancestral shrine will be destroyed. To give birth to you, one person, the whole Su family is ruined!"

As Su Hu was lamenting his fate, a messenger reported that Black Tiger was calling outside the city wall for a fight.

Su Hu refused to open the city gates.

Black Tiger waited and waited. But Su Hu would not come out. Black Tiger thought to himself, "My very dear friend Su Hu, why are you afraid of me? If you don't come out to see me, how can I help you out of this mess?"

Black Tiger returned to his brother's camp.

Tiger Duke suggested, "Since Su Hu refused to come out and fight, why don't we go on an offensive, using cloud ladders and climb the wall?"

"No, my older brother. We can simply blockade the city and cut off their supply from the countryside. The city will sooner or later be breached. My older brother can sit tight and wait for the Grand Duke of the West with his army."

*   *   *   *

Su Hu saw no way to save his beleaguered city, no place to go for help. Just then a messenger reported that general Zhen Lun had returned from his secret mission and was waiting to see him.

Zhen Lun saluted. "On my way here, I heard the trouble. I rushed back as fast as I could with my heart hanging in the air. What happened and what can we do?"

Su Hu recounted the story of that fatal morning in King Zhou's Court and its aftermath, his misgiving of Black Tiger's presence here with his brother, the Tiger Duke, and Total Loyal's capture.

Su Hu said in despair, "I know Black Tiger possesses black magic, all my generals and soldiers together would not be his equal. Yes, there are eight hundred dukes in the nation, but Su Hu knows not where to go for help.

"Well, my family has only four members. My son has been captured and may be killed already. I have made up my mind to kill my wife, my daughter, and myself. All of you, my dear and loyal friends, should pack up and go find your own salvation. Don't let me hinder your future!"

Zhen Lun cried out loud, "My Lord! You must have taken some wrong medicine and are turning crazy. You are uttering nonsense! In my eyes even if all the grand dukes and all the eight hundred regional dukes come together, they would not be any threat. Why do you belittle us so! I have been in your service since I was very young. Because you are fair and you care, I now wear this jade belt! It is my turn to fight, to end this injustice!"

Su Hu said to the other generals, "Zhen Lun must have met some unholy specters and is bewitched. Let alone all the eight hundred dukes, just Black Tiger by himself, with his black magic, is enough trouble! How dare we disparage him?"

Holding his sword, Zhen Lun said loudly, "My lord! I will capture Black Tiger for you! Or I will present you with my head before all these generals."

So saying, he mounted his golden-eyed beast, grasped his two large Evil-Taming bars, and rushed out. On the sound of a cannon, a city gate opened and out charged Zhen Lun and his three thousand black crow troops, streaming out like a black cloud sweeping over the earth. When they reached Tiger Duke's camp, Zhen Lun shouted, "Black Tiger, come out to see me!"

Leading his three thousand flying tiger soldiers, Black Tiger rode in front with a pair of banners. He saw the men and horses of Ji Region, stood like a patch of black cloud. A general who had a face like a purple plum, hair like golden needles, wearing a Nine-Cloud-Flaming helmet, bright red robe and jade belt; riding a golden-eyed beast very much like his own animal; and holding two Evil-Taming bars. But Black Tiger did not recognize him.

Black Tiger shouted, "General of Ji Region, announce your name."

"I am Ji Region full General Zhen Lun. You must be Black Tiger, Duke of Cao Region. You have captured my master's son. You'd better return him immediately or I will give you a what-for!"

Black Tiger blew his top. "Man! How dare you made such bold speech? Your master, having rebelled against the King, will have his body broken and his bones powdered. You, my friend, will enjoy the same fate!"

Black Tiger spurred his beast, waving his two axes, and charged toward Zhen Lun. Zhen Lun fenced with his two Evil-Taming bars.

Look!

War drums beating, multicolored banners fluttering, three armies shouting, thousands of arrows flying. Two generals on golden-eyed beasts, four arms flying with axes and bars. This one bellowed angrily like thunder, the other was born with a foolhardy character. This one had a face like the bottom of a kettle and a long flaming red beard. That other had a face like a purple plum and hair like golden needles. This one was like a tiger from the mountain, and that one was like dragon from the sea. This one had learned his magic from a Superior-man and the other had studied under a famous teacher in the Kunlun Mountains. This one could rearrange mountains and rivers, the other could change day to night. Red clouds faded and white fog thickened. We have seen many generals in battles but never like these two axes facing these two bars.

After their weapons clashed two hundred times, Zhen Lun saw the red gourd on Black Tiger's back and recognized it as the seat of Black Tiger's magic.

Zhen Lun himself studied under Superiorman Bubble Vaunter in the Western Kunlun Mountains. Bubble Vaunter knew that Zhen Lun was destined to help the founding of a new dynasty and thus would earn his rights to be invested later as a God. The magic trick he taught Zhen Lun was the shooting from his nostrils two jets, which could suck up an opponent's spirits and souls.

When Zhen Lun realized that he must use his own magic first, he waved his bars in the air, as his black crow soldiers formed a long line, each holding a long chain with a hook, shouting and running like lightning toward Black Tiger. While Black Tiger was thus distracted, a loud sound exploded as two jets issued from Zhen Lun's nostrils.

At the sound of the explosion, Black Tiger fell from his saddle, his golden headdress upside down, his two boot-shod feet dancing in the air. By the time Black Tiger came to, the black crow soldiers who were pushing him into the City of Ji to the triumphant beating of drums and gongs on the City Wall already bound him up.

A Superiorman on the mountain above the clouds and the sea,
Given special instructions and skill.
Ten thousand Tiger soldiers became useless,
Giving proof Zhen Lun's boast was more than real.

Su Hu was sitting in his court. On hearing the sudden commotion, he sighed with dismay. "Oh, this is the end of Zhen Lun!"

But a scout reported that Zhen Lun had instead captured Black Tiger and was waiting for Su Hu's order.

When Zhen Lun brought Black Tiger in, Su Hu got off his chair, walked down from his court, and personally untied Black Tiger.

Su Hu then knelt before Black Tiger, and said, "Su Hu deserves heavy punishment for his crime of offending the Son of Heaven. Now my Zhen Lun has offended you. Please let me take the full blame."

Black Tiger said, "We are old friends and our friendship is not so easily forgotten. Today, I am ashamed to be captured, and I do appreciate your treating me like an honor guest."

Su Hu let Black Tiger sit in the honor seat, and introduced Black Tiger to his generals.

Black Tiger said, "General Zhen Lun's military prowess is great. Today, he captured me. I will respect him all my life."

Su Hu related all his woes to Black Tiger.

Black Tiger said, "I came, first because my elder brother was in defeat, and second, because I want to help you out of your difficulty. I did not expect your young son wanted to fight and would not let me come to see you. So I captured him and for your sake and his safety, placed him in the rear of my camp."

*   *   *   *

In the other camp, eyewitness recited to Tiger Duke how Black Tiger was captured. As Tiger Duke was pondering, a scout reported that a messenger from the Grand Duke of the West had just arrived. Tiger Duke was annoyed but decided to see the messenger right away.

Counselor Easy Life of the Grand Duke of the West, in very plain clothes, came in to pay his respects.

Tiger Duke said, "Counselor Easy Life. Why is your lord sitting tight with his army and not fighting? Is this not disobeying the King's edict? Your lord does not seem to know his duty. What justification do you bring?"

Easy Life said, "My Lord Tiger Duke. My master said that soldiery is a weapon of cruelty! We should use it only as last resort. We cannot hurt the people and waste the national treasury just for little nothings. The populace is terribly disturbed by passing soldiers and their tax burden is already higher than ever. Moreover, many soldiers will be wounded and killed. Therefore, my master has sent me with this letter of truce to persuade Su Hu to send his daughter to the king. If he will not listen, then we will annihilate him. He cannot regret that we did not offered him an alternative."

Tiger Duke laughed aloud and said, "Your Lord Ji Chang knows he has disobeyed the King's order; now he is using this fancy scheme as an excuse to relief himself of the blame. I have come here first and engaged in many fierce battles; many of my generals were killed, and my army was destroyed. And you expect Su Hu to give up his daughter because this one piece of paper? I would like to see what Su Hu would do to you! And suppose Su Hu does not agree, what excuse will your lord use to save his own skin? You go ahead to the Ji Region!"

*   *   *   *

Su Hu was drinking with Black Tiger when informed that a messenger from the Grand Duke of the West had come. Su Hu ordered the city gate open immediately to welcome him.

Su Hu said, "Honorable Counselor come to my humble country with what advice?"

Counselor Easy Life said, "Your humble servant carries a message for you from the Grand Duke of the West. My master knows well your loyalty to the throne and therefore will not move his troops to disturb you. He sends you this letter. Please read it carefully and consider it seriously."

Su Hu opened the letter and read, "Greetings to the Duke of Ji Region from Ji Chang, the Grand Duke of the West. Chang learns that the relationship between the shore and the river is just like that between the ministers and the king. Today the Son of Heaven wants to select a beautiful concubine; dare any from the high to the very humble hide their daughters? Now you have a beautiful daughter; that the king wants her is quite appropriate. But you rebelled and wrote that poem on the wall of the Noon Gate. What did you expect? Your offence is unpardonable. You care for only your daughter; you forget your duty to your king. I have often heard you are an upright, just, and intelligent person. I cannot help but feel sorry for you. I would try my best to show you your folly with the hope of turning your misfortune into fortune. Please consider my words with an open mind.

"If your daughter is selected to the palace, there will be three points of fortune. Namely:

1. Your daughter will be the king's favorite, and you, the king's close relation with your position and wealth insured.

2. The Ji Region will be well protected from all harm.

3.   There will be no more war, soldiers will not be killed and the populace will not be sacrificed.

"However, if you stubbornly stick to your own plans, there will be three points of misfortunes. Namely:

1.   Ji Region will be annihilated; your ancestral shrine will be destroyed.

2.   The populace will suffer untold grief and loss.

3.   Soldiers and people will die without just cause.

"A gentleman will put priority on the big principles and sacrifice the petty. Is your personal sacrifice worth the extermination of your country? You and I both are officials of Shang Dynasty. I cannot help but have to point these facts out to you. Do consider them. I await your decision."

Su Hu finished reading, nodding his head in silence.

Seeing Su Hu sitting in silence, Counselor Easy Life added, "My Lord need not hesitate. If on account of this letter you promise to stop fighting, it is only obeying the king's order, agreeing with all the officials and keeping the populace from further sufferings. This is my master's good wishes. Please give your order to stop the hostility right now."

Hearing that, Su Hu turned to Black Tiger and said, "My friend, take a look at this letter. What the Grand Duke of the West says is the whole truth. He really is for the people, a loyal official and a true gentleman. How dare I not obey?"

Next day, Su Hu wrote a letter, and together with a great gift, sent Counselor Easy Life back to Western Foothills. He said to Easy Life, "I will go to the Capital City Morning Song with my daughter to redeem my crime."

Yes, a letter is stronger than ten thousand soldiers.
The tongue out talked hundred rivers and streams,

Sorting out matters bad or good, corrupt or clean.
A few lines of writing changed Su Hu's resolution,
No more nightmares but peaceful dreams.

CHAPTER 4

▼

A FOX SPECTER KILLS DAJI

Su Hu and Black Tiger discussed the letter from the Grand Duke of the West. Black Tiger said, "My friend, you have made your decision, so you had better get ready to send your daughter to the Capital City, Morning Song. A delay may lead to unforeseen incidents. I am now going back to my brother's camp to release your son. My brother and I will take our armies back to our own countries, and then inform the king so you may confess your crime to him. I hope there will not be any more happenings that may harm your health."

Su Hu replied, "Thanks for your friendship and the concern of the Grand Duke of The West. Just because my love for my daughter I have put my country and family in jeopardy! We do appreciate very much your releasing my son right away. My poor wife has been so aggrieved."

Su Hu and Black Tiger bid each other a very fond farewell.

Scout flew to report to Tiger Duke that Black Tiger had been released from Ji. Tiger Duke immediately invited Black Tiger to his tent, and said, "The odious Grand Duke of the West has still to send out his troops! He is still sitting there watching. Yesterday he sent his

Counselor Easy Life with a letter advising Su Hu to surrender his daughter to the king. I have yet to learn the result. All these on top of your being captured! I am so relieved that you are safely back. Please tell me all about what you saw and heard. What did Su Hu do to that counselor?"

Black Tiger replied solemnly, "My older brother, we came from the same father and the same mother, same ancestors for generations. We are of the same flesh and blood. But there is a saying that from the same tree, some fruits are sweet and some are sour. Sons from the same mother and father, some are intelligent and some are dull.

"In the king's court, you are one of the highest ranking officials. Yet you don't seem to do what is good for the king. You encourage the king to favor the bad officials, causing the populace to suffer. Yes, Su Hu rebelled. You were ordered by the king to annihilate him. So without investigating the truth, you led a big army to put him down and lost all your men and horses.

"It has been common knowledge to all in this kingdom that Su Hu is one of the most loyal and upright persons in the Court of Shang. Yet it never occurred to you to ask why a loyal official acted in the way Su Hu did, or whether this accusation was merely some trumped up charge.

"On the other hand, The Grand Duke of the West's letter has convinced Su Hu to surrender his daughter to the king. Your 50,000 strong army is not as good as the sheet of paper from the Grand Duke of the West. Are you not ashamed of yourself? You have dishonored our clan, my older brother! We say farewell today. I will never come to see you again!"

Turning to the guards, Black Tiger ordered the release of Total Loyal. Total Loyal came up to thank Black Tiger, "Thank you so much, my Uncle Black Tiger. I shall never forget your generosity."

Black Tiger said, "Do urge your father to hurry on his trip to the Capital City, Morning Song. I will carry his message to the king in order to give your father a chance to ask for the king's pardon."

After giving his older brother a piece of his mind, Black Tiger mounted his golden-eyed beast, and led his three thousand flying tiger troops back to his Cao Region.

Tiger Duke was so ashamed; he had nothing to say to his younger brother. He ordered his men to prepare to return to his country. He had to get ready to ask the king's pardon for losing the war with Su Hu.

*   *   *   *

Total Loyal returned to Ji. His father told him about the letter from the Grand Duke of the West, and his own decision to take Daji to Morning Song.

Su Hu said, "While I am gone, you will be in charge of Ji. Be kind and just. I shall be back soon."

When the mother learned of Su Hu's decision to send Daji to Morning Song, she wailed, "This daughter of ours has been so pampered and sheltered, she will not know how to serve the king and surely will get into trouble!"

Su Hu said, "We cannot help that. Let events take their natural course."

Husband and wife grieved all night.

Next morning, Su Hu ordered three thousand soldiers and horses, plus five hundred household servants, and a padded chariot to be ready for the trip. When Daji was told to get up early, she realized what had transpired and her tears fell like a heavy rain.

She said farewell to her mother and brother. The grief and sorrow, the pain and suffering of separation all showed on Daji's face like peony flowers in the mist, and pear blossoms in the rain. How to cut off a daughter from her mother, and a sister from her brother? The servants did their best to comfort them, pulling Madame Su Hu back to the mansion, and Daji to the padded chariot. Big brother accompanied the procession for five miles before returning to the city.

*   *   *   *

Father and daughter traveled to the Capital City, Morning Song, under a banner denoting royal business. They stopped to eat only when hungry, to drink only when thirsty. In the morning, they saw the sun came up from behind the pine and cedar groves. At the end of the day, they drove through the evening dust. They passed through the green willow-shaded high roads and the red almond flowered parks. They heard the crows calling in the spring morning, and the cuckoos crying in the shadow of the moon at night. They climbed high mountains and crossed deep waters.

One evening, they arrived in the En Region. Su Hu asked the manager of the hostel to have the place ready for a royal person.

The manager said, "I beg your pardon, my lord. Three years ago, there appeared a specter in this hostel. A lot of strange happenings occurred. No lord or lady passing by dared to stay here. Your humble servant suggests that you stay in your tent to save worry."

Su Hu scolded the manager, saying, "A royal person is not afraid of evil things. Where there is a hostel, why should we stay in a tent? Hurry and get the place ready!"

Su Hu put his daughter Daji and fifty maids to serve her in the inner section of the hostel, and the remaining household servants up front. He himself stayed in the central hall, and the three thousand soldiers set up tents surrounding the hostel.

Su Hu thought to himself, "This place is so crowded with our people, how is it possible to have any specters around? But the manager was serious about it, so we had better be prepared."

Su Hu put a whip of leopard's tail on top of his desk, and started to read. As the bell rang one, signaling the first watch, Su Hu became uneasy. He carried his leopard whip and walked to the inner court. Seeing Daji and her maids all quietly asleep, he felt a little easier. He returned to his room and continued to read.

The bell rang twice, and then rang thrice announcing the midnight watch.

Suddenly Su Hu's light dimmed momentarily, accompanied by a strange chilling draft. It was neither the growl of a tiger nor the scream of a dragon that penetrating his bones, but the draft so cold and full of evil intent.

Then horrid screams came from the inner court: "Specter! Specter! Specter is here!"

Su Hu, with his leopard whip in his right hand and a lamp in his left, rushed into the inner court. A gust blew out his lamp, engulfing him in total darkness. He returned to the main hall, called his servants to replace his lamp, and then returned to the inner court. The maids were all terrified.

He rushed to his daughter's bedside, lifted the bed curtain and asked, "How is my child? Did you see any specter?"

Daji, opening her phoenix's eyes and looking at Su Hu as if it was the first time she had ever laid eyes on this warrior, replied sweetly, "I was awakened from my dream by the cries of the maids about specters. When I opened my eyes, I saw lamp light. I did not know it is you,…my daddy. But I did not see any specter."

Su Hu said, "Thank goodness you are not disturbed!" Su Hu tucked his daughter back to sleep.

No one was the wiser, but the specter had come and it was the Thousand-Year-Old vixen! Between the blowing out of the lamp and its replacement, plenty of time elapsed. That was when Daji's soul and spirit were sucked up by the vixen specter, leaving Daji dead but for her body. This the vixen occupied and would use to bewitch King Zhou, to lay waste his beautiful rivers and mountains, to terminate his dynasty. We have a poem as proof:

> *Terrified by an evil draft and the scream of a specter, in the Hostel in Region En,*
> *Rushing to the inner court, Su Hu had his leopard whip and a blown out lamp.*

Daji's flesh and blood had been replaced by a thousand-year vixen,
Fooling him and the world to the very end!

Su Hu's pillow was not touched all night. His anxiety knew no bounds. Luckily his daughter Daji appeared unharmed; otherwise, he would be accused of deceiving the Son of Heaven again! How would he ever be able to explain that? Early in the morning, they left the hostel, and continued on to the Capital City. One day, they finally crossed the Yellow River and arrived in the Morning Song. They made camp outside of the city wall.

Su Hu sent a messenger to inform The Lord of National Security Prince Yellow Flying Tiger. The Prince ordered Su Hu to keep his men outside of the city wall, but he and his daughter Daji and her maids might come in the city and stay in the Golden Pavilion Hostel.

*   *   *   *

Again, the powerful king's favorite Middle Counselors Fei Zhong and You Hun noted that Su Hu did not send them any gift. They said to themselves, "The king's mood is controlled by us. Su Hu's fate therefore is also in our hands but he never seems to pay us any attention!"

King Zhou was in the Benevolence Dragon Court when these two Middle Counselors came to see him. Fei Zhong said, "Sire, Su Hu and his daughter are outside waiting for Your Majesty's decision."

King Zhou was furious, for he had forgotten the petition sent in by the Grand Duke of the West.

"How dare they come to see me! Tomorrow morning, take them both out and off with their heads!"

Fei Zhong added oil to fire, saying, "Yes, Sire. We all know that your laws and rules are for the good of the nation, and not for your own selfishness. If we don't get rid of this malcontent, there will be no law and order in the kingdom!"

Next morning, King Zhou saw his officials in the assembly as usual.

The bells were ringing
And the drums were beating.
In the Forbidden City, the Spring dawn was serene and warm,
Willows hanging softly and canaries singing songs.
Fragrance from the incense urns filled the air,
All were immersed in the haughty radiant fair.

The Officer of the Noon Gate reported, "Su Hu of Ji Region is here with his daughter to seek your pardon."

The king ordered Su Hu to be brought in. Instead of wearing his court regalia, Su Hu appeared in a prisoner's garb. He knelt before the throne and pleaded, "Criminal Su Hu incurred the death penalty!"

The king said, "Su Hu of Ji Region. You wrote a poem on the Noon Gate wall, declaring you would never honor Shang. And when Tiger Duke followed my order to discipline you, you fought the Imperial Army and killed many of them. Yet today, you have the audacity to come to my court! Take him out for immediate...."

Before the king could finish his sentence, Prime Minister Shang Rong came out to say, "Sire. Su Hu should definitely be executed. But just the other day, the Grand Duke of the West informed Your Majesty that Su Hu would bring his daughter to you to render his duty as an obedient subject. Now Su Hu is following the law. He has brought his daughter to the court to redeem his crime, an acceptable practice. To begin with, Your Majesty punished him because he would not give up his daughter. Now he brings his daughter and you also punish him. Certainly, this is not what you have in mind. Have mercy on him!"

As King Zhou hesitated, Fei Zhong came out to say, "Sire. The Prime Minister is right. Your Majesty can have Daji brought in to see whether her look is outstanding, her manner graceful and her personality attractive. If they are good enough to serve in your palace, Your Majesty can then pardon Su Hu. Otherwise, father and daughter should be taken to the marketplace and have their heads chopped off to show what a rebel's fate is!"

King Zhou said, "You are right!"

Daji entered Noon Gate, crossed the Nine Dragon Bridge, and came to the Nine Hall Court. Under the eaves, she called out, "Long live the king!"

King Zhou took a closer look. Daji had thick and shiny black hair piled high on her head, two apricot cheeks and a peach chin, curvaceous bosom like high mountains in the spring, and a caressing willowy waist. She was like a begonia enjoying the sun, or a pear blossom after a drizzle.

She was no less than the fairy from the ninth heaven, or the Moon Lady from the sky. Daji opened her mouth which was ringed with lips like a ripe cherry. When she called out her salutation to the king, her tongue twirled modulation and harmony. Her phoenix eyes were lively, animated like autumn waves in a tranquil pond, sending out intense feelings and passions.

She said to the king, "I am Daji, the daughter of your criminal minister Su Hu, here to pay homage to Your Majesty, and to wish you many ten thousand years!"

With these few words, Daji sent King Zhou's spirit and soul out to space. His spine turned to jelly, his ears burnt, and his eyes jumped. He did not know what to do. He got up immediately and pulled Daji to sit with him. Then he ordered his other palace females to help this "Niang Niang" to his Longevity Palace, to await his return.

He sent out his edict to pardon Su Hu of all his crimes and reinstated him to his former position. On top of that, he awarded him the title of Minister of National Relations, with an increase in salary of two hundred thousand bushels of rice each month. All in the king's court were to have three days of celebration complete with banquets and festivities. Also, Prime Minster Shang Rong was to send two civil and two military officials to accompany Su Hu on his return trip home.

Su Hu thanked the king for his generosity. But all the officials at the assembly were dismayed to see the king so taken by a woman. The king hurriedly left the throne-room and went to his Longevity Palace before anyone had a chance to say anything.

With resignation, the officials went to the celebration banquet. And Su Hu left for home, without even a chance to say good bye to his daughter.

The king's passion for Daji was sticky as glue and lacquer! Day and night, the king and Daji indulged in wine and lust, not once in three months did the king see his officials in the morning assembly or any other time, for that matter. His only pastime was to be with Daji. Messages from eight hundred dukes were piled up as high as a mountain. None in the country had been able to see the face of the Son of Heaven.

The whole kingdom was going to pot. Could it be any other way?

CHAPTER 5

▼

CLOUD DWELLER
PRESENTS A PINE WOOD
SWORD

King Zhou, entwined in Daji's physical beauty, was oblivious to everything else. The administration of the kingdom was completely neglected.

*　　　*　　　*　　　*

Now on Mount South End there lived a Superiorman who had been studying and training for thousands of years to achieve his status. He called himself Cloud Dweller.

One day, he took a walk to the Tiger Peak to look for medicinal herbs. As he walked on the cloud, he saw an unholy haze coming from the Southeast. He parted the cloud for a closer look, and said to himself, "Aha! That is the Thousand-Year-Old vixen, in a human form, sneaking around in King Zhou's Palace! If she is not eliminated, great disaster will befall the Red Dust! I must prevent this from happening!"

He called to his pupil, "Please bring me a section of that dead old pine wood. I will make a sword to get rid of this unholy specter."

His pupil asked, "Why not use your precious sword?"

"Not for that Thousand-Year-Old vixen. She is not worthy of it. A wooden sword will do the job fine," replied Superiorman Cloud Dweller.

*   *   *   *

For many months now, King Zhou had not been to the morning assembly to receive his ministers. The populace was getting restless and none of the high officials knew what to do.

Number One Grand Counselor Mei Bo spoke to Prime Minister, Shang Rong and Vice Prime Minister, Prince Bi Gan, "My friends, the Son of Heaven indulges in wine and lust, completely neglecting the administration of the kingdom. Memoranda from the dukes are piling up like a mountain. You both are the Prime Ministers of the kingdom. You should take it upon yourselves to rectify the situation. Why don't we beat the gong, gather all the officials of the kingdom and ask to see the king. Then we would at least have performed our duties as responsible high officials."

Prime Minister, Shang Rong said, "Yes! Thank you for reminding us." He then ordered the gong keeper to beat the gong and the drummers to beat the drums. The gong was to request permission to see the king while the drums were to summon the officials to the court. The Palace guard reported to the king that the gong had been sounded by the Prime Ministers.

King Zhou was very annoyed. Reluctantly he told Daji that he must go to the court. Daji accompanied him to the palace gate, eagerly urging the king to return quickly.

King Zhou came to his Throne-room. He saw hundreds of his officials waiting for him. Both Prime Minister Shang Rong and Vice Prime Minister Prince Bi Gan carried their Yahus [1]. The eight Grand

Counselors, as well as the Lord of National Security, Prince Yellow Flying Tiger, also carried theirs.

The king, having indulged too long in wine and woman, was rather exhausted. He was in no mood to listen to what were on the Yahus. All the king wanted was to get this over with as quickly as possible so that he could return to his Daji.

The Prime Minister and the Vice Minister were the first two to step out to speak, "Sire! Our kingdom is in trouble. There are uncontrolled floods and droughts. The populace is suffering and restless. All the memoranda from the dukes have not been attended to. Your Majesty has not come for months to the morning assembly. Many urgent matters await your decision."

The king said, "What are you talking about? I heard there is prosperity in the four seas, and all our people are happy. The only sore spot is in the North Sea, but Grand Old Master Wen Zhong is taking care of that. All other things are so unimportant, why bother me with them? Since the two of you are taking care of the day-to-day business, you can certainly do more of the administrative work and relieve me of this boring stuff! Even if I see you people every morning, it is only a matter of formality. Why all these complaints?"

As they were discussing this, a report came to the king that a Superiorman from Mount South End wished to see him. King Zhou thought to himself, "What a break! I can now cut short this unpleasant confrontation with all these disgruntled men!"

He said, "Invite the Superiorman in!"

Cloud Dweller, wearing a black kerchief hat with two ribbons flying in the back, a loose robe and soft cloth shoes, entered the Noon Gate, passed the Nine Dragon Bridge and came to the throne room. His complexion was like peaches and cream, his lips were blood red. He carried his flower basket in his left hand and a horse tail whip in his right. He walked to the edge of the court, barely nodded his head and said to the king, "Your Majesty, yours truly salutes!"

King Zhou was displeased when the Superiorman saluted him with barely a nod. The king thought to himself, "I am the Son of Heaven, I own the treasures of the four seas and all the people in my kingdom. Even though you are beyond my rule, you are now in my territory. Why then do you behave in such a disrespectful manner? If I punish you for your contempt, my people may think I am too narrow minded. Mind you, I will find a way to show you who is the boss here!"

So thinking, the king asked, "Where is this Superiorman from?"

"I am from the cloud-water," the Superiorman replied.

"What is cloud-water?" the king wanted to know.

"My heart is as much at ease as the cloud; my mind is fluid like the water," said the Superiorman.

The king, though exhausted, was still alert, and being basically an intelligent person, asked, "When the cloud is blown away, when the water is dry, where will you be?"

"When the cloud is blown away, the bright moon will shine in the clear sky; when the water dries, the pearl will appear," the Superiorman said.

When the king heard this, his anger turned to delight. He said, "A while ago, I was quite offended. Now after listening to you, I realize you really are a scholar extraordinary. You may sit down."

Cloud Dweller sat without apology. He said, "I know now that the Son of Heaven knows only the honorable position of the Son of Heaven himself. He fails to know that scholars of other philosophical disciplines are also very honored."

"How so?" Asked the king.

Cloud Dweller said, "Let me explain. There are three major philosophical schools of discipline, but the Dao (Tao in old spelling) is the most honored. They do not kneel to any king, nor take orders from any official. They are above the law and order of the land, and live quietly in high mountains like hermits. They care neither for material wealth, nor for power. They wear the stars as their hats, and bathe in the sun and the moon. They let their hair grow naturally, and go around naked and barefoot. Or they may wear cotton garments and shoes, as they please. They pick fresh flowers for decoration or fresh rush to repair their huts. They drink and brush their teeth from cool fresh mountain streams;, and chew on pine needles and cedar leaves for long life. They clap their hands and sing loudly. They sleep on the cloud after they dance. They discourse on philosophies when they are with mountain spirits. They drink wine, and write poetry when they are with friends. They laugh at the rat race below in the Red Dust world while enjoying their own worry-free life. Sometimes, three gather to ponder philosophical thought, or two to study the ancient history and discuss present trends. The change of the seasons seems to make them younger each year; their white hair returns to black. Most of their time, they would go with their flower baskets to the mountain top to search for medicinal herbs to relieve the suffering of the popu- lace in the Red Dust. They study the stars and predict the future. They can see the good and bad clearly in the hearts of men. For the good of all men, they will come down to the Red Dust when necessary to rid it.

"They are unlike the scholars of the school of discipline whose sole purpose is to study the classics, to gain high positions in the king's court. The Daoists consider wealth and high ranks as changeable as floating clouds; not worth the bother of a person of true intellect. And unlike those who play with black magic, the Daoist is the true magic.

"This is why I say, among the three schools of philosophical disci- plines, the Daoist is the most honored."

The king was delighted, and said, "To hear you is like breathing the mountain fresh air. Indeed, all material wealth is but billowing clouds. Where really is your residence and why are you here?"

"I am Cloud Dweller, I live in the Jade Column Cave, on Mount South End. I was picking herbs on Tiger Peak when I saw an evil spirit encroaching in your palace. So I decided to help you get rid of it."

The king replied, "You must be joking. Within my palace, there is tight security. It is absolutely impossible for any evil to gain entrance."

Cloud Dweller said with a faint smile, "No, Sire. If you know it is an evil specter, it certainly would not be able to gain entrance. But since you don't know, that is how it found its way in. If we don't get rid of it, there will be disaster! Let me read you a poem:

> Beautiful and gracious the epitome of charm,
> Stealthily replacing an innocent child, with intent to great harm.
> If it was known this was indeed an unholy specter,
> Much suffering and death would be avoided later.

King Zhou said, "What can we do to purify the palace?"

Cloud Dweller opened his flower basket, took out the wooden sword and said to the king, "Please let me tell about this wooden sword:

> A magic sword made of a magic pine tree,
> Untold power and magic no one could perceive.
> Within three days, it's a promise,
> Unholy specter forever in demise.

So saying, Superiorman Cloud Dweller presented the wooden sword to the king, saying, "Hang it over the door of the Longevity Palace."

The king ordered the wooden sword be hung as Cloud Dweller instructed, then said to him, "You must be a very learned man. Why not come down from your Mount South End to my court? I will reward you all the wealth and honor and power you so deserve. And behold, your prestige will last for many generations to come. Why settle for poverty and obscurity?"

Cloud Dweller replied, "Thanks but no thanks. I fully appreciate your generous offer, but I am so used to my lazy, leisurely life, I would not know what to do as an official in your court. I like to sleep until the sun is high in the sky. I enjoy walking barefoot and in the nude, going anywhere as I please."

The king said, "Is that so! What good is it? Now I offer you purple robe, gold belt, unlimited wealth for your wife and children, from generation to generation. Why settle for less?"

Cloud Dweller said, "Sorry but I have my own values in life. My body is free and my heart is content. I don't play with weapons, I don't deal with intrigue. I don't care about gossips. I love to plant my vegetables. To me, fame and wealth are like weeds in a rubbish heap. I could not care less for silk robes and gold belts. I would never permit myself to kneel down in the dust just to please you, or to bend the bow to shoot the arrow because you decree so. My children in generations to come will take care of themselves in manners befitting them. They will feel like I do that fame and wealth are nothing. My little cottage is not too narrow for me, and my simple garments are quite comfortable. I adorn myself with lilies and orchids. I care not who is who and what is what. I do as I please and enjoy every bit of it."

The king laughed, "You really are something!" The king gave the order to reward Cloud Dweller one pot each of gold and silver for his travel expenses."

Cloud Dweller said, "Thank you but no thank you again. Your gift has no use for me. I came out of the forest and down the mountain because there was a need. My heart is as pure as the moving cloud and the running of the mountain stream. I carry with me two rolls of my reading material, a three foot long sword, and my five string lute. My pockets are full of medicine which I dispense as I see fit. I write new poems when my mood wills it. What use will this gold and silver be to me?"

So saying, Cloud Dweller nodded to the king and was gone like a breeze.

Grand Counselor Mei Bo and the two Prime Ministers Shang Rong and Prince Bi Gan had finally got the king to come to the throne-room, but before anyone could say anything, they were interrupted by this Superiorman Cloud Dweller who took so much of the king's time. And as soon as the Cloud Dweller was gone, the king said,

"Enough for today. All dismissed!" and rushed back to his Longevity Palace.

*   *   *   *

Strange, why didn't Daji come to greet the king when he returned? King Zhou felt an uneasy premonition.

A palace servant reported to the king, "Sire! Su Niang Niang contracted a sudden illness and is now in a coma!"

Upon hearing this, the king rushed to the bed chamber. He opened the pink peony bed curtain, and saw Daji's face was yellow as gold, her lips white as paper.

The king moaned, "Oh, my beauty! This morning, when you said good-bye to me, you were like a blooming peony. What kind of illness has put you in such a state? Oh, what should I do? What could I do?"

As Cloud Dweller had anticipated, his wooden sword had caused this fox specter in Daji to be sickened. Had the fox specter been left to die, King Zhou's Shang Dynasty might have been saved. However, as destiny had it, it was King Zhou's fate to set the stage for the Chou Dynasty to come into being.

Daji opened her phoenix eyes a little and moved her white lips to force a sigh. "Sire," she said, "This morning when I said good-bye to you I was in perfect health. At noon, I went to the entrance to wait for your return, and saw a pine wood sword hanging there. I was so frightened, I came down with a cold sweat. That was how I contracted this sudden illness.

"Oh, it is fate! I had hoped to serve Your Majesty all my life. But it seems my life is ending. I am so sorry. Do please take care of yourself."

Tears rained down her yellow face.

The king, shocked for a long moment, did not know what to do. Then he said, "It was all my fault! The wooden sword was a gift from a Superiorman Cloud Dweller of Mount South End. He promised in three days it would vanquish any unholy specter in our palace. Little did I realize that it could terrify you so!" The king ordered the pine wood sword taken down and burnt.

Notes

1. A Yahu is a writing tablet, the equivalent of the modern memo pad.

CHAPTER 6

▼

THE BRONZE TOASTER

With the pine wood sword burnt, the vixen specter Daji regained her evil power; and grew even more beautiful. She continued her way with the king; but, completely forgetting the Snail Goddess's instruction not to harm others, she got more and more cruel, and ruthless in time.

At this moment, Superiorman Cloud Dweller saw the unholy haze gushing again from the palace. Sighed to himself, "I have tried but the king would not heed my warning. Well, if this is the scheme of things heaven and earth, let it be, let it be! But I would like to leave a few words for the future generations.

He took out his writing instruments and wrote on the wall of the National Astrological Observatory.

In the Palace, befuddled king dazed by unholy haze,
In the West, Heavenly virtues spread with divine grace.
  Tides of crimson flood Capital A B C,
High noon of year X Y Z.

Cloud Dweller then returned to his Mount South End.

A large crowd gathered to see what the Superiorman had written on the wall. They read and reread but no one could make any head or tail of it.

That day Royal Astrologer Du Yuanxi was coming to his office when he saw the milling crowd. He read the words on the wall, but he could not understand the mumbo jumbo either. He ordered the words washed off the wall and to disperse the crowd.

In his office Du pondered about the writing on the wall. He was certain there was deeper meanings than met the eyes. For several months now, Du had seen in the sky, a certain unholy plume around the star of the king. Could it be the evil spirit alluded to by the Superiorman Cloud Dweller the other day? Du saw many indications.

Du thought to himself, "Our king completely ignores the administration of the kingdom, readily accepts the flatteries of a few. Our land and people are plagued by floods, droughts, insects, and war. And despite all the sufferings, our king pays absolutely no attention to anything but Daji!

"Can I sit back, like the rest of the ministers, fearful of the king's anger and keep my silence? No! I cannot! I must warn the king before it is too late! Dare I speak the truth? Dare I keep my mouth shut? What is the best course to take? Will it do any good if I speak the truth and be killed? Can I live with it if I keep my silence and keep my head? What options do we have to save the country"

That was a soul searching and sleepless night for Astrologer Du. He made up his mind, "I must not think of my own head. I must warn the king!" He got up and wrote his memo to the king.

With his memo he went at dawn to the morning assembly. The king, of course had not attended the meeting for a long time. This morning, he was not there either.

Royal Astrologer Du learned that it was Prime Minister, Shang Rong's turn to read memos that day. He went to see him. Du said, "My Prime Minister. From my observatory, for several months now, I saw unholy mist around the star of the king. Bad things will happen.

Even as now, we all know that the Son of Heaven pays no attention whatsoever to the administration of the kingdom. This matter affects the whole country and our ancestral shrine. The dynasty may be in danger! I cannot stand by not trying to help. I wrote this memo last night. May I bother you to present it to the king?"

"For sure, my Royal Astrologer." Replied Shang Rong. "Since the king has not come today, why don't we go to his palace to see him on such a grave matter?"

Royal Astrologer Du, led by Shang Rong, walked through the Nine Hall Court, Virtuous Dragon Court, the Distinguish Joyful Court, the Perfect Happiness Court, and came to the Demarcation Building.

A young eunuch said to Shang Rong, "My Prime Minister. This is the forbidden area, the private quarters of the king. You may not come in!"

Shang Rong said, "Don't I know! That is why I am telling you that we wait here! Please inform the king that we have very grave matters to discuss."

The eunuch reported to the king. The king said, "What business has Shang Rong to come to my palace? Shang Rong is an outside minister, has no right to be in my inner court! However, since he has served the dynasty for three generations, I shall be generous this time. Send him in!"

Shang Rong entered. The king said, "What emergency brings you here?"

Shang Rong, holding Royal Astrologer Du's memo, replied, "Sire. The Royal Astrologer Du Yuanxi saw, especially last night, an unholy plume hovering over the star of the king, Your Majesty. Du does not dare not to inform you of this portent of impending calamity. Since Your Majesty had not come to the morning assembly, we dare to offend you to come to your inner court to present his memo."

The king read:

Memo
To: The King
From: Your Royal Astrologer Du Yuanxi.
Subject: Report on unusual haze surrounding the king's star in the sky.

"We heard that good omen abound when a country is prosperous and at peace. But when signs of evils are seen, we must take precaution to prevent calamity from happening. Last night, I saw in the constellation, some unholy haze hovering over Your Majesty's star. Your humble Royal Astrologer judged that something irreverent with evil intent has sneaked into your inner palace.

"Your Majesty may recall the incident of the pine wood sword presented by the Superiorman Cloud Dweller. Because the sword was burnt, the evil is not quenched. For the past several months, Your majesty had so completely ignored everyone and everything. It is like a thick cloud covering the sky. Even your high ranking officials have not seen your face for a long time.

"I am risking my life in pointing out what I saw in the sky, and hope you would see the light."

The king thought to himself after he read the memo. "He is right. But he mentioned the wood sword which almost cost the life of my Daji. Talking about evil spirits in the Palace again! I must ask Daji what to do."

The evil vixen specter Daji said to the king, "The other day, Cloud Dweller talked about unholy spirits bewitching Your Majesty. Now Royal Astrologer Du also talked about unholy spirits in the Palace. It is very obvious that they belong to the same conspiracy trying to destroy you! This kind of things must be dealt with at once. We must kill all the rumor mongers without mercy! Your Royal Astrologer Du must be executed in the marketplace, and his head displayed as a warning to all that whoever again takes up this subject will meet the same fate!"

"It will be done!" the king said, and ordered the immediate beheading of the Royal Astrologer.

Prime Minister, Shang Rong was so shocked, he could hardly believe what was unfolding before his eyes. He begged the king, "Sire. Your Royal Astrologer Du has served loyally the Court of Shang for three generations. His loyalty and integrity are beyond reproach. He is trying to save you, at the risk of offending Your Majesty, by telling you what he saw in the sky. When he dies, I am sure he will find his right place in Heaven. What I am concerned now is how will your four hundred high officials feel about Your Majesty's action toward your faithful Royal Astrologer? Is it just? For the sake of his exemplary record, spare him!"

The king said, "My Prime Minister. You just don't realize, if I don't kill him now, how are we to calm the populace? They will hear again and again the rumor of unholy spirits. They would not know what to believe."

Shang Rong tried again and again in vain. The king ordered Shang Rong to leave the palace.

Poor Royal Astrologer Du, waiting for Shang Rong at the outer court of the palace, not knowing that his head was soon to part company from his body!

Then the edict came! Palace guards unceremoniously striped Royal Astrologer Du of his red robe and his jade belt. They bound and pushed him toward the Noon Gate. On the way they met Mei Bo, the Number One Grand Counselor to the king. Mei Bo asked Royal Astrologer Du, "What crime had you committed?"

"I really don't know," Du replied. "Last night, as I was watching the sky, I saw a very unholy haze hovering over the star of the king. A bad omen definitely. I tried to warn the king. Instead, the king ordered me killed…Oh, my Number One Grand Counselor Mei Bo, fame and wealth are but dust."

Mei Bo said to the guards, "Wait! Hold it! Let me talk to the king first!"

Mei Bo went quickly. He crossed the Nine Dragon Bridge and bumped into Shang Rong.

Shang Rong said, "Du wrote a memo to the king about evil spirits in the palace. Su Beauty Daji insisted that Du was in league with Cloud Dweller and that they both spreading rumors."

Counselor Mei Bo held Shang Rong's hand and together they ran to the inner court and told the young eunuch that they wanted to see the king.

The king said, "Shang Rong is a very old minister who has served for three generations. When he came in here, I could pardon him. So call him in. But Mei Bo! What business does he have to come in here? Take him out and off with his head!"

However, Mei Bo followed Shang Rong in to see the king. The king asked, "What are you two here for?"

Mei Bo spoke earnestly, "I have just heard that the Royal Astrologer Du has committed a crime against the kingdom and is going to die."

The king said, "You heard it right. Both Cloud Dweller and the Royal Astrologer Du are rumor mongers. They must be killed without mercy so that the populace will know what to believe."

Mei Bo cried out, "Sire! How could you, my king! How could you think of the Royal Astrologer as a rumor monger? He has served brilliantly for three generations of the throne. He has been a most loyal civil servant. To kill a loyal minister without just cause would be like removing a beam from your house. Forgive him and save your kingdom!"

The king paused only for an instant and said to Shang Rong, "Mei Bo and Du belong to the same conspiracy. Both should meet the same fate. However, I will spare Mei Bo's life, but strip him of his rank so he will forever be a peon!"

Mei Bo shouted, "You foolish king! You are losing your people. To kill Du, you are not just killing him, you are killing the people of the country! And now you want to strip me of my rank. I could not care less! But I cannot stand by to watch the six hundred year Shang dynasty comes to an end just because you are so stupid! I realize the Grand Old Master Wen Zhong is still away in his North Sea campaign. But there are many other good and loyal ministers. Yet you rather listen to the few unscrupulous ones. How will you face your ancestors when you die?"

The king was fit to be tied. He said, "Take Mei Bo out and use the gold mallet and beat him to death!"

The palace guards were ready to take Mei Bo when vixen specter Daji spoke, "Don't do that. I have a better idea. Mei Bo is not just bad, he is evil! He tries to stir up people to act against you, my king. Put him in a cage first. I have a special design for a toaster to torture him to death."

"What kind of toaster?" the king asked.

Daji showed the king a design, and said proudly, "A bronze cylindrical device twenty feet tall and eight feet around. We remove Mei Bo's clothes, tie him to the toaster, and use hot charcoal to fire up the device."

"What an ingenious idea!" the king praised.

So it came to pass, that Royal Astrologer Du was beheaded in the marketplace, and Number One Grand Counselor Mei Bo was incarcerated in a cage, to await his fate with that horror of horrors, the bronze toaster.

Seeing how useless and helpless he had become, Shang Rong begged the king to let him retire. "Sire. I am old. I have served three generations of kings in the Shang Dynasty. Please let me go. I am no longer useful to Your Majesty."

King Zhou granted Shang Rong's wish with ample gold and silver, and ordered two each of civil and military officials to escort Shang Rong to return to his farm.

Many of the officials bid Shang Rong a tearful farewell and accompanied him to the edge of the Capital City, Morning Song; for he was one of the most liked and respected person of them all. And others were waiting for him ten miles outside of the capital. Among these were Lord of the National Security, Prince Yellow Flying Tiger, Vice

Prime Minister, Prince Bi Gan, the king's two older brothers, Princes Wei Ziqi and Wei Ziyan, and the king's half brother Prince Wei Zi.

Shang Rong got off his horse to greet them. They said, "We know you deserve to retire. But how can you leave us when we need you the most?"

With tears brimming in his eyes, Shang Rong replied, "My dear Princes and colleagues. I would be glad to give my life if I know it would do any good. You are the pillars of the country. Do your best to save the kingdom. Let us drink to old times and I know we will see each other again." Shang Rong wrote a poem to express his anguish:

> Our farewell is bitter and dolorous,
> Our wine full of mournful sadness.
> Continue to pray for our beloved country, my dear friends, someday,
> When we meet again, hopefully, we will be more joyful and gay.

*   *   *   *

The bronze toaster was completed and the king had the toaster brought in for Daji's inspection.

It was a golden bronze monster twenty feet tall, with three layers of fire from three levels of burning charcoal; and two wheels to move it around like a chariot.

The king praised Daji, "My Beauty must have received secret formula from the divine to be able to design such a perfect punishment device. We will let the Number One Grand Counselor Mei Bo have the honor to be the Number One User tomorrow!"

Next morning, the bronze toaster was standing at the corner of the throne-room. Everyone was puzzled and wondered what that was. And to the surprise of everyone, the king came to the morning assembly.

The king had Mei Bo brought in. He knelt before the king, and spoke softly, "Your Number One Grand Counselor salutes you!"

The king shouted, "You damn fool! You have insulted me and my Beauty Daji with your poisonous tongue. Today we will crisp you to cinder on this toaster. Anyone who dares to say anything unforgivable will be treated like Mei Bo. So hear you all!"

Mei Bo now exploded, "You stupid king! My death is as light as a feather. It matters very little whether I die or live. I am one of your highest ranking counselors. I have served three generations of kings in this dynasty. What crime have I committed? I only fear that Cheng Tang's glorious reign will end by your stupidity and cruelty!"

In a fury the king had Mei Bo stripped bare and bound to the bronze toaster. He ordered it fired up. Many big fans activated to hasten the burning of the charcoal. Mei Bo let out a blood-curdling scream as he died.

The throne-room was filled with horror, anguish and the sickening odor of burnt flesh. Mei Bo died for his loyalty to the throne and his love of his country.

Many officials prayed to retire.

At the Noon Gate, Vice Prime Minister, Prince Bi Gan, lamented with the other senior princes, the king's two brothers, half brother Prince Ji Zi, and The Lord of National Security, Prince Yellow Flying Tiger.

With his long beard in his hand and foaming at the mouth, Yellow Flying Tiger said, "My dear friends. What I saw today was not only the cruel death of Number One Grand Counselor Mei Bo. It was also the death of the Dynasty! Toasted and tortured was not only Mei Bo's body, but also the mountains and rivers of the Shang reign!

"As the saying goes, when a king treats his officials as his hands and feet, his officials will treat him as their hearts and lungs. But when a king treats his officials like dirt, then they will treat him as a criminal, an enemy!"

*   *   *   *

Pleased with Daji's toaster, King Zhou called for a celebration in the Longevity Palace. Music and songs continued throughout the night and into the wee hours. The celebration was heard by Queen Jiang in her Central Palace.

She asked, "Where is the music coming from at this hour?" When told of the torturing, the death, and the ensuing celebration, Queen Jiang felt she must have a talk with the king.

▼

CHAPTER 7

PLOT AGAINST QUEEN JIANG

Queen Jiang, under shining red lanterns and accompanied by her entourage, drove in her carriage to the Longevity Palace. This was reported to the king who, half drunk, told Daji to go to the gate to meet the queen.

Queen Jiang was the original wife of King Zhou and, alone among all the king's women, allowed by law to sit with the king. Daji, no matter how much the king favored her, could only stand on the side.

King Zhou lifted his cup to the Queen. "My Queen. I am so delighted you have come. I will order Daji to do a ribbon dance for you."

Gwen, Daji's Lady in Waiting lightly beat the sound board as silk ribbons fluttered in rhythmic sway in Daji's lovely slender hands. Twisting and weaving to the soft music, Daji's willowy body was like a light cloud caressing the tip of a mountain, a gentle wave moving in a tranquil pond.

Queen Jiang's eyes looked at her own nose, and her nose pointed at her heart. Seeing the Queen's refusal to look at the dance, King Zhou asked with a smile, "My dear Queen, time flies. We are no longer young. We must enjoy ourselves whenever we can. Daji's song and dance are so rare a treasure, unequaled in the world. Why are you so unhappy and not even looking at her?"

Queen Jiang left her seat, knelt before the king, and said, "Sire. Daji's dance is nothing rare and there is not any treasure to mention."

The king said, "If this joy of dance is not a rare treasure, what is it?"

Queen Jiang replied, "What are the treasures for the king? The sun, the moon and the stars are the treasures of the Heaven. The five grains and hundred fruits are the treasures of the earth. The loyal and able ministers and generals are the treasures of the kingdom. And the intelligent, healthy and dutiful children are the treasures of the family. These four are the true treasures for the king.

"Now the king indulges in wine and women, encourages lust and immorality, believes in flattery and castigates the loyal, penalizes the good and rewards the bad. Everything to satisfy this one woman's evil whims. This depending on a hen to announce the rising morning sun is the worst of all. And you consider that a rare treasure?

"From the deepest depth of my heart, I wish that my king regains his good senses, takes care of his people, and appreciates his loyal, and able ministers and generals so that our kingdom may once again enjoy peace and prosperity.

"I am but an uneducated woman, know not how to avoid taboo and thus dare to be candid, to speak the truth. We will be so grateful when our king returns to his former virtuous ways!" So saying, Queen Jiang returned to her Central Palace.

The drunken king said, "How dare she! That stupid woman does not know how to be gracious and appreciative! If she were not my Queen, I would have killed her with this gold mallet!"

The king asked Daji to dance once more. But Daji said, "Your Majesty. I do not dare to dance!"

"Why not?"

"Queen Jiang accused me as the evil woman who would destroy your dynasty. She might be right! You have bestowed your love on me, and I of course will never leave you. But if the Queen heard that my song and dance are bewitching you, even if I pull out all my hair, I will never be able to redeem myself." So saying, tears rained down her apricot cheeks.

The king was beside himself. He comforted Daji, "Don't you fret, my love. Just do as I wish. Tomorrow I will banish her and make you my Central Palace Queen!"

From then on, day and night the Longevity Palace was filled with song and dance, wine and feast.

The first morning of each month is a customary time for all concubines to pay their respects to the Queen in the Central Palace. That morning both Concubine Huang of West Palace and Concubine Yang of the Fragrant Happiness Palace were already there when Daji came in.

Queen Jiang sat in the middle; to her left sat Concubine Huang and to her right sat Concubine Yang. Since Queen Jiang had not asked Daji to sit, she could only stand on the side.

Referring to Daji, the two sitting Concubines asked Queen Jiang, "Is this Beauty Su?"

The Queen said, "Yes." She turned toward Daji and continued, "In Longevity Palace, The Son of Heaven carouses day and night, neglecting his kingly duties. You, with your bewitching song and dance, make him kill his loyal and able ministers. I will do my utmost to stop all this nonsense. You may go!"

Daji, controlling her intense hatred, managed to say a polite good-bye to the Queen.

*   *   *   *

Sitting on a satin cushion in the Longevity Palace, Daji gave a long sigh. Her Lady in Waiting Gwen asked, "My lady, why such a long sigh? Something displeased you?"

Gritting her teeth, Daji said, "I am the king's favorite. But the Queen haughtily humiliated me in front of the two concubines! How am I to avenge this?"

Gwen said, "My lady. Why are you so forgetful? Don't you remember the king promised to make you the Central Palace Queen? You certainly can do plenty to avenge yourself!"

Daji said, "Yes, the king said so. But Queen Jiang is still the Queen! Besides, not all the officials will agree, and some certainly will complain. We will never see the light of this, unless we get rid of her first. Do tell me if you have any good suggestions. You will not be forgotten when I am Queen!"

Gwen said, "Oh, My Lady. I am only a servant, how can I plan anything? Why not invite a minister to help you?"

Daji thought a little and said, "How can we invite an outside official here? Besides, is there any we can completely trust?"

Gwen said, "Don't you worry, My Lady. Tomorrow, when you are with the king in the garden, you can send a secret order to summon Middle Counselor Fei Zhong, and let me talk to him. You can promise him a great reward. He is known for his intelligence and he will not fail."

Daji said, "If he does not want to get involved, what then?"

Gwen said with confidence, "Middle counselor Fei Zhong is the king's favorite. Besides, your being here was on his recommendation. He will be glad to help."

Next day as Daji and the king strolled in the Imperial Garden, Fei Zhong was summoned to report to the Longevity Palace gate where Gwen met him.

Gwen said to Fei Zhong, "My Lady has a top secret mission for you. Here, take this letter home; study it carefully. My Lady will reward you very handsomely when the mission is accomplished. But hurry." With that she handed him the letter.

On returning home, Fei Zhong locked himself in his study and opened the letter. My goodness! Daji was asking him to plot the demise of Queen Jiang! Fear gripped his heart. He thought to himself, "As the king's original wife, Queen Jiang has, by law, a position equal to the king. Her father is the Grand Duke of the East, rules the great East Lu State, and commands a great army of tens of thousands. Besides, his son, her brother Jiang Wen Huan is a renowned warrior. How dare I touch her?

"If my plot fails, the consequence will be too horrible to contemplate. On the other hand, if I don't try, Daji would never forgive me. I am damned if I do and damned if I don't! I am done for either way."

For days, the matter worried Fei Zhong so much he could neither eat nor sleep. This matter weighed so heavily on his greedy and unscrupulous heart.

One afternoon as Fei Zhong was sitting in the Great Hall of his residence stewing in his worry, he was startled by a tall man with broad shoulders and big chest passing by his window.

Fei Zhong called out, "Who is there?"

The tall man came before Fei Zhong, bowed and said, "I am Jiang Huan."

"How long have you been in my household?" Fei Zhong asked.

Jiang Huan said, "Five years ever since I left East Lu State. I am grateful that I have been treated well here. I am sorry to have startled you, sir."

An unholy light flashed in his evil mind as Fei Zhong said, "I have a mission for you. If you do it well, there is great fortune."

"My lord, your wish is my duty even if I have to go through fire and boiling oil. I will carry out your wish without a moment of hesitation!" Jiang Huan replied earnestly.

Fei Zhong continued, "For days, I have not been able to see a way out. Little did I know it dwells upon you. When this mission is accomplished, I promise you untold wealth!"

Jiang Huan said, "My Lord. How dare I expect such reward? Whatever is your wish, it is only my duty and pleasure to obey."

Fei Zhong spoke into Jiang Huan's ear, "Such and so, this and that..."

"And remember, this matter is of utmost secret. You must be prudent all the time!" Fei Zhong emphatically reminded Jiang Huan.

After Jiang Huan left, Fei Zhong wrote out his plan in detail and sent it secretly to Daji.

The vixen specter Daji was overjoyed, and said to herself, "That will be the end of Queen Jiang and the beginning of my own ascendancy."

Next day, the king and Daji were spending some quiet moments in the Longevity Place doing nothing in particular.

Daji said, "Sire. You have been with me all these months now. Perhaps you should be at the Morning Assembly tomorrow to show your ministers how diligent you are at your administration."

"Of course, my love. By just listening to you we all know how virtuous you are!" said the unsuspecting king.

So next morning, as scheduled, the king and his entourage left the Longevity Palace, passed the Nine Dragon Bridge, and were going toward the Demarcation Building when suddenly, out rushed a tall strong man.

With kerchief on his head, and sword in his hand, he jumped swiftly like a wolf, screaming, "Befuddled king! I have the Queen's order to kill you to make sure Cheng Tang's reign would go to her father, the Grand Duke of the East."

But the many bodyguards quickly captured and bound him up tightly.

The king was both frightened and angered. When he reached the throne room, all the officials were waiting there as usual but none had heard about the incident.

The king called The Lord of National Security, Prince Yellow Flying Tiger, and Vice Prime Minister, Prince Bi Gan to come forward.

Both men stepped out into the aisle. The king said, "My friends, today on my way here a very strange incident occurred. At the Demarcation Building, there was an assassin trying to kill me. I would like to know who was behind this!"

Incredulous, Prince Yellow Flying Tiger asked, "Who was in charge of the guards last night?"

A general named Honest Hero stepped out, "I was in charge last night. There were no strangers around. Could it be that this man came in amid the officials in the morning and slithered to the Demarcation Building?"

Yellow Flying Tiger ordered the accused be brought in.

The king asked, "Who wants to question the prisoner?"

Fei Zhong quickly stepped out and said, "Sire. I will."

Fei Zhong was not an investigator, but since this was part of his plot to harm Queen Jiang, he volunteered in order to forestall a real investigation which might reveal the truth.

Fei Zhong took the accused Jiang Huan out to the Noon Gate and went through all the motions of asking questions. He then returned to the throne room to make his report. All the officials were holding their breath in anticipation, but Fei Zhong would not speak.

The king said impatiently, "Don't just kneel there, say something!"

Fei Zhong said, "Sire. I dare not speak out."

"Why not?" the king demanded.

"Only if Your Majesty grants me immunity."

"Granted," said the king.

Fei Zhong, making up his story with much embellishment and relish, said, "The assassin's family name is Jiang, same as our Queen of the Central Palace. His given name is Huan, as in a jade bracelet. He is a household member of the Grand Duke of the East. He was following Queen Jiang's order to assassinate Your Majesty. The plan was to take your throne and give it to her father the Grand Duke of the East. Fortunately, Heaven was watching and the attempt failed. Your Majesty should call in all the top nine Grand Counselors."

The king said, "Queen Jiang is my original wife, how could she possibly be so crude as to make an attempt on my life? To get rid of a bad official is child's play. But to get rid of someone whom I have loved and trusted all these years is something else. Send for Concubine Huang of the West Palace at once."

The king angrily returned to the Longevity Palace. But the four hundred civil and military officials lingered in the Nine Hall Court, speculating on what was true and what was false.

Number two Grand Counselor Yang Ren spoke to Prince Yellow Flying Tiger, "Queen Jiang has the reputation of being the most virtuous, kind and wise person. There must be some kind of intrigue to hurt her. Let us all stay to see what Concubine Huang finds out."

Queen Jiang, in her Central Palace, knelt to receive the king's messenger. The king's edict said, "Queen Jiang of the Central Palace is my original wife. Her rank is almost equal to mine, the Son of Heaven. However, she is not diligently cultivating her virtues to assist me; instead she is trying to rebel against me. She ordered Jiang Huan to assassinate me in front of the Demarcation Building.

Fortunately Heaven was watching over me, and Jiang Huan was captured and has confessed. He said that my Queen and her father, the Grand Duke of the East, intended to usurp my throne. This is treason!

"To plot against the king is a treason punishable by death. To plot to kill one's spouse is a moral crime, also punishable by death. Therefore, Queen Jiang, if found guilty, will be dealt with according to the law of the kingdom. She is now to proceed immediately to the West Palace for questioning by Concubine Huang."

As if struck by a thunderbolt from a clear sky, Queen Jiang cried out, "What is this all about? What kind of sick joke is this? Oh, my God, who is manufacturing such ridiculous, false accusations? What will my fate be?"

Queen Jiang knelt before Concubine Huang of West Palace, and said, "The Jiang family has been known for generations as the most loyal subjects of the kingdom. The Emperor of The Heaven and The Empresses of The Earth are our witnesses. I am now calamitously accused of a most hideous crime. You know me well, my Concubine Huang. Please help me to prove my innocence."

Concubine Huang said, "The king said that you ordered Jiang Huan to assassinate him, and to usurp the throne for your father, the Grand Duke of the East. This is a crime punishable by death for all your nine family branches."

Queen Jiang said, "My dear Concubine Huang. I am the daughter of the Grand Duke of the East, who is the head of the two hundred regional dukes. His rank is above all the Grand Dukes and other officials. I am the Queen, also the mother of the Crown Prince Yin Jiao who will inherit the throne when the king goes to Heaven. In that event, I will be the mother of the king. On the other hand, should my father become the king, I will be only the king's daughter. And when my father goes to Heaven, my brother will become the king and I will be the king's sister. Have you ever heard that being a king's daughter and a king's sister is higher in position than being the Queen and the king's mother? I may not be highly educated, but I am not that stupid. Besides, there are so many loyal dukes, ministers and generals. Will they stand by to let my father take over the throne? And how can my father and the Jiang family expect to survive that? Is it not clear enough that I cannot possibly be the instigator of such an atrocious move? I will be forever grateful if you will clear up this matter."

At this moment, Concubine Huang received orders from the king to speed up the inquiry. She hurried to the Longevity Palace.

The king asked, "What did that worthless slut have to say for herself?"

Concubine Huang said, "As you ordered, I have severely questioned the Queen. To my best knowledge, Queen Jiang was, and is, the most loyal and virtuous person. She is your original wife, has shared with you the burdens of administering the nation, has given you the Crown Prince. When you go to Heaven, her son will be king and she will be the king's mother. This is the highest position under heaven anyone could aspire to. Why would she risk the death of her nine family branches for a lesser position? Besides, her father is already the highest ranking Grand Duke. For them to plot any assassination is unlikely. Why should Queen Jiang give up what she already has to go for a wild goose chase of so much less? She is not that stupid. Further, in all these years, the queen has shown everything she did or does is the most proper according to the teaching of our sages. I beg Your Majesty to please see through the fallacy of this malicious accusation. For the sake of the Crown Prince, pardon Queen Jiang. The country will be forever grateful."

Concubine Huang's plea moved the king very much. He thought to himself, "What Concubine Huang says is logical. There must be more than meets the eye."

As King Zhou was on the verge of pardoning Queen Jiang, Daji, at the side of the king, gave a little snicker. The king asked, "My Beauty. Why are you smiling?"

The vixen specter in Daji replied, "My King. Concubine Huang has been hoodwinked by Queen Jiang. Usurping the throne is a capital crime. Queen Jiang certainly will not readily admit it. The accused assassin Jiang Huan is her father's man and has confessed to the crime. Jiang Huan pointed his finger at Queen Jiang and not at anyone else. Is that not proof enough of Queen Jiang's guilt? To obtain a confession from Queen Jiang, we must use some heavy tortures."

"What a keen observation, my precious!" the king said.

Concubine Huang cut in, "Su Daji! You cannot suggest that! The Queen is the original wife of the king. She is the mother of our country. Her rank is almost parallel to the king's. Since the reigns of The Three Sages and The Five Reverend Emperors, no torture has ever been used on a Queen, no matter what she is accused of!"

Twisting the law, Daji said, "The law was made in heaven, the Son of Heaven is only administering the law according to what has been set up. He cannot change the law to suit his own convenience. Furthermore, between the rich and the poor, the high born and the humble, there should not be any distinction in the eyes of the law."

In her true vixen spirit Daji said to the king, "If Queen Jiang refuses to confess, Your Majesty can have one of her eyes gouged out. The heart is connected to the eyes. When her eye is gone, Queen Jiang will definitely confess to her crime. This will warn all who might entertain thoughts of violating the law of the kingdom."

The king said, "Daji is right!"

Seeing the turn of events, Concubine Huang rushed back to her West Palace where the Queen was waiting. With tears running down her cheeks, she said to the Queen, "Oh, my dear Queen. Daji is the arch nemesis of your last hundred lives! She is urging the king to have one of your eyes gouged out! If I were you, I would confess just to gain time to clear up the accusation! Never before have we seen such cruel punishment befall any Queen! The worst ever was a banishment to the Cold Palace."

The Queen wept. "My dear sister, what you just said was for my own good. But all my life, my thoughts and my actions have always been to follow the teaching of the sages. How can I acknowledge such a detestable crime that would shame my parents and offend my ancestors! Furthermore, a wife plotting to kill her husband is a moral crime at its worst, an act that would make my father not only look like a disloyal and rebellious official, but also a very immoral man. My family name will forever be odious for thousands of years, and my son the Crown Prince will forfeit his right to the crown. With an impact of such magnitude, how can I lightly confess to a crime I have never committed? Gouging out my eyes or cutting me to pieces may be my fate to endure. They can grind up my flesh and my bones, but they can never make me confess!"

Queen Jiang then added bitterly, "I would rather die."

So it transpired that the king had Queen Jiang's right eye yanked out, leaving her crumpled on the floor in her own blood. Concubine Huang felt helpless, and could not stop her tears when she reflected on the vulnerability of her own position and her own possible fate.

As ordered, Concubine Huang took the Queen's eye to Longevity Palace. The king looked at the bloody mass, the eye of his Queen of many years! Oh, how the memories of those cherished years rushed into his consciousness. His soul, which had deserted him the instant he saw Daji, miraculously returned. For a moment the king's remorse was real, and he bent his head in silence.

Then he turned his head and berated Daji, "It was all because of your fickleness! I did as you suggested without thinking. And now the Queen has lost her right eye! And we still don't have a confession. How are we to convince the ministers and the generals that the Queen really did commit the crime, and that my actions was justified?"

Daji said, "My King. You are right! But we have come so far, it is like riding a tiger. How to get off safely? Well, we certainly cannot let Queen Jiang go now and risk rousing the nobles and officials."

Alas! In an instant, the king lost his soul once more when he heard Daji's voice! The soul-less king issued his edict to Concubine Huang, "If Queen Jiang does not confess, use the red hot iron on her fingers."

Concubine Huang rushed back to her West Palace where she howled with anguish.

The half unconscious Queen Jiang was lying on the floor, soaked in her blood when Concubine Huang sobbed, "My dear, dear Queen! What wrongs had you done in your past lives that had offended Heaven and Earth enough to incur such a fate? The king, goaded on by Daji, is going to put you to death by burning your fingers with red hot iron if you don't confess. How can I endure seeing you go through such torture?"

Her tears mixed with her blood, the now fully conscious Queen screamed out, "If I had done such wrong in my past lives, I would not be afraid to die. But you be my witness. I cannot confess to a crime I did not commit!"

The palace strong men, who were to carry out the king's order, urged Queen Jiang to confess. The Queen, her determination like granite, stood up to her conviction.

The king's men put Queen Jiang's fingers under the red hot iron. The odor of burnt flesh filled the West Palace.

In immeasurable agony, the Queen again fainted.

Concubine Huang felt that a knife had pierced her heart. She went back to Longevity Palace to report to the king. She said, "The cruel tortures have not been able to extract a confession from Queen Jiang. I am convinced more than ever there is intrigue to harm the Central Palace Queen!"

Startled and confused, at first the king seemed once again to accept his soul's return. But instead he turned to the vixen specter Daji, and said, "I have been doing as my Beauty suggested. What should I do now?"

Daji knelt down, "My king! Don't you worry! Accused assassin Jiang Huan is still here. We can have him confront Queen Jiang. She will find no more ways to avoid a confession!"

King Zhou's soul, after a flash, now disappeared forever! He ordered the Chao twins to take the accused Jiang Huan to the West Palace.

CHAPTER 8

▼

MUTINY OF THE PALACE GUARDS

Chao twins, Palace Honor Guards, brought the accused assassin Jiang Huan to the West Palace for questioning. Concubine Huang said to Queen Jiang, "My Queen, your accuser is here!"

Queen Jiang opened her one remaining eye and screamed at Jiang Huan, "You felon! Who has paid you to ruin me? You undertook this set-up assassination and then accused me of your crime! Both Heaven and Earth will condemn you!"

Lying, Jiang Huan said, "Oh, my Queen. You were the one who ordered me to do it! Could I not obey? This is a fact. Don't you deny it!"

Beside herself with fury, Concubine Huang shouted, "You liar! You assassin! Can't you see the Queen is near death from cruel torture? The Emperor of Heaven and The Empress of Earth will take your life for this trump-up accusation!"

*   *   *   *

Crown Prince Yin Jiao and his younger brother Prince Yin Hong were playing a game of chess in the East Palace when a eunuch rushed in, crying, "My princes, calamity! Calamity!"

The two paid him no attention for the Crown Prince was only fourteen, his younger brother twelve years, and they liked to play chess.

The eunuch had to repeat, "My Princes, please stop your game! Disaster has come to our palaces. Our home and country are being destroyed!"

Crown Prince Yin Jiao asked, "What are you so excited about?"

In tears, the eunuch said, "My dear Princes. Your mother the Queen is suffering the cruelest tortures. Her right eye is gouged out and her hands are burnt. And she stands accused of trying to kill the king. Please do something fast!"

Screaming, the Princes raced to the West Palace and found their mother on the floor in a pool of blood.

The Crown Prince cried, "Our Royal mother! What happened to you to suffer such tortures? You as the Central Palace Queen should never have to suffer any torture!"

On hearing her son's voice, the Queen opened her one eye and cried out, "My sons! My sons! My suffering is all because of that lying rat Jiang Huan, and the cruel Concubine Daji who is behind it all. For the sake of my love for you, you must clear my name and avenge my agony!" She then let out an anguished howl, and died.

The Crown Prince turned from his mother's gruesome corpse to a man kneeling nearby and knew instantly that he must be the hateful Jiang Huan. Drawing a sword from the wall he said, "You renegade! You dared to plot the assassination of my father the king, then accused my mother the Queen of your crime!" So saying, he severed Jiang Huan's torso from his legs. Blood splattered all over.

With the sword still in his hand, the Crown Prince then ran out of the West Palace, screaming, "I will kill that Daji to avenge my mother's death!"

Concubine Huang was much alarmed. She called to the younger prince, "Quick, go get your brother. I have important things to say."

The young Prince ran out, calling, "My Royal older brother, please come back!"

Meanwhile, after delivering Jiang Huan to the West Palace, the Chao twins were taking their time sauntering back to the Longevity Palace when they saw Crown Prince Yin Jiao running toward them with sword in hand. Thinking the Prince was coming after them, they turned and ran for their lives.

Yin Jiao returned to the West Palace with Yin Hong. Concubine Huang said, "My dear Crown Prince, you were too impatient. Now that the accused assassin is dead, we will never be able to find out who was behind all this. I was planning to burn his hands for his confession. Now it is too late. A dead man cannot talk!

"And then you carried a sword to the Longevity Palace. I am afraid when the Palace Guards report it to the king, calamity will strike!"

At the Longevity Palace the Chao twins reported to the king that the Crown Prince was rushing toward the Longevity Palace with sword in hand.

The king was furious, "Those unfilial curs! Their mother plotted to assassinate me and has not yet been punished. Now her sons dared to come here with their swords to kill me! Well, like mother, like sons. They are not worthy of me. You Chao twin brothers, take my Dragon-phoenix sword and bring back both their heads!"

The Chao twins took the Dragon-phoenix sword and went straight to the West Palace. When informed of the turn of events by a trusted eunuch, Concubine Huang hurried to her West Palace entrance as the twins arrived.

Concubine Huang asked nonchalantly, "Why are you coming to my West Palace again?"

Very self-importantly, the Chao twins replied, "We have the king's Dragon-phoenix sword. The king wants the heads of the two princes."

Concubine Huang lambasted them, "You stupid fools! I know your kind! Using the king's order as excuse to come to the forbidden area of my palace to seduce my maidens! If it were not for the Dragon-phoenix sword, I would chop off your dog heads! Both the Princes chased you out of the West Palace. The East Palace is where you should go! Now get out!"

The Chao twins were so intimidated they immediately left.

Concubine Huang rushed back to the two Princes. In tears, she said to them, "The king killed his wife and now wants to kill his sons. As a West Palace Concubine, I am not able to save you. You must run immediately to the Fragrant Happiness Palace where Concubine Yang will hide you for a couple of days. By then, we hope some loyal ministers might be able to save you from the wrath of the soul-less king."

Both Princes knelt before Concubine Huang, saying, "Dear Concubine Huang. We don't know how we can ever repay you for your help and compassion. Our mother is dead. We wish you would bury her. We will be forever grateful."

Concubine Huang said, "Leave quickly now. I will do what I can."

At the Fragrant Happiness Palace, Concubine Yang was at the entrance, anxiously awaiting news of Queen Jiang. When she saw the two Princes, she hurriedly took them inside. She asked, "My two Princes. What has happened to Queen Jiang?"

The two knelt before her. The Crown Prince told her as much as he knew and said, "Now Daji wants to kill me and my younger brother. Please, save us!"

Concubine Yang returned quickly to her Palace entrance to face the Chao twins, knowing that they would come when they could not find the princes at the East Palace. They came running like wolf and tiger with the Dragon-phoenix sword.

Concubine Yang called out to her own guards, "Men! Get these two trespassers out of here!"

She then said to the twins, "This is the forbidden area of the Fragrant Happiness Palace. How dare you come here!"

The Chao twins said arrogantly, "Concubine Yang. We are Palace Honor Guards of the Longevity Palace. Look at this Dragon-phoenix sword. We have the king's order to fetch the heads of the two Princes. We are not running without authority."

Concubine Yang bawled them out, "The Princes belong to the East Palace. Why are you here in my palace? If it were not for the king's Dragon-phoenix sword, I would certainly have you both killed here and now! Get out!"

Not daring to say any more, the Chao twins left the Fragrant Happiness Palace.

"What are we to do now?" they asked themselves." They decided to report back to the Longevity Palace.

Concubine Yang said to the two Princes, "This is not the place for you to hide. There are many eyes and ears. You both should go to the Nine Hall Court while the high officials are still there. Go see your uncles Prince Wei Zi, Prince Wei Zi Yan, and Prince Wei Zi Qi. And particularly, see the Vice Prime Minister, Prince Bi Gan and the Lord of National Security, Prince Yellow Flying Tiger."

After thanking Concubine Yang, the two Princes raced to the Nine Hall Court.

Concubine Yang was overwhelmed with extreme depression. She sat on a satin cushion to do some soul searching. "Queen Jiang was the original wife of the king, also the mother of the Crown Prince. Still she could not escape torture and death. What fate might a mere childless concubine like me have? Now the witch Daji is the king's favorite. If rumor reached the king that the two Princes were seen leaving my palace, the king will definitely blame me. How am I to stand the cruel torture? Even Queen Jiang died at their hands. What can save me from the same fate? Oh, I'd rather die now, rather die now!"

Devastated by her despondency Concubine Yang hanged herself.

Reports of her suicide reached the king. The king could not understand why, but couldn't care less. He granted that Concubine Yang's coffin might remain in the White Tiger Court.

Meanwhile Concubine Huang went back to the Longevity Palace to report that Queen Jiang had died professing her innocence to the very end.

Concubine Huang added, "The Queen's body is still in the West Palace. Because she was your original wife and is the Queen Mother of your Crown Prince, please grant her a coffin so that she can be laid in state and accorded the proper rites that neither the civil nor the military officials can fault."

The king, realizing his delicate situation, granted Concubine Huang's request.

Now the Chao twin brothers returned to Longevity Palace to report to the king, "We don't know where the two Princes are. They were not in the East Palace."

The king said, "Could they still be in the West Palace?"

The twins said together, "No, Sire. They were not in the West Palace. And we also went to the Fragrant Happiness Palace. They were not there either."

The king said, "If they are not in the three Palaces, then they must be in the Nine Hall Court. They must be arrested and punished according to the law! Go get them!"

$$* \qquad * \qquad * \qquad *$$

The two Princes ran toward the Nine Hall Court where both Civil and Military officials were still lingering anxiously since the morning assembly.

Lord of National Security, Prince Yellow Flying Tiger heard running steps, looked through the peacock screen and saw the two Princes running in his direction, shaking, and out of breath.

Yellow Flying Tiger walked up to them, "What is the matter? Why are you trembling so?"

Seeing Yellow Flying Tiger, the Crown Prince howled, "Prince Yellow Flying Tiger, save us!" Crying and holding onto Yellow Flying Tiger's robe, he sobbed out the story to all who were present.

In shock and in tears, the officials said, "When the mother of our kingdom is falsely accused and tortured to death, how can we stand by and do nothing? Let us beat the gong to ask for the king. We may be able to find the real criminal to clear Queen Jiang's good name."

Then suddenly like rolling thunder, there rose from the west corner of the Nine Hall Court where the lower rank officials stood, the stirring words: "The Son of Heaven has neglected his administration, killed his Queen and now wants to kill his sons as well. He killed the Royal Astrologer Du and tortured to death Number One Grand Counselor, Mei Bo, because they dared to speak the truth. The king has neither morals nor principles. He is not fit to be our king. We are ashamed to be his subjects. Let us rebel and find a new king. We may then be able to save our ancestral shrine!"

All eyes turned to see Fang Da and Fang Er as they spoke. Brothers, they were also Palace Security officials. Yellow Flying Tiger, pulling his rank conspicuously, shouted them down, "Shut up! You should not talk so presumptuously when there are so many here who are of higher ranks. What are your ranks?"

The Fang brothers did not dare to say any more. Yellow Flying Tiger's heart was heavy as he reviewed the state of the nation, particularly the reactions of the populace to the recent happenings in the king's Court. Vice Prime Minister, Prince Bi Gan and every other official ground their teeth, but no one dared to speak his mind.

Number Two Grand Counselor Yang Ren, who wore a red robe and a jade belt, broke the silence.

"Today's happenings were exactly predicted by Cloud Dweller, the Superiorman of Mount South End. When a king is not upright, there will be treacherous, disloyal persons around him. It has been only a few

days since the king killed the Royal Astrologer Du and Number One
Grand Counselor, Mei Bo. Today, he took black as white, accepted
falsehood as truth, tortured and killed his royal wife, the Queen of
Central Palace. And now he wants to kill his Crown Prince and the
younger prince as well. There must be someone plotting all these murders, and I am sure this person is laughing behind our back right this
moment! Cheng Tang's Reign is now crashing down fast, and our
kingdom is in such a ruinous state we will all soon become victims of
this plot!"

"My Grand Counselor Yang is correct," Yellow Flying Tiger sighed.
Other officials were silent. The two Princes sobbed softly.

Suddenly, a commotion from the back broke the tension. The Fang
brothers were pushing their way to the front, shouting, "King Zhou is
vicious and mindless. He killed his Queen, now he wants to kill his
two sons! We are rebelling! We brothers are taking these two young
princes to East Lu State to seek help."

Swiftly, each Fang brother scooped up one prince and ran out of the
Nine Hall Court toward the South Gate of the Capital, knocking
down all in their way. They were so strong no one could stop them.

All were flabbergasted by the turn of events. But Yellow Flying
Tiger acted as if nothing had happened.

Vice Prime Minister, Prince Bi Gan edged over to Yellow Flying
Tiger and said softly, "Lord of the National Security, the Fang brothers
have rebelled. Why don't you say something?"

Yellow Flying Tiger replied, "Isn't it too bad that none of us high
ranking officials has the guts of the Fang brothers! They are but low
ranking warriors, not much educated. Yet they could see the situation
clearly. Because of their humble ranks, they don't dare speak directly to
the king. The only way they saw open to them was to help the two
young Princes escape, to run for help. I think their action is commendable!"

The running steps that were now coming toward the Nine Hall
Court were those of Longevity Palace Honor Guards, the Chao twins.

Holding the Dragon-phoenix sword, they asked, "Lords, are the two young princes here?"

Yellow Flying Tiger said, "Yes, indeed. They were here a moment ago. They were telling us about the tragic death of their mother, and how they were pursued by the two of you. The Fang brothers have carried them out of the city. Since you are under the king's order to capture them, why not go after them? They can't be far."

On hearing of the names of Fang brothers, the Chao twins lost their wits from fear. They were no match and they knew it. The Fang brothers were over thirty feet tall, twice the Chao twins in size. One touch from the Fang brothers would be enough to send them to the next world. Clearly Yellow Flying Tiger was goading them.

"Better report back to the king." The Chao twins told themselves.

The king was furious over the escape of the two princes. He shouted his order, "Go get the Fang brothers!"

The Chao twins said timidly, "Sire. How can we possibly catch up? The Fang brothers are known for their superior strength. The only way to catch them is for Prince Yellow Flying Tiger to do it himself."

The king said, "Then rush my order to Yellow Flying Tiger."

They went back to the Nine Hall Court and handed over the king's Dragon-phoenix sword to Yellow Flying Tiger together with the king's order to capture the rebels.

Yellow Flying Tiger laughed, "I knew the Chao twins would turn the hot chestnut over to me."

Yellow Flying Tiger left the Nine Hall Court holding the Dragon-phoenix sword, after refusing many warriors who volunteered to accompany him.

*　　　*　　　*　　　*

The Fang brothers, with the two Princes on their backs, ran for thirty miles out of the Capital City before putting them down.

The Crown Prince said, "How are we to thank you?"

The older brother Fang Da said, "When we saw the injustice and the danger you were in, we could not help but get you out of there first. Now we have to see where can we go."

Even as they were talking, they saw Yellow Flying Tiger coming on his Five-Colored Magic bull, a beast that could easily run eight hundred miles a day.

"Yellow Flying Tiger is here to capture us. No doubt, when we get back to the capital, we will be executed," said Fang Da.

When Yellow Flying Tiger arrived, all knelt and asked, "Are you here to arrest us?"

Rolling off his Magic bull, Yellow Flying Tiger said, "All get up please. Yes, indeed, I have the king's Dragon-phoenix sword to arrest you! Please decide what you want to do. Not that I wish you any ill, but I am under the king's order. Do hurry."

The Crown Prince knelt again, said, "You know about the injustice and torture given my mother. Now the king wants to kill me and my brother. Pity us! Let us go so that we can avenge our mother's death, and clear her good name. We will be so grateful!"

Yellow Flying Tiger also knelt, but shook his head, "Let's plan a little. We all know how terrible the situation is. If I let you go, all nine branches of my family will be put to death. If I take you back to the capital, it would be completely against my will and conscience. Let us think!"

Seeing there was no way out, the Crown Prince said, "It is all right, my general. You should not be sacrificed for my sake. But may I ask you a favor?"

Yellow Flying Tiger said, "Please speak out."

The Crown Prince said, "You can take my head to the king to complete your mission. But I beseech you to spare my little brother. Let him have a chance to grow up and to avenge my mother's death. I will never forget your generosity, even in death!"

On hearing this, the younger prince stepped forward to volunteer himself. "Oh, no! My beloved elder brother. You are the Crown

Prince. I am but a younger son, too young to do much to help matters. Let Lord Yellow Flying Tiger take my head to appease the king. You then go either to East Lu State to see Grandfather, or to Western Foothills to borrow some troops from the Grand Duke of the West to seek our vengeance. My life is unimportant."

The Crown Prince embraced his younger brother as they sobbed their hearts out fighting to be the one to give up his head.

The Fang brothers cried out, "What tragedy!" And they too wept.

Seeing how loyal the two Fang brothers were, Yellow Flying Tiger said to them in tear, "Don't cry, my Palace Security Guards. And don't despair, my two young princes. This matter is known only to the five of us and we must keep it a secret. Fang Da, please come here. You escort the two young Princes to the East Lu State to see the Grand Duke of the East. Fang Er, you go to the Grand Duke of the South, first to tell him that I have let the Princes go to the East Lu State, then also ask him to send troops to rid the king's Court of traitors and avenge Queen's death. Don't worry about me, I know how to take care of myself."

Fang Da said, "My Lord. This morning we rushed out of the capital on the spur of the moment and are without any cash. How are we to proceed without money?"

Yellow Flying Tiger said, "Neither am I prepared for that." He thought for a moment. "But here. Take this piece of jade, pawn it for travel expenses. It easily can fetch at least one hundred ounces of gold. Take good care of the Princes. You will be handsomely rewarded when your missions are completed. My Princes, take care, and go with the Gods. I must rush back to report to the king."

So saying, Yellow Flying Tiger got back on his Five-Colored Magic Bull. It was dusk when he arrived in the capital. The officials were still in the Nine Hall Court waiting for news.

"How goes?" They asked.

Yellow Flying Tiger replied, to the secret delight of everyone, "Try as I did, I could not catch up with them."

Yellow Flying Tiger went to see the king, who asked, "Have you captured my unfilial sons?"

Yellow Flying Tiger replied, "No, Sire. I chased them for seventy miles when I reached the three-forked road. I asked about but no one had seen them. I was afraid I might take the wrong fork and completely miss them. So I came back."

The king said, "Well, we will wait until tomorrow. But they must be captured!"

Daji was most disappointed. She said, "It is too bad that Your Majesty let the Crown Prince go for the night. I am sure he is on his way to the Grand Duke of the East. Why don't you quickly send out two generals of the Palace Security with three thousand mounted soldiers to find the Princes? We must get to the roots if we want to get rid of the grass!"

The king said, "That is exactly what I have in mind!"

The king ordered middle ranked Palace Security Guards Generals Yin and Lei to lead three thousand mounted soldiers for the mission.

On receiving the king's order, the generals went to see Prince Yellow Flying Tiger for the troops.

Yellow Flying Tiger was in the back hall of his mansion, pondering how to deal with the terrible situation when Generals Yin and Lei came in. Yellow Flying Tiger said impatiently, "We left the Nine Hall Court only a moment ago. What now?"

The two generals said, "The king just ordered us to lead three thousand mounted soldiers to capture the Crown Prince at once."

Yellow Flying Tiger thought to himself, "If I let them go, they will no doubt capture the princes. I definitely cannot do that! He said, "It is too late for today! Come early in the morning and I will have them ready for you. Now go!"

The two generals dared not disobey, for Yellow Flying Tiger was the top-most general of the kingdom. The rest of the military were his underlings.

Yellow Flying Tiger then instructed his trusted aides to select three thousand of the most sickly and aged soldiers and horses they could find.

Next morning, Generals Yin and Lei led their three thousand good-for-nothing troops toward the East Lu State.

$$*\qquad*\qquad*\qquad*$$

After running for two days, the Fang brothers and their charges came to a crossroad. In spite of Yellow Flying Tiger's earlier instructions, they decided that each should now go his separate way to avoid detection and possible capture.

They talked to the Princes, "Not that we don't want to help you to the end, but if we continue to travel together on these busier roads, we will be discovered easily. If we separate, one of us may last long enough, perhaps even to right the wrongs."

The Crown Prince said, "You are right. But both my younger brother and I don't know our way."

Fang Da said, "This fork leads to East Lu State, and this to the South. Both are well traveled and you will not get lost."

The Crown Prince said, "Very well then. But where are you two going? And when will we meet you again?"

Fang Da said, "It does not matter where we go. We will take the byways, find some regional dukes who may take us in for a while. When you are ready to march on the capital, we will come to join you without fail."

They parted in tears. The Crown Prince said to Yin Hong, "I will go to East Lu State to see Grandfather. You go south to ask the Grand Duke of the South for help. I will send for you in due course." They embraced.

*   *   *   *

Walking and crying, hungry and tired, the younger prince now had to fend for himself. Remembering his happier palace days, he could not stop his tears. By and by, while passing through a village, he saw a family just sitting down to dinner. He walked up and demanded, "Bring me my dinner!"

The family saw a handsome boy wearing a red robe, with unusual manners. Although they did not know who he was, the head of the family Lou Wang said, "Please sit down. There is rice for you."

After dinner the Prince said, "Thank you very much for your hospitality. But I don't know when I can repay your generosity."

Lou Wang asked him, "What is your name? Where are you going?"

The Prince replied, "I am the younger son of the king, on my way to see the Grand Duke of the South."

The villagers immediately knelt, asking for pardon for not knowing who he was.

The Prince asked, "Is this the road south?"

The villagers assured him that it was.

Slowly, the Prince trudged southward. By and by, he came to a temple in the shade of tall pines. The sign at the door told him that this was the temple of the Yellow Emperor.

Softly, the young Prince prayed in front of the idol of the Yellow Emperor, "My dear Yellow Emperor. I am the thirtieth generation of Cheng Tang's children, King Zhou's younger son. My Royal father has violated the Three Principles and the Five Relationships. He ordered the killing of my mother. Now I am feeling his wrath. May I please sleep here at your court for the night? I promise to refurbish your temple when the present calamity is over!" Then immediately, the young Prince fell asleep.

*   *   *   *

Meanwhile, the Crown Prince walked some forty miles. Toward evening he saw the mansion of Prime Minister. He knocked on the door and called out. "Anybody home?"

Hearing no answer, he pushed the door open and walked in, calling again, "Anybody home?"

From the inner court, a voice asked, "Who is there?"

Dimly discerning an old man, the Crown Prince replied, "I am a traveler passing through. I wonder if you will let me spend the night here?"

The old man said, "Come in please. Your accent sounds like you are from the capital."

"Yes, I am indeed."

As the Crown Prince entered, he recognized the retired Prime Minister Shang Rong, who at the same moment, also recognized him.

Shang Rong knelt, "My Crown Prince. Pardon me. I did not know it was you. But why are you here alone? Is something wrong?"

In tears, the Crown Prince Yin Jiao related the situation to the old Prime Minister.

Wringing his hands, Shang Rong said, "Oh, dear me! I did not realize conditions had deteriorated so fast and to such a degree. I am enjoying my garden and leisure hours in my retirement, but my heart is still in the capital, in the king's court. Is there no one doing anything on your behalf? Tomorrow I will go with you to see what I can do."

Old Shang Rong then ordered his servants to serve the Crown Prince dinner.

*   *   *   *

The pursuing mounted soldiers had just arrived at the crossroad where the young princes separated. It had taken Generals Yin and Lei three days to get there.

General Lei complained, "At the rate we are going, we will never catch up with them. Why don't we station most of our good-for-nothing troops here, and each of us select fifty of the stronger ones to do the chasing? You go to the East Lu State and I will head south."

The generals agreed to meet again at the crossroads where the bulk of their troops were to remain.

CHAPTER 9

▼

MARTYRDOM IN THE GREAT HALL

General Lei and his fifty mounted soldiers rushed southward. At dusk, so tired some almost fell off their horses, when they spied a village beyond the pines. On closer look, they found the Temple of the Yellow Emperor. As they saw no caretaker, they pushed open the door and walked in.

By the light of their torches, they saw someone asleep in front of the Yellow Emperor's idol. General Lei quickly discovered it was no other then the younger Prince Yin Hong.

He called out, "Wake up, my Prince!"

Startled from his deep sleep, Prince Yin Hong opened his eyes. In the torchlight he recognized the General Lei and called out, "General Lei!"

Lei replied, "My Prince. I have orders to bring you back to the capital. But please don't worry. All civil and military officials have submitted leniency petitions on your behalf."

The young prince said, "My General. I know the score. I am not afraid to die. But the last few days, I have been so tired and hungry, I don't think I can walk any more. Is it possible that I may borrow your horse?"

"No problem, my Prince. My horse is ready. I will walk by you," the general said.

*   *   *   *

Meanwhile, rushing toward East Lu State, General Yin, and his fifty mounted soldiers came to the residence of the retired Prime Minister Shang Rong.

General Yin was once Shang Rong's student. Since it was customary for a student to go directly to his teacher, General Yin walked in without waiting to be announced.

At this very moment, Yin Jiao was eating dinner with Shang Rong. General Yin recognized the Crown Prince immediately. He walked up to pay his respects and said, "My Crown Prince! My Old Prime Minister! I have the king's order to escort the Crown prince back to the Palace."

Shang Rong said, "It's just as well you are here. I have been wondering where are the four hundred civil and military officials at the Court. In the midst of dire need it seems Civil officials have locked their mouths, military officials have chained their tongues, all silently enjoying their high positions and receiving their high emoluments from the national treasury. What kind of world is this?"

Once started on his speech, the old Prime Minister was unable to stop his torrent of indignation.

Trembling and pale, tears pouring down his face, the Crown Prince said, "Prime Minister. Please don't get yourself so upset and angry! I fully realize my life will not be spared once the General takes me back to the palace."

Old Shang Rong screamed, "Don't you worry, my Crown Prince. I am not dead yet! When I see the Son of Heaven, I know what to say!"

Shang Rong told his servants to get ready for a trip to the capital right away.

Worried that he might lose a fat reward and a big promotion, if the old Prime Minister was to accompany them. General Yin begged Shang Rong to delay his trip.

"My dear Prime Minister. Please let me escort the Crown Prince back to the palace now, and you can follow in the morning. Otherwise, the king may find fault with me."

Yin Jiao did not want to leave. He embraced the old man and sobbed.

Shang Rong said to the general, "Look here! I am handing you a healthy Crown Prince. Don't you dare harm him for your own gain! Heaven and Earth will condemn you if you do!"

The Crown Prince mounted a horse and went with General Yin. He thought to himself, "I will certainly die. But my younger brother will grow up and avenge us all."

When they reached the three fork junction, General Lei was already there. And when the Crown Prince walked into the tent, he saw his younger brother! They held each other, and both wailed, "We are not able to escape their net! Our mother's injustice will never be righted!"

The three thousand mounted soldiers also wept for them. Secretly congratulating themselves, the two generals urged their troops back to the Capital City, Morning Song.

*   *   *   *

When they arrived, they set up camp outside of the city wall while the generals reported to Lord of the National Security, Prince Yellow Flying Tiger. He was incensed over the capture of the two princes. He immediately invited the senior princes and the Grand Counselors to meet him at the Noon Gate. Bad news traveled fast. Other officials were also there, jostling for news.

Yellow Flying Tiger said to the Senior Princes and the Grand counselors, "My friends. Today's fate is in your hands! I am only a soldier, not much for eloquence. Please think of some way fast."

They had barely begun to discuss the matter when soldiers brought the two young princes to the Noon Gate, bound! The officials immediately paid their respects.

In response, the Crown Prince cried out, "My royal uncles! My loyal ministers and officials. Pity the thirtieth generation of Cheng Tang's children! I am the Crown Prince of the East Palace. Even if I have indeed committed mistakes, the worst punishment should be no more than an admonition! My head and body should never be separated! For the sake of Cheng Tang's ancestral shrine, I beg all of you to rescue us!"

King Zhou's oldest brother Prince Wei Ziqi said, "My Crown Prince, don't worry! All the ministers and officials have submitted petitions on your behalf. I hope that will be enough to save you."

Meanwhile, Generals Yin and Lei reported the capture of the two young princes to the king at the Longevity Palace.

The king said, "No need to bring them here. Just chop off their heads at Noon Gate and report back to me."

The Generals said, "We cannot do that without your execution order."

With his royal pen, the king wrote out the word EXECUTION and handed it to the generals.

When Yellow Flying Tiger saw the two generals come out with the execution order, fire burst from his heart and anger erupted from his gall. He stood in the middle of the Noon Gate blocking their way and shouted, "My dear General Yin and General Lei! Congratulations on your capture of the two young princes. You will certainly be invested as dukes and become very rich after you kill them. But I am fearful for you because high positions and great wealth may bring danger to your lives!"

As the two generals were about to reply, Grand Counselor Zhao Qi walked up, grabbed the EXECUTION order and tore it into thousands of pieces, screaming, "You villains are helping the licentious sovereign to do his cruelty! Who dares to kill the Crown Prince? Who dares to kill the future king? My dear ministers and officials, Noon Gate is not the proper place to discuss this matter. Let's go to the Great Hall and beat the gong for the king. We must tell him what we think of this!"

The storm of rising anger very much intimidated the two generals. They retreated to Longevity Palace to report to the king.

Meanwhile Yellow Flying Tiger ordered four of his most trusted generals to guard the two young Princes, to protect them from harm.

As the Palace Gong resounded, King Zhou asked Daji, "I know what they want. But how should I handle this?"

Daji said, "Execute the two young princes today. You will see the officials tomorrow."

*   *   *   *

In the scheme of things Heaven and Earth, destiny is set in Heaven, so is a nation's fate: The affairs of the kingdom flourish and decline, the fortunes of the country wax and wane, no one can change.

In Heaven the two young princes were marked for future investiture as gods. But their time had not yet come. First they must fulfill the duties assigned them in the Red Dust.

*   *   *   *

Riding their clouds on a stroll were two friends: Superiorman Red Nudist of Colorful Cloud Cave on Mount Grandiflora, and Superiorman Broad Achiever of Peach Stream Cave on Mount Nine Elves. As they were passing King Zhou's Capital, they found their way blocked by two piercing bolts of red beams from the Red Dust; beams only Gods and superiormen could see. On parting their clouds and looking down, they saw what was happening below.

Superiorman Broad Achiever said, "My friend, Cheng Tang's destiny is ending. See those two children? They have blocked our way with their red bolts. Their lives are not supposed to end yet. Shall each of us take one back to our mountain to educate and train? They can help found the new dynasty later."

Superiorman Red Nudist agreed, "Why not? But we had better hurry."

Superiorman Broad Achiever summoned his Yellow Kerchiefed Genii [1], "Bring those two young princes to our mountains," he said.

Yellow Kerchiefed Genii stirred up his magic whirlwind. Immediately flying sands and rocks reached up to the sun as the sky turned suddenly dark as night, sending soldiers and executioners alike, heads in their hands fleeing for shelter. Then with a loud thunderclap the tornado stopped as abruptly as it had started! And the sun once more shone on King Zhou's Capital City, Morning Song.

The two young princes had vanished without a trace! General Yin was about to carry out the executioner order when the tornado touched down. He was so frightened, his soul left him for a long moment. He opened his mouth but nothing came out. His eyes stared but he saw nothing. He and General Lei rushed back to Longevity Palace to report.

All the officials were in the Great Hall waiting to see the king. When news of the sudden tornado and the vanishing of the two princes came, all secretly heaved a sigh of relief.

The king sat in silence for a long while when heard of the disappearance. So taken by the event, the king could not make up his mind what his next move should be.

*   *   *   *

Retired Prime Minister Shang Rong arrived in the Capital City, Morning Song. There was a milling crowd when he got to the Noon Gate. As Shang Rong walked across the Nine Dragon Bridge, Vice

Prime Minister Prince Bi Gan and other senior princes and ranking officials walked up to greet him.

Old Shang Rong said, "My dear friends. I feel so guilty in quitting my position, and so selfish in enjoying myself in my retirement. But how was I to know the king's behavior has deteriorated so much in such short time! With so many ranking officials and ministers around, why had no one done anything to stop it?"

Yellow Flying Tiger said, "My old Prime Minister. The Son of Heaven does not come to the Great Hall at all. He simply sends his edicts by messenger! We have not been able to see him. It is as if he is ten thousand miles away. The two young Princes were to be executed. Luckily Grand Counselor Zhao Qi dared to tear up the execution edict. We beat the gong asking to see the king, but were told that the young princes were to be executed before the king would see us tomorrow. There is no more direct communication between the king and his officials. What can we do? Fortunately Heaven is watching. A great tornado took the two young princes away! Generals Yin and Lei have just come back from reporting to the Longevity Palace."

Shang Rong rushed up to Generals Yin and Lei. Shang Rong said, "Congratulations! You will certainly be promoted and awarded great wealth! Isn't it too bad the two princes were gone with the whirlwinds?"

The two Generals bowed to Shang Rong. General Yin said, "Don't blame us, Old Prime Minister! We are only doing our duty!"

Shang Rong turned back to other officials. "Today I came to see the king. My chance of surviving the confrontation is nil. Nevertheless I have made up my mind to tell it as it is. There is no other way out. Then when I die I will be able to face my ancestors without shame."

He called to the gong keeper to beat the gong. Oh, how the gong resounded for the second time in one day!

King Zhou was very annoyed by the insistent summons. He was uncontrollably furious when he got on his chariot for the short ride to the Great Hall.

"What now?" he hissed when he got on his throne.

Shang Rong, in white mourning garb, knelt before the king but said nothing.

The king asked, "Who is kneeling there?"

Replied Shang Rong, "Your retired Prime Minister Shang Rong."

The king was surprised. He said, "Why are you here? You have not been summoned. Don't you know it is against the law for you to be here in the Throne-room in the Great Hall?"

With tears in his eyes, Shang Rong said, "Sire. I do realize I am violating the law. But I cannot stand by to see our kingdom going down the drain. You have neglected the welfare of the kingdom; caroused day and night, killed the Queen, persecuted your loyal officials, and now you intend to kill your two royal princes. All this adds up to a dead-end for your reign! I have my memorandum here. I beg you to renounce your current course of action and return to your former virtuous ways. The whole nation will be forever grateful!"

The king was incensed at Shang Rong's no-holds-barred account. Tearing up the memorandum he roared, "Take him out to Noon Gate and smash him with the gold mallet!"

When the Palace Guards moved to grab him, Shang Rong shouted at them, "How dare you touch me! I was the highest ranking minister for three generations of kings. It was I who recommended King Zhou to the throne."

Shang Rong then pointed his finger at the king. "You slow-witted, boozing, licentious king! You are disrespectful of Heaven and of your Ancestral Shrine! You are a shame to all generations of your family, past, present and future. Queen Jiang, your sacred partner and the mother of the kingdom, had never done anything wrong. But you killed her with the cruelest of tortures! You have violated the Three Social Principles and have profaned the Five Cardinal Human Relationships. And what have the two innocent young princes done to be hunted like animals? I am so glad a tornado took them away. As for your torturing and killing of Grand Counselor Mei Bo and Royal Astrologer Du, what had they done but told you the truth?

"There is no more law and order in the kingdom. Bit by bit, you are cutting your own throat, bringing Cheng Tang's Dynasty to an end. How will you ever be able to face your ancestors?"

The king screamed, "Take him out and beat him to death!"

Defiant, Shang Rong roared back, "I am not afraid to die! But I must ask your late father, my old King Da Yi to pardon me, his old Prime Minister for recommending you to the throne. I am so sorry I cannot help anyone any more!"

So saying, Shang Rong banged his head against a column, killing himself in the Great Hall.

Pity how a seventy-five year old minister became a martyr for his beloved nation. His brain splashed all over the floor and his blood soaked his white garment.

The king, not feeling horrified but cheated, ordered that Shang Rong's body be thrown over the city wall. He warned, "Don't anyone dare to bury it!"

The Great Hall was shrouded in silence at Shang Rong's martyrdom. The grief-stricken Grand Counselor Zhao Qi, his eyes popping and his eyebrows flying as indignation filled his heart, broke the silence. He walked out to the aisle, shouting, "Along with Shang Rong, I also unwittingly recommended King Zhou to the throne. We made a disastrous mistake! I will now join Prime Minister Shang Rong in seeking the pardon of my late King Da Yi." He pointed his finger at King Zhou, "You dimwit ruler! You have wasted loyal and brilliant officials. You let everyone down! You believe in treacherous rumors and you neglect the Ancestral Shrine! You tortured the Queen to death and made Daji your new Queen without the advice and consent of the people! You tried to kill your own sons. Soon the kingdom will be nothing but a ghost! You are not fit to be our leader! You are a shame to us all! Damn you! Ten thousand times damn you! Death is too good for you!!!"

The soul-less king was fit to be tied! He banged on his throne and screamed, "Take him out and toast him to death!"

Grand Counselor Zhao Qi said, "I have no fear of dying. My death will let future generations know how I feel about your terminating Cheng Tang's reign! And your foul name will stink for millions of years!"

Joining Prime Minister Shang Rong, Grand counselor Zhao Qi hit his head against a column with great force. Another martyr for his beloved country!

The spirits and souls of the hundred attending officials flew out to nobody knew where. All were hushed in fear.

On returning to Longevity Palace, King Zhou held Daji's hand, and said, "Today, Shang Rong and Grand Counselor Zhao Qi killed themselves in the Great Hall. But I feel terribly humiliated by them. We need more cruel punishments to instill greater fear among the officials."

Daji said, "Please let me think."

The king said, "Your promotion to Queen is settled. I don't think the officials will dare to complain. What worries me is what the Grand Duke of the East will do when he finds out about the death of his daughter Queen Jiang. We may then really have trouble. Grand Old master Wen Zhong is still not back from the North Sea. We must prepare for assaults by the Grand Duke of the East!"

Daji said, "Sire. I am only an uneducated female, and my ideas are very limited. Why don't we call Middle Counselor Fei Zhong for consultation? He will think of something superlative."

Fei Zhong came quickly. On hearing of the king's fears, he said, "Yes, Sire. Your worry is understandable and very real. The death of Queen Jiang, the disappearance of the two young princes, the suicides of Shang Rong and Zhao Qi, all add up to an unsettling score of unhappy events. The ministers and officials are restless. News of these happenings will reach the Grand Duke of the East in no time. It is predictable how he will react.

"Why not summon all four Grand Dukes separately to the Capital City, then promptly use whatever convenient excuses you find and kill them all. This is the only way to get to the root of future troubles. Like a powerful serpent with its head chopped off, or a ferocious tiger with its teeth pulled, with their leaders gone, the eight hundred regional dukes will realize they cannot do anything but behave themselves. Then and only then will Your Majesty have peace."

The king was delighted, "You are truly a genius! No wonder Queen Su recommends you!"

King Zhou sent out four secret urgent edicts to summon the four Grand Dukes.

Notes

1. Yellow Kerchiefed Genii is a general term used to denote a group of mythical creatures who have untold magic and strength, are ever ready to do the bidding of their Superiorman masters. The yellow kerchief is their emblem.

CHAPTER 10

▼

THUNDER QUAKER BORN

Rolling with the wind and wallowing with the dust, a Messenger of the king rushed toward The Western Foothills of Mount Singing Phoenix. He did not dare to take more than a very brief break, for he knew well that he was delivering the king's secret and urgent summons.

One day, the scenery suddenly brightened. The Imperial Messenger saw happy farmers tending luscious green fields, fruit laden orchards, and corrals of healthy animals. He saw merchants going about their business in a calm and orderly manner, and people conducting themselves with politeness and respect.

The Imperial Messenger sighed, "We have heard that the Grand Duke of the West is a wise and virtuous ruler. Now, seeing his country, I feel I am back to the time of our Sage Kings Yao and Shan as told of yore."

Ji Chang, The Grand Duke of the West, led his officials to welcome the Imperial Messenger and knelt to receive the Imperial edict. It merely said, "With the rebellion in the North Sea still unsettled, and the increasing unrest among the populace, I am requesting that the

Grand Dukes of my kingdom come to my Capital City, Morning Song, to help me form a national policy. Please come in haste."

Next day, Ji Chang sent the Imperial Messenger off with some expensive gifts and said to him, "Dear sir, we will meet in the Capital City very soon."

Preparation for the trip to City Morning Song was in high gear. In his Righteous-Light Court, Ji Chang instructed his Grand Counselor, Easy Life, "In my absence, the administration of all internal affairs of our country will be your responsibility, and the responsibility of all external affairs will be jointly shared by Generals Southpalace Nimble-foot and Xin Jia."

Ji Chang then said to his eldest son, Bo Yi Kao, "My son, yesterday, on receiving the king's summons to make haste to City Morning Song, I sought enlightenment from the divination. The message was ominous. It says that I would have to endure seven years of suffering, but I will survive. You in Western Foothills must carry on according to the laws and standards I have set. Be harmonious with your brothers and officials. Be conservative in thoughts and, most important, don't ever seek selfish personal gain at the expense of others. Treat the populace with justice, benevolence and respect. When a bachelor is too poor to take a wife, help him with the cost so that he can get married, and have a home. When a maiden is not able to find a husband because she lacks a dowry, present her with a gift. Take good care of the old and the sick, so that they don't ever lack food, shelter and medicine. Take care of the young and the orphaned so they have proper care and education.

"I will be back after seven years. But you must not, I repeat, MUST NOT go there or send anyone to get me out of difficulty."

Bo Yi Kao begged his father, "My father. If you foresee seven years of tribulation, please let me go in your place."

"My son. I appreciate your thought. It is true, a wise man instinctively avoids disaster. However, in this case, our destiny has been set in Heaven. There is no way we can escape. Your going would only worsen matters. You stay home and concentrate on doing a good job as I have instructed."

Ji Chang then went to his inner courts to say good-bye to his mother Tai Jiang. She said, "My son. Last night, I had a divination session, and found you would suffer seven years of ordeals!"

Ji Chang said, "Yes, mother. I too sought enlightenment. I too found seven years of trial ahead. But I will survive and ride out the storm.

"This morning, I delegated responsibilities of the state to Grand Counselor Easy Life and the two generals, Southpalace Nimblefoot and Xin Jia, and instructed my eldest son to care for the populace.

"Mother, I am here to ask for your blessing. Tomorrow morning I will be on my way to City Morning Song."

His mother said, "My son. Be cautious in everything. Go with the Gods."

Ji Chang had four wives, twenty-four concubines and ninety-nine sons, but he went only to his Number one wife Tai Ji to say good-bye. He reminded his eldest son, Bo Yi Kao, "Remember, live harmoniously with your brothers and officials and my heart will be at ease."

*   *   *   *

Ji Chang and his fifty men rode hard. Each day they started with the sun and rested with the moon. One beautiful sunny day, near Mount Swallow, Ji Chang said to his men, "Quick, look for shelter! A big storm is coming!"

Taken by surprise, all his men muttered, "Such a beautiful day, how could it be possible…"

Before the sentence was finished, dark clouds appeared from nowhere. Ji Chang shouted, "Quick! Get to the woods!"

Oh, how it rained! For half an hour, torrents of water fell as if the sky had sprung a big leak. Ji Chang then added another warning, "Be careful of the big thunderbolt!"

Yes! A thunderbolt, loud and clear, shook the earth. In their fear, his men crowded into a tight circle around him.

The storm was over as quickly as it had come. The bright sun shone once more. The Grand Duke was soaking wet but said excitedly, "The thunderstorm has brought forth a miracle baby. My men, please search for him!"

All his men laughed out loud, "Where would we find a baby in this wilderness?"

Nevertheless, they fanned out to search for this miracle being. Someone heard the cry of a baby! Following the sound, they rushed to an ancient tomb. Behold, a new born infant was there! How absolutely extraordinary! Could this possibly be the very being they were looking for? Yes, it really was a living baby boy. His face was pink as a peach flower bud, his eyes shone like the evening stars. They took the baby to the Grand Duke.

Ji Chang was overjoyed. He thought to himself, "I already have ninety-nine sons, this makes it a great round number!" He ordered his men to search for a family in the village who would be able to take care of the infant. In seven years the Grand Duke would come and take him to The Western Foothills of Mount Singing Phoenix.

Just then an unusual looking Superiorman came walking toward them. The Superiorman nodded his head in a salute. Ji Chang was taken by surprise. He immediately rolled off his horse to return the greeting, saying, "I am so sorry to have missed greeting you. Please may I ask your name, your abode and why are you here? You must have some special advice for me."

"I am Cloud Dweller of Jade Column Cave on Mount South End. A while ago, a tremendous thunderstorm was to bring forth a miracle child to the Red Dust. I have come a long way to search for him."

Ji Chang ordered his men to bring the Baby forward.

Looking at him, Cloud Dweller said, "My miracle child, you have finally come."

He then turned to Ji Chang, "My Grand Duke. Please let me take this child to Mount South End, to raise and educate. When you come back in seven years, I will return him to you."

Ji Cheng said, "It is fine that he goes with you. But when we meet again, how will we identify him?"

Cloud Dweller said, "He was born when the thunder was quaking the earth. Why don't we name him Thunder Quaker? When you come back to claim him in seven years, he will announce himself. Don't worry."

And so Thunder Quaker went with Cloud Dweller to Mount South End and Ji Chang and his men resumed their trek to City Morning Song.

*   *   *   *

The Grand Duke of the West had the longest way to travel. When he finally arrived at the City Morning Song, he went directly to the Golden Pavilion Hostel, where other visiting high ranking officials stayed. The other three Grand Dukes were already there. They came out to greet him.

One more table was added to the dining hall. Ji Chang said, "My dear Grand Dukes, what kind of emergency prompted the king to summon the four of us here? Whatever the emergency, on the military side, there is Lord of National Security, Prince Yellow Flying Tiger who can handle any situation. And on the civil side, there is Vice Prime Minister, Prince Bi Gan who can convince anyone. Why then did the king call us in, claiming it urgent?"

It was not often that they gathered like this. So as they chatted, they kept on drinking. By evening, all of them were quite mellowed with wine.

The Grand Duke of the South, E Chong Yu, was known for his upright, forthright, and straight forward manner. He hated nothing more than avarice and unscrupulousness, which happened to be the very quality the Grand Duke of North was well known for.

As wine loosened his inhibitions, the Grand Duke of South said to the Grand Duke of the North, known as Tiger Duke, "My friend Tiger Duke. We are the four leaders under Heaven. But I feel you have not behaved like a respectable leader and set a good example for your people. You befriend unprincipled people such as Middle Counselors Fei Zhong and You Hun. You treat the poor without mercy but let big criminals go if they can put up the bribe you demand.

"My friend, for your own good, I do sincerely wish you would change your ways. Good luck and good fortune will then be yours forever more."

This riled Tiger Duke so much, smoke shot out from his eyes and fire spouted from his mouth. He screamed, "How dare you! E Chong Yu! We both are equal in rank. How dare you insult me in front of the others?"

Right then and there Tiger Duke wanted very much to use this excuse to get rid of the Grand Duke of the South, counting on the help of his good friends Fei Zhong and You Hun.

But Ji Chang interrupted, "Tiger Duke, my friend. What E Chong Yu said was good advice. If the shoe fits, wear it. If not, forget it. You should appreciate him even more because he respects you and wishes you well enough to tell it as it is, even at the risk of offending you."

On hearing what Ji Chang said, Tiger Duke did not dare to act up. But suddenly E Chong Yu threw his wine vessel over, hitting Tiger Duke in the face. Tiger Duke got up and grabbed him by the collar, ready for a free-for-all.

Again, Ji Chang stopped them, shouting, "Are you not ashamed of yourselves? Two Grand Dukes engaged in a fist fight!"

Ji Chang then said gently to Tiger Duke, "Come on, my dear Tiger Duke. It is getting quite late. You had better go to bed now." And so he persuaded the angry but simple minded Tiger Duke to retire to his room.

The three remaining Grand Dukes continued with their drinking and chatting. They had not seen each other for some time and there was much news to catch up on.

As the three dukes were enjoying their visit, a servant of the hostel was so moved that he murmured to himself, "Tonight there is much merriment. But tomorrow I fear blood-shed in the marketplace!"

In the quiet of the midnight hour, the murmur reached clear across the hall. Ji Chang asked, "Who is talking there? Who said 'blood-shed in the marketplace'?"

Kneeling, the hostel servants denied that anyone did.

"Every word was so clear, how could you deny it?" Calling in his men, Ji Chang threatened to kill the whole bunch for lying.

In fear, the hostel servants pointed their fingers at Yao Fu. Ji Chang said, "All right then. Yao Fu, you stay. All others may go."

Ji Chang continued, "What made you say that, Yao Fu? Tell me the truth. Otherwise you know what punishment to expect."

Yao Fu said in tears, "My Lords, it was supposed to be top secret. But I heard it accidentally. Disaster struck our kingdom. The torture death of Queen Jiang, the disappearance of the two young Princes in a strange tornado, the promotion of Concubine Su Daji to be Queen of the Central Palace—all were followed by secret edicts to kill all four of you Grand Dukes tomorrow. I felt so sad and miserable about the whole situation that I must have blurted out in an unguarded moment. Please pardon me, my Lords."

Then at the urging of the Grand Duke of the East, Yao Fu told all what he heard about Queen Jiang's death. On hearing the gory details of what had happened to his daughter and grandsons, the Grand Duke of the East felt his body knifed thousands of times and his heart thrown into boiling oil! He gave a loud scream and fainted to the floor.

Ji Chang revived him and said, "All of us must deal with this injustice. Tonight we will write a memo to ask the king what was behind all this."

In tears, the Grand Duke of the East said, "It is the Jiang family's misfortune. How can I trouble you all? I shall face the king myself to clear the matter."

The Grand Dukes had come to the Capital City, Morning Song, with only a few household servants. They had not seen the need to bring with them a big army when the Son of Heaven only wanted them to discuss national policy. So writing a petition was all that was left for them in confronting the king.

Ji Chang said to the Grand Duke of the East, with compassion, "It is all right. You write your memo and we three will write ours also."

*   *   *   *

Fei Zhong learned of the arrival of the four grand dukes. He secretly went through a side gate to see the king.

The king was delighted and agreed to Fei Zhong's plan, that the king would not read any of their memos but simply order the grand dukes to be taken out to Noon Gate for execution.

To the great surprise of the four hundred civil and military officials who, day after day, had waited in vain for the king to show up, this morning, he came to the Great Hall promptly at five.

The king was formally told that the four grand dukes were waiting at the Noon Gate. The king said, "Bring them in!"

Holding high his yahu, the Grand Duke of the East handed his memo to Vice Prime Minister, Prince Bi Gan who in turn handed it to the king.

As planned, the king put the memo aside, saying, "Jiang Haun Chu, don't you know what crime you have committed?"

The Grand Duke of the East said, "In my East Lu State, I dedicate my life to taking care of the affairs of the state, following the Sage's teaching, and serving my king loyally. I have committed no crime. It is you who, to please a new favorite concubine, cast aside your sacred vow to your original wife and put her to death by means of the cruelest torture. You who want to kill even your own sons. You who burnt your loyal officials to death. You have changed for the worst without shame. I am not afraid of the consequence of my straight talk. But if you finally see your own folly, then even in my death, I and all those who were killed unjustly would forgive you!"

Beside himself, the king roared, "How dare you speak so! You who ordered your daughter to kill me so you could be king! You forgot all the favors you received from this court. Guards, take this ingrate out and beat him to death with the gold mallet!"

The guards quickly bound The Grand Duke of the East and took off his red robe and hat. But he kept screaming his defiance and indignation as he was pushed out to the Noon Gate.

Unfazed by what was happening to Grand Duke of the East, Ji Chang, along with Grand Dukes of the South and North came forward with their memos. Ji Chang said, "Sire. We have a memo here for you to read. We can vouch for the Grand Duke of the East. He is the most loyal to your reign. The charge of his trying to usurp your throne is utterly false. Please investigate to find the truth."

With not even a glance, the king brushed all memos aside.

CHAPTER 11

▼

GRAND DUKE OF THE WEST INCARCERATED

The king had ordered to take the Grand Duke of the East out for execution. Unfazed, the three remaining Grand Dukes calmly begged the king to read their joint petition.

Vice Prime Minister, Prince Bi Gan opened and displayed it before the king. It said in part:

Memo
From: The Grand Dukes of the West, South, and North.
Subject: To rectify the laws of the nation
To restore the moral standards
To rid the unscrupulous

We know that a good king rules his kingdom with justice and benevolence. He is appreciative of his good ministers and wary of the bad ones. He is frugal with the national treasury and generous in his treatment of the populace. Therefore he does not indulge in wine and women, but diligently administers his kingdom's business with care. That was how King Yao and King Shun managed to govern so well without even leaving their thrones. The people were happy and the kingdom prospered.

...With our sincere love of our country, we recommend that you banish Middle Counselors Fei Zhong and You Hun, and put Daji to death..."

As he read the recommendations, the king tore up the petition, and foaming at the mouth, screamed, "Take these three traitors out! Chop off their heads and hang them in the marketplace!"

As the palace guards bound up the three Grand Dukes, Fei Zhong and You Hun stepped out, asking for permission for a brief report.

"What report?" The king asked.

Fei Zhong replied, "The four Grand Dukes have all committed unpardonable crimes. But Your Majesty may have overlooked the fact that the Grand Duke of the North has been loyal and honest, giving his heart and liver to serve Your Majesty. What he is doing now is merely from peer pressure, not truly from his heart."

As Fei Zhong and You Hun were his favorites officials, the king again granted their implied wish and pardoned the Grand Duke of the North.

At this turn of events, seven senior princes led by Lord of National Security, Prince Yellow Flying Tiger and Vice Prime Minister, Prince Bi Gan, came out to report.

Prince Bi Gan said, "Please listen to us! A minister is the king's arms and legs. The Grand Duke of the East in the East Lu State has contributed very outstandingly to the kingdom. There is no proof whatever that he tried to assassinate Your Majesty.

"The Grand Duke of the West has administered the Western Region with extraordinary results, earning the respect of all in our kingdom and the fame of 'The Sage of the West'. His loyalty is beyond reproach.

"As to the Grand Duke of the South, he has served with full devotion. His region has contributed very substantially to the Royal treasury.

"We beg Your Majesty to pardon them all."

The king said, "One attempted to usurp the throne, the others used foul language to humiliate me. Their crimes are not pardonable!"

Yellow Flying Tiger said, "They are all important ministers and have never done anything really wrong. The Grand Duke of the West Ji Chang is a very conscientious man. He has, in particular, special ability in divination; in the calculation of the Trigram; and interpretation of the oracle bones.

"And the Grand Duke of the South has contributed greatly to the National Treasury. Without him, our kingdom would have been much poorer. Now if they are executed, how are we to explain it to the world?

"Besides, they all have tens of thousands of troops. Will their armies stand still? If they make a move, especially when Grand Old Master Wen Zhong is still trying to quench the North Sea rebellion, how are we to protect the kingdom?"

The king thought a little, finally saying, "Ji Chang may be all right. For your sake, I will pardon him. But if he later rebels, you seven will be fully responsible! But I will not spare the other two. No more words from any of you!"

The king sent out his edict to pardon Ji Chang, and ordered the immediate execution of Jiang Huan Chu and E Chong Yu.

Jiang Huan Chu was beheaded. E Chong Yu's hands and feet were nailed on a board and he was beaten to death!

Sobbing bitterly, Ji Chang thanked the seven senior princes and asked them to bury the bodies of Jiang Huan Chu and E Chong Yu in temporary graves, to await future development.

Needless to say, by this time the family servants of the two executed grand dukes had already fled home to report the tragedy.

Next morning, the king met his ministers in the Distinctive Joy Court. Prince Bi Gan reported on the burial of the two grand dukes, then requested permission to send Grand Duke of the West, Ji Chang, back to Western Foothills of Mount Singing Phoenix. The request was granted.

After Bi Gan left the court, Fei Zhong said to the king, "Sire. May I warn you of Ji Chang? He looks honest and loyal, but he is actually most cunning and ambitious. To let him go home is like letting a tiger return to his mountain, or a dragon back to his sea! I am certain he will later cause you trouble. It is not a good idea to let him go!"

The king said, "But I have already issued my edict. Everyone knows about it. How can I take it back?"

Fei Zhong revealed his plan: "I am sure Ji Chang will go to the National Ancestral Shrine to express his gratitude before leaving for home. And other ministers and officials will be there to bid him farewell. Let me join them to find out the truth."

The king agreed.

*   *   *   *

After leaving the court, Prince Bi Gan hurried to the hostel to see Ji Chang. Bi Gan said, "The king has given permission to let you go home. Tomorrow after you pay your respect to the National Ancestral Shrine, I beseech you to leave as quickly as possible before some unforeseen event occur."

Next morning, as soon as he went through the thanksgiving ritual at the National Ancestral Shrine, Ji Chang led his retinue out of the West Gate. But when he reached the Ten Mile Pavilion, he saw hundreds of ministers and officials, among them Yellow Flying Tiger and all the senior princes, waiting to say their farewell.

Ji Chang got off his horse. Yellow Flying Tiger and Prince Wei Zi said to him, "First of all, we want to express our good wishes to you. Second, we want a little promise from you."

Ji Chang said, "Please tell me your wish."

Wei Zi said, "We know the Son of Heaven has mistreated you. But for the sake of our past kings, please do not be bitter. And most of all, please do not ally yourself with the others to make trouble for the kingdom. Then we would all be grateful to you."

Ji Chang said, "I am living now because of the generosity of the king, and the kindness of all of you. How dare I cause you trouble? You have my promise."

They drank to their parting. Ji Chang had a good capacity for wine. Even if he drank with each of the hundreds of officials, he could take it very well. And when good friends gathered, there was endless talk. No one wanted to leave.

Fei Zhong and You Hun now arrived with their own wine. Others were annoyed and, one after another, they left.

Now alone with the two, Ji Chang said, "My dear Counselors, how do I deserve the honor?"

Fei Zhong said, "We heard you are going home with honors. We came especially to say good-bye with some of our watery wine, and we are sorry we are late. We hope you will overlook that."

Always an honest man, Ji Chang accepted their wine as graciously as he would from his true friends. Ji Chang could out drink anyone. But by now he was getting careless.

Fei Zhong said, "May I please ask, my Lord? We have heard your lordship is highly versed in the interpretation of signs; the Trigram; and other divinations. Do they really have meaning?"

Replied Ji Chang earnestly, "But of course, my Counselors. The designs of Heaven and Earth are fixed. But if we see a bad sign and do something constructive to avoid it, we may avert the trend."

Fei Zhong said, "Suppose our present Son of Heaven wants to know what is the future of his reign, can it be predicted?"

Divination was Ji Chang's favorite subject, but because of the wine he had consumed, he clearly forgot the evil intent of these two counselors.

He said without hesitation, "Pity, our nation is at the end of its luck. This is the last generation of this reign, and it is not even a good end." As sadness overcame him, he continued, "How can I sit quietly without pointing this out to the king?"

Fei Zhong persisted, "How soon would the end come?"

Ji Chang said, "In seven to ten years, I fear." Fei Zhong and You Hun pretended to be saddened. They urged the Grand Duke with more wine.

Fei Zhong then asked again, "Will you read in your Trigram and foretell what would happen to the two of us?"

Ji Chang had always treated the high and low alike; without guile. He did the same today. He consulted the Trigram. He was very puzzled by what he saw. He kept murmuring to himself, "How strange, how strange."

Both Fei Zhong and You Hun said, "What is so strange?"

Ji Chang said, "Our destiny is fixed in Heaven. We die either from some sort of illness within, such as trouble of the heart or lung; or some force from without, such as fire, flood, or hunger. But I could see no clear sign in your case. The way you will die is neither here nor there, neither this way nor that. It is very mysterious."

Smiling, Fei Zhong and You Hun said, "How so? How will we die?"

Ji Chang said, "I saw ice all over you. It looked like ice pits."

You Hun remarked, "How true, we were born when our time came. We die where and when as Heaven wills."

As they drank some more, Fei Zhong again asked, "Have you ever looked into your own future?"

"I certainly have." Ji Chang was still unaware of the trap set by the two.

You Hun asked, "Tell us about it?"

Ji Chang said, "Well, I think I will die a natural death."

The two felt very ugly about the prediction of their death in ice pits. But they pretended to be very impressed and congratulated the Grand Duke. Finally they bade him good-bye.

When the two returned to the court, the king asked, "How did it go? Did he say anything about me?"

Fei Zhong replied, with relish, "Did he ever! He was most abusive when he talked about Your Majesty! He should not have been pardoned!"

The king said, "That ungrateful maggot! What did he say about me?"

You Hun replied, adding more salt and spice, "As you know, Ji Chang knows how to calculate and interpret the Trigram and other divinations of the future. He said your reign would end within seven to ten years, and you would have a terrible death."

The king asked, "Did you ask him how he will die?"

"Yes. He boasted he would die a natural death. As you know, he is very cunning. He can create rumors to fan the populace. He knows well that his life depends on the whims of Your Majesty, yet he believes he will have a natural death. This shows he has some evil plans in store. When we asked him about us, he said we both would die in ice. How ludicrous! Not only are we under Your Majesty's special protection, even a peon, under your glorious and prosperous reign, would never die in ice! Your Majesty should promptly get rid of this quack before he can do more harm."

The king agreed and sent the Chao twins of the palace guards to get him.

After the two Counselors left, Ji Chang realized he had spoken too freely and honestly to them. He urged his men to rush forward before something else happened.

Alas! It was too late! The Chao twins were already in sight, and Ji Chang knew the score!

Turning to his men, the Grand Duke told them to hurry home. He assured them he would return in seven years. They were to remind his oldest son of his earlier instructions. Most important of all not to come or send anyone to the Capital City, Morning Song, in the next seven years!

*   *   *   *

Ji Chang was taken prisoner. The news reached Yellow Flying Tiger. He first sent a trusted general to call all the senior princes to the Noon Gate, then he himself rushed there. Ji Chang was there before him, waiting for the king's summons.

Yellow Flying Tiger asked Ji Chang, "Why have you come back?"

Ji Chang said simply, "I was summoned."

As Ji Chang knelt before the angry king, he heard, "Good God! I pardoned you and let you go home. How dare you bad mouth me? What have you to say for yourself?"

Ji Chang replied, "Sire, even if I were stupid, I would still know: up there is Heaven, and down here is earth, and in between, there is the Sovereign. The ones who gave me life are my parents, the ones who educated me are my teachers. The Heaven, the Earth, the Sovereign, the parents, and the teachers, these five are always in my heart. How is it possible for me to say anything derogatory about Your Majesty? Do you think I want to court death?"

Still angry, the king said, "I can see you are very eloquent. You used the Trigram to predict the future, to humiliate me and to curse me. Your behavior is unpardonable!"

The Grand Duke said, "No sire. I did not invent divination. Our Sacred God of Agriculture invented it to foretell the changing balance of natural forces. All predictions are clearly stated in the configuration of the Trigram which our Sage Emperor Fu Qi designed. They are not made up by me."

The king said, "Then you should do some reading and calculation here right now to show me what you mean."

The Grand Duke said, "No, sire. I did one for Middle Counselors Fei Zhong and You Hun which turned out to be rather bad. I have already incurred their hatred. I would not dare to incur Your Majesty's displeasure!"

The king said, "You told them I will die an unnatural death while you yourself will die a natural one. How interesting. Just to prove you wrong, I will have you die an unnatural death right this moment!" So saying, he yelled, "Take Ji Chang out to Noon Gate for execution!"

Shouts were heard as the guards made ready to take Ji Chang out. The king turned to the noise and saw the seven senior princes, led by Yellow Flying Tiger, coming into the throne-room.

"You cannot do that! Let us have our say!" They knelt and continued, "Sire, you have pardoned Ji Chang and let him return to his country. Your populace sang your praise for that. As to his using divination, he was only trying to interpret what our Sage Emperor Fu Qi showed us in the Trigram. If the prediction is correct, so much the better. However, if it is in error, well, that can happen too. Ji Chang was not using flowery language to charm anyone. He told what he saw. Your Majesty is too great a person to fault him for that. Let him go, we beseech you."

The king said, "Ji Chang is flaunting his knowledge of the Trigram and divination, and using them to humiliate his king. How can he be pardoned?"

Prince Bi Gan said, "We are not trying to save Ji Chang. We are thinking of the welfare of the kingdom. Ji Chang is widely known for his knowledge of divination. When he sees something that may be beneficial to our country, we should heed his advice. Why not let him show us? We can then judge whether he is truly a wise man. Your Majesty then can deal with him as you see fit."

The king could not argue further. He said, "Let Ji Chang demonstrate a divination game here."

Ji Chang took out a few gold coins and cast them on the floor. Alarmed at the resulting configuration, he let out a little cry, "My God! Fire will destroy our National Ancestral Shrine tomorrow! Sire, please order the contents be removed immediately from the building."

Unimpressed, the king asked, "What time tomorrow?"

"High noon, sire."

The king said, "Very well then, we will see. Put Ji Chang in prison for the night."

Before taken to prison, Ji Chang thanked the seven senior princes for saving his life once more.

Yellow Flying Tiger asked, "My friend, do you have any contingency plan if the fire does not occur tomorrow?"

Ji Chang said, "Our fate depends on what Heaven wishes."

Meanwhile, the king asked Fei Zhong how to deal with Ji Chang's prediction.

Fei Zhong said, "Order the shrine guards to put out all fires and incenses in the shrine from now until tomorrow night. How then can there be a fire tomorrow?"

The king sent out his order accordingly.

Next day, Yellow Flying Tiger and the other senior princes were at the Nine Hall Court waiting for high noon. As usual, the timekeeper reported on the hour each hour. When he shouted, "High Noon!" they became very apprehensive.

At that very moment, a sudden thunderclap boomed from the sunny sky, shaking the earth. The Fire Marshall rushed in to report that the Shrine was on fire!

Prince Bi Gan remarked, "When the National Ancestral Shrine burns, it is a sign that Cheng Tang's reign is ending!"

Everyone went out to watch. Oh, what a fire!

When the news came that the fire had broken at the exact predicted time, the king was in his Virtuous Dragon Court, chatting with his favorite middle counselors. How devastating it was to those who had wished it otherwise.

The king conceded, "Ji Chang's prediction comes true!"

"So what?" Fei Zhong said. "It is just coincidental! Your Majesty cannot let him go! And you must stop the senior princes from petitioning on his behalf."

At this very moment, the seven senior princes came in to see the king. Prince Bi Gan said, "Now that Ji Chang has proved his worth, please let him go home."

Said the king, "Oh yes. He was right this time. So I will take back his death sentence. However, he cannot go home yet, not until peace comes to the kingdom. Meanwhile, I want him confined to Youli District, outside of Capital City, Morning Song."

The senior princes thanked the king and went out to Noon Gate where Ji Chang was waiting. They consoled him with the thought that his house arrest at Youli District would only be temporary, for they would put in a petition on his behalf again at the opportune time.

*   *   *   *

The populace of Youli were overwhelmed with joy when they heard that the Grand Duke of the West was coming to their district. Young and old, and all ages in between, brought wine and sheep and goats as gifts. They knelt on the roadside to welcome him.

They chanted, "Youli is very honored to have the Grand Duke of the West here!"

Ji Chang settled in the house assigned him. He lived quietly and treated the local people as his own, with love and respect.

Relieved of all burden of administration, he now had time to research further into the Trigram. From the basic eight diagrams, he elaborated them into sixty-four then to three hundred and eighty-four.

He lived contentedly, never uttering a bitter word toward the king or his administration.

*   *   *   *

Back in the Capital City, Morning Song, The Lord of National Security, Prince Yellow Flying Tiger, received ominous reports. In the East, the son of the late Grand Duke of the East had rebelled. In the

South, the son of the late Grand Duke of the South did the same. On top of that, four hundred regional dukes of the East and the South had joined them in the rebellion.

Yellow Flying Tiger sighed, "With all these rebellions, what will happen to the people?"

CHAPTER 12

▼

NEZHA BORN

Commander Li Jing had studied at Mount Kunlun under the Superiorman Danger Skipper. Among other things, he learned how to travel underground in a hurry, undetected, for thousands of miles. But lacking the karma for the making of a Superiorman, he was sent back to the Red Dust to serve in King Zhou's Court. After many years of distinguished service and many promotions, he became Commanding Officer at Old Pond Pass.

His wife Yinshi bore him two sons. Ten years later, Yinshi was again pregnant. After three years and six months had gone by, there was still no sign of imminent birth. The couple were very worried. They feared something evil.

One night, Yinshi dreamt of a strange Superiorman, with his hair in a top-knot, in a loose fitting gown and soft sole cloth shoes. He walked into her bedroom without ceremony.

Yinshi was both startled and angry. "Get out!" she shouted. "This is the private chamber of a lady, how dare you come in?"

The Superiorman said, "Madam, you are about to have a wonderful child this very minute. I am here to deliver him to you."

So saying, the Superiorman threw a little bundle at Yinshi.

Yinshi woke up with a jolt. So scared was she that she called her husband to her room to tell him her dream. But, before she could finish her tale, she felt the labor pain coming in earnest.

Li Jing dashed out to call the midwife, while thinking to himself, "With such a prolonged pregnancy, and such a bizarre dream, nothing good can come from it."

Then a servant came rushing out to report, "My lord, Madam has given birth to a monster!"

With his sword in hand, Li Jing hurriedly returned to his wife's bedroom. He was confronted by a strange red glow filling the bedroom, and a overwhelming heavenly fragrance permeated the air. A huge meatball was rolling around in mad circles like a wheel. In shock, Li Jing slashed the meatball with his sword.

It broke open! Out jumped a three and a half year old boy child who began running around the room. Pulsating with vitality, his body glowed red, though his face was so fair it looked powdered. On his right arm he wore a gold bracelet. And wrapped around his body was a red silk scarf.

Li Jing scooped up the child of flesh and blood. How could this possibly be a monster or a demon? Oh no! This was truly his third son! It was love at first touch.

Next day, among the people who came to congratulate Li Jing on his new addition to the family, was a man who introduced himself as Superiorman Paragon, of Mount Champion, Golden Light Cave. He came to see the baby.

Holding the child in his arms, Superiorman Paragon asked, "When was he born?"

Li Jing said, "Two o'clock in the morning."

Paragon said, "Bad hour!"

Li Jing asked worriedly, "You mean we may have trouble raising this child?"

"Oh no," said Paragon. He paused, then changed his mind, continued, "Yes, for it is a sign that he is destined to kill many; in fact one thousand and seven hundred killings. Have you given him a name?"

"Not yet." replied Li Jing.

Paragon said, "In that case, it would be my pleasure to give him a name. But you must let me have him as a student. How many older children have you, and what are their names?"

Li Jing said, "I have two older sons. My eldest is Jinzha; he is a student of the Superiorman Broad Altruist, of Mount Five Dragons, Cloud Top Cave. My second son is Muzha, a student of Superiorman Universal Converter, of Mount Nine Courts, White Egret Cave."

Paragon said, "Very well. Your third son is named Nezha."

Li Jing said, "Thank you very much. We will be honored if you stay for a humble meal with us."

Superiorman Paragon said, "Thank you but no thank you. I must be going. I have too many things to take care of."

*   *   *   *

Back in the Capital City, Morning Song, Lord of National Security, Prince Yellow Flying Tiger, issued orders to the commanders of all Border Passes. They were to be on full alert and readiness to guard against the rebellious armies of the Grand Dukes of the East and South, plus their four hundred regional dukes.

Everyday from then on, as at all Border Passes, Li Jing at Old Pond Pass had training sessions with his army.

Perhaps because of the reputation of the commander, seven years had elapsed and no rebellious army had tried Old Pond Pass. By now Nezha was fully ten and a half years old, counting his three and a half years at birth. He had grown to be a husky six foot tall boy.

One sultry day, Nezha was bored and wanted to get out the Old Pond Pass for a little excursion. He asked his mother for permission.

His mother, Yinshi, like all indulgent mothers in the world, said, "My son, we are on full alert. It is not safe to go out of the Pass. However, if you really want to go, you must take a few strong servants with you. Don't stay out too long. Your father may want to see you when he comes back from his training session with his men and horses."

Nezha took only one servant with him. The day was so hot, it was more like a late summer day than the fifth moon of the year. They walked no more than a mile, and Nezha was dripping with sweat. He asked his servant to look for a place to cool off.

They got into a cluster of willows where there was a cool breeze. Nezha loosened his clothes and sat down on the ground. That was when he heard the sound of running water. Following the sound, he and his servant walked deeper into the woods when they found a stream with crystal clear water rushing over large and small pebbles. This was the Nine Curve River; it emptied into the East Sea.

Delighted, Nezha took off his clothes to bathe. He sat on a stone at the edge of the stream, dipped his silk scarf into the water and began to wash himself.

When Nezha's scarf touched the water, he unwittingly started a shock wave of red glow through the East Sea, rattling the Crystal Palace in its wake.

*   *   *   *

In the watery realm of the Crystal Palace dwelled a tribe who ruled the East Sea. Like his counterpart on land, East Sea Dragon King Ao Guang, also ruled under the mandate of Heaven. Ao Guang was a good king until a few years back when he acquired a taste for human flesh, and had become addicted to it since. His craving, in fact, had progressed from just an occasional treat to an insatiable appetite. The erstwhile tranquil East Sea was now stormy and turbulent. Fatal shipwrecks were now frequent. Since no one survived them, no one outside of the Crystal Palace knew of Ao Guang's dark secret.

Dragon King Ao Guang had finished a boat load of shipwreck victims and was taking his after meal nap when he was awakened by the clattering of windows and doors. He made a quick calculation, murmured to himself, "Strange, the earth is not supposed to quake at this time. What's going on?"

Night Face was sent up to investigate. The whole river was bathed in a beautiful red glow. At its edge, a husky child was playing with a red cloth. "Um, this child would make a delicious meal for the dragon king," thought Night Face.

He shouted, "Hey, you there! Who are you and why are you disturbing the tranquility of the Crystal Palace?"

Nezha turned toward the shouting, and saw in the water a monster with an indigo face and mercury red hair, its long teeth protruding outside the mouth. It held a large trident.

Nezha said, "Hey yourself, strange beast! Are you speaking to me?"

Night Face was angry at the way he was so addressed. "I am Night Face, here to patrol the shore of the Nine Curve River, by the order of the East Sea Dragon King. I am not a beast!"

So saying, he jumped out of the water and pounced on the naked Nezha. To fend off the swinging trident, he threw his gold bracelet at Night Face, forgetting that it was not an ornament but a lethal weapon. Poor Night Face died instantly on the spot.

Laughing, Nezha picked up his bracelet and continued his bath with the red cloth. Shock waves emanating from the bracelet and the red cloth almost tumbled the Crystal Palace.

At this moment, a dragon soldier reported to East Sea Dragon King that a husky child on shore had killed Night Face. King Ao Guang thought to himself, "Night Face was given us by the decree of the Supreme Jade Emperor of Heaven. How dare anyone kill him? I had better investigate the matter myself."

His third son Prince Ao Bing entered and asked, "Why is my Royal father so angry?"

After hearing the story, Ao Bing said, "My Royal father, please let me go instead."

*   *   *   *

Prince Ao Bing was a rain God who brought rain to the world. In time past he had earned praise for his reliability. But he since had been corrupted by his father, the Dragon King. And in recent years the world suffered both devastating floods and disastrous droughts. For fear of offending the royal family of the Sea, these failings had never been reported to the Jade Emperor. Instead, each year, the people made sacrificial offerings to appease them. So far, this royal family had gotten away with their crime.

*   *   *   *

Dragon Prince Ao Bing got on his water beast and led his dragon soldiers to the Nine Curve River. As he went, the water parted for him, creating steep waves. Nezha stood up to look at the rising water. Oh, how interesting! A water beast was carrying on its back a vicious looking man in full armor.

The man called out, "Who killed my Night Face?"

Nezha relied, "You mean that strange looking creature? If so, I think my bracelet hit him."

Ao Bing asked, "Who are you?"

"I am Nezha, the third son of the commander of Old Pond Pass. I could not help it that he died."

Ao Bing was furious. "What a self-righteous cur you are," he shouted. "Night Face was sent to us by the decree of the Jade Emperor of Heaven. You killed him and still think you have no blame!"

So saying, Ao Bing came at Nezha with his spear. Nezha dodged neatly, then turned around and said, "Please stop. Who are you? Announce yourself and listen to my side of the story."

"I am Prince Ao Bing, third son of the East Sea Dragon King."

"Oh, yeah?" Nezha said. "Don't be so arrogant! I was just taking a little bath, minding my own business. Your man yelled at me for no reason, then he charged at me with his trident. So I threw my bracelet at him. You think you are invincible, right? Don't get me mad or I will kill you too. As for that puny mud fish, your father, I will take the skin off him."

Ao Bing screamed in rage, "How dare you!" So saying, he lunged his spear at Nezha.

Nezha flung out his red scarf to ward off the spear. The scarf opened up like a fire ball, came down on Prince Ao Bing and his water beast, plucking them both out of the water. Nezha ran up and stepped on Ao Bing's head, then hit him with his bracelet.

Stretched stiffly on the ground, dead Ao Bing returned to his true form: a dragon, now dead, of course.

"My! My! A dragon!" Nezha was surprised but unmoved. He thought to himself, "Well, since it is already dead, I might as well take his tendons for a bow string for my father."

Nezha pulled the tendons out, and returned home as if nothing unusual had happened. But his servant was so frightened of the events, he could hardly walk.

Dragon King Ao Guang got the news of his third son Ao Bing's death: not only was he killed, but his tendons were pulled! In grief and anger, Ao Guang wondered how anyone could kill him. His son, after all, was a deity who carried rain and wind to the populace.

Ao Guang thought to himself, "The killer is said to be Li Jing's son! Oh yes, I remember who Li Jing is. I met him at Mount Kunlun when Li was a student there."

So Ao Guang changed himself into human form and went directly to see Li Jing.

*   *   *   *

Commander Li Jing had come back from his daily training session. He was sitting with his armor off, reflecting on how King Zhou had turned his kingdom upside down, causing the four hundred dukes to rebel. For seven years now, day in and day out, along with all other commanding officers defending the Passes, he had to drill his men and horses, had to keep them on full alert. The soldiers were getting tired and the suffering of the people was getting worse. When Ao Guang's visit was announced, Li Jing hurriedly put on his clothes to receive the East Sea Dragon King.

Ao Guang was in rage and rancor, "My dear friend Li Jing. You do have some great sons!"

Li Jing said, "We have not seen each other for years. Why such language? Yes, indeed, I have three sons. Number one is Jinzha, number two is Muzha, and the young one is Nezha. Each has a Superiorman as teacher. Even though they are not particularly outstanding, they are honest and upright. Please don't be prejudiced against them."

Ao Guang said, "I am prejudiced against your sons? Well! Well! It was one of your sons who took a bath in the nine Curve River today. I don't know what he did, but he almost toppled my Crystal Palace. I sent my scout to investigate. Your son killed him without provocation. Then my third son went to investigate, and your son killed him too, and even pulled his tendons!"

With tears streaming down his cheeks, Ao Guang screamed, "And you have the audacity to say I am prejudiced!"

Li Jing tried to calm his visitor. "My dear friend, I am sorry to hear that. However, it could not have been my sons. My oldest son is now on Mount Five Dragons; my second son is on Mount Nine Courts; and my third is only ten years old and very seldom ventures out of the house. How could such a thing have happened?"

Ao Guang said, "Yes, it was your third son Nezha!"

Li Jing said, "Please be patient. I'll call him here to see you."

Li Jing hurried to the family quarters to look for Nezha. His wife told him that Nezha was in the garden; but she did not dare mention that she had given Nezha permission to go out of the Pass.

For more than twenty minutes, Li Jing searched for Nezha, but he was nowhere to be seen. As a last resort, Li Jing went to the begonia hot house where Nezha was never known to have gone before. The door was locked. Li Jing called and called. Nezha finally opened the door and came out.

Li Jing asked, "What are you doing here, my son?"

"I was enjoying the begonias, father."

"Where were you before?"

"I did not have anything to do, so I went out of the Pass to the Nine Curve River for a walk. The weather was hot, so I bathed in the river. I did not expect to meet the monster Night Face. He screamed at me without provocation and charged at me with his trident. So I killed him. Then someone calling himself Prince Ao Bing, claimed to be the third son of the East Sea Dragon King. He lunged at me with his spear. So I used my scarf to pluck him out of the water, put my foot on him and hit him with my bracelet. He died and turned into a dragon! I know dragon tendons are good material to tie things, so I pulled them. Here, my father, my gift for you."

The father was struck dumb and could not utter a word for a long moment. After regaining his senses, he shouted at his son, "You little beast! How could you! You have incurred the worst calamity ever! Come with me to see your Uncle Ao Guang!"

Still acting the child, Nezha said, "Do not worry, my father. I have not used the tendons yet. I will return them to him, and that should settle the matter."

Nezha hurried out to the front Hall to meet Dragon King Ao Guang. Very politely, Nezha bowed and said, "My honorable Uncle Ao Guang. Please pardon your uninformed nephew who did not know any better and so made a grave mistake. I am very sorry. Here are the tendons. Please take them back."

Looking at his son's tendons, Ao Guang wept bitterly, saying, "You and your evil son! A while ago, you accused me of wrongly pointing my finger at him. Now he has confessed, with evidence in hand. What can you say for yourself? My son Ao Bing was a deity, and my scout was sent to me by the decree of Jade Emperor of Heaven. How dared you kill them?

"Tomorrow I will report directly to the Jade Emperor and we will see how he wants to settle the score."

The Dragon King left in a huff.

Li Jing howled with grief, "We will never live through this!"

Yinshi heard her husband's crying and asked the servants what was going on. She then rushed to comfort him. Li Jing said, "Unfortunately you have given birth to this little devil! Our family will be destroyed because of him! The East Sea Dragon King rules the East Sea and Nezha had killed his third son and his favorite scout. The Dragon King is going to see the Jade Emperor of Heaven for revenge. In a day or two, we will be ghosts under knives!" Husband and wife wept bitterly.

Pointing at her son, Yinshi said, "I carried you for three years and six months, with endless sufferings, before you were born. Whoever thought you would bring our family to an abrupt end!"

Seeing his parents so grieved, Nezha knelt and said, "Daddy and Mommy. I have to tell you the truth after all. I am not an ordinary person. I am The Magical Pearl. My bracelet is the Omnipresent Ring and the red scarf is the Amalgam Silk Ribbon. Both are the treasured weapons of Mount Champion. Dragon Prince Ao Bing and Night Face never had a chance against these weapons. Now I had better go back to seek help from my master Superiorman Paragon. Please do not worry. I will take all the blame coming."

Nezha picked up a handful of earth, threw it into the air and disappeared from sight.

*   *   *   *

At Mount Champion, Nezha knelt in front of his master Superior-man Paragon. Paragon asked, "You are supposed to be at Old Pond Pass. Why are you here?"

Nezha said, "My honorable Master, by your instruction, I was born at Old Pond Pass. It has been seven years. Yesterday, I went out for a walk and inadvertently killed Ao Bing. His father, the East Sea Dragon King, Ao Guang, is going to take my parents to the Court of Supreme Jade Emperor. My parents are very frightened. I don't know what to do. Please help us."

Paragon thought to himself, "In the scheme of things Heaven and Earth, the death of the Dragon Prince, Ao Bing, was unavoidable. It is time the people got a more benevolent and reliable Rain God. But it is too bad that Nezha had to be the killer. I could pretend that I do not know, yet how can I? It is so clearly shown in the configuration of the stars. As to the East Sea Dragon King, he is behaving as any indulgent father: never a moment's thought of the failings of his son. In fact he never seemed to know his son had done so much harm to the world. No matter, it is always a great sorrow to lose a son. Perhaps I should be compassionate toward Ao Guang on this; however, my priority is to help Nezha out of his present predicament."

Paragon asked Nezha to open his garment. On Nezha's chest, Paragon drew with his finger an "invisible juju", a sign that would confer on Nezha the ability to become invisible. He then instructed Nezha, "Go now to the Precious Virtues Gate, and wait for Ao Guang. When he shows up, you do this and that. Afterward, go back to your parents to reassure them that no harm will come to them. Everything will be taken care of by your master. Now go!"

*   *   *   *

Nezha left Mount Champion and went directly to Precious Virtues Gate. Since this was first visit to Heaven, he was greatly bedazzled by the beauty he saw there.

It was still early. The Dragon King had not yet arrived, and the Precious Virtues Gate was not yet open. Nezha waited impatiently.

Soon, Ao Guang arrived in his full court regalia, his jade pieces, pearls, and other ornaments twinkling as he walked. He was annoyed when he saw the Gate was still closed.

On seeing Ao Guang, Nezha's bottled up concern turned to anger. He walked over to Ao Guang and pounded him with his gold bracelet, knocking him down. Nezha then put his foot on the Dragon King.

CHAPTER 13

▼

MADAM ROCKIE, THE EVIL ROCK

Using his "Invisible Juju" Nezha, sought to be invisible. However, the East Sea Dragon King, Ao Guang, could still faintly make out Nezha's outline. Nezha's foot was so firmly planted on him, he could not move. His anger knew no limit.

"You scalawag," he screamed! "You are still wet behind the ears, and your milk teeth are still in. By killing my son and my Night Face, you have committed an unforgivable crime already. Now you dare come to the Precious Virtues Gate to torment me! Do you think you can get away with it?"

It would have been too easy for the impetuous Nezha to kill Ao Guang, but Superiorman Paragon had forbidden him from doing so. As Ao Guang hurled more insults, Nezha stepped on him harder. Beating him more rapidly, Nezha said, "You little old mud fish! You think your screams and profanities will help you? By chance, I was bathing in the Nine Curve River, minding my own business. Your son and Night Face insulted me. They even tried to kill me. You want to make a mountain out of such an insignificant mole hill? You want to sue my parents in the Supreme Jade Court? Even if I also kill you, mud fish, the Supreme Jade Court should still not be bothered with such little nothings!"

Ao Guang screamed even louder, "You little cur! Stop beating me!"

Nezha, using his bare fist, beat Ao Guang ever harder, saying, "If I want to beat you, I will and you cannot stop me. So there!"

To torment Ao Guang even more, Nezha tore off Ao Guang's robe and started to pull out scales from his dragon body. Blood gushed and the pain was so excruciating that Ao Guang begged for his life.

Nezha said, "Well, I will let you go only under one condition. You must now go back to Old Pond Pass with me, and forever forget about the Nine Curve River incident. Otherwise, just a touch of my bracelet will finish you off. My master is completely behind me."

Ao Guang knew he was not in a bargaining position, and the pain was killing him. So he said, "All right. I will go back with you."

Nezha said, "I know you can change your shape, form, and size. If you disappear, it would be a bother to find you. How about changing yourself into a small snake so that I can carry you with me?"

Ao Guang could not argue, so he became a small green snake. Nezha left the Precious Virtue Gate with this snake and returned to Old Pond Pass.

*   *   *   *

Nezha said to his father, Commander Li Jing, "I went to the South Heaven Gate to invite the Honorable Uncle Ao Guang to return to earth and begged him not to sue you in the Court of the Supreme Jade Emperor."

Not believing and already upset, Li Jing began to shout, "You deceitful snoot! Who do you think you are to be able to go to Heaven?"

Nezha said, "Daddy, please don't be angry. Uncle Ao Guang is my witness."

Li Jing said, "What nonsense! Where would you find Ao Guang?"

"Right here." Nezha produced the little green snake and threw it to the ground. In a breeze, Ao Guang appeared in human form.

Startled, Li Jing bowed and said, "How is my friend Ao Guang?"

Ao Guang replied acidly, "You and your vicious son!" Ao Guang then showed his wound to Li Jing while relating what Nezha had done at the Precious Virtue Gate.

"We the dragon kings of the four seas will bring a joint complaint to the Supreme Jade Emperor. We will see how you get away with the indignity you have given me!" With these words, Ao Guang disappeared.

Stamping the ground, Li Jing moaned, "It is getting worse and worse!"

Nezha knelt in front of his parents. "Please don't worry," he said. "My master will come to our rescue. He said that I am not here by accident. I was sent down to the Red Dust for a purpose. Even if all the dragon kings join forces, it would not matter at all. My master promised me that."

*   *   *   *

The massive Kunlun Mountains were the favorite abodes of Superiormen of many cults. All had intimate knowledge of the matters of Heaven and Earth. Li Jing had been in training with one of these superiormen, so he too understood the intricacy of such matters. Besides, as Ao Guang attested, Nezha did go to Heaven, so there must be some truth in what Nezha said. Still, he was resentful of the way Nezha behaved. On the other hand, Yinshi felt very miserable seeing her husband being so hard on their son. She tried to get Nezha out of her husband's hateful sight, suggesting, "Son, why don't you go to the garden?"

Nezha wandered into the garden, trying to entertain himself. He walked here and there, looking at this and that. The day was hot, and he was soon soaked in perspiration. He walked over to the fish pond where it was a bit cooler. As he bent over to look at the fish, he saw something in the water. What was that? Ah, the reflection of the Watchtower! Nezha had never been up there before. Why not? Why not indeed?

Nezha climbed up the high Watchtower. What a wonderful breeze! What a beautiful view! On one of the walls he spied a bow and three arrows. These were no ordinary weapons. They were, in fact, The Cosmic Bow and The Heaven Quaking Arrows. The Yellow Emperor had used them to conquer the powerful and savage Chief Ignoramus. Since then, no one had been able to even lift the bow, so heavy was it. They became the talisman of Old Pond Pass. But Nezha had never heard this story.

Just for the fun of it, Nezha took an arrow, put it on the bow, and shot it toward the southwest sky. The arrow disappeared into the clouds with a loud thunder clap.

*   *   *   *

Under the Southwest sky, on Skeleton Mountain, there lived Madam Rockie, a superiorwoman in her own right. She had been trained in the Kunlun Mountains for thousands of years. She was as powerful in her magic as any other superiorman. However, she belonged to the school of discipline that ran counter to the other three main schools. To Madam Rockie, there was no such thing as moral or immoral. Hers was the school of the Me. It was Me alone that mattered, and anything or anyone else be damned.

The truth was that Madam Rockie was originally an old rock—a rock that had been nurtured by the sun's light and the moon's beam, and by the blood and flesh of the innocence victims whose bones and skeletons she made into her abode. Madam Rockie had achieved the status of a Superiorwoman. Oh no, rather a superior-specter: more powerful, more evil, and amoral, than any ordinary specter. She could change into whatever form she wanted, but she liked the human form best. She depended on her regular diet of human flesh and blood to sustain her life and vitality.

$$*\qquad*\qquad*\qquad*$$

Of all places, where did Nezha's arrow go? Yes, you guessed it. To Madam Rockie's Skeleton Mountain!

One of Madam Rockie's disciples, on her way to the mountain top, died instantly when the Heaven Quaking Arrow pieced her throat.

On examination, Madam Rockie recognized the arrow as a Heaven Quaking Arrow. Anger rose in her heart. She said, "That was from Old Pond Pass! Li Jing! How could you? I had recommended to your master that you be sent down to the Red Dust to enjoy the material richness. Now that you have become a Commander, instead of being thankful, you repay me with this vicious arrow, killing one of my girls. Such an ingrate!"

Madam Rockie jumped on her Green Bird and came directly to Old Pond Pass. She yelled from mid-air, "Li Jing, come out this very instant!"

Li Jing heard the call. He rushed out, and saw Madam Rockie. Li Jing knelt and said, "Pardon me, Madam Rockie. I did not know you were coming, and therefore did not come out to welcome you."

Madam Rockie said, "You and your good deeds! I can see you also have a very eloquent tongue!" She ordered her Yellow Kerchiefed Genie to take Li Jing back to her mountain.

"Li Jing! What is your gripe?" Madam Rockie could hardly contain her anger. "I know you may be unhappy because you could not become a superiorman. But you have managed in the Red Dust quite well. Instead of repaying a kindness, you resorted to violence, killing one of my girls without cause. What do you have to say for yourself?"

Like a tidal wave rising from a tranquil sea, the accusation stunned Li Jing. He said, "Madam Rockie, I really don't know what you are talking about."

Raising her voice, Madam Rockie said, "You killed one of my girls with your arrow and still feign innocence!"

Bewildered, Li Jing asked, "May I please see the arrow?"

Madam Rockie threw the arrow at Li Jing, shouted, "See for yourself!"

Startled, Li Jing murmured, more to himself than to Madam Rockie, "How incredible! Who had the strength even to pick up the bow, much less shoot with it!" He begged Madam Rockie to let him go home to find the culprit.

"Very well, if you don't come back with the perpetrator, you know the consequences!"

Using the underground traveling trick learned at Mount Kunlun, Li Jing was back in Old Pond Pass in a shake. His wife Yinshi had been terrified when a whirlwind sucked up her husband. Now miraculously he was back! She stopped her wailing to ask what had happened.

Li Jing's tale of the bow and arrow frightened her even more. She cried out, "You mean our Nezha has already caused a second calamity, even before we could ride out the first?"

Li Jing said, "I am afraid so, my love. Our luck has been so bad lately; nothing seems to go right. Since the time of the Yellow Emperor, the bow and arrows have become the talisman of the Old Pond Pass. No one had ever been able to lift the bow, much less shoot it.

"As it was one of these arrows that took the girl, Madam Rockie insisted it was my responsibility to repay the life that was lost. My dear wife, after twenty-five years of service to my king, who could have known my career would end with such bad luck?"

Li Jing called for Nezha, who came quickly and stood silently before his father.

Setting an ambush, Li Jing said, "My son. I remember you said you were sent here by your master of Mount Champion to assist in the founding of a new dynasty. Why don't you practice such warfare skills as shooting arrows?"

Nezha said, "Yes, my father. I did just that a while ago. I was on the watchtower and saw on the wall an old bow and three arrows. I shot one arrow and it disappeared beyond the clouds."

Li Jing thundered, "You foolish boy! You killed third dragon prince, a matter we have not resolved. And now you have caused another calamity!"

Yinshi was sobbing nearby. Nezha, not knowing what had aroused anger in his father, said timidly, "What is the matter, Daddy?"

Li Jing said in tears, "Your arrow killed one of Madam Rockie's disciples. Madam Rockie took me to her Skeleton Mountain for questioning. Now you must come with me to see her."

Father and son went by disappeared under ground and reached Skeleton Mountain in haste.

Li Jing went in the White Bones Cave to see Madam Rockie while Nezha waited outside. Nezha could not understand how it was possible that he had killed Madam Rockie's girl. He thought to himself, "They are going to punish me for a crime I did not commit. It is better I do something to them before they do it to me!"

So thinking, Nezha threw his bracelet at the first person coming out of the cave, who let out a blood-curdling cry and slumped to the ground.

Madam Rockie rushed out of her cave and found another of her girls on the ground, grievously wounded.

"You louse! You hurt another of my pupils!"

Madam Rockie, a handsome woman of uncertain age, had a fish tail gold tiara on her head, the design of the Trigram on both front and back of her bright red robe, and a white silk sash that showed off her small waist. She wore soft soled red linen shoes. She came toward Nezha with her Satellite-sword in one hand. Nezha threw his bracelet at her. She caught it in her bare hand. "Oh!" she said, "So it is you!"

Nezha was surprised that someone could take his bracelet with such ease. He hurriedly flung open his silk scarf, but it too fell easily into Madam Rockie's sleeve.

She called out, "Nezha! Any more of your master's treasures left?"

Nezha had no more. So he picked up his feet and started to run. Madam Rockie called over her shoulder, "Li Jing. You are all right now. Go home."

Madam Rockie took off after Nezha. They ran like lightning through the clouds. Nezha had no place to go but to Mount Champion, to his master the Superiorman Paragon.

"Why are you here?" Paragon asked.

"Master, save me! Madam Rockie is chasing me with her Satellite-sword. She has already taken my Omnipresent Ring and my Amalgam Scarf. She is now outside. Please, Master, save me!"

Paragon said, "You silly pup. Go wait in the garden. Let me see what is going on."

Paragon saw Madam Rockie coming toward him in full fury, Satellite-sword in her hand. Paragon saluted her, "Welcome to my Cave, Madam Rockie."

Madam Rockie returned the salute, saying, "My Elder Brother-in-learning! Your student Nezha, flaunting your treasures and magic, killed one of my girls and gravely wounded another. He even used the Omnipresent Ring and the Amalgam Scarf on me. If you call Nezha out and punish him in my presence, we may still be friends. If you try to protect him, then you will have to take the consequences!"

Paragon said, "No problem. Nezha is in my garden. However, I think you had better go first to see my master of Vacuous Jade Palace. If he says to give Nezha to you, I will hand him over. Nezha was born under order of the Supreme Jade Emperor to assist in the founding of a new dynasty. He is really not under my command."

Madam Rockie said with a grimace, "Don't you use your master to intimidate me, my dear Elder Brother-in-learning. Do you mean you are going to let your pupil do as he pleases? Even to kill without cause? He killed my girl, and you want to use your master to cow me? Don't you think you are a bit too presumptuous? We all know that my Persuasion, my Cult, is as good as yours. Why do you think you can do such a thing to me?"

Paragon said, "Madam Rockie, listen to me. You belong to The Incisive Cult, while I belong to the Elucidation Cult. We have all been sent to the Red Dust to help some worthy cause in order to redeem ourselves for some of our violations of Heaven. You do remember when the three cults, yours and mine included, agreed to the list of the Investiture of Gods? My master had then ordered me to assist in the founding of the new dynasty. Do you realize that Nezha is no other but the Magical Pearl, ordered to be born as a human to help Jiang Baby Tooth in his effort to terminate Cheng Tang's Dynasty? Nezha was sent down by Heaven. Your girl's life was fixed to end sooner or later anyway. So what is the big deal?

"People like you who have not a worry in the world should not bother yourselves with such insignificant matters and upset the Scheme of things Heaven and Earth! Sooner or later, you will finish your own training and receive your rewards from Heaven. So what is the fuss?"

Fixed or not, that girl was one of Madam Rockie's favorite disciples. More importantly, Paragon was too casual in dismissing her cult, her persuasion. She could not suppress her anger.

"Just what are you implying?"

Paragon said, "Well, everything has its place and there is such a thing as priority!"

Now mad as a wet hen, Madam Rockie raised her Satellite-sword at Paragon. Paragon stepped aside and rushed into his cave. He took out his own sword and put something in his pocket. Then, facing Mount Kunlun, he knelt, saying softly, "My master. I am going to kill someone today."

Then he came back out and said to Madam Rockie, "I am afraid your training does not befit your violent behavior, my dear Madam Rockie!"

Again, she raised her sword.

Paragon cried, "Look out!"

Furiously they fought, changing the colors of the clouds at every clash of their swords. Madam Rockie turned and threw the Trigram Scarf at Paragon, trying to catch him with it.

Paragon said, "Good guys don't worry about bad gals!"

He chanted while pointing his index finger at the scarf, stopping it in mid-air.

Upon losing command of the magic scarf, Madam Rockie's angry face turned as red as a pomegranate blossom. Now her sword came as fast as a blinding blizzard! At last, Paragon pulled from his pocket the Nine-dragon-fire-net and threw it over Madam Rockie who saw it coming too late. Alas! Madam Rockie was caught in the net! With nine encircling dragons spewing fire, she was reduced in a few moments to her original form: an ancient fire-forged, weather-beaten rock!

This rock was born when the world was first formed. It had gone through the disciplines of water, fire and wind, and had attained the magic of a superior-specter. As such she was a selfish, and amoral creature. To sustain her own life, she killed and sucked the blood of the innocent. It was inevitable, according to the larger scheme of things Heaven and Earth, that she had to come to an end. Paragon felt bad because he had to be the one who put an end to Madam Rockie.

Paragon took back Nezha's bracelet and scarf, both of which Madam Rockie had taken for herself.

Nezha saw what happened. He wanted the net very much, but Paragon thought differently. It was not time yet for Nezha to have it.

He said to Nezha, "The dragon kings of the four seas have reported your misdeed to Jade Emperor. They are picking up your parents at the Old Pond Pass this very moment."

Tears ran down Nezha's face when he thought of the sufferings his parents had endured because of him. He begged Paragon to help.

Paragon bent and whispered into Nezha's ear that Nezha must do this and that, such and so in order to save his parents.

Nezha left Mount Champion and instantly returned to Old Pond Pass.

*   *   *   *

A large crowd of people were milling around in front of Commander Li Jing's residence. When they saw Nezha, they cried out to Li Jing, "Third master has returned!"

Nezha walked up to the four dragon kings and said, "I am fully responsible for what I did. Please don't implicate my parents."

He then said to East Sea Dragon King Ao Guang, "I am The Magical Pearl on order from the Supreme Jade Emperor to be born in human form. Today, I will open my body, and return my life to my parents. Please let them go. If you disagree, we can then go to see the Supreme Jade Emperor. What do you say?"

Ao Guang said, "I see you are trying to save your parents by sacrificing yourself, so you are not really too bad. All right, we agree."

The four dragon kings let go of Li Jing and his wife Yinshi. Nezha took a knife in his right hand and cut off his left arm first. He then proceeded to cut open his body, took out his heart, lungs, kidneys, stomach and liver. He died then and there.

Mollified, the four dragon kings left. Nezha's parents buried his body.

However, his spirit and soul were originally from the supernatural, as such, they lived on, but floating, here, there, and nowhere, because there was no body for them to cling to. Eventually they soared back to Mount Champion.

CHAPTER 14

▼

NEZHA ACQUIRES A LOTUS BODY

A servant reported to Superiorman Paragon that Nezha was wandering outside of the cave. Paragon knew immediately what that meant.

He came out and said to Nezha, "This is not the place for you. Go back to Old Pond Pass. Tell your mother when she dreams that she must build a temple for you. A meadow on top of the Green Screen Hill, about forty miles from Old Pond Pass is the right place for it. You then will have a place to stay, to receive incense offerings. Your body will regain its essence and you will live in human form again. But you must hurry."

That night, Nezha appeared in his mother's dream. He said to her, "Mother dear. I am your young son Nezha. Since my body is gone, pity my soul floating around without a place to call its own. Help me please. About forty miles from here on the Green Screen Hill, there is a meadow. Please erect a temple there for my soul to receive incense offerings so that my body can regain its substance. I will be forever grateful."

Yinshi woke up in tears. Her husband Li Jing asked why she had cried in her sleep. Yinshi told him about Nezha's request.

Li Jing was cynical, "It is all in your head. When you think of something hard enough, it will appear in your dream. Nezha has caused us enough grief, so much so that we almost lost our lives. You are not going to erect any temple!"

Yinshi dared not say any more. But next night, then the next, and the next, every time she closed her eyes, Nezha was there pleading. She was so sad and helpless.

When Nezha was alive, he had always got his way with his mother. In death, he became even more determined. He even told her he would make life miserable for the whole Li family forever and ever until he got his temple!

After many trying and sleepless nights filled with fear and sadness, Yinshi finally took her own money and secretly instructed a servant to engage someone to build a temple on the Green Screen Hill meadow, and place a clay idol of Nezha in it.

To attract attendance to his temple, Nezha revealed his magic to the local populace who daily flocked to the temple with their incense offerings.

As Nezha's reputation spread, the crowd coming to the Green Screen Hill got bigger and bigger. Whatever their prayers, they were always answered.

*   *   *   *

Time flew like an arrow. Soon half a year had passed since the completion of the temple.

One day, returning from a business trip, Li Jing happened to pass by the Green Screen Hill and saw people going up the hill, thick as ants. He inquired, and was told of the temple and its miracles. Something faintly flashing in his memory, he asked, "What is the name of this wonderful god?"

Upon hearing Nezha's name, Li Jing ordered his men to hold their horses while he raced his horse up the hill to see for himself. As he approached, people stepped aside to make way for him.

There above the doorway, he saw the words NEZHA'S TEMPLE. Inside was the idol of Nezha, in perfect likeness, with clay servants standing on each side.

Pointing at the idol, Li Jing blared, "You impudent fraud! You brought harm to your parents when you were alive. Now in your death, you try to make fools of the populace!"

Then with the full sweep of his whip, Li Jing knocked the idol to the floor, smashing it to smithereens. Next he kicked down all the other idols and ordered the temple burnt!

He told the people who had come to offer incense not to be fooled by this imposter. Frightened by what Li Jing did and said, they hurried down the hill to their homes.

Returning to Old Pond Pass, Li Jing scolded his wife, "You and your no good son! Was it not enough that he harmed us? And now, behind my back, you erect a temple for him to fool the populace! Do you want me to lose my jade belt as well? Should the news of Nezha's temple get to the Capital City, Morning Song, all my past hard work and glories would go down the drain in a hurry! You stupid woman! What made you think you could get away with doing such things behind my back? Well, for your information, I have destroyed the whole thing today. So there!"

Yinshi dared not utter a word.

*   *   *   *

Nezha was away when his temple was destroyed. That night he was shocked to find not only that there was no idol to receive offerings, but there was not even a temple! The mountain was red and the ground was black. What had happened?

Two of his clay servants came to him crying, "It was commander Li Jing. He charged up the hill in a fit of anger, destroyed the idols and burnt down the temple."

Nezha thought to himself, "Why, Li Jing! How could you do such a thing? By returning my body to you, I have saved you from the four dragon kings. I can no longer incriminate you because you are no longer my parent. So why did you deprive me of my clay idol that I need for my soul and spirit?"

After some thought, Nezha decided to take a trip to Mount Champion. His master Superiorman Paragon asked him, "Why are you here? You are supposed to be in your temple to receive incense offerings."

Nezha knelt. He told Paragon what had happened and begged him to do something.

Paragon thought to himself, "Li Jing, you are too petty! Nezha has returned his body to you. There is no more kinship between the two of you. You in turn should leave him alone, as Jiang Baby Tooth is coming soon and will need Nezha's help."

Paragon said, "Very well. I will have to do something drastic."

He called to his servant to bring from the lotus pond two fresh pink lotus flowers and three fresh lotus leaves.

Paragon built the head, face, brain and other organs from the flower petals, and the bones and body from the stems and leaves. He then put a magic pill on top of the heap. Using his magic to gather up Nezha's soul and spirit, he hollered, "Nezha, why are you waiting! Turn into a human form Now!"

In a thunderclap, out jumped Nezha with a face as fair as the lotus blossom, and eyes twinkling like shining stars. Fully grown and husky, Nezha was now sixteen feet tall!

Imagine, a flesh and blood human being, transformed from two lotus flowers and three lotus leaves!

Paragon took Nezha to the garden and taught him magic incantation and the use of a Fire-tip spear. In a leopard skin bag, he put

Nezha's Omnipresent Ring, Amalgam scarf, and a gold brick. Then he gave him two wind-fire wheels.

"Go to the Old Pond Pass," Paragon instructed Nezha.

*   *   *   *

After thanking his master, Nezha put the leopard bag on his back, picked up the Fire-tip spear, stepped on his new wind-fire wheels, and went directly to Commander Li Jing's residence in Old Pond Pass.

"Bring Li Jing out to see me immediately!" shouted Nezha.

The servants scurried to report to Li Jing, "My lord. Outside is third young master on two fire wheels, holding a fire-tip spear. He dares to call you by your name."

Li Jing scoffed, "Nonsense! A dead person could not return to life."

Before he could finish his words, more servants came rushing in, shouting, "Master! He is coming in!"

Enraged, Li Jing picked up his long handled knife, got on his green horse and charged out of his residence. What he saw was no longer a child but a tall, grown, menacing Nezha.

Shocked, Li Jing exclaimed, "You vermin! When you were my child, you caused untold calamities. Why do you reincarnate and disturb the peace?"

Nezha said, "Li Jing! I have returned my flesh and bones to you and no longer owe you anything, so why did you destroy my temple?"

Nezha came directly at Li Jing. Li Jing fought with his knife, but he was hardly Nezha's match. After only a few passes, the exhausted Li Jing turned his horse and fled toward the southeast.

Nezha gave chase on his wheels, shouting, "Don't even think you can outrun me!"

Of course, Li Jing's green horse could never compete with Nezha's wind-fire wheels for speed. Seeing Nezha was catching up, Li Jing jumped off his mount and disappeared under ground.

Nezha laughed, "So you think no one else can do that?" Nezha tunneled after him. Desperately trying to find a place to hide, Li Jing surfaced. Just then he heard someone singing.

Bright moon in the water waving,
Green willows and peach flowers dancing.
A few colorful clouds in the sky,
Oh, yes, what a different world at this height.

The singer was a young man with hair in a top knot, wearing a loose cotton garment with silk sash, and linen shoes, all very much in the style of a superiorman.

To Li Jing's great relief, the young man turned out to be his second son Muzha, who had been studying with Superiorman Universal Converter on Mount Nine-Court, White Egret Cave.

Li Jing screamed, "My son Muzha, save your father!"

Muzha shouted at his brother, "You stop! Don't you know the punishment for killing one's own father? Go away before I do you in!"

Surprised, Nezha Said, "Who are you to interfere with me?"

"You mean you don't know me? I am Muzha!"

"So you are my second elder brother! Apparently you don't know what was going on between father and me."

Nezha told Muzha about the returning of his body to his parents, the temple on the Green Screen Hill, the burning and destruction of the place he had hoped to use to rebuild his body.

Muzha said, "Nonsense! There is no such thing as a parent doing wrong!"

Nezha said, "I have already returned my blood and bones to them. We are no longer related. How could he still be my father?"

Muzha was furious. He came directly at Nezha with his sword, shouting, "Shut up!"

Nezha blocked the sword with his Fire-tip spear, and said, "Look, Muzha. There is no animosity between you and me. Step aside and let me finish with Li Jing."

Muzha, in return, yelled, "How sinful! You are going to kill your own father?"

So saying, Muzha swung his sword at Nezha. The two brothers fought a most fearsome battle.

As they fought, Nezha saw Li Jing taking off. So Nezha took out his gold brick and threw it at Muzha, knocking him to the ground.

Li Jing saw Muzha fall and ran even faster. Like a bird breaking from a forest fire or a fish thrashing to escape from a raising net, Li Jing had never moved so fast in his life.

Nezha now taunted him, "Even if you run into the sea, you will never get away from me this time!"

Realizing there was no way out, Li Jing was ready to kill himself to keep his dignity. As he poised his sword to cut his own throat, he heard someone shouting, "Stop! I am coming!" Then the man sang,

> *The breeze in the field blowing,*
> *The flowers in the pond floating.*
> *Where do we come from?*
> *Home is deep in the forming clouds.*

The singer was Jinzha's master Superiorman Broad Altruist of Mount Five Dragons, Cloud Top Cave.

Li Jing begged, "Master, save me! Please!"

Broad Altruist said, "Go into my cave. I will wait for him."

Presently the arrogant Nezha appeared. He asked, "Hey, Monk, did you see a general just passing by?"

Broad Altruist replied, "You mean General Li Jing? He went into my cave. Why?"

Nezha said, "Now listen you! He is my archenemy! If you let him come out, you will not be involved. If you let him escape, well, you can expect three cuts from my Fire-tip spear!"

"Tough, eh?" said the old man. "You mean you are going to hurt me?"

Not knowing the monk was a superiorman, Nezha said, "Old man, don't you dare look down on me! I am Nezha, the favorite disciple of Superiorman Paragon of Mount Champion!"

"Oh, yes? I have never heard that Superiorman Paragon had a favorite disciple named Nezha. Young punk, if you want to have a temper tantrum elsewhere, that is your business. However, if you want to have it here, I will give you three hundred lashes and hang you in my peach garden for three years!"

Reckless and hot tempered, Nezha came straight at Broad Altruist with his Fire-tip spear. Broad Altruist stepped aside, and hoping that Nezha would then go away, went into his cave. But Nezha kept up his pursuit.

Broad Altruist reached into his sleeve and brought out the "Seven Treasure Golden Lotus" and threw it over Nezha's head.

A whirlwind of fog, sand and stone engulfed Nezha. He passed out. When he came to, he found himself firmly immobilized, with his neck and legs cuffed by gold rings attached to a gold post.

Broad Altruist said, "What do we have here? Jinzha, please bring me my whipping board."

Jinzha was Nezha's eldest brother, who had been studying under Superiorman Broad Altruist for many years. When Jinzha brought out the whipping board, Broad Altruist said, "Please flog him for me."

What a flogging Nezha got! Nezha screamed bloody murder, but who cared?

Yes, this whole episode was arranged by Nezha's master, Superiorman Paragon of Mount Champion. Paragon had asked Broad Altruist to help tame Nezha, to cut down his haughty arrogance.

As Nezha smoldered in frustration and humiliation, a superiorman wearing a loose garment with a silk sash and linen shoes sauntered past. Recognizing his master, Nezha hollered, "Master! Save me please!"

But Paragon did not seem to hear him and went directly into Cloud Top Cave to see Broad Altruist. "My appreciation to you for disciplining Nezha," he said to his host.

Broad Altruist asked Jinzha to bring Nezha in.

"Your master wants to see you," Jinzha said to Nezha.

Still cheeky, Nezha said, "Don't you sass me! You know well I cannot move!"

Jinzha replied with a smirk, "Ah, that's so! Close your eyes and we will see what can be done."

When Nezha reopened his eyes, the gold rings had disappeared. He was free.

He went in with Jinzha, and saw his master Paragon sitting to the right of Broad Altruist. His master was lower in rank than this detested Broad Altruist!

Paragon said, "Nezha, come over to pay homage to your elder Uncle-in-learning."

Nezha, hating it in his deepest heart, knelt down before Broad Altruist, then turned and knelt before his own master Paragon.

Now Li Jing came out and knelt before Broad Altruist, who said, "From now on, no more quarrels between the two of you. Li Jing, you may go."

Li Jing thanked the two superiormen and left. Nezha was so angry that he could scarcely contain himself, but he dared not make a sound.

Paragon said, "Nezha, you may return to our cave now. Your elder Uncle-in-learning wants to play a game of chess with me. I will be back when we finish."

Seeing a chance to go after Li Jing, Nezha regained his animation. Flowers seemed to bloom once more in his heart. He said good-bye to both superiormen, and his eldest brother Jinzha. Then, on his wind-fire wheels he left like a speeding arrow to chase after Li Jing.

Li Jing saw Nezha coming but thought of no way he could possibly save himself. He was again ready to commit suicide when at this very desperate moment, Li Jing heard someone calling from the top of the hill, "Hey you down there, are you Li Jing?"

Li Jing looked up and saw standing next to a pine tree a superiorman. Li Jing begged, "Master, save me please!"

The superiorman said, "Come up here and stand behind me." Li Jing scampered up as Nezha came on the scene.

Nezha laughed to himself when he saw Li Jing standing behind a superiorman. "Don't tell me I have to deal with this again!" He shot up the hill on his wind-fire wheels.

"Is that Nezha coming up the hill?" the superiorman asked.

"So it is!" Nezha replied. "Why are you shielding Li Jing?"

"Why are you chasing him?"

Nezha related the Green Screen Hill incident.

The superiorman said, "I thought this problem had been resolved in the Cloud Top Cave. It is not good for you to rekindle your revenge again."

Nezha said, "That is none of your business. Out of my way!"

The superiorman said, "Itching to fight, eh?" He turned to Li Jing and said, "Go ahead and fight him!"

Li Jing begged, "Please, Master, save me. He is so strong, how can I fight him?"

"It is all right. Don't worry. I am here to watch over you." So saying, superiorman first spat on Li Jing and then patted him on the back.

Li Jing raised his long handle knife and came straight at Nezha. They fought like two tigers battling for a mate. With the superiorman's assurance and magic, Li Jing gave a credible show; even Nezha felt the pressure.

"That must be because of that trick." Nezha thought to himself. "The way to win over Li Jing is to destroy that superiorman first."

Nezha deliberately missed Li Jing and came directly at the superiorman. When the superiorman opened his mouth, a white lotus spouted out to stop Nezha's Fire-tip spear.

Putting up a hand to stop Li Jing, the superiorman then turned to Nezha, "What is the matter, young man? You and your father were fighting, why did you try to kill me? Good thing my white lotus stopped your spear in time. Otherwise, as a bystander, I would have become a ghost for no good reason!"

Nezha said, "You know well that Li Jing is not my match. What trickery are you using to help him? And you say you are not involved?" So saying, Nezha came at the superiorman again with his spear.

This time superiorman raised his sleeve and a purple cloud appeared and fell over Nezha, capturing him inside a tiny tower! The superiorman gave the tower a little tap, starting a fire inside and roasting Nezha. He yelled for mercy to no avail.

The superiorman asked, "Nezha, do you recognize your father now?"

Just to gain some relief from the fire, Nezha said, "Yes, Master. I do."

The superiorman said, "All right. I will let you go." So saying, he lifted his sleeve and the tower disappeared.

Nezha looked over his body. Nothing was burnt.

"Kowtow to your father, Nezha!" the superiorman said.

Still untamed, Nezha refused. But when he saw the superiorman ready to raise his sleeve again, Nezha knelt, resentment all over his face.

The superiorman said, "Nezha, tell your father you are sorry."

Again, Nezha refused.

"Well, then I will have to use the tower again."

"My father, I am sorry," Nezha hurriedly said, but in his heart, he was planning to get even with Li Jing once this abominable superiorman was out of sight.

Now the superiorman said to Li Jing, "Kneel in front of me. I will teach you the secret Juju of this golden tower. Should Nezha ever again be disobedient, use it on him without hesitation."

Nezha's horror now knew no bounds. He would forever be at the mercy of this odious superiorman's magic golden tower!

The superiorman said, "Nezha, listen to me. From now on, you and your father will live in harmony. When the right time comes, both of you will assist the new ruler to found a new dynasty. Mind you, I am watching you all the time. Go back now to Mount Champion." Nezha left without a word.

Li Jing knelt and said, "My master. May I know your name and your abode?"

"I am Superiorman Lamp Lighter of Mount Condor, Intuition Cave. Even though you did not have the right karma to ever become a superiorman, fate has decreed that you enjoy honor and material reward in the Red Dust for many years.

"Right now King Zhou is doing everything to terminate his own reign. Return to Old Pond Pass and resign from your post. Keep a low profile. Wait for the ripe moment then help in the founding of the new Chou Dynasty."

CHAPTER 15

▼

BABY TOOTH'S ROTTEN LUCK

Jiang Baby Tooth was a mild-tempered and good-natured man, intelligent and diligent. He got along well with his fellow students and all other dwellers on Mount Kunlun. Under the strict but benevolent tutelage of his master, Superiorman Primordial Supreme, he had made excellent progress in his studies. Life had been good and he was content.

One day, his master, Superiorman Primordial Supreme, said to him, "Jiang Baby Tooth. You are a good man and have been a good student here. You lack, however, the right Karma to ever become a superiorman. But you do deserve some wealth and honor in the Red Dust. Besides, you are needed down there to help to establish a new dynastic reign. So go and do your best. You must leave right away."

"Oh, please, my master," Baby Tooth pleaded, "don't send me down there. I have been here since I was thirty-two years old. After forty years, I have no family or relatives that I can return to. And I don't know how to make a living down there. Please, let me stay. I will study harder, and I will endure any hardship."

Superiorman Primordial Supreme said, "No, Baby Tooth. We must not upset the scheme of things Heaven and Earth. Someday, you may have a chance to return here. Go now with my blessings."

He then gave Baby Tooth eight lines of his prophecy to guide him in the Red Dust.

> *Ten difficult years in the wilderness,*
> *Be patient and endure whatever fate doles out.*
> *Atop a stone at a river bank fishing,*
> *Someone special comes advice seeking.*
> *Assist the founding of a new dynasty,*
> *At age ninety-three, heads the Prime ministry.*
> *Be responsible for the investiture of gods when made,*
> *At the age of ninety-eight.*

Baby Tooth had neither brother nor sister, neither uncle nor aunt. His parents had died many years ago. On leaving Mount Kunlun, he was like a bird who had lost its forest and there was no tree in sight.

He thought and thought, feeling lost and dejected. Then he recalled an old friend, Soong Spectacular, who used to live on a big ranch outside of the Capital City, Morning Song. Baby Tooth prayed hard that this friend was still around.

With only his lute, his sword and a few belongings, Baby Tooth traveled by the underground method, and in a jiffy he arrived in front of Soong Spectacular's ranch.

The ranch had not changed; surrounding the house were the luscious green willows and red flowering trees that as he remembered.

Baby Tooth sighed, "Will the faces of the people inside be the same?"

He knocked on the door. "Is Mr. Soong Spectacular home?"

"Who are you, sir?" a servant inquired at the door.

"Just say Jiang Baby Tooth has come to visit."

*   *   *   *

Soong Spectacular was a rich man. He owned a huge acreage of farmlands, gardens, restaurants and other business enterprises. His friendship with Baby Tooth dated back to their childhood. Baby Tooth was a poor orphan who tried to learn how to read and write by stealthily standing outside the windows of a classroom where children of the rich were having their lessons. Intelligent and diligent, Baby Tooth was soon discovered by Soong Spectacular's philanthropic father, who underwrote Baby Tooth's tuition so that he could study inside. Baby Tooth and Spectacular became fast friends.

Then one day Baby Tooth disappeared. No one knew where he had gone. Rumor had it that Baby Tooth was kidnapped by bandits and had been killed because he refused to join them. Others said that Baby Tooth was eaten by a tiger when he went to the high mountains.

*   *   *   *

Soong Spectacular greeted Baby Tooth with the same enthusiasm and warmth Baby Tooth so fondly remembered, "My goodness! I have thought of you often. Why such a long silence? I am so happy to see you again!"

Baby Tooth told Spectacular about his life on Mount Kunlun and why he came back to Capital City, Morning Song.

Spectacular asked, "How long were you there and what did you do?"

Baby Tooth said, "Ah, forty years. I really did not have much to do. I fetched water for the peach garden; I watered the pine trees and kept the fire of the elixir oven going."

Spectacular said, "These do not take special skills. They are the chores for the servants. Now that you are back here, forget your wishful thinking of becoming a superiorman. Why not let me help you get into some kind of business? We are old friends, you don't need to move, you will stay with us. Make yourself at home here."

"Yes, thank you." Baby Tooth was grateful.

Spectacular continued, "The most important thing in life is to have a family and children."

Baby Tooth said, "Oh, no. Please. I don't want to get married."

Next morning, Soong Spectacular rode his donkey to the Ma Ranch to see Mr. Ma Hong. The Ma family and the Soong family had been friends for generations. The Ma Ranch was large but not quite as grand as the Soong Ranch.

Ma Hong received Spectacular warmly, "What winds brought my favorite friend here?"

Spectacular said, "I have come especially to make a match for your daughter Li Li."

"My friend, who do you have in mind?"

Spectacular said, "My very old friend Jiang Baby Tooth, by-name Flying Bear. We have been friends since childhood."

Ma Hong said, "I appreciate your concern and respect your judgment. If you think it is a good match, I have no objection."

As an engagement gift, Spectacular presented four gold ingots to Ma Hong, who set up an engagement banquet to entertain Spectacular. They drank until quite late.

When Spectacular returned home that evening, he said to Baby Tooth, "Congratulations, my friend."

"Whatever for?"

"I have made a very good match for you today."

Baby Tooth was dismayed. "It is not a good day. The stars are in the wrong positions."

"Don't be so superstitious," Spectacular chided.

Baby Tooth became curious. "Whose daughter is the bride to be?"

"She is Ma Hong's daughter, very capable and not bad looking. Li Li is sixty-eight years old and a virgin, just right for you."

The wedding took place a few days later. Neighbors, friends and relatives of both the Ma and Soong families came and brought gifts to congratulate the newlyweds.

$$* \quad * \quad * \quad *$$

Homesick for Mount Kunlun, Baby Tooth was restless. He could not fully appreciate his new life. Instead of the orderly and tranquil daily routine, he was now stuck with a complaining wife. She seemed to have a talent for needling him about his lack of money-making skills and his inability to support her in the style she was accustomed to in her father's home. The fact that their life with the Soongs was quite comfortable did not seem enough for her. Although the Soongs who treated them as family, she longed for a place they could call their own.

After two months, Mrs. Baby Tooth could not contain herself any longer. She asked her husband, "Is Cousin Soong your Aunt's son?"

"No, my dear. Spectacular is my god-brother."

"Well. Even if he is your blood-brother, there comes a time when each should have his own home and business. We cannot depend on them forever, even if they don't seem to mind. I think we had better do something about making a living," Li Li suggested. Baby Tooth agreed.

"What can you do?" his wife asked.

"I really don't have any skill. But I do know how to weave bamboo sieves."

Li Li said, "Good. Everyone uses bamboo sieves. We don't even need any capital since there are bamboo groves in the garden. You can sell the bamboo sieves in the Capital City, Morning Song. A few pennies here and a few pennies there, not much to speak of, but it will be some kind of business of our own."

So Baby Tooth cut some bamboo, made the finest threads and weaved them into the nicest sieves. After he finished a batch, he took them to sell in the Capital City, Morning Song, some thirty-five miles away.

After a full day in the city, Baby Tooth did not make a single sale. He was hungry and tired when he returned home with all his sieves. His wife Li Li was so disappointed. She asked him what had happened but he cut her short by shouting at her, "You stupid woman! It was all your dumb idea to take this heavy load to the Capital! A round trip of seventy miles and not one sold!"

Li Li said, "Everyone uses bamboo sieves. It was you who did not know how to sell. Why blame me?"

The two quarreled through the night. Spectacular inquired with concern next day.

Baby Tooth told him about their wanting to be independent; and his business venture with bamboo sieves.

Spectacular said, "Why bother with such things? Let alone just the two of you, even if there were five hundred people, I have enough here to support them all in style."

Mrs. Baby Tooth said, "Elder brother. It is very generous of you. We are grateful. But we have to establish some means of self-support."

Spectacular said, "You are right. I have plenty of wheat. Why not let the servants grind some, and you can take the dry flour to the market to sell in the Capital. It will certainly fetch a better price than the bamboo sieves."

*   *   *   *

Baby Tooth took two basketfuls of flour to the Capital, hawking it all around but no one wanted any. As the sun was getting low and the shadows long, a man approached Baby Tooth wanting to buy one penny's worth.

"One penny's worth of flour? Well, it beats no sale at all," thought Baby Tooth to himself.

He put down his load and started to measure out flour. Being inexperienced, he neglected to tuck in the cords tied to the basket. As Baby

Tooth bent down, a startled horse came charging towards him from nowhere.

Someone shouted a warning. Baby Tooth was able to step aside to save his life but the hoofs of the horse caught the baskets by their cords, dragging them some sixty feet and spilling the flour all over. While trying to save his flour, a sudden gust of wind dusted Baby Tooth from head to toe with the white powder.

The would-be buyer left without even a backward glance. A dejected Baby Tooth went home with his empty baskets.

Mistaking the empty baskets for a successful day, Mrs. Baby Tooth greeted her husband with a big smile. "The capital people liked your flour." she exclaimed.

The frustrated Baby Tooth walked up to his wife, threw the baskets at her and screamed, "It's all your fault, you stupid woman!"

Bewildered, she said, "Why, you sold all the flour, how come I get blamed again?"

Baby Tooth told her about the rampaging horse and the whirlwind that ruined the day.

Still feeling hurt, Li Li retorted, "You are just a good for nothing rice tub!"

Baby Tooth snapped back, "How dare you call me names!" He picked her up and started to beat her.

Soong Spectacular and his wife came running to pull them apart.

Spectacular took Baby Tooth to his library where Baby Tooth related the day's event.

"When one has bad luck, nothing seems to work. I am grateful, my elder brother. You have been so generous in taking care of me and my wife. But what can I do to better ourselves?"

Spectacular said, "Yes, it is true, much of what we do depends a lot on luck. But bemoaning past happenings will not do you any good. As the saying goes, even the Yellow River has days when the water is clear. So why can't people have lucky days too? Let me think. I have thirty five restaurants in the Capital City, Morning Song. I will introduce you to the managers, and ask them to let you take charge on their day off. That would give you a steady job and a steady income. What do you think?"

*   *   *   *

A few days later, Spectacular led Baby Tooth to the restaurant at the South Gate, in the busiest district of the City Morning Song. Nearby was the drill ground for the troops of Lord of National Security, Prince Yellow Flying Tiger. After their daily drill, generals and soldiers would mill around and eat at nearby restaurants. It was the prime location.

To start Baby Tooth's new venture with a bang, Spectacular ordered special dishes, slaughtering more pigs, sheep, goats and fowls than usual. Baby Tooth sat in the manager's chair, eagerly waiting for his customers.

But on that day, a sudden unseasonable storm pounded the drill ground for many hours. Prince Yellow Flying Tiger canceled his daily drill session. After the storm, the weather turned unusually hot and muggy, and by late afternoon the food began to turn bad and the wine turned sour. Forlorn, Baby Tooth told his helpers to eat as much as they wanted before the food completely spoiled!

In the evening, Spectacular asked how business was for the day. Baby Tooth said, "My dear elder brother, I am so ashamed. Today was a total disaster. We did not sell a single dish!"

Laughingly, Spectacular comforted his depressed friend, "Don't lose heart. Everything depends on luck. Apparently today was not your lucky day. You must be patient. Let's try something else."

Spectacular took out fifty ounces of silver, told Baby Tooth to go to the country with a servant to buy horses, pigs, goats and sheep to sell in the City Morning Song.

"Living animals can't possibly turn sour," Spectacular assured Baby Tooth.

*   *   *   *

A few days later, all matters were ready and Baby Tooth led his animals to City Morning Song. He did not know that King Zhou, on a whim, had decreed that no beast nor fowl was to enter the City Morning Song that particular day! Baby Tooth was stopped at the city gate and charged with violating the king's decree! He fled for his life, but all his animals were confiscated.

Spectacular saw Baby Tooth come running home with his face the color of earth. "What happened?" he asked solicitously.

Baby Tooth heaved a long sigh, "My dear elder brother. You help me at every turn so generously. But what can I do with my bad luck? Today, I found out too late that the king had decreed no animals were to enter the City. I was lucky to escape with my life. But all the pigs, sheep, horses, and goats were confiscated! I am so sorry."

The ever patient and generous Spectacular smiled and said, "The loss of a few ounces of silver is nothing to worry about. Come with me to the garden. Let us drink and forget about the whole thing."

CHAPTER 16

▼

JADE PIPA, THE
FAT-BELLY GUITAR
SPECTER

This was one of Spectacular's private gardens which Baby Tooth had never seen before. It was enclosed by a ten-foot high wall and covered by blooming vines. It was truly a wonderland.

Spectacular and Baby Tooth strolled along the two lines of tall golden willow trees, passing the pink, white and red begonia beds where a swing named CARE-FREE was swaying gently in the breeze. Here and there, small groups of flowering trees set forth their blooms in a colorful tableau: the fiery red pomegranates, the purple myrtles, the pink and white camellias, the yellow primrose jasmines, and the multicolored rhododendrons.

They walked through the flaming red hibiscus hedge, and went into the gazebo named POSY-APPRECIATION which housed Spectacular's extensive exotic orchid collection. From the back gate of the gazebo, they sauntered through the rose garden toward the TOUCH-THE-CLOUD pine grove. Deep in the pineland, lotus flowers paraded their finery in a pond where myriads of fish darted around as if in celebration of a fine spring day. Encircling the pond and covering the entire terrace was a wisteria arbor hosting thousands of dancing butterflies.

A clearing suddenly appeared at the edge of the pine grove. There, a huge patch of thousands of peonies in bloom. And there, quite appropriately, stood the PEONY PAVILION.

Spectacular took Baby Tooth into the pavilion to rest as servants served wine and snacks.

Looking around, Baby Tooth suddenly became very excited. He pointed his finger toward the other side of the peony bed and exclaimed, "Look over there, my elder brother! I see a perfect setting for a five room villa!"

Spectacular was startled by Baby Tooth's unexpected animation. "A five room villa?"

"Yes, indeed!" Baby Tooth replied, so excited as if in a trance. "I have failed so far in finding, even in a very small way, something to repay your generosity and kindness. Here is my chance. According to my geomancy reading, that spot holds thirty-six jade belts, and as many gold belts as the number of sesame seeds in a ten gallon measure! In a lay person's terms, that means a most suitable location for a five room villa. These jade and gold belts will insure the rightful and deserving owner of unending prosperity and untold happiness."

"Do you know geomancy?"

"A little."

Spectacular said, "To tell you the truth. I had a villa built on that very spot several times before. But each time, it was destroyed by fire before it was even completed. I had given up the thought of ever building on that spot."

Baby Tooth said confidently, "Don't worry. Let me find a good date to start a new villa. When the workers are ready to raise the main beam, I will be in the garden watching for any problems."

*   *   *   *

Ground was broken, and the building started as planned. On the day when the roof beam was to be raised, Baby Tooth sent Spectacular away. It was a beautiful sunny day. Baby Tooth seated himself on the front steps of the Peony Pavilion, expecting something to happen.

A sudden tornado materialized, bringing flying sand and rolling stones. In the whirlwind, a flame of fire illuminated five beasts with fearsome colored faces floating in midair.

Baby Tooth stood up, let loose his hair and pointed his sword at the beasts. "How dare you!" he shouted. "Get down here this instant!"

With a thunderclap, the tornado stopped as suddenly as it had started. Kneeling in front of Baby Tooth were five fearsome beasts, their faces colored in black, white, red, purple, and yellow-green. They wailed and begged for their lives.

The Red-Colored-Face devil said, "My lord. We did not know you were here. We have been living and playing in this garden for many years and that spot is our favorite game field. We did not want any building there. We meant no harm to anyone. Please spare us and let us go. Have mercy."

Baby Tooth said, "What an evil bunch you are. You have destroyed this building many times before, and are trying again. You like to play here but you have no right to destroy the rightful owner's property. There is no mercy for the likes of you!"

So saying, Baby Tooth raised his sword, ready to chop them up. But the pitiful wailing and begging softened Baby Tooth's heart. He finally said, "I will give you a chance to redeem yourselves. Listen to me carefully. Go directly to The Western Foothills of Mount Singing Phoenix, and wait there for my order. Don't you ever harm this place again!"

Mrs. Baby Tooth and Mrs. Spectacular were also in the garden when the thunderstorm struck and drove them to the Peony Pavilion.

They saw Baby Tooth standing at the front steps with his hair loose, holding his sword and mumbling to himself.

Embarrassed, Mrs. Baby Tooth remarked sarcastically, "See what I mean? A man who stands in front of the pavilion with his hair down, holding a sword and mumbling to himself! How could such man be any good at making a living?"

She walked up to Baby Tooth and shouted, "What are you doing here?"

Baby Tooth looked up and saw his wife and Mrs. Spectacular. He bowed to them and said quietly, "I just vanquished some fearsome beasts."

Mrs. Baby Tooth hissed, "Daydreaming again! What kind of fearsome beasts?"

Baby Tooth said calmly, "Trying to explain it to you would be a waste of time. You would never understand. I don't know much about anything, but I do know geomancy."

Mrs. Spectacular asked, "Younger brother. Do you know fortune telling?"

"Yes, that is my forte. How I wish I had a studio to practice it."

Meanwhile Spectacular came back and asked, "Younger brother, did you hear the thunderclap? Did you see anything?"

Baby Tooth recounted his encounter with the five beasts. Mrs. Spectacular put in, "Younger brother Baby Tooth is very versed in casting horoscopes and telling fortunes. Why don't we find a house and let him use it as a studio?"

*   *   *   *

Soon a house at the South Gate of the Capital City, Morning Song, was ready for Baby Tooth. The South Gate was the busiest district in the city, an ideal location for such business as fortune telling.

For decoration, many couplets were posted. On the door, was:

Within my sleeves, a domain as complete as the cosmos and the universe.
Within my teapot, a realm as everlasting as the sun and moon.

On one wall, was:

Comprehending the mystics
Preaching no folly.

On another wall:

An iron mouth speaks the good and the bad.
A pair of magic eyes sees the ups and the downs.

Opening day came and went. For months, day after day, Baby Tooth faithfully sat in his newly decorated studio, waiting. But not a single customer showed up.

Yes, he who gave oracles to all the world was not wise enough to look into his own fortune.

Then one day, miracle of miracles, someone stopped!

A firewood cutter named Liu Quin passed by and saw the couplet on the door. He put down his firewood, walked into the studio where Baby Tooth was bending over his desk, taking a nap. Liu banged loudly on the desk. Baby Tooth woke up with a start. He found standing before him a muscular man, looking at him with unfriendly eyes.

"Well, my friend. What will it be today?" Baby Tooth asked.

"What is your name?" Liu said.

"My name is Jiang Baby Tooth, by-named Flying Bear."

"Let me ask you. What do you mean by the couplet on your door?"

Baby Tooth replied, "*Within my sleeve, a domain as complete as the cosmos and the universe* means I know the past and the future, everything in the cosmos and the universe.

"*Within my teapot, a realm as everlasting as the sun and the moon* means that I possess the art of living forever."

Liu said, "Bragging, eh? If you can tell the past and the future, then your fortune telling skill must be great. Tell me my fortune for this day. If accurate, I will give you twenty coppers. If not, I will give you my fist so that you will never make a fool of anyone again!"

Poor Baby Tooth. His first customer turned out to be such a bully.

Liu took out a joss stick from the container and handed it to Baby Tooth. Baby Tooth looked at it and said, "Well, well. Your fortune for this day is not bad. But it can only be accurate under one condition: You must follow my instructions exactly."

"All right. I promise I will do as you instruct. What is my fortune?"

Baby Tooth wrote out the prediction in four lines and handed it to Liu. It said,

> Toward the southeast go thee
> An old man under the willow tree you'll see
> Four pieces of cake and two bowls of wine
> Plus one hundred and twenty coppers for your find.

Liu looked at the paper and remarked, "Impossible! I already know this is going to be wrong. I have cut and sold firewood for twenty years, and no one has ever given me cake and wine!"

Baby Tooth said with a grin, "Do as I say. I guarantee everything will come true."

Liu picked up his firewood and walked toward the southeast as Baby Tooth directed. Soon he saw under the willow tree an old man who was calling to him, asking the price of his firewood.

So far so good, thought Liu. But I must not let Baby Tooth have his satisfaction. So instead of one hundred and twenty coppers that he knew his firewood was worth, Liu asked for one hundred.

The old man said, "The firewood seems to be very good and dry. All right, one hundred coppers it shall be. Please deliver it to my wood-shed."

Liu carried the firewood to the woodshed; the old man disappeared into the house.

Liu had always been a fastidious person. While waiting in the messy woodshed for his pay, he picked up a broom and swept the floor clean.

The old man returned and noticed the clean floor. "Eh, my servant is diligent today." he remarked.

Liu said, "No, sir. It was I who swept the floor."

The old man said, "My friend, today is my son's birthday. And I meet a nice person such as you. That is a good omen." So saying, the old man disappeared once more before paying Liu.

Soon a young servant brought a dish with four pieces of cake, a jug of wine and a large wine bowl. He handed them all to Liu, saying, "With my master's compliments."

Liu's astonishment knew no end. For the first time in his life, a customer gave him cakes to eat and wine to drink! But he must not let Baby Tooth get full mark for his prediction.

Liu deliberately poured the wine into the bowl as full as he could without spilling, hoping to leave the next bowl half full. But to his amazement, the second bowl was as full as the first.

After Liu finished his wine and cake, the old man reappeared, handing Liu one hundred and twenty coppers, and saying that because today was his son's birthday, the twenty extra coppers were for Liu to have a drink on the house.

Liu thanked the old man, picked up his things and raced straight to Baby Tooth.

*   *   *   *

That morning, when Liu was consulting Baby Tooth, a crowd had gathered to hear the prediction. After Liu left, someone kindly advised Baby Tooth to leave because Liu was a notorious bully and might carry out his threat.

Baby Tooth assured them not to worry.

Soon Liu came breathlessly to the studio, screaming at the top of his lungs, "Mr. Jiang is the best fortune teller who ever lived! In fact, I think he is a demigod from heaven. Now that we have such a genius among us, no one needs to suffer any more anxiety."

Baby Tooth said, "In that case, my friend, where is my money?"

Liu said, "Twenty coppers is too little for your prediction. I mean to pay you more."

Baby Tooth persisted. This, after all, was the very first income he had ever earned. Still, Liu tarried and stood in front of Baby Tooth's studio, waiting for something.

By and by, there came a man in a neat cotton garment with a leather belt, walking in a great hurry toward South Gate. Liu stepped out and grabbed the man, pulling him toward the studio. The man fought to get away, screaming, "Let go of me! I am busy and have no time to play games. I say let go, you idiot!"

Liu said calmly, "I just want you to let Mr. Jiang tell your fortune."

The man tried hard to pull loose, saying, "I have urgent official business. I don't have time!"

Liu would not let go. He said to the man solicitously, "I am doing you a favor. This Mr. Jiang really is marvelous."

The man, getting more impatient by the second, said, "Let go of me! If I don't want my fortune read, that is my business!"

"Sorry about that, my friend." Liu's tone changed into anger. "Are you or are you not going to have Mr. Jiang read your fortune?"

"Emphatically no!" the man replied hotly.

"Then I will commit suicide by jumping into the river and will take you with me."

So saying, Liu pulled the poor man with all his might toward the river.

People watching the drama stepped in and said to the man, "Oh, friend. Just take a minute to have your fortune told. Mr. Liu here is sincere in his recommendation. It would not hurt you to be a good sport."

Giving up his struggle, the man walked into Baby Tooth's studio, pulled out one joss stick and handed it to Baby Tooth.

Baby Tooth asked, "What do you want to know?"

"I am a tax collector on my way to collect delinquent taxes. I hate my job!"

"In that case, congratulations!" Baby Tooth wrote out four lines on a piece of paper and handed it over to the tax collector. He wrote:

> *The timing is becoming*
> *The money is waiting*
> *One thousand and three ounces of silver*
> *Ready to be handed over*

The tax collector asked, "How much do I owe you for this prediction?"

Liu cut in with authority, "This is a very special prediction. Pay Mr. Jiang one half ounce of silver please!"

"You are not Mr. Jiang. What business is it of yours?" The tax collector was still smarting.

Liu, unruffled by the man's scorn, said, "I am doing you a favor! The silver will be refunded if Mr. Jiang's prediction does not come true."

The tax collector hurriedly weighed out the silver and took his leave. People milled around to wait for the outcome of the new prediction.

An hour passed. The tax collector came back breathlessly, and went directly to Baby Tooth's studio.

"Mr. Jiang. I am so happy. Your prediction is completely correct. The half ounce of silver is the biggest bargain I have ever had in my life. I collected one thousand and three ounces of silver as you have predicted; without any trouble."

Baby Tooth's fame spread near and far. Horoscopes were cast, joss sticks read, and geomancy studied. At a half ounce of silver per transaction, Baby Tooth's income was quite substantial. His wife was happy that her husband was finally making money. Spectacular was also happy that Baby Tooth had found his calling.

*   *   *   *

Remember the three specters from the tomb of the Yellow Emperor? The Thousand-Year-Old vixen, Daji, the Nine-Headed Pheasant, Splendor, and the Fat-Belly Guitar, Jade Pipa? And do you remember they had a special order from the Snail Goddess Nu Wa Niang Niang to undermine King Zhou's reign?

It was common knowledge that specters were female. And it was also common knowledge that for a specter to stay alive, she must absorb the essence of the human male or eat human flesh and blood. That was why specters were forever so eager to seduce the human male at every chance.

Yes, the Thousand-Year-Old vixen specter had killed Su Daji, and using Daji's body, had sneaked into King Zhou's palace. For many years now, Vixen specter Daji had been sapping King Zhou's essence to maintain her evil existence. She had no need to consume human blood and flesh. But her cravings remained strong.

When her specter friends, the Fat-Belly Guitar, Jade Pipa, and Nine-Headed Pheasant, Splendor, came to visit, vixen specter Daji had often treated them to a feast on the flesh and blood of unsuspecting palace maidens. The remains of their victims were buried at the bottom of the Lotus Lake in the Imperial garden; no mortal was the wiser.

One day, on her return from a visit with Daji, Fat-Belly Guitar, Jade Pipa, passed by South Gate, and saw a crowd in front of Baby Tooth's studio. Thinking to have some fun by making Baby Tooth a fool, or perhaps seducing him, she turned herself into a beautiful young widow in full mourning. As she walked sedately toward the studio, the crowd opened a path for her.

The moment Baby Tooth saw her, he knew immediately that she was an unholy specter!

Baby Tooth said to his other customers, "My friends. Please bear with me. Let me take care of this lady first."

After she sat down, Baby Tooth asked, "Please may I see your right hand?"

"Do you read palms too?" Jade Pipa asked.

"Yes," said Baby Tooth. Picking up Jade Pipa's hand, he immediately applied pressure to capture her inner spirit, to keep her from changing her present form.

Jade Pipa realized what Baby Tooth was doing. "What is the matter?" she shrieked. "Why are you holding my hand and not saying a word? I am a woman from a good family. Don't you dare have any evil ideas!"

On hearing what the woman said, the crowd joined in and chanted: "Baby Tooth. Let go of her! You are too old to play this kind of game. Shame on you!"

Calmly Baby Tooth said, "Please listen to me. I am not trying any funny business. This is not an ordinary woman. She is a specter!"

"Nonsense!" said a man in the crowd. "It is as clear as day she is an ordinary woman, only more beautiful. Let go of her, you old goat!" they demanded.

Baby Tooth thought to himself, "If I let go of her, she will disappear into the crowd and I will never have a chance to establish my innocence. Better hold tight and do a good deed for the populace as well."

Baby Tooth then picked up his stone ink well and smashed it against Jade Pipa's head, making a big hole. She was beyond a doubt quite dead. But strangely there was no blood. Baby Tooth held onto the hand ever tighter. He was more than certain now that this was not any ordinary young female but a truly evil specter.

Pandemonium followed the momentary shocked silence. The crowd screamed, "The fortune teller killed a woman!"

"Get the constable!"

"Don't let him get away!"

At this very moment, Prince Bi Gan happened to pass by and asked his servants what was the trouble. Someone in the crowd saw Bi Gan, and shouted, "Here comes the Vice Prime Minister. Let us take Baby Tooth to him!"

Bi Gan reined in his horse. A public-minded person came out and knelt before the Vice Prime minister, saying, "My lord. Here we have a fortune-teller named Jiang Baby Tooth. A while ago, a young lady came to have her horoscope cast. Apparently overcome by her beauty, Baby Tooth tried to seduce her. The virtuous lady refused. Jiang killed her with his stone ink well."

Several people also came forward to tell the same story.

Bi Gan was furious. He ordered his aides to bring Baby Tooth forward.

Still holding on to Jade Pipa, Baby Tooth came to kneel before Bi Gan.

Bi Gan said, "I see you have a head of white hair already. Don't you know the laws of the land? How dare you seduce a virtuous lady in front of all these people and kill her when she refuses you? This is a capital crime. What do you have to say for yourself?"

Baby Tooth said calmly, "My lord. Please hear my side of the story. I learned to read and write when I was very young. I do know the laws of the land. But this is not an ordinary person. She is a specter who, with other unholy specters, bring much calamity to the populace. Being a loyal subject, I feel it my duty to help get rid of these unholy elements when I see them. Please, my lord. Do investigate the matter and you will know I am telling the truth."

All in the crowd knelt and the public-minded man said, "My lord. Please don't listen to this charlatan. He knows how to speak with flowery language, but we have seen this murder with our own eyes. If you let him get away with it, that poor woman's soul will never rest in peace."

Bi Gan asked Baby Tooth, "The woman is already dead. Why are you still holding her hand?"

Baby Tooth said, "My lord. The woman seems dead, but the specter is not. If I let go, the specter could easily disappear. What then can I do to prove my innocence?"

Bi Gan told the crowd, "This is not the place to try such a serious case. Let me talk to the king and see what can be done."

Surrounding Baby Tooth lest he run away, the crowd followed Prince Bi Gan to the Noon Gate.

Bi Gan went directly to the Star-Picking Belvedere, asking to see the king.

King Zhou asked, "I did not summon you. Why are you here?"

Bi Gan said, "Today, a fortune teller killed one of his customers with his ink well. He claimed the customer was a specter. A crowd saw what happened and insisted the woman was killed because she refused his advances. Both stories have merit and I could not decide which is true. So I brought them here for further questioning."

Behind the screen, Daji heard Bi Gan. She swore under her breath at the turn of events:

"Oh, pity my poor little sister Jade Pipa! Why didn't you go home directly? Why were you so foolish? I will seek revenge for you. I promise!"

Daji walked out to speak to the King, "I heard Vice Prime Minister's report. Please give the order to bring in the fortune teller and his victim. One look and I will be able to tell which story is true and which is false."

Still tightly holding onto Jade Pipa and pulling her with him, Baby Tooth knelt at the foot of the Star-Picking Belvedere.

The king looked down from the terrace, asking, "Who is there?"

Baby Tooth respectfully replied, "I am Jiang Baby Tooth, a native of East Sea District. I have studied under famous teachers in Mount Kunlun for many years and learned the art of fortune telling and geomancy. I set up shop at the South Gate. Unfortunately I met this woman today and immediately saw she was not an ordinary person. She was a specter who had harmed untold numbers of innocent victims. I felt duty bound to my king and my fellow countrymen to get rid of this unholy specter."

King Zhou said, "I can see this was a very ordinary woman. What made you think she was a specter? What was her original form?"

Baby Tooth said, "If Your Majesty wishes to find out the original form of this specter, we will have to burn her."

The king ordered it be done.

To prevent her from changing form, before loosening his hold, Baby Tooth put a juju on her head, then one on her chest, one on her back and one on each of her four limbs for good measure. Firewood was then piled on and around her.

What a fierce blaze! But even after two hours, the body did not show any hint of ever being in a fire! Not even one hair was singed.

King Zhou asked Bi Gan, "What is the matter with the fire?"

Bi Gan said, "As I see it, Baby Tooth may have told the truth. That means he is a remarkable man. But what kind of specter this is, I think only Baby Tooth can find out."

▼

CHAPTER 17

THE SNAKE PIT, THE WINE POOL, AND THE MEAT FOREST

With total concentration of his inner strength and spirit, Baby Tooth brought forth from his eyes, nose, and mouth, a triple divine fire. Yes, of all the energy in Heaven and Earth, nothing was more powerful. No one, nothing under Heaven, had ever survived a Triple Divine Fire!

The fat-belly guitar, Jade Pipa struggled with all her might, but could not escape the Triple Divine Fire. She screamed in terror, "Baby Tooth! Have I ever done anything to you? Why are you using your cruel fire on me!"

King Zhou was so terrified when he heard a voice from the fire, he almost fell from the railing of the Star-Picking Belvedere.

Baby Tooth said, "Your Majesty, please go quickly inside. Thunder and lightning are coming."

As Baby Tooth opened his hands, jagged lightning and a deafening thunderclap erupted from his fingers. Then just as abruptly, the storm evaporated into the burning fire. What was there in the ash? A beautiful jade fat-belly guitar!

Hatred and regret filled Daji's black heart, and revenge was her vow. However, she said lightly to the king, "Why, Baby Tooth seems to be quite a remarkable man. Why not keep him in the Court and make good use of his talents?"

"Oh, by the way," Daji continued, as if it was only an afterthought, "May I keep that jade fat-belly guitar? I can have it strung and play for Your Majesty."

And so Baby Tooth became a Lower Counselor. Soong Spectacular set out a banquet to celebrate the event.

Baby Tooth did not have a mansion of his own in the Capital City, Morning Song. He stayed with the Vice Prime Minister Prince Bi Gan at Bi Gan's invitation.

*   *   *   *

It became Daji's favorite passion to restore Jade Pipa's life. Day and night, from the height of the Star-Picking Belvedere, Daji diligently gathered the energy of the sun, the essence of the moon, and the anima of the earth, distilling them for her dear dead friend the fat-belly guitar specter, Jade Pipa. Five years of perseverance of Daji's devotion finally paid off. The fat-belly guitar, Jade Pipa, became once more a specter. When time came, together with vixen specter Daji and the Nine-head-pheasant specter Splendor, she would undermine King Zhou's reign.

One day, Daji and the king had a special celebration. To the king it was a special party with Daji playing new songs on the jade fat-belly guitar. But to Daji, it was to celebrate the rebirth of Jade Pipa. Daji gave one of her best performances. The king and, of course, all the palace attendants, applauded with enthusiasm. But, alas! Among the crowd were seventy-two maidens who not only did not applaud, but actually had tears in their eyes!

Enraged, Daji demanded an investigation.

"Yes," the investigator reported, "they are the former Queen Jiang's servants. They claim they are sad because many of their companions disappeared and were never heard from again!"

Poor wenches. Without Queen Jiang to protect them, they had been disappearing at an alarming rate. From more than one thousand in Queen Jiang's day, their numbers had plummeted to a measly seventy-two. They knew sooner or later their doomsday would come like the plague. None would escape this cruel fate.

Only Daji knew where those maidens had gone. They were the flesh and blood on which Daji and her specter cronies feasted.

Daji hissed, "Your mistress was put to death for her treason. How dare you show any resentment? To keep the likes of you in the palace is dangerous and disgusting!"

King Zhou agreed, as always. He ordered the maidens be beaten to death with the gold mallet.

Daji said, "That would be too easy for them. Put them in the Cold Palace while I think of a new torture."

Daji designed a snake pit to be dug under the Star-Picking Belvedere. Twenty-five feet in diameter, the pit was to be filled with venomous snakes and poisonous spiders.

"Your Majesty can levy from each household in the Capital, four snakes and four spiders to fill the Snake Pit," Daji suggested.

The king's edict was out. The pit was dug. The populace was running like crazy here and there to fill their quota lest they be killed by the king's men. But there were simply not enough snakes and spiders in the Capital City, Morning Song. Families had to trudge hundreds of miles to the countryside, and many had to skimp on food to pay for them.

*   *   *   *

Sitting in the Counselor's Chamber one day, Grand Counselor Jiao Ge saw people, two or three together, each person carrying a basket, streaming toward the Nine Hall Court. He asked his aides what was going on and was told that the his subjects were bring in their quota of snakes and spiders for the king.

"What for?" Jiao asked.

"We don't know, sir."

Jiao walked out to inquire, but no one knew. He returned to the counselor's Chamber. He asked the seven senior Counselors.

Lord of National Security, Prince Yellow Flying Tiger said, "This morning, after the training session with my men, I saw people in the South Gate district fighting to buy snakes and spiders. I also saw the king's edict posted on the wall. The people are suffocating under the present taxes already, and now this!"

None of the other senior counselors knew anything either. Yellow Flying Tiger ordered an aide to gather all the information he could find.

Ten days passed. All quotas were filled and the Snake Pit was ready.

Daji said to the king, "Round up the seventy-two servants from the Cold Palace, strip off their clothing, shave off their hair, bind them together and throw them into the Snake Pit!"

When the maidens saw the horrible slithering snakes with their tongues flicking in and out, and the enormous hairy spiders crawling everywhere, they let out long, pitiful screams, begging for mercy.

Grand Counselor Jiao Ge heard them from the Counselor's Chamber. He walked out to investigate. At this same moment Yellow Flying Tiger's aide rushed in breathlessly, stuttering, "My lords. All these snakes and spiders are for the Snake Pit under the Star-Picking Belvedere. And all of the former Queen Jiang's servants are being dumped into the pit to feed these vermin!"

Jiao Ge was so shocked he immediately went to see the king. He passed the Virtuous Dragon Court and through the Demarcation Building to reach the Star-Picking Belvedere. He saw the seventy-two maidens being readied for the Snake Pit. Their pathetic begging for mercy fell on deaf ears.

Jiao shouted, "How can such a thing be allowed? May I speak to the king?"

The bewitched King Zhou was waiting excitedly for the torture to begin. When he saw Jiao, he asked, "Why are you here? I did not summon you."

Jiao said, "Sire! What crime have these maidens committed to deserve such a fate? These are disastrous and calamitous times all over our kingdom. But Your Majesty does not seem to see or care! On top of the heavier than ever taxes, now Your Majesty creates this Snake Pit for which many families had to skip meals for many days to pay for. We all know that when people are too poor to eat, they become thieves, then robbers, then cutthroats. May I remind Your Majesty that the rebellions of the Grand Dukes of the East and the South, and all the dukes of these two regions, are not yet settled. And Grand Old Master Wen Zhong is still not able to crush the North Sea rebellion. This torture device here, what is it called? From what dynasty did it come from?"

The king said, "When servants show disloyalty, they deserve cruel torture. This is obviously a snake pit, invented by your Queen Su!"

Jiao Ge pleaded, "The four limbs of a person are of flesh and blood. Though they are not as important as the five viscera, they are parts of a person's body. The king is the head of his people, and his people his limbs! How can you possibly let the snakes and spiders chew up your limbs? Besides, these are only lowly servants, what can they do to harm anyone? Pity them. Let them go!"

The king said, "Grand Counselor Jiao, you do give a good speech. But these seventy-two wenches are still carrying Queen Jiang's torch!

How can I punish them with an ordinary device? Don't under-estimate the power of a woman's spite!"

Jiao howled with agony, "How can you ignore my plea? Don't you remember the Grand Duke of the East with an unparalleled record of service to your Majesty? You tortured him to death because you believed in flowery words and false accusations! Remember the Grand Duke of the South who contributed more than anyone to the national treasury, and now you killed him because he was so loyal to his king? If you don't care about yourself, don't you care about the National Ancestral Shrine of the kingdom? I am not asking any favor for myself. It is the kingdom I am thinking of. How long can you expect this cruelty to go on and still keep your throne intact?"

The king exploded, "Throw him into the Snake Pit!"

As the palace guards rushed over, Jiao shouted, "Dare you touch me!" He then pointed his finger at the king, "You no good bird-brain! Your stinking name will be linked with cruelty and stupidity for tens of thousands of years! And you will meet your end in the worst manner ever!" Jiao then leaped over the railing and plunged to his death from the Star-Picking Belvedere. Another martyr for love of country and respect for humanity!

Humiliated by Grand Counselor Jiao, King Zhou was angrier than ever. He ordered the seventy-two condemned maidens thrown in the Snake Pit at once. Their harrowing screams could be heard hundreds of miles away as the spiders and snakes made short order of them.

The king said to Daji, "I am glad we have the Snake Pit. How else can we control the malcontents!"

*   *   *   *

Daji spread before the king a new drawing: A circular mini-park around the Star-Picking Belvedere, with the Snake Pit as the center. On the left side was a pool filled with wine, and on the right a small hill covered with trees from which hung an assortment of freshly roasted pigs, goats, geese, chickens and ducks.

"This," Daji proudly proclaimed, "is called The Wine Pool and Meat Forest."

"Oh, Your Majesty," Daji continued. "You must have this Wine Pool and Meat Forest to show that you are above all the nobles in the kingdom!"

*   *   *   *

Pity the populace, already struggling under heavy taxes and conscript labor, and now having to support yet another insane project.

To celebrate the completion of the Wine Pool and Meat Forest, King Zhou and Daji had another banquet.

But, alas! Song and dance, feasting and carousing had become old hat to Daji. She was bored but she had a new game to demonstrate the wonders of her new Wine Pool and Meat Forest. Daji explained to the king, "fifty eunuchs and fifty palace maidens are selected. Take off all their clothing, tie a eunuch to a maiden to make fifty pairs and let them frolic in the Wine Pool and the Meat Forest. They are to play games like foot races or swimming. They are to drink the wine from the pool and eat the meat from the trees. They must get drunk and have fun. At sunset when we are tired of watching them, each day a few pairs will be beaten to a pulp and stored in the new pulp trough. Then new ones will take their place."

But of course no one knew or dared to find out what had happened to the pulp in the pulp trough. It simply disappeared over night. And of course everyday new pulp was ready to fill the empty trough.

Why a meat trough? Because the Thousand-Year-Old vixen specter Daji needed constant feeding on human flesh and blood to maintain her vitality. For years, she had the king's essence to enrich her existence. However, she still needed at least one human a day to satisfy her and to maintain her life. At night, she would change back to her original form, and leave her palace to eat just one maiden from other palaces, in particular, those of the former Queen Jiang. As the king got older and less able to supply her his essence day and night, Daji's craving for human flesh and blood increased. Right now she wanted a change of taste, drunken human flesh pulp!

An atmosphere of doom enveloped the servant's quarters in the palaces. No one knew when he or she would be the chosen one for the Wine Pool and the Meat Forest. On top of that, they were forever aware of the Snake Pit.

One day, it suddenly dawned on Daji that fat-belly guitar Jade Pipa's humiliation and burning had not yet been avenged. She must think of some pretense to torture and kill Baby Tooth.

She showed King Zhou an architectural drawing, her latest scheme. It was a design for a Deer Gallery. The structure was to be fully forty-nine feet high, with floors of marble, columns of jade, railings of south sea corals, and roof and ceiling of precious jewels.

She very easily convinced the king that the Son of Heaven must have this Deer Gallery.

"Why," she said disparagingly, "The Star-Picking Belvedere is a mere twenty feet high! This Deer Gallery is much taller, so tall that when the king dines there, heavenly maidens would descend to keep him company. And even the humble Daji herself would benefit from these encounters. They would enjoy long lives and heavenly repast forever and ever."

The king was very impressed, "Such a gigantic endeavor! Who can handle it?"

Daji said, "No one other than Lower Counselor Jiang Baby Tooth. He is versed in the craft of construction and the art of geomancy. Only he is qualified to handle this project."

Baby Tooth, on receiving the king's summons, secretly read a joss stick to see what was in store for him. He then went to see his host, Vice Prime Minister, Prince Bi Gan.

"My dear Prime Minister," Baby Tooth said. "You have been so kind to put me under your wing. I have learned a lot from you. Today, I am summoned to see the king. I have put a letter under the ink well for you. It is my token of appreciation. Please open it only when there is trouble. I don't know when I will see you again!" Tears welled in his eyes.

Bi Gan said, "Why so depressed? You are new in the Court and could not have made many mistakes."

Baby Tooth said, "I looked at my joss stick and foresaw, with trepidation, the events ahead. Do take care of yourself, Sir!"

"Perhaps I can talk to the king on your behalf?"

"No, please. Fate has set its pattern and no one can change it. I appreciate very much your kind offer but it would only make matters worse."

Baby Tooth got on his horse and went directly to the Star-Picking Belvedere where the king and Daji spent most of their time.

King Zhou said to Baby Tooth, "Here is an architectural drawing for a Deer Gallery. I want you to be in charge of the construction. When the job is well done, you will be richly rewarded."

Baby Tooth looked at the drawing and the specifications, fully realizing that his days in King Zhou's Court had come to an end. How to escape and save his life was all Baby Tooth could think about.

CHAPTER 18

▼

TWO HELPING HANDS

Baby Tooth studied the drawing, contemplating how he could prolong his days on earth. He said to King Zhou, "Sire, this is a remarkable design. It is forty-nine feet high and the construction is most intricate. When it is done according to the detailed specifications, it will be the most outstanding building in the world, unrivaled in history. However, we do need many years to gather the materials and meticulously follow the specifications. In my humble estimation, this project would take at least thirty-five years to do it justice."

The king said to Daji, "My dear royal wife. Baby Tooth estimates that it would take at least thirty-five years to build this Deer Gallery. Time is flying, by then we will be too old to enjoy it. What good will it be to build such a thing?"

Daji said, "How could it take thirty-five years? He is a liar! He should get the Bronze Toaster treatment!"

Baby Tooth said, calmly, "Sire, please listen to me. I am not lying nor am I talking nonsense. It will take a new tax and more conscript labor to build this Deer Gallery. In dire times like these when the national treasury is empty, the people are going hungry, and the wars with the regional dukes are still touch and go, it is not an auspicious time to build such a structure. If Your Majesty will delay this for a few years, I am sure it will be much better."

King Zhou reproached him angrily and ordered Baby Tooth be put to death at once.

As the palace guards started toward him, he turned and ran down the steps.

"What a coward!" snickered the king. "Where does he think he can go? After him!"

Baby Tooth ran with all his might, the palace guards hot on his heels. He passed the Nine Hall Court, the Virtuous Dragon Court and reached the Nine Dragon Bridge. He jumped off and disappeared without a ripple.

The guards peered into the water and saw a big hole closing with not even a wavelet. They kept looking, thinking Baby Tooth would surface but he never did. Of course he had escaped by traveling underground, and no one was the wiser.

While studying on Mount Kunlun, Baby Tooth had learned, among other things, how to travel underground undetected. However, he was told by his master that he should never use this trick except in life threatening situations. Being a law-abiding person, Baby Tooth had never once abused his master's trust. Yes, he did use that trick to come to the Soong Ranch when he was sent down from the mountain, but he had special permission for that.

At that moment, Grand Counselor Yang Ren was on his way to the Grand Counselor's Chamber. He saw the commotion and asked the guards what was going on.

"Lower Counselor Jiang Baby Tooth has committed suicide by jumping into the river," they told him.

"Why?" Yang Ren asked.

"We don't know, sir."

Ever since the king stopped coming to the early Morning Assembly, the task of reading the petitions from both the populace and the officials was assigned to the grand counselors. Today it was Yang Ren's turn.

The king asked Daji, "Now that Baby Tooth is gone, who should be in charge of the Deer Gallery construction project?"

Daji said, "I think the only capable one is the Grand Duke of the North, Tiger Duke."

A messenger was sent to summon Tiger Duke to the Capital City, Morning Song, without delay. However, before leaving, the messenger went to see Grand Counselor Yang Ren.

Yang Ren asked, "Why did Baby Tooth commit suicide?"

The messenger said, "The king wanted Baby Tooth to take charge of the construction of a Deer Gallery. Baby Tooth estimated it would take thirty-five years to build. Unhappy with the estimate, the king ordered Baby Tooth killed at once. Baby Tooth ran away and jumped into the river from the Nine Dragon Bridge."

"What is Deer Gallery?" Yang Ren asked.

"That is Queen Su's newest project. The structure was to be fully forty-nine feet high, with floors of marble, columns of jade, railings of south sea corals, and roof and ceiling of precious jewels. Now the king wants Tiger Duke to be in charge of this project. I have heard so much about the empty national treasury and the sufferings of the people. I hate to deliver the king's edict. That is why I stopped by to see you first, hoping you would talk to the king."

Yang Ren said, "All right. Delay delivery. I will see what I can do."

Yang Ren went directly to the Star-Picking Belvedere.

"Why are you here? I did not summon you," the king said.

Yang Ren said, "With our kingdom in so much trouble, I am shocked to hear Your Majesty is planning a gigantic new project. Your Majesty must be aware that we are in the midst of three great perils.

"First, Jiang Wen Huan is rebelling to avenge the deaths of his sister Queen Jiang and his father, the Grand Duke of the East.

"Second, E Chun is rebelling to avenge the death of his father, the Grand Duke of the South. On both of these fronts, our generals have not been able to stop them.

"Third, after fifteen years, Grand Old Master Wen Zhong has not been able to crush the North Sea rebellion. All these rebellions have drained our national treasury and squeezed the populace dry. How then can Your Majesty think of a project like the Deer Gallery?

"Please, sire. Listen to your loyal ministers and forget the whole idea, at least for the time being."

The king cursed, "You stupid bookworm!" then shouted his order, "Gouge out his eyes!"

Yang Ren fainted to the floor, now covered with his own blood. But his outraged spirit pierced the clouds to reach the Superiorman Insouciant, of Mount Green Top, Purple Cave.

In response, Superiorman Insouciant sent his Yellow Kerchiefed Genie to rescue Yang Ren. Yang Ren's body vanished without a trace in a sudden tornado and thunderclap.

Now with Yang Ren's body before him, Superiorman Insouciant deftly placed some magic potion on each of Yang Ren's eye sockets. Summoning up his own inner energy, Superiorman Insouciant gently blew on Yang Ren's face, then shouted, "Up! Yang Ren!"

Two hands sprouted from Yang Ren's eye sockets. And in the palm of each hand was an eye that could see from heaven to hell, and everything in between! Each hand could turn independently a full circle of three hundred and sixty degrees to canvas the world.

Groggily Yang Ren stood up and soon became aware of the two strange hands protruding from his eye sockets and the presence of a Superiorman before him. Timidly Yang Ren asked, "Honorable sir. Am I in the realm of death?"

"No such thing, my man!" Superiorman Insouciant said. "You have been unjustly punished for your loyalty, and since the years allotted you by Heaven are not supposed to end yet, I decided to give you two helping hands."

Yang Ren thanked the Superiorman and begged to remain as a disciple.

*   *   *   *

Tiger Duke was now in charge of the building of the Deer Gallery, carrying out his assignment with great severity. He levied more taxes and conscripted more labor. Regardless of any possible health problems, all males thirteen or older were accountable. One son was exempted when a family had more than three sons. Where there was no son, the male head of the family would be conscripted, regardless of age. Should there be no male in the family, the women would serve regardless of age. The young, the old and the infirm were first to die under Tiger Duke's relentless drive, and their bodies were used as fill under the Deer Gallery. The people lived in fear and hopelessness. Many were starving and many fled.

*   *   *   *

Baby Tooth surfaced at the Soong Ranch. His wife was surprised but glad to see him.

"Why are you home?" she asked.

"I have left the court. I am no longer an official."

Shocked, Mrs. Baby Tooth asked again to be sure of what she had heard, "What did you say?"

"Well," Baby Tooth replied quietly, "the son of Heaven wanted me to be in charge of building a Deer Gallery, a structure forty-nine feet high. I advised him not to build it. King Zhou got angry and fired me. I had never thought he was my true master anyway. I left his court without regret. We will go to the Western Foothills of Mount Singing Phoenix. I am certain my luck is changing for the better. And who knows, I may even become a prime minister someday."

"Damn fool!" shrieked Mrs. Baby Tooth. "You are day dreaming again! You are not a scholar, how in the world will you ever become a prime minister? You are lucky to be a lower counselor, sitting pretty and drawing a salary but doing no work. You should be grateful. Instead, you behave as if you were better than anyone else! And you dared to tell the Son of Heaven he was wrong and you were right? Who are you and what do you think you are?"

"My dear wife," soothed Baby Tooth. "Someday, I really will be a prime minister and you will be the prime minister's wife, eligible to wear a pearl bonnet and silk satin. Now please pack up so that we can start on our journey."

Mrs. Baby Tooth taunted, "So that's it! You gave up the bird you had in your hand and want to hunt for the two in the bush? You could not even hold on to a ninth rank position, and you are dreaming of a first rank prime minister!

"Letting you be in charge of the construction gave you a special opportunity to upgrade yourself. But your stupidity has finally done you in!"

"My dear wife, please listen to me," said Baby Tooth, ever so patiently. "My luck is due to change soon. Please have faith in me. Look a little further into the future. We do have a very good future if you just do as I say."

"Thank you but no thank you," said Mrs. Baby Tooth. "Our days together have come to an end. I was born in the Capital City, Morning Song, and I intend to die in the Capital City, Morning Song! If you insist on going to the Western Foothills, you go ahead without me! I have had enough of your foolishness! I thought you had finally come to your senses and found your place in the world. But you threw it away! From now on, you go your own way and I go mine!"

"My dear wife. You are wrong! When a lady marries a chicken, she follows the chicken; when she marries a dog, she follows the dog. You married me, you will go where I go. How can husband and wife go their separate ways?"

Mrs. Baby Tooth said hotly, "Write me a divorce declaration! I will never leave the Capital City, Morning Song, where I was born!"

Baby Tooth pleaded, "Please, listen to me. Don't let your emotion carry you away. I promise you, someday, we will be rich and we will become nobles."

"No! My mind is made up! Write me the divorce paper and I will go home to my father. If you don't write that paper, I will call my brothers to give you a beating!"

The Soongs came to mediate the quarrel. To Baby Tooth, Spectacular said, "If your wife insists on leaving, my dear younger brother, please write that paper and let her go. When the heart is gone, there is no sense keeping the body around. You will find another wife."

Baby Tooth said, "My dear elder brother and sister-in-law, I have lived with this woman for almost ten years now. Although I have not been able to provide her with a high social position, I do love her. If both of you think I should write that divorce paper as she demanded, I shall obey."

Baby Tooth held the divorce paper in his hand and said to his wife, "My dear. Here is the paper. If you leave it in my hand, we are still man and wife. Once you take it, our relationship is finished! Please don't be rash."

Mrs. Baby Tooth reached over and grabbed the paper without hesitation.

Baby Tooth sighed, "There are ways to counteract the venoms of the most poisonous snake bite and the deadliest bee sting; but there is no cure for a woman's scorn."

And so the marriage ended. The former Mrs. Baby Tooth returned to her father's ranch, and resumed her maiden name Ma Li Li. And Baby Tooth went on to the Western Foothills.

*   *   *   *

It was a long and arduous way to the Western Foothills of Mount Singing Phoenix. He trudged on, confident of his future. At the Lin Tung Pass, Baby Tooth came to some eight hundred people, old and young, men and women, crying, sobbing, and weeping. Baby Tooth inquired what the matter was. Someone recognized him, and said, "Oh, Mr. Jiang. We are fleeing the Capital City, Morning Song. We could not take it any more. We gave up everything we had and are on our way to the Western Foothills. But the commander of the troops garrisoning this mountain Pass would not let us out. Please, Mr. Jiang. Help us! If we are sent back to the Capital City, we will be killed for certain."

Baby Tooth comforted them, "Stop your crying. I will see what I can do. I too am on my way to the Western Foothills."

The Commander heard that a Lower Counselor had come to see him, and thought, "Well, this Lower Counselor is a civil official from the Capital City. He may do me some good someday. Better make a good impression on him."

When the Commander saw Baby Tooth in his common people's garb, he asked, "Who are you?"

"I am Lower Counselor Jiang Baby Tooth."

"Why are you not in your official robes?"

"Well," Baby Tooth said. "I have resigned from my post. I am, along with the hundreds of people out there, on my way to the Western Foothills. Why don't you let them go? As you know, they can no longer bear the burden of the new taxes and the conscription, and are giving up everything to seek a new life elsewhere. Please have mercy."

The Commander was not only disappointed but angry when he found out Baby Tooth was no longer a counselor. "You damned charlatan!" he shouted. "The king made you a lower counselor and you lost it, claiming that you have resigned! I know better. You must have done something bad and got fired! What did you do? Now you are on your way to join the rebels! And you have the audacity to ask me to let that bunch go out of this Lin Tong Pass! I want you to know I am a loyal soldier! I will send all of you back to the king for the punishment you deserve."

The people were devastated when they saw Baby Tooth came out of the Commander's office without an exit permit. They knew, once they were sent back to the Capital City, Morning Song, they would all be slaughtered.

Baby Tooth said, "Don't despair. I will do something to help you."

"If you cannot even get out of here yourself, how can you help us?" some pessimists cackled.

Baby Tooth said, "If you really want my help, stay with me until sundown and do as I direct."

When evening came, Baby Tooth told them to close their eyes as tight as possible and not to open them until he said so. He let loose his hair, then knelt, facing Mount Kunlun, and mumbled some incantation.

The people heard the sound of a piercing wind blowing, but, scared as they were, they kept their eyes shut. A few moments later, Baby Tooth said, "You may open your eyes now. This is the Mount Golden Rooster, outside of both the Lin Tong Pass and the Flood River Pass. You are now in the Western Foothills territory and safe from the cruelty of King Zhou."

*   *   *   *

They climbed over Mount Golden Rooster, Mount Sun's Head, Mount Swallow and passed the White Willow Village. Then twenty days later on a fine morning, they arrived in the Phoenix City, Capital of the Western Foothills of Mount Singing Phoenix, home of the Grand Duke of the West Ji Chang.

In Phoenix City they saw beautiful and clean streets, prosperous and friendly people. Everything was as they had heard. They petitioned the local authority, asking for asylum.

Ji Chang was imprisoned by King Zhou in Yuli. So this morning, the petition came to Bo Yi Kao, Number one son of the Grand Duke of the West.

Bo Yi Kao instructed Grand Counselor Easy Life, "These people have trudged a long way to come to us. Please see to it that they are taken care of. Give them shelter and food, and some money until they find suitable livelihood."

Seeing all these refugees from the Capital City, Morning Song, Bo Yi Kao thought of his own dear father, who had been imprisoned there for seven long years. How his father must have suffered! Yes, his father had emphatically told him not to go to the Capital City, Morning Song, for seven years. But it had been seven years now. "I must do something," he said to himself. "I must go to see my father!"

Bo Yi Kao said to Easy Life, "My father has been in prison long enough. I think I should go there to ransom him."

Easy Life countered, "The Grand Duke had told us repeatedly not to seek his release. He said to be patient and wait here in the Western Foothills. After seven years, he will come safely home. Please don't do anything contrary."

"It is seven years already," Bo Yi Kao said. "When I think of my father's suffering, how can I sit here any longer? I must go!"

Easy Life said, "If you are worrying about his health, you can send a servant to inquire. But please don't go there yourself. The Grand Duke had said over and over not to."

"But the seven years is up! My father has suffered enough. I am his number one son, and if I don't go, what good is it for him to have ninety-nine sons? I must bring him home!"

CHAPTER 19

▼

HEIRLOOM TREASURES

Number one son Bo Yi Kao was determined to go to the Capital City, Morning Song, to ransom his father. No one, not even his Grandmother, his mother or the Grand Counselor Easy Life was able to change his mind.

Bo Yi Kao left the Western Foothills with only a few servants, but carried with him three family heirloom treasures as tributes to King Zhou. After many arduous days on the road, they arrived in the Capital City, Morning Song.

Early next morning, Bo Yi Kao went to the Noon Gate with his petition in hand. He was dressed in white, as befitted family members of criminals. He stood outside the Noon Gate, waiting for a chance to get in.

Soon, Vice Prime Minister, Prince Bi Gan came by on his horse. Bo Yi Kao walked up and knelt before Bi Gan. Bi Gan reined in and asked, "Who is kneeling?"

"Sir, I am Bo Yi Kao, a son of the Grand Duke of the West Ji Chang."

Hearing the name, Bi Gan rolled off his horse and took Bo Yi Kao's hand, pulling him up, and said, "My dear young sir. Why are you here?"

Bo Yi Kao said, "My Prime Minister. We are grateful to you for saving my father's life. Now that seven years have passed, I feel deeply that my father has suffered enough. That is why I have come with three heirloom treasures as tribute to the king in the hope of gaining my father's release. Please help us. We will forever remember your kindness."

"What kind of treasures?" Bi Gan asked.

"They are the Eight-Direction Chariot, the Anti-Drunk Rug, and the White Face Monkey."

"What are these treasures good for?"

"The Eight-Direction Chariot is equipped with a device that points to the desired direction. In ancient time, there was Chief Ignoramus, Chi-You, who ruled his tribe with absolute cruelty. He was a warmonger and made much trouble for his neighbors. But because he had the fog-making magic power, no one could fight him. He was finally vanquished when the Yellow Emperor invented the compass. The Eight-Direction Chariot is equipped with the original compass which Yellow Emperor used.

"The Anti-Drunk Rug has unusual power. When a drunken person lies on it, he would be revived in minutes."

"And the White-Face Monkey is an exceptional beast trained to sing and dance with a repertoire of three thousand songs and one thousand ballads. It specializes in dancing on the palm of a man. It is a very good entertainer at banquets."

Bi Gan sighed sorrowfully, "They are treasures all right. But they will only add to the king's debaucheries. He is already deep in wine and women, song and dance. Well, there is nothing we can do about it. I will take you to the king."

*   *   *   *

Bi Gan said to the king, "I have a petition from the son of Ji Chang, the Grand Duke of the West. He has brought with him heirloom treasures as tribute, to redeem his father's crime."

King Zhou gave the order to bring in Bo Yi Kao.

Bo Yi Kao walked all the way from the Noon Gate on his knees, then climbed to the Star-Picking Belvedere, also on his knees.

The king said, "Ji Chang's crime against his king is unpardonable. But it is commendable that his son is so devoted."

Bo Yi Kao said, "My father committed a crime against Your Majesty, and Your Majesty spared his life. We are ever so grateful. I am here to beg Your Majesty to let him come home, so that our family can be whole again. We will be ever and forever singing your praise."

King Zhou thought well of Bo Yi Kao's good faith. He gave Bo Yi Kao permission to stand up.

Daji heard the melancholy voice pleading with heartfelt sincerity. She looked through the bead curtain which kept her from public view, and saw Bo Yi Kao standing outside of the balustrade. "My, oh my, how handsome and young he is," Daji thought to herself. She saw eyes as fluid as an autumn lake, enhanced by clearly etched eyebrows, and even, pearly white teeth, showing off deep red lips.

"Roll up the bead curtain!" Daji ordered her servants.

On hearing Daji, the king said, "My dear royal wife. We have the son of the Grand Duke of the West, bringing tributes to redeem his father's crime. I think it very commendable."

Daji said, "I heard Bo Yi Kao of the Western Foothills is a virtuoso on the lute."

The King was curious, "How do you know?"

"When I was in my father's house, I heard of his virtuosity. If Your Majesty doesn't believe me, simply ask Bo Yi Kao to play one song and you will see."

The king presented Bo Yi Kao to Daji. Daji said, "I heard that you are a virtuoso on the lute. How about playing a song for us?"

Bo Yi Kao said, "I beg your ten thousands pardons. But with my father suffering in prison, my mind is far away, and my heart is as confused as a tangled ball of flax. It would be impossible for me to make any sense of the lute. How dare I fool around with discordant noises to offend your Royal Highness?"

The king said, "Go ahead and play. If I like your music, I will pardon your father and let him go home with you."

Overjoyed, Bo Yi Kao thanked the king and sat on the floor, putting the lute on his knees, and slowly began to play. Delicately caressing the strings, ten slender fingers played the melody called "The breeze in the meadows."

Weeping willow swaying in the evening flow,
Half opened peach flowers reflecting the sunlight glow.
Green grasses softly nodding in the meadow,
Care not wherever horses and chariots go.

"What a splendid musician!" The king was delighted.

"I knew it!" Daji put in.

King Zhou ordered a banquet and Bo Yi Kao was ordered to entertain them.

All evening, Daji sent her stealthy glances toward Bo Yi Kao. She was drooling over his youth and his strong body, finding how revolting it was to look at King Zhou's old and decrepit carcass! Yes, King Zhou was once also young and virile, strong and handsome. But after so many years of wine and carousing, what could one expect?

Scheming how to seduce Bo Yi Kao, Daji said to the king, "It is very generous of you to pardon Ji Chang and let him go home. Too bad Bo Yi Kao will also be going with him and we will never hear his music again."

"That is regrettable. But I have already promised."

"I know one way to help. Your Majesty can keep Bo Yi Kao here for a while and let him teach me how to play the lute. When I have mastered it, then let him go home and we will not miss his music."

Bo Yi Kao was ordered to stay.

Daji schemed further and deliberately got the king to drink more than usual. As soon as the king was drunk, he was immediately put to bed.

Daji ordered her servant to bring another lute. Very seriously, Bo Yi Kao explained the theory of the lute to Daji. But Daji's mind was elsewhere. She was trying to get closer so that her face might touch Bo Yi Kao's. To Bo Yi Kao, this was the only chance he might have to win his father's release. So no matter how unsavory it was to give music lessons to Daji, he would never dare to disobey the king's order. He concentrated on explaining the intricacy of the lute, and paid absolutely no mind to what Daji was trying to do.

Not at all discouraged, Daji said, "It is so difficult to understand. I simply cannot comprehend so much at once. Let's take a rest and have some wine first."

Daji ordered fresh wine and food. She invited Bo Yi Kao to sit next to her.

"How dare I?" said Bo Yi Kao, alarmed. "You are the queen, how dare the son of a prisoner sit next to her!"

Daji said, "You are absolutely correct. As the son of a prisoner, you definitely may not sit next to me. However, since you are my teacher, you certainly are allowed to. No question about that."

Now fully aware what was in Daji's mind, Bo Yi Kao tried his utmost to find a way to escape her entrapment. Oh, how he wished his dear father was there to advise him! He had never missed his father more than at this moment. Bo Yi Kao refused both wine and food.

"It is all right if you don't want to drink or eat. But with me sitting up here and you sitting down there, don't you think it rather difficult for me to learn? Why not come up here and sit next to me?" Daji coaxed.

Bo Yi Kao said, "You cannot expect to learn to play in one day. You have to practice constantly to master the art."

Daji cajoled, "Come up here and sit behind me, hold on to my fingers and guide them on the string. That way I will learn quickly."

Bo Yi Kao realized his plight. If he wanted to keep his body and soul intact, the only way out was to tell her off and then commit suicide if need be.

He said calmly, "I am sorry. But you are treating me like one of those shameless beasts, trying to take advantage of you. I would like to remind your Royal Highness that you are the mother of our nation. If rumor goes out that I tried to seduce you, how will I ever clear my name? Please be patient and keep on practicing your lute. You will be able to master it someday."

Daji's disappointment turned to regret, but she kept her cool, still hoping Bo Yi Kao would change his mind. She said lightly, "You may go now."

When Daji lay down next to the drunken king, in her lust, the regret turned to hatred. She swore, "I have tried to compliment the moon, the moon turned out to be so full of crevasses! You just wait, Bo Yi Kao!"

Next morning, the king asked, "How was the music lesson last night?"

Daji said indignantly, "Don't even mention it! Last night, Bo Yi Kao did not have any mind to teach me music. He was trying to seduce me instead!"

The enraged king summoned Bo Yi Kao immediately.

"Last night, why didn't you concentrate on the teaching the music?"

Bo Yi Kao said, "Sire. One must be pure and sincere in heart to learn to play the lute."

Daji cut in, "The art of playing the lute is intricate, we all know that. If your teaching was a little better, I would have learned more. But your instruction was so muddy. You simply did not put your heart in the teaching!"

The king did not mention what Daji told him. Instead, he said to Bo Yi Kao, "Play another song for me."

Bo Yi Kao sat on the floor, played the lute and sang,

My loyal heart facing the Heaven high,
My king's good health and long life pray I.
Harmonious wind and seasonal rain,
A unified kingdom and a glorious reign.

The king found the song most agreeable and felt no reason to punish Bo Yi Kao. Sensing the king's attitude, Daji said, "I heard Bo Yi Kao has a monkey which can sing and dance. Has Your Majesty seen it?"

"No. Tell Bo Yi Kao to show us his monkey."

*   *   *   *

Bo Yi Kao handed a sound board to the white-face monkey as it came out of the red lacquer cage. White-face monkey lightly hit the sound board and began to sing. It sang like an opera star in volume and range. Its high notes were like the song of phoenix praising the sun; and the low notes were like that of the canary mourning a death in its sob. On hearing the monkey's song, a sad person would loosen his knitted brow; a happy person would clap his hands in joy, and a weeping person would stop his tears.

The king and Daji were in ecstasy. In her delirium, Daji lost control and revealed her fox specter self. Luckily, everyone was so engrossed that no one saw any change. No one, alas, except, the monkey who, agitated at the sight of a fox specter, threw his sound board to the floor and leaped over to grab Daji.

Daji instinctively stepped behind the king. King Zhou hit the monkey with his fist, killing it instantly.

Daji regained her composure as the ever so beautiful Queen. She cried out, "Bo Yi Kao is trying to use the Monkey to assassinate us! Fortunately Your Majesty's quick reflex saved the situation!"

The king was incensed. He shouted, "Throw Bo Yi Kao into the Snake Pit!"

"Injustice!" Bo Yi Kao screamed as the palace guards grabbed him.

Hearing that, the king stopped the guards and said to Bo Yi Kao, "You ungrateful cur! We all saw what the monkey did. What do you mean injustice?"

"Sire," said Bo Yi Kao, with tears running down his cheeks, "the monkey was a beast from the wild. Even though he was taught human language, his character was still that of a wild beast. He loved fruits and saw in front of Your Majesty so many luscious ones, he could not help but want to grab some. He did not have a single inch of iron, how could he possibly attempt an assassination? I have too much gratitude toward Your Majesty to do anything so evil as that. Please investigate so that the innocents are not unjustly punished."

The king thought for a moment and said to Daji, "My royal wife. I think Bo Yi Kao is right. The monkey is a wild beast, and without any iron in his hand, how could he be guilty?"

Daji was not appeased. "Since you are pardoning Bo Yi Kao, then let him play one more melody," she said. "If we can detect any disloyalty in the music, he should still be punished."

Fully realizing a trap was again set for him, Bo Yi Kao was determined to protect his soul and body. He sat on the floor. Again he placed the lute on his knees and started to play gently. He sang,

> *Luminous head of the Nation,*
> *Practice justice and benevolence.*
> *His kind heart would never permit the matters,*
> *Of high taxes and tortures.*
> *Lo, of the Bronze Toaster,*
> *Flesh and bone turn to cinder.*
> *Lo, of the Snake Pit,*

The condemned forever lost their body and spirit.
Ten thousand families' blood and tears,
Into the Wine Pool they pour,
Bitter harvests from the four corners,
Become the meats hanging in the Forest.
Spindles are emptying,
The Deer Gallery treasures are brimming.
Plows are worn-out,
To build bridges and to fill the Grain House.
To my luminous king I pray,
Be rid of the wicked and send the unscrupulous away.
Rejoice with the populace in the former virtuous way.

The king enjoyed the music and the song. He could find no fault. But Daji, with the evil intent to hurt, shrieked, "How dare you, you scamp! You are using your music to satirize the king!"

The king said, "I like the music. I don't see anything wrong."

Daji explained, twisting his words and adding spice to his tale, tightening her grip and closing the trap on Bo Yi Kao.

"Please, Sire." Bo Yi Kao said. "There is one more stanza. May I sing it to Your Majesty?"

Pray to my luminous Lord,
Return our nation to order and law.
Away from the debauchery,
Strive to be virtuous.
Rid of things unholy,
Return to prosperity.
Divorce the licentious and lewd,
Populace live in atmosphere of chastity and purity.
Murder Yi Kao, but he is not afraid,
Dispatch Daji, all under Heaven will sing your praise.

After the song, Bo Yi Kao stood up and threw the lute directly at Daji. Dishes from the table flew everywhere. Daji ducked and fell to the floor.

"Throw him into the Snake Pit!" the king roared. His anger knew no bounds. Daji got up and said, "Definitely not. Take him away. Nail him to a board and scrape him away bit by bit to the bone!"

Bo Yi Kao screamed back at Daji, "You spiteful woman! You tried to seduce me but in vain. I only regret that I cannot expose you to the world. My name and body will forever be clean, and yours will stink for tens of thousands of years!"

In no time, Bo Yi Kao became a pot of meat pulp! King Zhou ordered it dumped into the Snake Pit.

The fox specter Daji would have loved to devour him alive, or at least to savior the pulp of his flesh. But she had a more hateful idea. She said, "People kept saying that Ji Chang is a wise man, knows the art of the Trigram and divination, and can predict the future. Have the pulp of Bo Yi Kao's flesh made into meat cakes and send them to Ji Chang. If he eats them, that proves he is not a wise man but a charlatan, and should be killed immediately. No wise man could eat his own son's flesh. If he refuses to eat them, he is disobeying Your Majesty's order and also should be killed immediately."

And so with the compliments of the king, meat cakes were sent to Ji Chang, The Grand Duke of the West, at his Youli prison.

CHAPTER 20

▼

SECRET BRIBES

The Grand Duke of the West Ji Chang had been under house arrest in Youli District for seven years now. Although he was allowed to move freely within the Youli District, he was forbidden to have any communication with the outside world; and in particular, with the Western Foothills. The local people received him with honor and friendship. In turn, he taught them the meanings of loyalty, moral integrity, trust, and filial piety.

Now relieved of all administrative duties, he spent his time in the study of the Trigram. He wrote a book on the subject, a book that is now known as YI JING, or the BOOK OF CHANGES.

Never in those seven years had he murmured a word of complaint, nor once did he comment on the injustice that he had befallen. He prayed for the king's good health and prosperity for the kingdom.

One day, while Ji Chang was playing his lute, the main string gave forth a sudden discordant sound. Alarmed, he stopped his music and cast a few gold coins. As he read the configuration, tears rained down his cheeks, "Oh," he moaned. "My son Bo Yi Kao went against my advice to beseech King Zhou and now he has been butchered! Today, the king is sending me some meat cakes made of his flesh! My son! My son! How am I to eat your flesh? But if I don't, I will be killed instantly. I am not afraid to die. But if I die now, the world will never know what happened, and the injustice and cruelty of this reign will never be righted. I must live to tell the story and to right the wrongs!"

His servants stood by silently, not comprehending the sudden change in his mood. Ji Chang hurriedly wiped away his tears and calmed himself. He told his servants to be ready for the king's messenger.

Soon the messenger arrived with a box of meat cakes, saying that the king had gone hunting yesterday, had killed some deer and wished to share them with Ji Chang.

Ji Chang thanked the messenger for bringing the cakes. He then opened the box and ate three of them with apparent relish. Carefully closing the box, he asked the messenger to convey his appreciation to the king.

Aware of the true content of the meat cakes, the messenger was flabbergasted to see Ji Chang not only eat but enjoy them! The messenger sighed to himself, "Ji Chang being wise is nothing but rumor! How can a wise man eat his son's flesh and not know it? And he ate it with such gusto too!"

After the messenger left, Ji Chang wrote out his anguish:

> Departing from the Western Foothills,
> I left words not to come to my rescue.
> Your filial piety and love,
> Prompted your suffering for your father.
> Not comprehending the king's mind,
> Is another matter!
> A pure and gallant youth wasted and gone,
> Pity your grieving father's heart forlorn.
> Your virtuous soul and your courageous sacrifice,
> Forever in history the bold and enduring granites.

Ji Chang fell sick over his son's death. His servants stood helplessly by not knowing where to turn.

*   *   *   *

In his Virtuous Dragon Court, The king was playing chess with Fei Zhong and You Hun, now known as Higher Counselors, having been promoted at Daji's recommendation on Queen Jiang's death. They have become very rich and more powerful than ever.

The messenger reported back to the king that Ji Chang had eaten the meat cakes and thanked the king for his generosity.

The king remarked to Fei Zhong and You Hun, "I have heard that Ji Chang was a wise man, knew the past and could predict the future. But now he has eaten his son's flesh without knowing it! Well, I think I will let him go home. He has been in Youli for seven years. I should think he has suffered enough."

Fei Zhong said, "Don't be fooled, Sire. He is a very cunning man. Even if he knew what was in those meat cakes, he had to make you believe that he didn't. You see, if he refused to eat them, he would be disobeying Your Majesty and would be put to death. He had no choice but to eat them."

The king said, "Ji Chang is reputed to be a wise man. If he knew the meat cakes were of his son's flesh, he would never be able to swallow them, no matter what! His eating them proves he is not wise."

"No sire." Fei Zhong said. "Ji Chang has a very honest exterior, but his heart is full of cunning and treachery. He fools everyone. Let the bird stay in the cage, the tiger remain in the pen! It would only be a matter of time, but trouble would surely come if Your Majesty lets Ji Chang go home."

The king conceded. And so The Grand Duke of the West remained a prisoner in Youli.

*   *   *   *

Bo Yi Kao's servants fled home with the sad news. They went directly to see his younger brother Ji Fa, who was at that moment in the Great Hall, talking to his ministers.

Ji Fa fainted after hearing of his brother's horrid death. General Southpalace Nimblefoot cried out, "I have had enough of this! It has been seven years since our master was imprisoned, and now our young master is murdered! How can we idly stand by? Let's join the dukes of the East and the South!"

Many joined in, shouting, "Nimblefoot is right!"

All present were so agitated, sound and fury filled the Great Hall. But no one had any constructive suggestions on how to rescue the master.

Grand Counselor Easy Life finally said, "My Lord Ji Fa. May I say something? My Lord should send Nimblefoot out the front gate and have his head chopped off!"

"Why so?" Ji Fa was shocked.

Addressing all the ministers, Easy Life said, "This rabble rousing will compromise our master's loyalty. Have you ever thought what this kind of bravado without wit and brawn without brain will lead us to? Not to mention entering the Capital City, Morning Song. Our master would be murdered before we could reach the first mountain pass. Therefore I say, Nimblefoot must be killed first!"

The whole group was sobered; even Nimblefoot hung his head in shame.

Easy Life continued, "Lord Bo Yi Kao refused my advice not to go. On top of that, he refused my advice to take gifts to the two most powerful and unscrupulous Counselors Fei Zhong and You Hun. And now the worst has happened!

"When our master left the Western Foothills seven years ago, his divination foretold seven years of tribulation, and he repeatedly warned us not to try to rescue him. His words are still clear as the day he spoke them. But, alas, circumstances have changed. We cannot bring Bo Yi Kao back to life. Now we must think carefully, yes, very carefully.

"My suggestion is, first send expensive gifts secretly to Fei Zhong and You Hun, asking them to help secure the release of our master! Only after our master is safely home can we join with others to get rid of this cruel and execrated King Zhou!"

Everyone agreed. Ji Fa gave order to get things ready. Two envoys, along with letters written by Easy Life, were dispatched secretly to Capital City, Morning Song. The two envoys traveled incognito as common merchants.

*   *   *   *

Fei Zhong came home one night and found an envoy from the Western Foothills waiting to see him.

Fei Zhong asked, "Who are you? Why are you here?"

"I am General Mountaintop of the Western Foothills. I came on the order of our Grand Counselor Easy Life, to bring Your Lordship a few insignificant trinkets as an expression of our gratitude for your saving our master Ji Chang's life. Here is Grand Counselor's letter."

Fei Zhong read:

"The humble Counselor Easy Life of The Western Foothills salutes the Honorable Higher Counselor Fei Zhong. My master Ji Chang, the Grand Duke of the West, spoke inadvertently and committed the unpardonable crime of offending the Son of Heaven. We are very grateful that Your Lordship helped to spare our master's life. We in the remote wilderness, The Western Foothills, long to have our master back so that in his declining years he can be with his family, especially his aged mother who is anxious to see her son once more before she dies.

"I have taken the liberty of sending our General Mountaintop to secretly bring you some very insignificant baubles as our token of appreciation. We hope this meager fare will not offend Your Lordship. Enclosed:

One pair of white jade disks
Two thousand and four hundred ounces of yellow gold
Four bolts of silk satin brocade cloth"

Fei Zhong read the gift list and quickly calculated its worth. Quite satisfied, but keeping the feeling to himself, he said causally, "Please inform your Counselor Easy Life that I will do my best to help. It would not be convenient for me to write a thank you note. I know your counselor will understand."

That same night, envoy General Hong Yao was seeing Counselor Yu Hun. He carried a similar letter and identical gifts and got practically the same response.

Both envoys were gratified that their missions, so far, were progressing as hoped. Again, traveling incognito, they quickly returned home to report.

Neither Fei Zhong nor You Hun showed any sign to each other that they had received gifts from Easy Life.

*   *   *   *

One day, again the king was playing chess with Fei Zhong and You Hun. The king won two games in a row. To celebrate, the king invited both to a banquet. During the feast, the king reminisced about how beautifully Bo Yi Kao had played the lute and how delightful were the songs the White-Face Monkey sang. Then the king rambled to how strange it was that a wise man like Ji Chang could have eaten his son's flesh!

"How can anyone claim that he can predict the future! What nonsense!" the king remarked.

As if on cue, Fei Zhong said, "I have always been suspect of Ji Chang's intent. Therefore, a few days ago, I sent someone secretly to spy on him. The report was rather astonishing. It said not only that he never uttered a word of complaint about his incarceration, but that he actually prays for Your Majesty all the time. In seven years of imprisonment, he has always shown his loyalty and integrity beyond the slightest doubt."

The king said, "Just the other day, you told me that Ji Chang was a most treacherous man. What changed your mind?"

Fei Zhong said, "It is indeed difficult to discern the false from the true. So I had to find out for myself. And it is true that Ji Chang is loyal to Your Majesty. As the saying goes, only after a long journey do we know the strength of the horse; only after a long association, can we find out the true character of the man. So that's how it is."

The king asked You Hun, "What is your opinion, Counselor You Hun?"

You Hun said, "I think Lord Fei Zhong is right. I heard that Ji Chang not only never complained, but he also taught the populace of Youli the meanings of loyalty, moral integrity, trust, and filial piety. In fact, I would have mentioned them had Lord Fei Zhong not said it first."

The king said, "Since both of you think that Ji Chang is a loyal person, I intend to let him go home. What do you think?"

Fei Zhong said, "That is a serious question that only Your Majesty can decide. But if Ji Chang can go home now, his gratitude would be doubly boundless. Instead of being executed, he gets his life back. Instead of being homeless, he gets his home back. Now he owes his life and everything else to Your Majesty. I know he will serve Your Majesty even more loyally than ever."

Hearing Fei Zhong, You Hun knew for certain that Fei Zhong must also have received gifts from Easy Life.

Not to be outdone, You Hun said, "Since Your Majesty is going to pardon Ji Chang and let him go home, why not also promote him to a higher rank to insure his fullest loyalty? His help is especially critical right now because both the East and South regional dukes are rebelling, and our generals have not been able to stop them. If Your Majesty gives Ji Chang your Battle Ax and has him lead the fighting, the rebellious dukes will lay down their arms at once. As the saying goes: promote a good one, the evil ones will dare not show up."

The king praised his two counselors for their brilliant suggestions and sent out his decree to pardon Ji Chang.

*   *   *   *

Ji Chang was deep in grief from his son's untimely demise. A sudden gust of wind blew two loose tiles from the roof, clattering them to the ground. Startled out of his reverie, Ji Chang almost jumped out of his skin.

"What is that!" he asked himself.

He cast a few gold coins to seek enlightenment from the divine. The configuration quickly quieted his pounding heart. He told his servants to pack their things and be ready to go home. They thought he was going mad.

Soon, the messenger came with the king's edict to pardon Ji Chang and to summon him to the Capital City, Morning Song.

Ji Chang left immediately with his servants. The roads to the Capital City, Morning Song, were lined with people, young and old, men and women, carrying gifts to bid him farewell.

They were all in tears, so happy for him now that he was going home; at the same time, so sad that he was leaving them.

Also with tears in his eyes, Ji Chang said to them, "I am grateful that all of you have received me so graciously and treated me with honor. I don't have any gift for you, but please remember what I taught you about loyalty, moral integrity, trust, and filial piety. And I wish you will live in peace and prosperity."

As Ji Chang arrived in the Capital City, Morning Song, officials were waiting at the Noon Gate to welcome him. Among them were the seven senior princes and the eight Grand Counselors.

Ji Chang, in good health and high spirit, saluted them, "I am free today and I thank you all."

In his white garments Ji Chang knelt before the king and said, "I am very grateful to be pardoned and permitted to go home. I wish Your Majesty good health and longevity of tens of thousands years."

The king said, "In seven years of confinement you had not uttered a single word of complaint. Not only that, I heard you prayed for the prosperity of my reign and my good health. I also heard that you got along well with the populace and gave them a good education. All these showed clearly indeed that you are a loyal official. It was I who might have treated you a little too harshly. I want to make up for the past. You are hereby promoted to the first rank as King Wen of the West, and you will have my Battle Axe to represent me in putting down the rebellions of the East and the South regions. Your headquarters will still be the Western Foothills. You will receive two more each of civil and military ministers, plus ten thousand more bushels of rice each month. Now you will be entertained at a banquet in the Virtuous Dragon Court. We will then have three days of celebration and parading in this Capital City, Morning Song."

Ji Chang was glad to see his old friends again at the banquet. They were all happy for him.

*   *   *   *

On the first day of celebration, the streets of Capital City, Morning Song, were jammed with people. They all sang Ji Chang's praise.

Yellow Flying Tiger, the Lord of National Security, came to see the parade and asked Ji Chang to come to his private residence for a drink afterward.

"Are you out of your mind? Haven't you learned anything after seven years of imprisonment?" Yellow Flying Tiger said urgently. "The Capital City, Morning Song, is not the place for you to linger. Get out of here as soon as possible! Right now, this very moment, before anything unexpected happens!"

"But how will I get through the city gate at this hour?" pleaded Ji Chang like a lost child awakened from a euphoric dream but now fully alarmed at what Yellow Flying Tiger had said.

Yellow Flying Tiger handed Ji Chang the Bronze Passport, which was good for Ji Chang to go through all five mountain passes on his way to the Western Foothills. Yellow Flying Tiger then helped Ji Chang change his parade finery to ordinary clothing, and ordered two trusted aides to open the city gate. He sent Ji Chang on his way, alone on a horse.

CHAPTER 21

▼

TWO RIPE APRICOTS

Ji Chang had checked in at the Golden Pavilion Hostel. Alarmed when Ji Chang did not return after the first parade day, the manager reported this to Higher Counselor Fei Zhong. Fei Zhong realized the seriousness of this turn of events. He immediately invited You Hun to his home to map out a plan to cover their own asses.

"Stop worrying so much," You Hun said. "We can simply tell the king that Ji Chang turned out to be more cunning than we thought. We can suggest a chasing party to capture that ingrate and this time punish him as he deserves!"

Upon hearing what had happened, the angry king said, "I was following your recommendation. Now what?"

Fei Zhong said soothingly, "Sire. We know, and we are very sorry. As the saying goes, the bottom of a pond appears when the water dries out; but no one can see the heart of a man even after his death. We had recommended his pardon in good faith. But he could not have gone far. Why not send out three thousand flying troops to capture him?"

Quickly, Generals Yin and Lei were dispatched to lead three thousand of the king's personal troops. Yin and Lei had not forgotten how humiliated and disappointed they were when a tornado snatched away those two princes. This time, they swore that they would not let such a thing happen again. They knew exactly which route the Grand Duke must be taking. So this time they felt that promotion and great wealth were again within their grasp.

Although traveling as fast as he could, Ji Chang was still losing ground. After he crossed the Yellow River and came within twenty miles of the Lin Tong Pass, he heard thundering troops at his heels. He knew what that meant. He looked up to Heaven and sighed. "How will I ever get out of this?"

Superiorman Cloud Dweller of Mount South End had a sudden foreboding. He looked down at the Red Dust and saw Ji Chang in dire mortal danger. He told his young disciple Thunder Quaker, "Your father needs help!"

"Who is my father?" Thunder Quaker had never been told. "He is the Grand Duke of the West. He adopted you at Mount Swallow right after you were born in a thunderstorm. Now hurry over to the cliff and get your weapon first."

Thunder Quaker looked here and there, but did not know what kind of animal or thing his master called "weapon".

A whiff of a strange fragrance distracted Thunder Quaker. A delicious smell now propelled him to follow his nose to the edge of the cliff. There hanging on a tree were two beautiful apricots! They were too tempting for a seven year old boy. He reached over and picked both fruits, thinking to himself, "I'll eat one and take one to my master."

After he finished the first one, he found to his dismay he had absent-mindedly started biting into the second.

"Well, how can I take a half eaten fruit to my master? I might as well finish it."

And that was exactly what he did. Oh, what satisfying eating it was!

While continuing his search for this "weapon" thing, Thunder Quaker felt something strange sprouting out of his left shoulder. It was a wing long enough to reach the ground. He was so frightened he picked up his feet and started to run back to his master. Then another wing sprouted out of the right shoulder!

Not only that, without his being aware of it, his face began to change. His eyes popped out, his nose arched into a hook, his front teeth extended beyond his lips and, worst of all, his face turned indigo blue and his hair flame red!

Crying, he ran to his master the Superiorman Cloud Dweller, who was waiting for him. The master smiled and comforted Thunder Quaker, "Oh, don't cry. It is not as bad as you think. Come now with me to the garden."

Cloud Dweller gave Thunder Quaker a golden rod and taught him how to use it. On the left wing he wrote the word WIND, on the right THUNDER; then he mumbled some incantation.

Suddenly Thunder Quaker rose, spread his wings and soared into the sky. When Cloud Dweller waved his hand, Thunder Quaker landed softly and knelt before his master.

"Your father is in trouble." Cloud Dweller said. "Go quickly to Lin Tong Pass and fly him over the five mountain passes. Take him to Mount Singing Phoenix so that he can return home. Come right back after that. I have other things for you to learn."

*   *   *   *

From his soaring height, Thunder Quaker saw an old man on a horse, racing frantically, but barely ahead of a large chasing party.

Thunder Quaker landed on a mountain slope nearby and shouted, "Down there, are you the Grand Duke of the West?"

Ji Chang heard someone calling his name, the deafening echo reverberating from the surrounding mountains. Ji Chang looked around but could not tell where the voice came from. "Even the mountain ghosts are mocking me," he sighed.

But the voice came again, "Are you the Grand Duke of the West?"

This time Ji Chang saw, on the slope of the green mountains, a red dot that faintly looked like a person. What else was there to do but admit his identity?

"Yes, I am," Ji Chang shouted back as he climbed up the mountain slope to see what kind of creature had spoken.

"How do you know me, my brave one?" Ji Chang asked.

Thunder Quaker knelt and said, "My father. Pardon me for being a little late in attending to your suffering."

"Why do you call me father? Who are you?" Ji Chang was flustered.

"I am Thunder Quaker, the child you adopted on Mount Swallow."

"If you really are Thunder Quaker, you should be with Superior-man Cloud Dweller," Ji Chang said.

"I have orders from my master to get you over the five mountain passes," Thunder Quaker said.

Ji Chang was not sure whether to trust this strange winged creature. But seeing the soldiers coming up after him, Ji Chang said, "My son. Please don't harm the Royal troops. They are under the king's order to capture a criminal."

"Don't worry, my father," Thunder Quaker said. "My order is only to get you over the five passes."

Once again, Thunder Quaker soared and this time landed in front of the soldiers. Brandishing his golden rod, he shouted, "Stop!"

The frightened soldiers ran back to report to their generals. Generals Yin and Lei refused to believe them. They rushed up front to see for themselves what kind of monster dared to block the Imperial Army.

CHAPTER 22

▼

THREE WHITE RABBITS

"Who are you? How dare you block our way!" General Yin shouted with bravado.

Thunder Quaker said, "I am the youngest son of the Grand Duke of The West. My father is a righteous man, a loyal minister, a benevolent ruler and a trusted friend. He was unjustly imprisoned for seven years. Now he is pardoned and on his way home. What business have you to chase him like a common criminal? If you want to keep your skin, go back and leave him alone—or else!"

"Braggart!" General Lei snickered. "Or else what?"

With his golden rod, Thunder Quaker gave a mountain peak a little whack and it came crashing down. "Is your head harder?" Thunder Quaker asked.

Scared out of their wits, the king's men turned their horses and ran for their dear lives.

Thunder Quaker turned back to the Grand Duke. "My father. Let's go."

Ji Chang said, "I have this bronze Passport. I will be able to get out through the passes without a problem now that the chasing party has gone."

Thunder Quaker said, "My father, please don't delay. There may be more soldiers coming. Please let me help you before things turn bad again."

"What should I do with my horse?"

"Forget it." Thunder Quaker said urgently. "Your life is more important. Besides, the horse will not die. He will find another master. Come on, let's go!"

With tears brimming, Ji Chang patted his horse gently and said, "I am so sorry. Please go find yourself a new master."

"Please, my father, hurry!"

Ji Chang got on Thunder Quaker's back and held on tightly. Ji Chang closed his eyes. He could hear the wind sweeps by, but he was not afraid. They soon landed on top of the Golden Rooster Mountain, inside of the Western Foothill territory.

"My father, you are now safe. Now I must say good-bye and return to Mount South End. Please take care of yourself. I will see you again someday." So saying, Thunder Quaker soared away.

"You cannot leave me here alone!" Ji Chang wailed to no avail. The sun had set and it was getting dark and cold. Ji Chang had to sleep on the mountain to wait for morning. At daybreak, he was still exhausted because he had not eaten since he left Yellow Flying Tiger. He started to walk toward Phoenix City. In the evening, he eventually found a small inn for the night.

Next morning, he told the young innkeeper that he had no money to pay for either food or lodging, but he promised, when he reached the Phoenix City, he would send someone back with the full amount plus interest.

The young man was enraged. "How dare you cheat us like this? We in the Western Foothills are law abiding people. We do not tolerate cheaters."

Hearing trouble up front, the inn owner came out and saw a sturdy and distinguished looking old man. The owner asked politely, "Sir. What business do you have in the Western Foothills?"

Ji Chang said, "Kind man, I am no other but the Grand Duke of the West himself. I have been imprisoned in Youli for seven years. Now I am pardoned and on my way home. My son Thunder Quaker helped me over the five mountain passes. I am sorry I have no money with me. When I reach Phoenix City, I promise I will send someone to bring you all I owe and more."

The inn owner knelt in a hurry, pulling down his son with him. The father said, "My lord. We beg your pardon. We did not recognize you. Please come inside, meet my family, and have some tea with us. I will accompany your lordship to Phoenix City."

"What is your name?" Ji Chang asked.

"My name is Shen Jie. This is my son Ho. We have been here for over five generations."

"May I borrow a horse?" Ji Chang asked.

"My lord. We are poor people. How can we afford to keep a horse? But we do have a donkey to help us grind our wheat. We can put a saddle on him if you don't mind. I myself will serve you on your journey," the inn owner said earnestly.

Ji Chang was again on his way back to Phoenix City. It was mid autumn, but the weather had already turned cold. The foliage had changed from green to yellow and red, and some had already fallen. Morning dew had become frost, and the wind was getting sharp.

For seven long years, day and night, Ji Chang had longed for this land of prosperity and tranquility. Mountains, rivers, fields and streams were all still the same, but his beloved son Bo Yi Kao would never again be with him! This saddened his heavy heart.

The closer they came to Phoenix City, the slower the donkey's pace seemed to become. It steadily and patiently plodded on, but no amount of urging would quicken his pace.

*   *   *   *

Brooding in her quarters, Ji Chang's mother suddenly perceived a strange vibration in the rustle of the autumn wind. She burned some incense, then cast a few gold coins to seek enlightenment. The configuration of the coins told her that her son the Grand Duke of the West was coming home! She happily informed her household. The good news spread like wild fire. Everyone in the Western Foothills was mad with excitement and anticipation.

Ji Chang became sadder as he got closer to home. But what was that up ahead? Two red banners were fluttering in the wind!

"Yes, they have come to welcome me home!" Ji Chang exclaimed happily.

Yes, there was Ji Fa, his second son, followed by Grand Counselor Easy Life, General Nimblefoot, and all of the other ministers.

Tears of happiness rained down every face.

Easy Life said, "In the olden days, Cheng Tang was imprisoned by the cruel Xia Jie for a long time. After he was released, he trained his people and finally defeated Xia. Then he founded the Shang Dynasty. Right now, after six hundred years, history is going to repeat itself! Who knows, perhaps your seven years of incarceration will end as happily as Cheng Tang's did."

Ji Chang said, "My dear Grand Counselor is wrong. How can we think of such a parallel? We are loyal to the present king, no matter how unjust and brutal he is. It would be against my heart to ever think of disobeying his order! From now on, please don't ever harbor such disloyal thoughts."

Ji Fa helped his father change into his court regalia and mounted his own chariot. Ji Chang asked the inn owner, who had accompanied him, to come along.

What a joyous procession! The populace came to cheer; they brought gifts and burnt incense. To give the people a better view of himself, Ji Chang got off his chariot and rode on his horse.

As they approached his official residence, Ji Chang saw all his ninety-seven sons lined up in either civil or military attires, kneeling to welcome him home. He was reminded afresh of Bo Yi Kao who would never be among his brothers again! Ji Chang also remembered the meat cakes he was forced to eat. How could he forget? He had never really swallowed them. They had been stuck in his chest ever since.

A sharp pain stabbed at Ji Chang's heart. Tears poured down his cheeks. Letting out a loud cry, "This pain is killing me!" Ji Chang fell from his horse!

Ji Fa caught his father before he hit the ground and rushed him into the house where they tried to revive him. The minutes passed ever so slowly; no one dared to breathe. Then suddenly the Grand Duke threw up a mouthful of slobber. It tumbled to the ground, sprouted four feet and two long ears, turned into a white rabbit and ran away off toward the west. Ji Chang threw up two more slobbers which also turned into white rabbits and ran off to join the first. Yes, they were the flesh of his dear Bo Yi Kao's!

*   *   *   *

Days passed into months as Ji Chang recuperated slowly. On the day he was completely well he met his ministers in the Great Hall. Ji Chang recounted the vicissitude of his seven years of incarceration, the horrible death of dear Bo Yi Kao, his close call at Lin Tong Pass, and the miraculous rescue by Thunder Quaker. Then finally he instructed the Grand Counselor Easy Life to reward the inn owner and send him home.

Easy Life said, "Now that you are safely home, we in the Western Foothills are most gratified. As I see it, it is only a matter of time before a new ruler replaces the accursed King Zhou.

"I am fully aware that you are the most loyal minister in King Zhou's court," Easy Life continued, "but the world is looking for a new leader and they are looking to you. It is a mandate and a responsibility that you are entrusted with, whether you want it or not! As the saying goes, *He who seeks not receives, and he who schemes comes out empty handed.*"

A voice from the west corner of the Great Hall chimed in, "That's right! Now that you are safely home, we should think of how to avenge the murder of our young master Bo Yi Kao! We in the Western Foothills are an army of forty thousand strong, with sixty generals. Why don't we take King Zhou to task. In particular, why not kill Fei Zhong and You Hun, and Daji in the market place, and set up a new, benevolent king? I am sure all under heaven will join in this glorious and noble deed!"

Displeased, Ji Chang said sternly, "Please, gentlemen! I have always believed you are the most loyal and level-headed. How can you harbor such thoughts? Much less utter such talk? The king heads our nation, even when he is wrong. As in a family, a son does not disobey his father when the father makes a mistake! From ancient time, when the king summons, no one dares to delay; When the king says 'die!' no one dares to live! I was so foolish to speak against the king's wishes, and courted seven years of dreadful imprisonment! I am lucky to keep my life and would never utter a word of complaint again. Let us do the best we can under current circumstances, and rejoice with our people in the Western Foothills."

General Nimblefoot said, "My Lord. We do not agree. Our young master took tributes to the king, and the king killed him! I don't think that is fair! It was outright murder without provocation, downright brutal murder without cause."

"I know how you feel, General." Ji Chang said. "My son did not listen to me. Alas, he thought that his love for me would overcome anything!

"To be in harmony with the universe, we should follow the right path, do the right thing. So we must observe the laws of the land to the best of our ability, and treat everyone with justice and benevolence. Let King Zhou do whatever he wants. Sooner or later there are bound to be people who will fight the injustice.

"Now that I am home again, I shall devote myself to teaching my people the meanings of the Five Cardinal Human Relationships and the Three Principles of Social Order. Rejoice with our people in peace and prosperity. We don't want to hear of murderous war cries, to see wanton bloodshed. We don't want any misuse of our national treasury or any unnecessary sacrifice of lives. Let our people devote their energies to the cultivation of fields and virtues. That is what I call true justice."

"By the way," Ji Chang added, "I would like to build an Inspiration Belvedere at the south southwest corner of the Western Foothills. This will enable me to observe the celestial constellations more clearly and set up a more conducive environment for my divination study, which helps guide the course of our country, but I worry about the expense."

Easy Life said, "The belvedere will benefit our country. I am sure our people will not object. In fact, loving you as they do, they will surely want you to have it, even insist that you have it."

"I suggest using volunteer labor for this project," Easy Life continued. "Those who volunteer will be paid a fair wage. They can either work full or part time, so building it will provide opportunities for the energetic ones to earn some extra income."

Ji Chang said, "I am glad you agree. Please get the ball rolling right away."

Soon advertisements for volunteer labor and the rates of pay were posted throughout the Western Foothills.

CHAPTER 23

▼

THE FLYING BEAR

At the public square, the people of the Western Foothills jostled to read what was on the posters the soldiers were putting up. They read:

Announcement
From: Ji Chang, King Wen of the West
To: The populace of the Western Foothills:

"The Western Foothills is a country of law and order, trust and justice where all live in peace and prosperity. Now that I have come home from my seven years of incarceration in the Youli District, I see we still have problems of water shortage and insect control. When I try to pray for seasonal rain and harmonious winds, I find no proper edifice for this and similar functions.

"Recently, I located a parcel of public land on the west corner of the Western Foothills. According to geomancy, this is a most suitable site for an Inspirational Belvedere.

"From this belvedere, I will be in a better position to observe the motions of the stars and thus able to augur the course of our nation.

"To avoid the extra burden this project may cost my people, I have decreed that no one will be conscripted, and all who wish to help will

do so strictly on a voluntary basis. You may work full or part time, and
will be paid a fair wage."

The people were excited over the announcement. They said to each
other, "Why, King Wen wants to pay us to build an Inspirational
Belvedere to benefit us! His benevolence and justice have enabled us to
live in peace and prosperity. We have not yet really shown him how we
appreciate him. This is our chance to do so. Let us build it without
pay!"

Grand Counselor Easy Life reported the people's sentiment to Ji
Chang. Ji Chang said, "Just the same. All workers will be paid as promised. Please get the ball rolling."

*   *   *   *

The building of the Inspirational Belvedere went into high gear:
architectural plans were drawn, ground broken, and the work begun.
Under the able and conscientious direction of the chief engineer and
his assistants, the stone cutters, masons, wood carvers, and myriads of
other artisans and skilled hands worked eagerly and with precision.
Trees were cut and made into logs, stones were quarried and the
ground leveled. Even those without special skills were doing their best
in serving tea, meals and running errands. There was a beehive of activ-
ity, full of cheer and enthusiasm.

In less than ten months, the Chief engineer reported the project was
completed.

Ji Chang was very pleased. He took his officials to inspect this new
Inspirational Belvedere and to meet the people who had contributed
their labors. They found a twenty foot tall, round edifice of three levels,
with the observation and praying platform in the center of the highest.
Many rooms were designed for specific purposes: the observation of
changing weather, the movement of the stars, the study of the Trigram,
the reading of the oracle bones and tortoise shells, and the divination of

impending junctures. All these rooms had bronze incense urns and offering vessels. There were also a kitchen and sleeping quarters for Ji Chang, his ministers, and attendants. From intricately carved and painted beams, columns, windows, and screens, to the well appointed furniture on the beautifully tiled or carpeted floors, everything revealed the care, skills, and love of the workers who had given their best.

But Ji Chang was pensive. Easy Life was concerned. He asked, "Why is my lord so silent?"

Ji Chang said, "I am not unhappy. But this belvedere lacks a water pond to complete the Fire and Water combination required in geomancy. If I add this feature, I worry it would be too much of an additional burden for our people to bear."

Easy Life said, "My lord worries unnecessarily. A pond is a very small work to that of the gargantuan Inspirational Belvedere."

Easy Life related Ji Chang's wish to the workers, who, without a moment's hesitation, shouted, "Don't you worry, my lord. We will get this pond done in no time."

Under the supervision of the Chief Engineer, work began immediately, and enthusiastically. As the workers dug deeper, they came across a set of ancient human bones. Without much thought, they unceremoniously threw the bones away.

"What are they throwing away?" Ji Chang asked.

"Some old human bones," Easy Life said.

"Tell them to gather all the bones in a box and re-bury them in higher ground. It is a sin for me to expose them," Ji Chang said.

The workers cheered, for their King Wen was so kind and benevolent, even to the long dead. They buried the bones as directed.

The sun had now set and it was too dark to return to Phoenix City. Ji Chang and his entourage spent the night in the new Inspirational Belvedere.

In his deep slumber, Ji Chang saw a winged white-faced tiger appear suddenly from nowhere, diving directly toward him. He screamed for help as a roaring flame shot skyward from behind the Inspirational Belvedere.

Ji Chang woke with a start. The night watchman was beating the gong thrice, signaling midnight. It was difficult for Ji Chang to get back to sleep again. He sat up until dawn, pondering. In the morning, Ji Chang described his dream to Easy Life.

Easy Life said, "Congratulations, my lord. It is an omen that my lord will get a wise man as a minister!"

"How so?" Ji Chang asked.

"The Xia King dreamt of the flying bear and later events brought his very able and famous prime minister. Now your winged tiger seems nothing but a flying bear, and the flame behind the Belvedere signifies the unequivocal success of whatever endeavor my lord is going to undertake."

*   *   *   *

Jiang Baby Tooth had been in The Western Foothills for a while now. As a hermit, he had been quietly living in the woods, reading scriptures on terrestrial matters. For food, he would fish the River Pan. He was eighty-six years old, in excellent health, and at perfect ease with the world. He was confident that someday soon, he would be discovered by his true master.

One lovely day, Baby Tooth sat fishing the River Pan under his favorite willow tree. Admiring the clear running water, he sighed, "Only the green mountains and the clear river will forever be the same; all others will change and be gone in time!" He heard a firewood cutter singing:

> Over the hills I chop my wood,
> Carrying my ax and cut whenever I feel I should.
> In front of the cliff, rabbits chasing each other,
> Behind the woods, deer napping without a bother.
> Colorful birds singing on a branch,

Their beautiful songs hard to match.
Passing over the evergreen pine and cedar towers,
Say hello to the plum and peach flowers.
With neither trial nor stress,
Why lament you are not a success?
Selling a load of firewood,
In exchange for a day's food.
Seasonal vegetables are my fancy,
A jug of wine is my delicacy.
Inviting the moon my repast I share,
The enjoyment is no less than that of a millionaire.
I do whatever I please,
Because I am not tied down by a leash.

Finishing his song, the wood cutter put down his load and sat next to Baby Tooth, saying, "Old Uncle. I see you often fishing here. Let us have a chat."

"What kind of a chat?" Baby Tooth asked.

"How about a fisherman and a wood cutter chat?"

"Sounds fine to me," Baby Tooth said.

"That is wonderful." said the wood cutter. "Now let me ask you, what is your name? Where did you come from?"

"I am a native of the Eastern Sea District. My name is Jiang Baby Tooth, by-name Flying Bear."

The wood cutter started to laugh. Baby Tooth asked, "What is your name and where did you come from?"

"My name is Wu Ji. I am a native of the Western Foothills."

"Why do you laugh when I tell you my name?"

"Because you said your by-name is Flying Bear. That is why."

"I don't understand," Baby Tooth persisted.

"From ancient time, only famous people, learned people, or very rich people have by-names. Why do you think you need to have a by-name? I see you fishing here often, that means you don't have a regular job. Why then would you be so pretentious with a by-name?"

Wu Ji lifted up Baby Tooth's fishing line, and found the fishing hook was but a straight needle. Wu Ji said, "How can you catch any fish with a straight needle? Let me tell you how. You put this needle into the fire, when it turns red hot, you beat it into a curved hook. On the hook, you put some bait. When the fish try to eat the bait, you pull up the line to snatch your fish. With a straight needle like this one you are using, don't say in three years, even in one hundred years, you will catch a fish."

Baby Tooth said, "You only know the obvious but not the subtle. I am fishing here, but my aim is not catching fish. If the fish is kind enough to offer itself to me, I am glad to enjoy it. But I will never use cunning to trick it. So far, I would like you to know that I have never been hungry for lack of a catch. Do you know what I am really fishing for? No, not the little fish. I am fishing for a high official position in the court."

Wu Ji again laughed, "You want to be a noble lord with your monkey face? You are pulling my leg. You really are funny."

Baby Tooth said with a smile, "I don't think your face is so good looking either!"

Wu Ji protested, "My face is better looking because I am a happy person. Let me sing you a song:

Selling my firewood on the long street,
Fetch some wine to my mother I treat.
Cutting firewood I know how happy I am,
Forget the restless world outside my cant."

Baby Tooth said, "I don't mean your physical face. I mean your spiritual face. From what I see, it is not very good."

"What do you mean?"

"Your left eye is green and your right eye is red. Today, you will kill someone dead!" Baby Tooth said seriously.

"We were just joking. How can you curse me like this?"

Wu Ji picked up his firewood and left in a huff.

"Be careful, my young friend." Baby Tooth shouted after him.

*   *   *   *

At the South Gate, Wu Ji met Ji Chang and his ministers who were on their way to the Inspirational Belvedere to pray for rain. The soldiers were marching through the City Gate and Wu Ji was trapped in a corner, with hardly enough room to avoid colliding with the soldiers. He tried to make way for them by shifting his load from one shoulder to the other. But alas, his firewood inadvertently pierced a soldier's throat, killing him instantly!

Wu Ji was immediately collared and brought before King Wen. On his horse, Ji Chang asked, "Young man, what is your name? Why did you kill this soldier?"

Wu Ji said, "My lord. I am a subject of the Western Foothills. My name is Wu Ji. When I saw you coming, I tried to make way for your soldiers by shifting my load from one shoulder to the other. It accidentally hit this soldier and killed him. I am terribly sorry. I did not mean it."

Sternly Ji Chang said, "Our law is an eye for an eye. You have taken this man's life, you will have to pay for it with your own."

According to local custom, found only in the law-abiding Western Foothills, a line was scratched on the ground around Wu Ji to serve as his prison. And a stick was planted inside to represent a prison guard. three meals a day would be provided for Wu Ji while he awaited his execution.

Imprisoned thus for three days, Wu Ji worried about his mother, alone at home waiting for him to bring food.

"She must be starved to death by now!" The more he thought, the sadder he felt. He started to weep which soon became a wail.

Easy Life happened to pass by and asked why he was wailing.

Wu Ji said, "My lord. It is justifiable that I should pay my life to the soldier whose life I accidentally took. I have no complaint. But my seventy-eight year old mother is home alone waiting for me. I am her only son and her sole supporter. I fear she must be dead by now without food and care."

Easy Life thought for a moment and said, "I understand. I will ask King Wen to let you go home for now. You have to come back in the autumn for the execution."

Easy Life related this incident to Ji Chang, adding, "Since the killing was accidental, and the widowed mother did not even know her son was in trouble, she could be dead by now."

Ji Chang concurred. Wu Ji was given permission to go home to see his mother until autumn.

*   *   *   *

His mother was standing at the door, sobbing forlornly. When Wu Ji showed up, she was overjoyed. She dried her tears and said, "My son! My son! I was so worried you might have been eaten by a wild tiger or bear in the mountain. I could neither eat nor sleep. Thank heavens you are back!"

Wu Ji embraced his mother. He recounted the happenings of the last three days and, with tears, added, "My mother. I have to go back for my execution in the autumn. I am so sorry to abandon you to fend for yourself!"

Beating her heart, looking at the sky, the mother again wailed, "My son has been dutiful, upright and kind. He was never in any trouble. Why has a curse like this befallen him? Oh, Heaven! Let me die in his stead! When my son dies, I will die for sure."

Wu Ji said, "Mother, now that I think of it, someone did curse me." He told his mother about his encounter with Baby Tooth.

His mother asked, "Who is this Baby Tooth? Instead of being your adversary, I think this Baby Tooth could be your salvation! If he could predict your trouble, he may be able to help you out of it. Go quickly to seek him and beg him to help you! He is the only hope we have."

Chapter 24

▼

A Beautiful Spring Day

Baby Tooth was enjoying his fishing at River Pan when he heard someone calling his name.

"Good morning, Mr. Jiang," Wu Ji called, walking up to Baby Tooth timidly.

"Aye, aren't you the wood cutter Wu Ji?" Baby Tooth turned toward the sound of the voice.

"Yes, sir."

"Didn't you kill someone on the day after you left me?"

At once, Wu Ji knelt in front of Baby Tooth and sobbed out what had happened. He begged Baby Tooth to save him and his mother.

Baby Tooth said, "Well, you killed someone, and you will have to pay for it. How can I save you?"

Wu Ji's continued begging and profound anguish softened Baby Tooth, who finally said, "Well, unless you become my disciple, I can do nothing."

Without hesitation, Wu Ji knocked his head on the ground soundly three times, saying, "My master. Your new disciple is prostrating himself before you!"

Baby Tooth said, "Now that you are my disciple, I have no choice but to try to save you. I don't promise anything. It will depend on your karma whether you deserve to be saved or not."

Baby Tooth then told Wu Ji to go home at once and do this and that, such and so.

Wu Ji raced home. Mother and son followed Baby Tooth's instructions to the most minute detail:

In front of Wu Ji's bed, they dug a hole four feet deep, and long enough for Wu Ji to lie down comfortably. In the evening, Wu Ji laid down in the hole while his mother loosely covered him with straws, then sprinkled a handful of rice on top. Two lit lamps were placed on either end of the hole. That was how Wu Ji spent the night.

Meanwhile, at midnight, Baby Tooth knelt, facing Mount Kunlun. With his hair loose and his sword in his hand, he mumbled an incantation. He was calling up a divine force which would temporarily cover up Wu Ji's star so that to all appearances, Wu Ji was dead.

The next day, Wu Ji returned to his master Baby Tooth.

Baby Tooth said, "From now on, get up one hour earlier, gather your load of wood, and sell it for the day's food. Then come back here to study with me. Cutting and selling firewood should not be your life's work. Now that four hundred dukes have rebelled against King Zhou, you should get ready to be useful."

"Master, which regional dukes have rebelled?" Wu Ji asked.

Baby Tooth said, "Both the East and the South regions. The king's forces have not been able to stop them. I can see from the stars, our Western Foothills will soon also be involved. We must be ready to serve."

Each day, after attending to his mother's needs, Wu Ji spent the rest of his time with Baby Tooth, studying Statecraft and military stratagem.

Autumn came and went, but Wu Ji did not return for his execution. Easy Life, who helped Wu Ji gain his release, was most annoyed and reported it to King Wen. Ji Chang studied the configuration of his cast coins. "Oh, dear!" he exclaimed. "Poor Wu Ji! He has committed suicide! What a pity! I had planned to pardon him on his return since his killing was truly accidental. Poor thing!"

And so the matter was dropped.

*   *   *   *

That winter had been one of the most severe in recent memory. However, under the tutelage of Ji Chang, all in The Western Foothills were able to live in relative ease. Starving people from other regions fled to the Western Foothills in droves. Yes, the Western Foothills became the true haven for those refugees who were lucky enough to reach it.

Spring finally arrived and the frozen earth came back to life once more. Ji Chang invited five hundred of his officials to an outing.

Easy Life said, "My lord. Remember your dream of the flying bear? This could be a good time to seek this wise man while we enjoy the outdoors."

What a beautiful day it was:

> *Lazy breeze gently wafting,*
> *Sleepy rosebuds awaken, blushing.*
> *Golden willows greening with envy,*
> *Arrogant peaches flaming without apology.*
> *Pushing up with fearful energy,*
> *Young grass lining up like a triumphant army.*
> *Butterflies gathering for a masquerade ball,*
> *Each one showing off its best overall.*
> *Some fluttering alone in haughty air,*
> *Others dancing gaily in dazzling pair.*
> *Flaunting their exotic melodies unashamed,*

Spring has sprung, the birds proclaim.
Farmers plowing their fertile ground,
Silk-worm raisers rushing their mulberry round.
Tea-pickers quickly filling their baskets,
Merchants busily earning their profits.
Washing clothes in the river, maidens singing songs new and old,
Playing bamboo flutes, cowherds riding their water buffalo.
Picnic hampers full of chicken dinners,
No one worries about leftovers.
Seniors drinking, commenting on the present, reminiscing about the
past,
Juniors frolicking, as if this day will forever last.
Yes indeed, spring has sprung,
Let us rejoice under the balmy sun.

Ji Chang and his entourage came to a hill surrounded by a fence with red banners fluttering and guarded by soldiers. Inside the fence were hunting eagles and retriever dogs.

Ji Chang asked, "What is this place? Why is it being guarded?"

"This is your hunting ground, especially set up by General Nimble-foot for you to enjoy," Easy Life told Ji Chang.

Sternly, Ji Chang said, "Too bad! On this beautiful day, I've come out to enjoy the greening of the earth, not to harm innocent creatures! In the ancient days, when grains were few, our Sage Kings Yao and Shun did not even eat animal flesh. Now, we have an abundance of grains, vegetables and fruits; we should not kill nature's creatures to satisfy our gluttony. Just think, each creature has its own parents and children! Please remove this hunting set-up immediately!"

Picnickers, both young and old, cheered on hearing Ji Chang's benevolence. Some passing fishermen sang:

Defeating the Xia with many battles great,
Chang Tang's banners brought peace and a new mandate.
Pity six hundred years of glorious reign,

Soon will come to its horrid end.
Red wine flow in Pool and roasted meat swing in Forest,
Starving populace forced to supply their best.
Deer Gallery garnering blood and tear,
Populace living in constant dread and fear.
Putrid odor from within to without spreads,
Diffused by corrupt and unscrupulous aristocrats.
I am but a peon from the district of East Seas,
Washing the pathetic whimpers of the stateless from my polluted ears.
Following the ripples of river and stream,
With my straight needle I fish for my dream.
Heaven high and earth here,
My charioteer will soon appear.

Ji Chang heard the fishermen's song and said to Easy Life, "I can hear an unusual undertone in this song and feel there is a wise man among the singers. I would like to meet him. Please send someone to investigate."

A general shouted from his horse, "Hey, you there! Who taught you this song? My master wants to see him."

All the fishermen knelt and said, "We are law abiding subjects. We fish and sell our catch. We learned it from an old man at the River Pan, about thirty-five miles away."

Ji Chang said, "Thank you. You may go."

A phrase in the song kept haunting Ji Chang. "Washing my ears, to get rid of the whimpers of the stateless." He could not get it out of his thoughts.

Easy Life said, "My lord. Please explain this allusion to us."

Ji Chang said, "This is the story of Sage King Yao courting Shun to succeed him to his throne. King Yao knew his son was unworthy, so he went out to the countryside in search of a virtuous man to take over the governing of the country. King Yao's search led him to a very remote area where he saw a man playing a gourd under a tree.

"Why do you keep turning the gourd like that?" Yao asked the man.

The man replied, "Ah. Don't you see I am enjoying myself? I have seen through the rat race of the Red Dust, and have given up everything to live a life of contentment and tranquility here!"

Yao thought to himself, "This man has no desire for high position and no greed for fortune and fame. He must be a very wise and virtuous man."

So thinking, Yao told the man, "My dear sir. I am no other than Emperor Yao himself. I would like to give you my throne."

On hearing this, the man stomped on his gourd, shattering it. Then he covered his ears and ran to the watering hole to wash them.

A cowherd came by, hollering, "Make way so my buffalo can drink!"

Paying no attention to the cowherd, the man kept on washing his ears.

"What's the matter with your ears?" the cowherd asked. "The way you are washing them, they must be very dirty."

The man replied, "You just don't know! See that man over there? He offered me his throne! Ugh, dirty politics!"

On hearing what the man said, the cowherd took his buffalo away.

"Isn't your buffalo thirsty anymore?" the man shouted.

"Are you kidding? How can I let my buffalo drink that water you have so polluted? I am taking him up stream." the cowherd shouted back.

So, that is the allusion of the whimpers of the stateless. Ji Chang finished his explanation with stories of olden days, how the new replaced the old when the mandate of heaven changed.

Later, a small band of firewood cutters passed by, singing,

Lacking no phoenix or is Qilin [1] rare,
Polluted court is filled with traitors and lackeys and stinking air.
Dragon soaring in the cloud, tiger roaring in the wind,
Populace is urgently seeking the just and wise who will win.
Don't you see toilers and workers,
Rather forever stay humble than serve the wrong masters?
Don't you know before Chang Tang's third visit,

That certain scholar preferred to act stupid?
Plenty of samples of rag to riches,
Why worry forever hanging around water's edge?
Imitating the carefree cowherd riding in style,
Playing the flute to praise the blue sky.
In the mist of bewilderment,
My smiling eyes upon the new Son of Heaven!

On hearing the song, Ji Chang said again, "Among them must be a wise man. Please find him."

The little general again shouted, "Hey you there! Who taught you this song? King Wen likes to meet him."

One of the woodcutters said, "My lord. We learned it from an old man fishing at the River Pan, about ten miles from here."

Then they sang another song:

Spring water gently flowing,
Spring grass eagerly growing.
Gold fish enjoying the spring thaw of the pond,
Has yet to meet the old man fishing at the River Pan.
With a straight needle sits he under the willow tree,
He knows a lot more than he would tell you and me.

Ji Chang sighed, "There must be a wise man here!"

Easy Life now took a closer look at the woodcutters. He immediately recognized Wu Ji, the one who was thought to have committed suicide.

Easy Life cried out, "By jolly! Look, sir. That cunning Wu Ji!"

"Impossible, Wu Ji is dead," Ji Chang said.

"But sir, this is he in person, very much alive!" Easy Life said, pointing at the woodcutter.

Too late to avoid being seen, Wu Ji knelt by the side of the road. Easy Life collared him and brought him to Ji Chang. Ji Chang was especially angry because Wu Ji had loused up his divination.

Ji Chang said to Easy Life, "If the divination is defiled, how else can we depend on it? We must thoroughly examine this fellow to see what other trickery he knows, and he must be punished accordingly."

Wu Ji sobbed out his confession: "My Lord. I am a law abiding subject. Because I accidentally killed someone, I sought help from an old man at the River Pan, about three miles from here. His name is Jiang Baby Tooth, by-name Flying Bear. He told me to do such and so. My kind Lord, even an ant wants to live. I did not want to die when there was no one to take care of my mother. I never meant to fool you."

Easy Life instantly caught the by-name Flying Bear, and said to Ji Chang, "Congratulations, my Lord. Flying Bear is here waiting for you! Please pardon Wu Ji so he can take us to him."

Wu Ji ran with all his might. He led King Wen and his entourage into the woods to find Baby Tooth. But to his consternation, his master was not where he usually was.

"Where does he live?" asked King Wen.

"Over there," said Wu Ji, leading the way to Baby Tooth's hut.

King Wen touched the door but dared not knock lest he disturb the wise man.

A young boy opened the door.

Ji Chang asked, "Is your master home?"

"No, sir," said the boy. "He has gone out with friends."

"What time do you expect him?"

"Hard to say. He may come back right away, or not for a long time," the boy said.

Easy Life said to Ji Chang, "My Lord. I don't think we are doing it correctly. We should not just drop in like this. May I suggest that your lordship go home first, undertake three days of penitence, then make a special trip to seek him. The Sage Emperors Yao and Shun did it this way in the olden days."

"How right you are. Let us go home now," Ji Chang said.

General Nimblefoot said, "Why does my Lord have to do that? We don't even know this Baby Tooth is really a wise man. Why not let me come back tomorrow and take him back with me. If he is what we think he is, then my Lord can bestow on him the honor. If not, we can scold him and let him go."

Easy Life said, "Will you please shut up, General Nimblefoot! Nowadays, the wise and able keep themselves away from the limelight. They are not your everyday bookworms, flaunting their knowledge, prostituting their talents! The truly wise and able deserve our utmost respect. Now, this Flying Bear appeared in King Wen's dream, a most promising omen from heaven. We must not do anything to upset the situation!"

And so everyone in the court of Ji Chang undertook a three-day penitence to cleanse all impurity from their thoughts and bodies. Thus cleansed and in appropriate court regalia, Ji Chang led all his ministers to seek the wise man.

*   *   *   *

Ji Chang sat in his own chariot, while bringing another prepared especially for the use of Baby Tooth. All dismounted as they approached River Pan, and walked softly on foot into the woods.

Fishing at his usual place, Baby Tooth instinctively knew Ji Chang was coming, but pretended not to hear the approach. Baby tooth softly hummed to himself,

> *West wind blowing, white clouds fly,*
> *The year ending, my head turns white.*
> *Songs of five phoenixes heralding the coming of a new mandate,*
> *I fish with a straight needle and will soon land my accolade.*

Ji Chang stood in front of Baby Tooth and said to him, "How is the fishing?"

Baby Tooth immediately knelt.

Ji Chang continued, "I have heard about you and I am here to make your acquaintance. I had come before, but realized I did not follow the correct etiquette. This time we have all purified ourselves. Now that we meet, I feel honored."

Easy Life helped Baby Tooth up. With a broad smile, Baby Tooth said, "I am but an old man. How can I deserve such honor? My book learning is not good enough to help with your administration and my military training is but nil. I really don't know what to say."

Easy Life said, "You are being modest, Mr. Jiang. Under the leadership of King Wen, the Court of the Western Foothills has done penitence for three days to show our sincerity in seeking your help. As you already know, King Zhou grossly abused and neglected his reign, leading the whole kingdom to its worst suffering in the history of this nation. Don't you feel some compassion in your kind heart to help alleviate their distress?

"My master has been so concerned that he neither sleeps well nor has much appetite for food. Now that he has found you, Mr. Jiang, please come to the court of the Western Foothills. With your help, we know there will be ways to save our kingdom from complete ruin."

Easy Life opened the gift package King Wen had brought for Baby Tooth. Baby Tooth nodded to his young disciple, who took the gift into the hut. Easy Life then invited Baby Tooth to ride on the special chariot. Baby Tooth steadfastly refused the honor.

After repeated invitation and repeated refusal, Easy Life suggested a horse. So that was how Baby Tooth, an eighty-six year old man, accompanied King Wen back to the Phoenix City, the capital of the Western Foothills.

People lined the streets to see the wise man whom their King Wen had just discovered. At the Great Hall, Ji Chang invested Baby Tooth as the Prime Minister, and his disciple Wu Ji as a new general.

Notes

1. A Qilin is a mythical animal that is a symbol of loyalty, justice and ability.

▼

DAJI ENTERTAINS HER SPECTER CRONIES

News of Baby Tooth's investiture as Prime Minister of the Western Foothills reached the Floodwater Pass Commander, Han Yong. Without delay, he transmitted this news to the Court of King Zhou. This event could be an early indication of the Western Foothills' intention.

That day, it was Vice Prime Minister Bi Gan's turn to read court reports. Han's report caught Bi Gan's attention immediately.

He thought to himself, "Baby Tooth is a very able and ambitious man. For Ji Chang to invest in him such high position and power means there will soon be trouble. I had better report this to the king."

Bi Gan went directly to the Star-Picking Belvedere. The king asked, "What do you have there?"

"The Commander of the Floodwater Pass reported that Baby Tooth is now Prime Minister of the Western Foothills. Both the Grand Dukes of the East and South are at war with us. If Ji Chang joins in, we will really be in great trouble, especially in view of our empty National Treasury, restless populace, and the inability of the Grand Old Master,

Wen Zhong, to vanquish the North Sea Territory. Something has to be done quickly," Bi Gan said.

"All right, I will talk to the full court tomorrow," said the king.

Next morning, as King Zhou was discussing this vital matter with his ministers, Tiger Duke, the Grand Duke of the North, wanted to see the king.

Turning to Tiger Duke, the king asked, "What do you have here?"

Tiger Duke, whom the king had entrusted with building the Deer Gallery, said proudly, "It has been two years and four months since we started building the Deer Gallery. I am happy to report that it is now completed."

The king was very pleased. "That fast? Without your effort, it would never have been done so quickly. You have my appreciation."

"Thank you. We have been working day and night, never dared to rest."

The king said, "I just received report that Baby Tooth is now Prime Minister of the Western Foothills. What do you think of it?"

"Fancy that," snickered Tiger Duke. "Ji Chang thinks he is a big shot! But he is just a frog looking up from the bottom of a well. And as for Baby Tooth, he is but a provincial swindler with paltry talents. How far can the light of a glowworm shine? You will only legitimatize them if Your Majesty sends an army to face them. Forget about them before Your Majesty becomes the laughing stock of the world!"

Always bored by the business of governing, the king eagerly agreed.

Tiger Duke continued, "Now that the Deer Gallery is completed, we wish Your Majesty's inspection."

"Delighted!" said the king. "You go ahead and I and my queen will come right away."

*   *   *   *

With a huge entourage, King Zhou and Daji went to the Deer Gallery in the Eight-Direction Chariot, a gift brought by the late Bo Yi

Kao, the number one son of the Grand Duke of the West. What an edifice Deer Gallery was:

The forty-nine foot tall structure of green marble gleamed in the sun. Supporting green marble columns lined up like a well ordered forest, while the yellow tile roof reached to the sky. Carved yellow marble steps led up to an open terrace with a yellow marble floor and red marble balustrades. Beyond, was the Great Hall. The ceiling was of red coral, pearls and other precious jewels, to reflect the sun and the moon. Luscious soft silk brocade satin was everywhere.

After the formal inspection, all the officials were dismissed. The king reminded Daji, "You said heavenly maidens would join us in our celebration every night when the Deer Gallery was completed. Are they coming tonight?"

The ever so cunning Daji had lied about the heavenly maidens. She quickly thought of something, and said with aplomb, "Heavenly maidens will come only during the full moon. We must be patient. They will come, I am sure, when the time is right."

The king said, "How wonderful. Today is the tenth; that means only five more days to full moon. Oh, I can hardly wait."

Two days before the full moon, Queen Daji thought of a plan to hoodwink the king. That night, after getting the king dead drunk, she changed back to a fox and stole back to her old haunt, the tomb of the Yellow Emperor.

There she found her fox cohorts whom she considered as her fox children. Many had also achieved the specter status, but many were still young and learning the tricks.

The most accomplished specter among them was not a fox but the Nine-Headed Pheasant named Splendor, whom Daji, a thousand year old fox herself, considered her best friend.

Seeing the Thousand-Year-Old Vixen, the Nine-Headed Pheasant Splendor said, "Welcome back. You are enjoying a good life in the palace, with an endless supply of human flesh and blood. Why are you here tonight?"

"My dear friends," said the Thousand-Year-Old Vixen. "I have never forgotten any of you even though I am in the palace. Now that the Deer Gallery is completed, I would like to invite all of you to a banquet. Any of you who can change into human shape may come. Others will have to wait."

Splendor tallied a total of thirty-nine who could come to the banquet.

After giving them detailed instructions, the Thousand-Year-Old Vixen rushed back to her palace and changed back to Daji, lying next to the snoring king.

To King Zhou, time seemed to pass ever so slowly. He kept asking, "Will the heavenly maidens be here tomorrow? It will be full moon."

"Let us hope so," Daji said, and ordered the preparation of a most sumptuous banquet to be held on the terrace of the Deer Gallery. Thirty-nine tables, one for each guest, were set in three rows of thirteen. Daji asked the king to summon a high ranking minister who was known to have a large capacity for wine, to serve as wine tender.

The king said, "As far as I know, only Vice Prime Minister, Prince Bi Gan can qualify."

Bi Gan was summoned but did not understand what the king was talking about. The king told him directly, "Never mind what. You just come tomorrow evening to the Deer Gallery to serve the heavenly maidens."

*   *   *   *

The day of the full moon finally arrived; everything for the banquet was in order. So restless was the king, he appeared to be sitting on an ant hill. While waiting for the evening to come, he cursed the sun for not yielding the day to the moon.

Daji said, "Now, look here, Your Majesty. When the heavenly maidens arrive, it would be best that Your Majesty stay inside until they wish to see you. Otherwise, they may refuse to land."

The king submitted to Daji's every trick and demand. Finally, the moon came up. There came a sudden breeze. Daji rushed the king inside as her guests began to land at the Deer Gallery terrace. They were her specter cronies. They all had the ability to change their external form and to travel by air. On Daji's instructions, some came as young maidens, and some as noble matrons. All were beautiful and in their best finery, and a few even came in rather attractive nun's attires.

With a pounding heart, the king peeped through the bead curtain. So excited was he that he wet his royal pants.

Splendor, the leader of the group said, "Salutations, dear king. We thank you for your invitation."

Bi Gan was now to serve the wine. In the dim moonlight, the visitors were truly most beautiful. Could they really be heavenly maidens? Bi Gan was confused.

From behind the bead curtain, Daji ordered Bi Gan to drink a cup of wine with each guest. Poor Bi Gan, a prince, and the highest ranking minister, had to obey Daji's order.

Splendor said, "May we know who you are?"

"I am the Vice Prime Minister, Prince Bi Gan."

"We appreciate your being here. Cheers! Let us drink with the big cups."

Bi Gan could not refuse and drank anew. But as he went from one guest to another, he smelled a distinct body odor. Bi Gan thought to himself, "Strange. Heavenly people are supposed to be purity itself. Why this unmistakable fox odor? Well, when the morals of a kingdom collapses, even heavenly beings stink!"

As the third round of wine was served, the guests began to become mellow and their control became lax. Their tails were first to show, and the fox odor was now overwhelming. But the nauseated Bi Gan dared not show his feelings. Methodically, he continued to serve the guests. As they got more intoxicated, more tails were wagging under the tables.

Looking through the curtain, Daji suddenly realized the younger specters were losing control and she quickly dismissed Bi Gan.

Leaving the Deer Gallery behind, Bi Gan hurried to the Noon Gate where he bumped into the special night patrol, led by Lord of National Security, Prince Yellow Flying Tiger.

"What emergency kept you here so late?" Yellow Flying Tiger asked.

Bi Gan related the whole episode in detail, especially the fox odor and the waving tails.

Yellow Flying Tiger said, "You go on home and take a bath. I will take care of the matter."

Anticipating these specters to be too drunk to fly home with the wind, Yellow Flying Tiger ordered four trusted generals each to lead twenty of his own household servants to stand guard at the four gates of the city. They were to follow the specters back to their lair.

When all specters had returned to their lair in the ancient tomb of the Yellow Emperor, Yellow Flying Tiger immediately had huge piles of firewood stacked against all entrances and set them on fire! By noon next morning, his men reported the total destruction of the lair.

Bi Gan and Yellow Flying Tiger went out there to see for themselves. They found many specters were burnt to cinders. But the fur of a few older ones was intact.

Bi Gan said, "Why not use these skins to make a wrap for the king? It may shock him out of his stupor!"

CHAPTER 26

▼

BI GAN LOSES HIS HEART

On the first snow, Vice Prime Minister, Prince Bi Gan went to the Deer Gallery to see the king. The king asked, "What have you here?"

Bi Gan said with a beguiling smile, "The snow comes early this year. It may mean another severe winter. Your Majesty's residence in the Deer Gallery is so high, it must be much colder than in your other palaces. So I had this fur robe made especially for you, as a token of my love and respect."

The king said, "You, my royal uncle, are older. You will need this wrap much more. Why, your giving it to me indeed shows you really love me. Thank you. Put it on me."

Bi Gan opened the red lacquer gift box, carefully took out a robe of gold silk satin, beautifully lined with fox fur. He put the robe on the king. With unexpected pleasure the king felt the instant warmth engulfing him.

The king exclaimed, "Why had I not thought of such a coat before!"

So delighted was the king, he invited his uncle to have a few drinks with him. Bi Gan thanked the king and took his leave after enjoying his host's hospitality.

Meanwhile, through the bead curtain, Daji followed Bi Gan's every move. Being a fox specter, she sensed a menacing threat from Bi Gan, like a knife stabbing her heart.

She cursed Bi Gan under her breath, "Damn you, Bi Gan! This time you have overplayed your hand! Just you wait! You will never get away with this!"

She quickly regained her composure as the king walked in to show her the new robe. "Look what Bi Gan just brought me. It is so light and warm. I am so delighted."

"Yes, it is indeed very good looking. However, may I say something?"

"Of course," said the king. "You would like to have one just like it?"

"No, thank you," said Daji. "I just wish to point out to Your Majesty that you, being the Son of Heaven, you would be lowering yourself to the level of the peons when you wear fox fur!"

The king conceded this dubious point and had the new coat put away. Meanwhile, Daji thought of a scheme to kill Bi Gan: Mind you, not just to kill him, but to make him suffer great pain as well!

*   *   *   *

One day she skipped some of her make-up in order to look a shade older and rather haggard. The king was shocked, thinking to himself, "What has happened to my Beauty?"

"Sire, what is the matter? Why are you staring at me like this?" Daji asked. "Is it because I am getting old and ugly?"

"Oh, nothing of the sort." The king lied to cover his embarrassment. "Your beauty is as lovely as ever!"

Daji said, "Beauty is in the eye of the beholder. Because you love me, that makes you think I am beautiful. However, compared to my adopted little sister Splendor, I am just a plain person. Splendor is the true beauty in my family."

Instantaneously excited, but purposefully showing little interest, the king asked, "Where is your younger sister now? Why have I never heard of her?"

Daji said, "My sister is a nun. When we were both young, living in my father's house, we loved each other dearly, just like real sisters. Then she decided to go to the mountains to be a nun. We cried at parting. She promised me that once she learned her magic, she would send me a magic incense so that whenever I wished to see her, I could simply burn the incense to summon her. I received the incense, but I have never had an occasion to use it because I was summoned to serve Your Majesty."

"Quick, get the incense out! I want to meet her!" the king said excitedly, barely containing himself.

"Now, now. Please. My sister is a nun and we cannot simply just summon her. Sire, Your Majesty must be patient. Tomorrow night after I take my specially perfumed bath, I will set out a table of luscious fruits before I burn that magic incense."

As the king drooled over the prospect of meeting a new beauty, he drank more than usual and was soon helped to bed.

*   *   *   *

Reverting again to a fox specter, Daji sneaked out of the palace grounds and rushed to her old lair. She found it in ruin and all her fox cronies burnt to death except the Nine-Headed Pheasant, who was indeed a very established specter. Together, the two old friends hashed over that hateful event.

"Did you know they made a robe out of the fox skins?" said the Nine-Headed Pheasant indignantly.

"Yes. That is why I am here. We must do something to avenge their death. I need your help, and in turn you will enjoy an unlimited supply of human flesh and blood at the palace. You may also enjoy some of the king's essence. Mind you though, the king is my property and only on occasion are you to sleep with him!"

"You know I can never refuse your request, especially with such attractive fringe benefits," said the Nine-Headed Pheasant. "Of course I will come."

*   *   *   *

So anxious to meet this Splendor, the king counted hours and minutes the next day, again cursing the sun for not yielding its place to the moon in the sky. Oh, how long must he suffer this torture of a parched man's longing for a drop of heavenly nectar?

After much urging from the king, Daji got ready to light the magic incense.

She said, "Your Majesty. Please listen to me. We must handle this visit carefully. My sister is a nun and she may not like to meet with a man. When she first appears, will you please stay away so that I can explain the matter to her? Otherwise, she might just leave and never return again."

Then suddenly, a wind came from nowhere, and the bright moon was covered by a huge black shadow.

Daji said, "Please, Sire. Go inside quickly. I think Splendor has arrived."

As the jade ornaments clinked musically, there came the soft sound of someone landing. A most sensual female voice called out, "My dear sister. My salute."

Now the moon shone once more. Peeping through the curtain, King Zhou saw, in the light of the silvery moon, a most lovely lady in a nun's attire. She wore a bright red robe with the designs of Trigram on both front and back; around her slim waist was a silk sash that accentuated those extra full bosoms; her little feet encased in red linen shoes.

Her fair complexion was aglow with translucency, and her eyes were deep blue like an autumn lake.

* * * *

We recall that this enchanting Splendor was of course the Nine-Headed Pheasant specter, one of the three specters chosen by the Snail Goddess Nu Wa Niang Niang to undermine King Zhou's reign.

Among the three specters, the Thousand-Year-Old Vixen was the most cunning. She had killed the real Daji, while Daji was on her way to meet the king; and had usurped Daji's body and became Daji to all the world. The Thousand-Year-Old Vixen thus became the king's favorite woman. Yes, she did bewitch him totally as decreed by the Snail Goddess. But she completely forgot the Snail Goddess's proscription not to harm anyone but King Zhou. All under heaven were suffering from her inhuman cruelty. Many of the nation's best minds were killed because they saw through her ungodliness. And the flesh and blood of many of the palace maidens were the nightly repast she needed to sustain her specter vitality.

Of the other two specters, the Fat-belly Guitar Jade Pipa was vanquished by Baby Tooth. Even though Daji had managed to renew its life, Jade Pipa had not regained her full evil power.

Now the Nine-Headed Pheasant, Splendor, joined the Thousand-Year-Old Vixen to bewitch King Zhou, to undermine his reign, as the Snail Goddess decreed. But Splendor too had forgotten the Snail Goddess's decree to harm no others.

* * * *

Welcoming Splendor, Daji said, "My little sister. You have come!"

"I would have come much earlier, but I did not dare to disturb you," said Splendor.

A feast was spread. The two sisters seemed to have so much to catch up on after all these years of separation.

Watching through the curtain, the king was getting very restless. He so wanted to hold Splendor in his arms! He made little coughing sounds, hoping Daji would notice his impatience.

Daji turned her head toward the curtain, winked at the king and said to Splendor, "My dear little sister. I have a favor to ask but I don't know whether it is appropriate."

Splendor said amiably, "Please, my elder sister. Ask me anything you have in mind."

"The other day," Daji said, "I mentioned you to the king. He dearly wants to meet you."

"Oh, it will be rather awkward," replied Splendor. "I am a woman, how can I dine with a man?"

Daji said, "You are wrong, my little sister. You are a nun, above the Red Dust and therefore not bound by such convention. And you are my sister, the king is my husband, and therefore he is your brother-in-law. A brother-in-law is equal to a brother. How can it matter for you to dine with your brother? Moreover, the king is the Son of Heaven, he owns the four seas and everything within them. Therefore, he owns you as well. Why then, how can you refuse to see him?"

Playing along, Splendor said, "My elder sister, you are right. Of course I will be delighted to see the king."

Without waiting to be invited, the king walked out, and nodded to Splendor. In return, Splendor lightly returned the nod and said, "Your Majesty. Please be seated."

The king could not take his eyes off Splendor. Yes, She looked more beautiful than any moon maidens could ever be! Look at that red cherry mouth! Look at those peach chin and apricot cheeks! Look at those deep fluid eyes and long moth eyebrows! Look at the well coiffed indigo blue hair! Look at that creamy fair complexion and the slender long neck! And above all, look at that voluptuous body inside the nun's costume! And finally look at those dainty feet!

Daji saw through the king's lewd craving. Following her game plan, she discreetly left him alone with Splendor.

The king poured a cup of wine and presented it to Splendor. As she was taking the cup, he squeezed her hand. Splendor smiled but did not protest.

The king said, "Let me take you for a walk around the terrace."

"As Your Majesty wishes," cooed Splendor.

As they walked, the king said, "Why not give up that mountain cave and come join me in the palace, and enjoy the best life has to offer? I would love to have you by my side forever and ever!"

Splendor did not make a sound but kept on smiling. King Zhou's hand which was first holding Splendor's waist, had slyly crept up to hold her breasts. What breasts! Two soft mounds so full of warmth and bounce! Again Splendor did not seem to mind. Quickly the king took her into a nearby room and, oh me oh my, what a storm of clouds and rain they generated!

Much later, as they were putting their clothes back on, Daji walked in and feigned surprise at Splendor's shortness of breath and disheveled hair.

Daji asked, "What is the matter, my little sister?"

The king said, "To tell you the truth, Splendor has agreed to give up her mountain cave and come to serve me. Now with the two of you by my side, I am the happiest king in the world! I do appreciate your getting Splendor here."

New feast was spread, and many new jugs of wine. They drank until dawn.

Now Splendor shared the king's bed with Daji. Day and night, lust and wine occupied the king's full attention. Communication between the inner palace and the outside became nonexistent, even as the war with the four hundred rebellious regional dukes raged on.

*   *   *   *

Although given full responsibility of the defense of the kingdom, Lord of the National Security, Prince Yellow Flying Tiger, could do just so much without the direct involvement of the king. Communiqués from all fronts were nothing but bad news. The forces of the Grand Duke of the East had taken the Wild Goose Mountain, and were now coming down on Old Pond Pass. In the south, the forces of the Grand Duke of the South were gaining victory after victory. And still there was not much news from the Grand Old Master, Wen Zhong, in the North Sea where rebellion had festered for too long.

The forty-eight thousand troops garrisoned at the Capital City, Morning Song, were the only force that Yellow Flying Tiger could count on to defend the Capital, and the king. But the king, oblivious to all, couldn't care less.

*   *   *   *

One morning, in accordance with a prearranged plan, as the two specters were eating breakfast in the Deer Gallery, Daji suddenly screamed and fell to the floor. Her face turned purple, her eyes closed tightly and she vomited much blood. It appeared she was dying in short order.

The king was scared out of his wits while Splendor calmly said, "Oh, dear. My elder sister's old affliction has returned."

"Do you know what it is?" the king asked anxiously.

"Yes, of course," sighed Splendor. "When we were young, my elder sister suffered often of a heart ailment. But we had a most remarkable physician, who really was a deity incarnated. He would prescribe a bowl of soup made of a slice of a magic human heart. Every time my sister drank that, she recovered promptly."

"Quick, send for the physician!" said the king.

"Oh, no," said Splendor. "He lives so far way, it would take at least one month for him to get here!"

"What else can we do?"

"As I see it, the only thing we can do to save my sister's life is to find a magic heart in this capital city. Let me see," said Splendor, as she continued her part of this deadly game. "I have learned how to calculate this kind of matter."

With her fingers, Splendor went through the motions of a calculation and said, "Well, according to my figures, the only person in the capital city who possesses such a magic heart is the Vice Prime Minister, Prince Bi Gan. But I wonder if he would consent to give up a slice of his heart."

"Why, of course he will," said the king. "He is not only a high ranking minister, he is also my uncle and he loves me. I am sure he would want to help my dear queen." So saying, the king summoned Bi Gan to the Deer Gallery.

The urgent summons from the king interrupted Bi Gan in his deliberation of the affairs of the kingdom. But before he could get up to answer the first messenger, a second summons arrived, then four more, one right after the other. Bi Gan could not comprehend the nature of such an emergency.

He asked the sixth messenger, who said, "My dear Prime Minister. Unusual things are going on in the Deer Gallery. Most recently, the king found a new love, a nun named Splendor who supposedly is the younger sister of Queen Su. No one outside of the Deer Gallery knows about this. Today, Queen Su suddenly fell sick. Splendor told the king that only a bowl of soup made from a special kind of human heart can help the queen. And that only your lordship possesses such a heart. It is urgent that you go to the Deer Gallery so that they can cut a slice of your heart to make the soup."

Hiding his fear and indignation, Bi Gan dismissed the messenger calmly. He then went to his inner halls to tell his wife the nature of the king's summons.

In tears, he said, "Please take good care of yourself and the children, my dear wife. After I am gone, do remember my teaching and bring up our children accordingly. Try never get into trouble. There will not be anyone who can help you!"

His prescient son, who was standing by, reminded his father of Baby Tooth's parting gift.

"Please don't despair, my dear father. Don't you remember what Baby Tooth once told you? He said when we are in trouble, look under the stone inkwell for the letter he left us. We are in trouble now. Let's read Baby Tooth's letter before you go to see the king."

After reading the letter, Bi Gan said, "Quick! Please bring me some fire."

He burnt the juju Baby Tooth left for him, put the ash into a bowl of water and drank it. Then he left for the Deer Gallery.

*   *   *   *

At the Noon Gate, he met yet another king's messenger. Many ministers had heard of the summons. All of them wanted to know the nature of these urgent calls. They gathered at the Noon Gate and went to the Deer Gallery with Bi Gan. Bi Gan was ordered to go up to the Deer Gallery at once.

The king said, "My royal wife is very sick, and urgently needs a slice of the magic heart to save her life. You are the only person in the capital with such a heart. I am asking you for a slice of it. You will be amply rewarded for your good deed."

Bi Gan said, "What do you mean a slice of the magic heart? What is a magic heart?"

The king said, "It is your heart. The one inside your chest."

Bi Gan was incensed. "How can a man pull out his heart? The heart is his life. Without his heart, he would certainly die. I have not committed any crime to deserve such punishment!"

The king whined, "I thought you loved me! I only want a slice of your heart, not the whole thing. Don't you think it is your duty to contribute to the welfare of my queen? Without this slice, she will surely die. How can you refuse?"

Bi Gan was really angry now. He said, "You damned fool! How dare you take my life because of that harlot of yours? Our kingdom is rotten and fast declining. And I am the one who has been trying to repair that rot. Without Bi Gan, there would not be a kingdom today!"

The king shouted at Bi Gan, then to the Palace guards, "When the king says 'die!,' how dare you live? Take out his heart!"

As the guards rushed over, Bi Gan said, "Daji, you filthy wench. I die but I can face my ancestors without shame. But you will be burnt by the Triple Whammy Fire and forever rot in hell!"

Bi Gan shouted for a sword. Holding the sword and looking up at the sky, he said, "My Honorable ancestors. King Zhou, your twenty-ninth generation offspring is ready to terminate the six hundredth year of Cheng Tang's reign, not because I have not tried to stop him."

So saying, Bi Gan opened his robe and plunged the sword into his chest, pulled out his heart and threw it on the floor! All this without losing a drop of blood because of Baby Tooth's magic juju.

Pulling back his robe, Bi Gan ran down the Deer Gallery, jumped on his horse and raced out of the North Gate, not saying a word.

CHAPTER 27

▼

GRAND OLD MASTER'S TEN RECOMMENDATIONS

Sustained by Baby Tooth's magic, Bi Gan pushed his horse at top speed. But he suddenly reined in at the sight of a woman hawking water spinach [1].

Bi Gan asked the woman, "Can a man live without his heart?"

The woman said, "The water spinach have no heart but they live. A man with no heart will die!"

The spell of Baby Tooth's Juju was broken! Bi Gan let out a scream, fell from his horse and expired with his eyes wide open, looking west.

Bi Gan's death shocked the kingdom. A funeral pavilion was built at the site where he died, and white mourning curtains were hung. White banners fluttered as various ministers came to pay their last respects. Bi Gan had been one of the most loved ministers.

A sudden excitement stirred among the mourning crowd: News that Grand Old Master had triumphantly returned, sparking a rush of the ministers from Bi Gan's wake to the Ten-Mile-Welcome Gazebo. There they were told that the Grand Old Master would meet them at the Noon Gate.

*   *   *   *

Grand Old Master Wen Zhong was destined to play a very important role in the scheme of things Heaven and Earth. By the decree of
Jade Emperor of Heaven, Wen Zhong was given an extra eye. Located
on his forehead, the magic eye could, among other things, pierce
through lies and falsehoods. He was also given an imposing and fierce
physique.

His mount was the miraculous black qilin, a mythical animal with
the build of a horse and the appearance of a dragon that could both
run and fly. Grand Old Master, flying over the funeral pavilion, was
shocked to learn of Bi Gan's death. He was even more shocked when
he entered the city and saw the gargantuan Deer Gallery piercing the
sky. At Noon Gate, he smiled as he saluted his waiting colleagues.

As he entered the Nine Hall Court, Grand Old Master saw
inch-thick dust and the mountain-high unread memos. He pointed to
the unholy bronze toaster in the corner and asked, "What is it?"

Yellow Flying Tiger recounted briefly the happenings of the fifteen
years since Wen Zhong was sent to the North Sea: the tortures, the
deaths, the blood, the tears, and the suffering as well as the tales of
strange banquets and the most recent death of the Vice Prime Minister, Prince Bi Gan.

As the story unfolded, the Grand Old Master became increasingly
enraged, his magic eye wide open, probing and searching.

"Beat the Gong!" he roared. "We want to see the king!"

*   *   *   *

Meanwhile, Daji continued to play her game of regaining her
beauty. She was very pleased with herself. A specter of her caliber could
easily manipulate its shapes and appearance, and the Thousand-Year-Old Vixen was particularly adept at her role. And with the

backing of the Snail Goddess Nu Wa Niang Niang's decree, the Thousand-Year-Old Vixen had no fear of anyone or anything!

But the Snail Goddess had also decreed that no one but King Zhou was to be hurt. And this constraint the Thousand-Year-Old Vixen specter had completely ignored.

Now virtually a puppet, King Zhou attended only to his pleasures. On hearing of the return of the Grand Old Master, he was jarred into a long silence. Finally he said, "Get me ready to go to the Throne-Room in the Nine Hall Court."

The king said to Grand Old Master Wen Zhong, "I am so delighted you are finally home with triumphant news. You have my appreciation."

Grand Old Master said, "After fifteen years of very hard fighting, I am glad to report a total victory. All rebellious giants and monsters of the North Sea are now vanquished. However, in these fifteen years, I have heard many rumors about Your Majesty not attending to the business of the governing. Now that we are face to face, tell me personally whether they have any truth in them."

The king said, "All rumors! All lies! I assure you. Everything is all right."

"Are you telling me the truth?" asked Grand Old Master, his magic eye focusing on the king.

"Well," the king stammered, "The Grand Duke of the East and his daughter Queen Jiang tried to assassinate me and to usurp my throne. So they were punished. The Grand Duke of the South rebelled against me, so, he too was punished. Now their sons are fighting me. They should be punished also."

"All these may be allegations. Were there any witnesses? Did you give them a fair trial?" Grand old Master persisted.

The king had nothing to say. Grand Old Master continued, "What is that ugly object in the corner over there?"

The king said, "Oh, that is the Bronze Toaster, designed by my new queen Su Daji. You just don't know how badly some of the grand counselors behaved. They did not seem to remember that I am the Son of Heaven, owner of the four seas and the head of the kingdom. They used foul language to humiliate me and the throne."

"And what is that monstrous green marble edifice over there?" Wen Zhong asked.

The king said, "Ah, that is the Deer Gallery. You know, during the hot weather, I need a higher place to catch some breeze. There really is nothing wrong for the Son of Heaven to have a little comfort. Is it not? Besides, from there, I can see near and far, the better to govern my kingdom."

Indignation filled Grand Old Master's heart. "Your Majesty has not faced reality for a long, long time. All these years, you lived in a dream world, in a self-imposed isolation. Permit me to look into the whole situation and report to Your Majesty when I reach the heart of the matter."

After the king left, Grand Old Master said to his colleagues, "Come to my residence and we will map out some plans to save our nation."

*   *   *   *

"My dear colleagues," said the Grand Old Master, "I was asked by our King Da Yi on his deathbed to oversee the care of the kingdom. I gave him my solemn promise and I will do so without fear from anyone! I would like to hear what happened during my absence."

A counselor said, "My Lord. We are too many mouths wanting to speak. To save time and confusion, I suggest you let Lord of the National Security, Prince Yellow Flying Tiger, sum up the situation."

All agreed. Yellow Flying Tiger rose and related the events, starting with how during a pilgrimage to the Temple of the Snail Goddess Nu Wu Niang Niang, the King had insulted the Goddess with his dirty poem. How the rebellion of the Ji Region, and the presentation of Daji, daughter of Su Hu, Duke of Ji Regional, came about. The subsequent visit of the Cloud Dweller; the murder of Royal Astrologer Du;

the torture death of the Grand Counselors; the false accusation against Queen Jiang and her horrible death; the disappearance of the two young princes; and the martyr deaths of the Prime Minister Shang Rong and Grand Counselor Zhao Qi. Then there was the execution of the two Grand Dukes of the East and South; the imprisonment of the Grand Duke of the West. The building of the Snake Pit, the Wine Pool, and the Meat Forest. And finally the building of the Deer Gallery, the lavish entertainment of the fox specters and their kind, and how Prince Bi Gan discovered the fox specter lair which could have led to his subsequent murder.

"Right now the king is secretly consorting with his new concubine, a nun who seems to have come from nowhere," Yellow Flying Tiger concluded.

After hearing the report, Grand Old Master ordered that he be not disturbed for three days, promising his recommendations on the fourth.

On that day, everyone came extra early for the morning session with the king.

Routinely the king said, "Anyone with reports report. Or you may all go back to your duties."

Grand Old Master stepped out. "Sire. I do have a petition." So saying, he presented it to the king.

The king dared not ignore it. The first few paragraphs were nearly the same as those that had cost the lives of several ministers and counselors. The king was getting more and more uneasy as he read, but dared not display a childish temper tantrum.

To prompt the king to act at once on the recommendations, the Grand Old Master had brought writing brush and ink for the king to write his approval under each listed recommendation.

The following were the recommendations and the king's dispositions:

1. *Tear down the Deer Gallery to mollify the populace.*

No, not approved. The Deer Gallery has cost a lot to build. It would be too big a waste to dismantle it. Let's talk about it later.

2. *Get rid of the Bronze Toaster so that loyal ministers dare to tell the truth.*

    Approved.

3. *Fill up the Snake Pit so that the palace servants can live in peace.*

    Approved.

4. *Fill up the Wine Pool with earth and dismantle the Meat Forest to spare the people of this extra burden to supplying wine and meat.*

    Approved.

5. *Kill Daji and thus eliminate the source of all the cruelty and trouble.*

    No, not approved. How can we kill someone who has never done anything wrong? She is such a virtuous person and has served me so lovingly. We will discuss this later.

6. *Kill both Higher Counselors Fei Zhong and You Hun to pacify the populace.*

    No. We cannot do that. They have served me so loyally and brilliantly. We will discuss this later.

7. *Open up the National Grain House to feed the starving people.*

    Approved.

8. *Send envoys to seek truce with both the East and South regions.*

    Approved.

9. *Send scouts to the countryside to recruit the wise and able to fill the gaps left by the murdered ministers.*

    Approved.

10. *Open all roads and mountain passes so that the people can travel freely and encourage commerce among all regions*

Approved.

Dissatisfied by the king's rejection of three of his recommendations, the Grand Old Master became insistent, "Sire. Your decision is not complete. Recommendation Number One, to tear down the Deer Gallery, is a must. It cost so much suffering to build it. Letting it stand one more day would mean one more day of hate and curses.

Recommendation Number Five cannot be delayed. Daji is the sole cause of your bewilderment and befuddlement. She is the designer of cruel torture devices, the instigator of the murder of Queen Jiang and other loyal ministers, the squanderer of the National Treasures and the unholy polluter of the principles and morals of the kingdom. One more day she is in the palace means one more step in bringing our kingdom closer to ruin. She must be dispatched at once.

Recommendation Number Six. Executing both Fei Zhong and You Hun is urgent. These two corrupt, unscrupulous parasites milked the country for their own gain, and in the name of the king abused their positions for profit. They must be executed immediately in the market place to sooth the hatred and resentment of the populace. We cannot delay this recommendation!"

The king said timidly, "Why, of your ten recommendations, I have already approved seven. I think you have done well. Let's not talk about the other three now."

Grand Old Master Wen Zhong said, "No, Sire. We must not let these three go undecided. They are vital issues!"

Just then, the arrogant Higher Counselor Fei Zhong stepped out for the king's attention. But the Grand Old Master did not recognize him. "Who are you?" he asked.

"I am Higher Counselor Fei Zhong!"

"So YOU are the infamous Fei Zhong! What do you have to say?"

"I say that you, Grand Old Master, with pen in hand, are forcing the king. Is this proper procedure? You insisted that the king get rid of the queen, who is virtuous and has never done anything wrong. Is that not presumptuous? You recommended the execution of two higher counselors who served the king brilliantly and loyally. Is that not lawless and barbaric? I think you are bullying our king, and that is a crime in itself!"

Grand Old Master Wen Zhong's magic eye flashed in red anger, his long beard stood erect. "How dare you!" he shouted. "You have befuddled the king long enough, and are still trying, even in my presence."

Swift as lightning, Grand Old Master slapped Fei Zhong who spiraled downward as his face turned black and blue.

The foolhardy You Hun now jumped up and shouted, "Your Majesty. How can you allow anyone to hit your most loyal minister in your presence? It is like hitting Your majesty personally!"

The Grand Old Master asked, "Who are you?"

"I am Higher Counselor You Hun!"

"So YOU are the other one of the evil pair!" Grand Old Master laughed. Without any ado, Grand Old master slapped him so hard, You Hun was thrown twenty feet!

"Take these two to the Noon Gate for execution immediately!" Grand Old Master commanded.

The king sat silently, not daring to say a word. But all the ministers were secretly enjoying the scene.

The king thought to himself, "I wish they had not confronted the Grand Old Master head on. Even I do not dare to cross him!"

Grand Old Master now turned toward the king and said, "I have ordered the execution of these two scoundrels. Please give your edict, Sire."

The king would not part with his favorites. He pleaded, "Please, my Grand Old Master. Both Fei Zhong and You Hun have never done anything against me. I don't think we should kill them."

Grand Old Master changed his tactics. "All right. We will talk about these three recommendations later. Meanwhile, put these two dogs in prison!"

And so Daji, the two higher counselors and the Deer Gallery had their reprieves—at least for now.

No sooner had the Grand Old Master arrived home than he received an urgent report from the East Sea that Duke of Pingling has rebelled.

Yellow Flying Tiger came to see the Grand Old Master immediately.

The Grand Old Master asked, "Would you or should I squash him?"

"It is up to you," replied Yellow Flying Tiger.

Grand Old Master said, "It is better that I go. It should not take me too long for this campaign."

The king was very relieved to hear the Grand Old Master was again going to war. He gave the Grand Old Master his Battle Ax. When the troops were ready to leave, the king presented him with a cup of wine in a mock gesture of appreciation.

Taking the wine from the king, Grand Old Master turned around and gave it to Yellow Flying Tiger, saying, "Your Majesty. I think this cup should go to the Lord of National Security, Prince Yellow Flying Tiger."

After Yellow Flying Tiger drank it, the Grand Old Master said, "Now that I am going away, you are the only one here to take care of the country. Please do your best and tell the king the truth."

Turning to the king, Grand Old Master said, "I am sorry, but I will be gone for no more than half a year. Please, Sire. Listen to your good ministers, and especially to Prince Yellow Flying Tiger for advice. I wish you well."

Amid the sounds of trumpets and cannons, the Grand Old Master was once again on the war path.

Notes

1. Water spinach, (Ipomoea aquatica) is a delicious vegetable in the sweet potato family. Its tender, edible stems are hollow, like drinking straws. It is also known as "No heart" vegetable.

CHAPTER 28

▼

WAR ON TIGER DUKE

King Zhou, blaming Grand Old Master's bad temper and banking on his long absence from the capital, released both Higher Counselors Fei Zhong and You Hun, and restored them to their former positions. The senior princes protested vigorously to no avail.

After an especially hard winter, the spring burst with vitality, even in King Zhou's Capital City, Morning Song. The Imperial Peony Garden was in its glory. The king invited Yellow Flying Tiger and all his ministers to a peony appreciation party.

To the king, this party was to celebrate Daji's regaining her health. To Daji, it was more than a celebration. It was a wish fulfilled, a vow attained. She had eaten Bi Gan's heart, and felt that her fox children's death was avenged!

But the ministers were ill at ease. Soon, they started to leave, one after another. The king, who had been drinking at the upper level with Daji and Splendor, came down to drink with his ministers, trying to keep the rest from leaving.

Evening came, lanterns were lit and the garden took on an added dimension of festivity.

By midnight, Daji and Splendor were so drunk they lost their self-control, and inadvertently reverted to their specter beings. Hungrily they stalked the garden for human flesh and blood.

Nearly all of the people in the party were too mellow to notice the change. Someone suddenly shouted, "Specters! Specters!"

Yellow Flying Tiger was immediately alert and stood up, just in time to see a hoary vixen charge at him. Since no one was permitted to carry a weapon to the party, Yellow Flying Tiger threw his chair at the vixen while calling for his hunting falcons. The vixen ducked and turned on him again. The falcons were on the attack, and one of them managed to scratch the vixen's face before she disappeared under the water lily pond.

The sudden turn of events shocked the king out of his drunken stupor. And in one of his rare moments of clarity, he ordered his men to dig under the lily pond.

What they discovered shocked the world! The king's memory was jarred as he recalled the many, many warnings of unholy activities in his imperial gardens and palaces. And he had executed all those who mentioned the word "specter". Could all these human remains be the work of those specters? Were there other burying places in other parts of the garden and palace? Were there really specters in his royal domain? The king puzzled.

Next morning, the king noticed a scratch on Daji's face and voiced his concerned. In the deepest darkness of Daji's heart, she damned Yellow Flying Tiger and swore to get even with him. She replied lightly, "Nothing important. Yesterday while Your Majesty was drinking with your ministers, Splendor and I took a walk around the garden and a bush scratched me."

The king said, "Don't go to the garden again. Last night, Yellow Flying Tiger saw an old vixen. Luckily his hunting falcons scared it away. One of them scratched the vixen's face; some fur still remained in its claw. And we discovered a huge pile of human remains buried under the lily pond. I don't think it is safe for you and Splendor to set foot there. There really are specters around."

Strange (or was it?) the king never suspected the creature sleeping by him was the cruelest of specters! And poor Yellow Flying Tiger! He had, unknowingly and undeservingly, become the next target of Daji's vengeance.

*   *   *   *

In the distant Western Foothills, Baby Tooth was reading the latest news from the other regions of the kingdom. The Southern and Eastern regions had rebelled against King Zhou. In the Northern Region, allied with the two corrupt Higher Counselors Fei Zhong and You Hun, Tiger Duke had intensified his oppression and cruelty.

Baby Tooth reported the developments to Ji Chang and recommended that Tiger Duke be cut down to size.

The ever loyal Ji Chang said, "I realize how terrible and oppressive Tiger Duke is. But he and I are the same rank. I really don't see how I can do anything about him."

Baby Tooth said, "After you were freed from Youli, for your loyalty the king invested you with the title of King Wen of the West, and gave you his Battle Axe; you are empowered to do what is best for the kingdom in the king's name. Have pity on the tormented people, my Lord. Have a heart for the glorious Cheng Tang's reign. Once we put Tiger Duke away, the king may regain his senses."

Grand Counselor Easy Life agreed. And so Ji Chang declared war on Tiger Duke. Ji Chang's troops were so well disciplined that neither a rooster nor a dog was disturbed as they marched north. The populace in every city and village en route came out to welcome them. And many brought wine and food. Soon Ji Chang and his troops came in sight of Tiger Duke's Capital, Tiger Town. They made camp ten miles outside of the city.

Tiger Duke was away in the City Morning Song, and had left his son Young Tiger in charge. Young Tiger was enraged on learning of Ji Chang's invasion, and vowed to capture him.

Next morning, under the direction of Baby Tooth, General Nimblefoot led his men and horses to Tiger Town city gate and demanded to fight Tiger Duke.

In a blare of trumpets, the city gate opened and out rushed Tiger Duke's army, led by Tiger Duke's number one general Huang Yuanji.

General Nimblefoot shouted insults, "Huang Yuanji, you small potato, get out of my way! I only want to fight the real Tiger Duke himself!"

With his long knife, Huang charged straight at Nimblefoot. Nimblefoot confronted Huang with his broad knife. Oh how the clashing knives resounded in the morning air! But Huang was hardly Nimblefoot's match and soon was knocked off his horse; his head was severed by Nimblefoot's soldiers for a trophy.

Nimblefoot and his men triumphantly returned to camp.

Young Tiger swore to capture Ji Chang to avenge Huang's death. Early next morning he led a charge into Ji Chang's camp, and demanded Ji Chang by name.

On his horse and surrounded by his eight generals, Ji Chang came out in full armor to confront Young Tiger. Galloping ahead was Baby Tooth, in a white robe with golden Trigram design, with silk sash and linen shoes.

His white hair flying and his sword in hand, Baby Tooth shouted, "Anyone who wants to see King Wen of the West must see me first!"

Young Tiger shouted back, "Who and what are you? How dare you come into my territory without invitation?"

"I am Baby Tooth, the Prime Minister of King Wen of the West. You father and son have behaved worse than predatory wolves and tigers! You rob your people to fatten yourselves. You use flattering tricks to befuddle the king. You allied yourselves with the most corrupt ministers. Even a three-foot tall child can recite your evil deeds. My master has the king's Battle Axe to capture you."

"So you are that stupid old fool who fished with a straight needle at the River Pan!" Young Tiger snickered. "Boasting will not get you any-where!"

Before he finished, Ji Chang came forth, shouting, "Young Tiger. Don't you dare to talk big. You know full well what foul deeds you and your father have done. What is the sense of your fighting? Come down from your high horse and let me take you back to my Western Foot-hills!"

Young Tiger was beside himself, shouting to his men, "Go get this old thief!"

In response, Wu Ji, a general from Ji Chang's side, dashed out in fury. "You will have to go through me first!"

How the two generals fought! Seeing his man losing, Young Tiger ordered other generals to join the fight. In retaliation, Baby Tooth did the same.

In the end Young Tiger's army was badly beaten. Baby Tooth wanted to press on and attack the city. But Ji Chang disagreed. "No, we will not do that! We are here because we want to alleviate the suffer-ing of the people. If we attack the city, we will do just the opposite."

Baby Tooth had to think of another way to get rid of Tiger Duke. He wrote a letter to Tiger Duke's brother, Black Tiger, the Duke of Cao Region, and sent General Nimblefoot to deliver it.

CHAPTER 29

▼

ACCESSION OF KING WU

Black Tiger read Baby Tooth's letter.

Baby Tooth, the Prime minister of the Western Foothills salutes the Honorable Duke of Cao, Black Tiger.

As the king's ministers, we know well our duties are to help with wise administration and to steer him clear of rumors and unscrupulous actions. The good of the kingdom and the welfare of the populace should be uppermost in our minds and hearts. Yet your brother Tiger Duke, one of the kingdom's highest ministers, never seems to understand his duties. He forfeits his position when he milks and bullies the people, particularly during the building of the Deer Gallery.

To alleviate the suffering of the people, my master Ji Chang, King Wen of the West has declared war on Tiger Duke.

We do know there are good and bad members in every house. You are the intelligent, honest and loyal one in your family. We sincerely request your cooperation in lifting the oppression your brother represents.

I fully know by so doing you may incur the displeasure of your ancestors. But would that not be easier to endure than to incur the hatred and wrath of the populace and the consequent annihilation of your whole family Tribe?

The welfare of our nation depends on your immediate decision. Please let us know as soon as possible.

With our best wishes and regards.

Black Tiger read and reread the letter, nodding his head. "Baby Tooth has a very convincing point," he thought to himself. "Indeed, we need to keep alive the good name of our Tiger Clan."

He turned to Nimblefoot and said, "My dear General. Please inform your prime minister that I will do as he instructs."

Black Tiger then made immediate preparation. In a few days he was in Tiger Duke's capital, Tiger Town, with his troops.

*   *   *   *

Young Tiger was overjoyed to see his Uncle Black Tiger. Young Tiger said, "We really don't know why King Wen of the West attacked us. But now that you are here, I am sure we will manage to send them packing."

Next day, with Baby Tooth's plan very much in mind, Black Tiger came to Ji Chang's camp spoiling for a fight. Baby Tooth sent Nimblefoot out to face him.

After a sham battle, Black Tiger softly said to Nimblefoot, "That is enough for the show. I will bring my brother to your camp as soon as I capture him. Please feign defeat, I will not chase."

Nimblefoot said aloud, "All right, you devil Black Tiger! I am not your match today, I'll let you win this round!" So saying, he retreated to his own camp.

Young Tiger was watching the fight from the battlement and could not understand why Black Tiger gave up and let Nimblefoot get away.

"Are you kidding?" said the uncle when asked. "Baby Tooth is a disciple from Mount Kunlun, with a bag full of high magic. I certainly don't want to confront him head on. Anyway, we have won today.

"I will write to your father at once, and urge him to come home quickly to squash Ji Chang." Black Tiger continued. "And you should write a report to the king about Ji Chang's unprovoked war on us."

*   *   *   *

Tiger Duke roared when he read Black Tiger's letter, "The ingrate Ji Chang! He has been in trouble many times and each time it was I who had saved him!"

Tiger Duke immediately informed the king, who granted him three thousand troops to take home.

Meanwhile Black Tiger stationed some of his men at the city gate and some at Tiger Duke's mansion, with instructions to do such and so on prearranged signals.

Young Tiger had gone ahead to meet his father outside the city. As they entered the city gate, Black Tiger pulled out his sword. At this signal, Black Tiger's men rushed up and bound Tiger Duke and his son.

The unsuspecting Tiger Duke said, "Why? I have never heard of a younger brother binding up his own elder brother!"

Black Tiger said, "I have had enough of your outrageous behavior! You don't seem to remember my warning when I left you not so long ago. In the last few years your actions have been getting worse. Don't you ever hear the crying of the people? Don't you ever see the agony of the poor and the old? Don't you ever stop to think how you have shamed your family and the name of the Tiger Clan? You are one of the top ranking ministers of the kingdom. Yet you allied yourself with the despicable wolves of the Court. It is time I do something before the whole Tiger Tribe is annihilated and our ancestral shrine is destroyed! I know our ancestors would understand and approve of my action!"

Tiger Duke gave a long sigh but had nothing to say. Did he finally realize his stupidity?

Meanwhile, Black Tiger's men in the mansion had bound up Tiger Duke's wife and daughter. Black Tiger took the Tiger Duke's whole family to Ji Chang's camp.

Baby Tooth thanked Black Tiger and took him to see Ji Chang.

Addressing Ji Chang, Black Tiger said, "My elder brother Tiger Duke has been most cruel and ruthless. He deserves your full punishment."

Ji Chang was shocked and thought to himself, "How can you do that to your own brother?"

Sensing his inner struggle, Baby Tooth said, "My lord. Tiger Duke's crimes are so hideous that even a three-year-old can recite them. It is very commendable that Black Tiger put loyalty to the people before his love for his brother."

Baby Tooth then ordered the immediate execution of Tiger Duke and his son, Young Tiger, lest Ji Chang might order their release.

Ji Chang had never hesitated to chop down an opponent on the battlefield. But never in his life had he faced such a morally difficult situation as the present. The grisly heads of Tiger Duke and Young Tiger so sickened and disquieted him that he almost fainted!

As Tiger Duke's women were blameless, Baby Tooth asked Black Tiger to take good care of them. He also suggested that Black Tiger come to take over Tiger Duke's rule.

Black Tiger freed the women and invited Ji Chang to take inventory of the city.

Ji Chang said, "No, thank you. I came to get rid of a tyrant, not to conquer a territory. With your invaluable help, my mission is now accomplished. Tiger Town is yours and your family's."

Ji Chang and his army returned home to a stirring welcome. But soon he fell ill and his health worsened with each passing day. His spirit had been waning ever since the repugnant sight of Tiger Duke's head. Whenever he closed his eyes, he would see a tearful Tiger Duke kneeling before him.

Meanwhile, Ji Chang's feat spread near and far. One after another, the regional dukes formerly under the Grand Duke of the North declared their allegiance to the Western Foothills.

Soon the news reached King Zhou's outpost at the Floodwater Pass and was at once transmitted to the Capital City, Morning Song.

The information came first to Senior Prince Weizi. He was both happy and worried. Happy because Tiger Duke was now dead but worried because the Northern Region would soon be a big headache when they joined the rebelling East and South regions.

He thought to himself, "Yes, this should be reported to the king. But what good would it do? The king would never understand its significance. Well, just the same, I will tell him."

The king was furious over the fate of Tiger Duke whom he considered a most loyal minister!

"I am going to annihilate the Western Foothills myself and then punish Black Tiger!" the king roared.

His favorite ministers Fei Zhong and You Hun cautioned him, "Yes, Tiger Duke was a very capable minister, but we don't see any need in Your Majesty personally going to fight for his sake."

His impulsive anger soon passed, as the king decided he would rather stay with his Daji and Splendor.

*   *   *   *

Ji Chang's health worsened. One day, with the affairs of state and nation very much in mind, he summoned Baby Tooth to his inner quarters. "The Shang line, now represented by King Zhou, has long been a benefactor of my family since my ancestor helped found the Dynasty." Ji Chang said. "I feel deeply that no matter how bad King Zhou is, we are still his ministers, and so must serve him loyally. Although I had the king's Battle Axe, it bothers me greatly that we killed Tiger Duke without the king's explicit permission, no matter how justified it seemed. Ever since, I have not had a good night's sleep. I keep seeing him in my dream. I know I will not be long in this life. What I worry most is how to keep the Western Foothills on its course of peace and loyalty after I am gone.

"Will you promise me that we will never start a war without the king's order?" Tears rained down Ji Chang's drawn face as he spoke.

"Of course, I will do as you wish," said the kneeling Baby Tooth. "I give you my solemn promise."

At this moment, Number two son Ji Fa came in to see his father. "Come here, my son. I was just this moment going to send for you. When I am gone, you should keep yourself close to Prime Minister Baby Tooth and Grand Counselor Easy Life, and heed their advice. Now to make sure of that, I want Baby Tooth to be your 'Honor Uncle'. You will discuss with him any move you make."

Ji Chang then directed Baby Tooth to a chair and ordered Ji Fa to prostrate himself before his new Honor Uncle.

In tears, Baby Tooth accepted this honor and the grave responsibility.

Ji Chang said to his son, "We all know that King Zhou is unjust and cruel. But we are still his ministers. We must remember never to make war on anyone, particularly the king. Remember, my three principles: Be benevolent to the people, be conscientious in your duties, and never fear to be just. Following these principles, you will go far. You have more than your share of kinfolks. You must be dutiful to your elders and live harmoniously with all your brothers."

And as his mind wandered back to the seven years he was under house arrest in the Youli District, he sighed, "Please convey my regards and love to the people of the Youli."

Ji Chang died at the age of ninety-seven, in the mid winter of the twentieth year of King Zhou's reign.

As Ji Chang's body laid in state, his council of ministers earnestly discussed the question of accession.

The question was not who, because Baby Tooth informed the council that Ji Chang's choice was his second son Ji Fa. The question before the council was accession to what?

The livelihoods of the populace in too many of the regions of the kingdom had been most seriously disrupted. The rebellions of the East and South regions were the signs of the general mood and temper. The competence and promise seen in the early years of King Zhou's reign had all long been dissipated in his lust, greed and corruption. The current Son of Heaven had forfeited his rightful mandate. The council decided it was time for bold action, Ji Chang's will notwithstanding.

Led by Grand Counselor Easy Life and General Nimblefoot, the council recommended the accession was to the throne of the Son of Heaven itself. So Ji Fa, the new lord of the Western Foothills, was crowned King Wu. The new king awarded his late father King Wen of the West posthumously King Wen, a one rank promotion to every minister and general across the board, and decreed a general amnesty. Baby Tooth now officially assumed the title of Honor Uncle.

News of Ji Fa's accession as King Wu reached Higher Counselor Yao Zong who passed it to Senior Prince Weizi. Weizi said, "Now that Ji Fa called himself King Wu, we can safely predict all the regional dukes will soon rally to his banner. The king will never comprehend the gravity of this bitter truth. So why bother?"

Yao said, "I understand your feelings. Still it is our duty to inform the king." So saying, Higher Counselor Yao went to see the king.

CHAPTER 30

▼

YELLOW FLYING TIGER REBELS

Higher Counselor Yao said to the king, "Ji Chang is dead and his son Ji Fa has crowned himself King Wu. He has the allegiance of all his regional dukes. As I see it, Your Majesty needs to squash him immediately, or else more regional dukes may go over to him."

The king said disparagingly, "That young punk is still wet behind the ears. What can he do?"

"Ji Fa may be young, but on the civil side he has such brains as Baby Tooth and Easy Life; on the military side, he has such brawn as Nimblefoot. We should not write him off."

"What is Baby Tooth but a mere country bumpkin with a few amateurish tricks!" the king sneered.

Frustrated, Higher Counselor Yao sighed as he left, "The one who terminates the Shang line will be no other but Ji Fa!"

*   *   *   *

King Zhou himself was crowned on New Year's day; it was also his birthday. So when the New Year came, marking the twenty-first year of his reign in the Shang line, there was much festivity in the court.

As custom decreed, on this day the wives of the high ranking ministers were to pay respects to the reigning Queen, Daji. For Mrs. Yellow Flying Tiger, this was also the only day she was permitted to visit her husband's sister Concubine Huang Shi of the West Palace. This once a year visit was treasured and longed for by both women. But by custom, Mrs. Yellow Flying Tiger must first pay her respects to Queen Daji.

As Mrs. Yellow Flying Tiger was announced, Daji's only thought was how she had suffered at the hands of Yellow Flying Tiger during that garden Party when he set his falcons on her.

"Ha! I would like to see how you, Yellow Flying Tiger, suffer now that your wife is in my hands!"

After the required formalities, Mrs. Yellow Flying Tiger was anxious to be on her way to the West Palace. But the cunning Daji invited her to stay for tea, an invitation she would not dare refuse.

"How old are you, my dear?" Daji asked.

"I am thirty-nine."

"Well, you are eight years older than I. I should call you elder sister," Daji said with much counterfeit warmth.

"Oh, how dare I? You are the queen and I am but the humble wife of a minister. How can a phoenix and a chicken be grouped together?"

"Why not? I was but a little girl from the humble region, and you are the sister-in-law of a King's concubine. We are almost equal. Let's take a vow to be fealty sisters!" Daji insisted and ordered a banquet.

As they began their toasts, it was announced that the king was coming to visit. Frightened, Mrs. Yellow Flying Tiger asked Daji, "Where should I go?"

"Don't worry, you can hide in the back room."

Daji told the king she was entertaining Mrs. Yellow Flying Tiger, and added, "Your Majesty should see how beautiful she is."

The king said, "No. A king is not allowed to see the wives of his ministers."

"This is different," Daji said. "Mrs. Yellow Flying Tiger is the sister-in-law of your West Palace Concubine Huang Shi. That means you and she are relatives. So why can't you see her? She is really a beauty. How about Your Majesty resting for a few moments while I take her to the Star Picking Belvedere. Then you show up there suddenly. She will have to face you and you can see for yourself how attractive she really is. What do you say?"

*　　　*　　　*　　　*

As they approached the Belvedere, Mrs. Yellow Flying Tiger was terrified by the sights of the Snake Pit, with white bones piled all around. Grand Old Master had recommended the Snake Pit be removed, but it was never done. The Pit was still there to threaten the palace personnel.

"You know, those palace malcontents are fed to the snakes here in the pit," Daji said as a matter of course. Then she ordered wine.

"Please, may I be pardoned? I cannot drink anymore," begged Mrs. Yellow Flying Tiger.

"Well, I know you are anxious to go to the West Palace to see Concubine Huang Shi. But since you are already here, please drink with your new sister a little longer."

At that moment the king showed up. Frightened, Mrs. Yellow Flying Tiger stood up but found no place to hide.

Daji said, "Don't worry. I will introduce you to His Majesty."

Still, Mrs. Yellow Flying Tiger ran to stand outside of the balustrade.

The king asked, "Who is standing outside?"

"That is Mrs. Yellow Flying Tiger," Daji said and called her in to meet the king.

314 Tales of the Teahouse Retold

Apprehensive, Mrs. Yellow Flying Tiger came in and knelt. The king leered at the matured but still attractive woman and thought to himself, "She should be a novelty, and a nice change," but said, "Please have a seat."

Alarmed and ill at ease, Mrs. Yellow Flying Tiger stood instead on the side.

Daji said, "My dear elder sister, please sit down."

The king turned to Daji, "Why do you call her sister?"

"Yes, she and I have sworn to be fealty sisters."

"In that case," the king said, "you are my sister-in-law. Please sit down."

The defenseless Mrs. Yellow Flying Tiger now realized that she was tightly snared in Daji's trap. Feeling utterly helpless, she knelt and said, "Please let me go."

"But first, how about a cup of wine?" said the king. Waving his cup, he tried to grab Mrs. Yellow Flying Tiger with his other hand.

Terrified and enraged that the king should behave so shamefully, she took the cup of wine and threw it at him, screaming, "You befuddled king! My husband risks his life constantly for you. And yet you now try to seduce his wife! You and your Daji will be burnt for ten thousand years in hell!"

The king shrieked, "Tie her up!"

"Dare you touch me?" Mrs. Yellow Flying Tiger shouted as she walked over to the balustrades. Then she said loudly, "My dear husband, I die to keep my virtue for you! Do take care of my children!" She then jumped to her death from the high Belvedere.

*   *   *   *

Concubine Huang Shi was very worried when she first heard Daji was detaining her beloved sister-in-law. Now she cried bitterly on hearing of her death. Gathering herself, Concubine Huang Shi rushed over to the Star Picking Belvedere.

Pointing her finger at the king, she screamed, "You damned fool! See what you have done? My father and brother risk their lives to conquer the barbarians both south and north to protect you and the kingdom. What more do you expect from our clan? Yet you tried to seduce my sister-in-law and caused her death. You violate not only the five cardinal human relationships, but also the three social orders! You are shaming your ancestors through and through!"

Turning to Daji, the concubine screamed, "And you, Daji, the polluter of the morals of the palace! I only hope that you will die in your own snake pit and your soul rot forever and ever in hell!"

So saying, she pulled Daji down and started to beat her mercilessly, revealing her training in the martial arts as befit a daughter of a military family. All the anger and indignation engendered in her since the torture death of the rightful Queen Jiang now boiled over.

Walking over, the king tried to stop the beating. "My dear Concubine Huang Shi, that was not Daji's fault."

In her fury the Concubine swung with all her might at Daji, but her blow landed on the king's face instead as he stepped in between them. Turning ugly, the king picked the concubine up and threw her down the Star Picking Belvedere to her death!

*   *   *   *

Meanwhile, Yellow Flying Tiger was home celebrating the New Year quietly with his two brothers, his four favorite generals and confidants, and his three young sons.

Report of the tragedies at the Star Picking Belvedere struck them like thunder in a clear sky. The young sons howled with pain while their father was struck dumb.

Radiance, one of the generals, said, "My dear friend, why are you waffling? What happened is crystal clear. Haven't you ever heard that when a king does not behave like a king, his ministers should look for a new leader? What are we waiting for? How much are we to endure? We are rebelling!"

So saying, the four generals got on their horses and left.

Awakened from his shock, Yellow Flying Tiger ran after them, shouting, "Come back! If you want to rebel, don't you think we better plan a little? Just walking out like this is no way to deal with such a grave matter!"

The four turned around as Yellow Flying Tiger struggled with his loyalty and his grievous loss.

"What do you mean rebelling?" he demanded. "My family have been loyal ministers for seven generations. How dare you ruin our reputation? Besides, what are the deaths of my sister and my wife to you? Don't tell me we give up our good name just because of that? You are just using this as an excuse. Don't you remember how you earned your gold belts? So you want to join the bandits in the forest?"

Trying to lead his Prince out of his confusion, Radiance teased, "You are absolutely right. That really is none of our business. We shouldn't have been bothered!"

So saying, the quartet moved to a table and started noisily drinking and making merriment.

With the sobs of his three young sons tugging at his heart, Yellow Flying Tiger screamed, "How can you make merriment under such circumstances?"

Teasing further, Radiance said, "Why not, my Prince? Today is New Year's Day. What do you mean we cannot make merriment?" And they started to laugh and sing.

"What are you laughing for? How can you sing at a time like this?" shrieked Yellow Flying Tiger, getting more angry.

Commence, another of the generals, said calmly, "Well, to tell you the truth, my Prince, we are laughing at you!"

"Laughing at me? What for? I am one of the highest ministers and hold the military power of the nation. What is there to laugh at?" Flying Tiger said wrathfully.

Commence said, "Yes, indeed. We all know you earned them with your prowess and valor. But some might think your beautiful wife took advantage of her good looks with the king to advance her husband's career!"

Suddenly seeing the light, Yellow Flying Tiger shrilled, "Damn the king! Let's fight our way out of this rotten capital!"

Immediately his brothers made ready by summoning one thousand of the Yellow family's best warriors and packing the family's valuables onto four huge carts. As they were ready to leave, Yellow Flying Tiger asked, "Where to?"

Radiance said, "Where else? Have you not heard King Wu of the Western Foothills has the allegiance of two thirds of the nation? Why don't we join them?"

He then continued, "Before we go to the Western Foothills, why don't we give King Zhou a what for?"

The generals were thinking to themselves, "We better burn our bridges behind us before Yellow Flying Tiger changes his mind."

Still very much distracted by his grief, Yellow Flying Tiger impulsively agreed.

And so while his brothers and two of the generals were leading one long column out of the West Gate, Yellow Flying Tiger, Radiance and Commence were leading another column heading toward Noon Gate and the king's palace.

As the morning began to dawn, over the palace complex, Commence shouted, "Tell the king we want an explanation of what happened yesterday to Mrs. Yellow Flying Tiger and Concubine Huang Shi!"

The king was remorseful, and had fretted all night. Now in Yellow Flying Tiger, he saw a scapegoat on which to vent his anger and frustration at losing his chance at a beautiful woman. He put on his full armor and came out himself.

Facing the king, Yellow Flying Tiger hesitated as he silently struggled with his inner turmoil.

Seeing the vacillation, Commence bolted out on his horse and shouted, "You cruel and evil king! You killed your minister's wife because she refused your seduction. What do you have to say for yourself?"

The king rushed toward Commence. The king was once a mighty warrior of unmatched strength. Now after many years of orgies, his form might still be there but the strength was not. Trailing his weapon behind, the king raced back inside the Noon Gate.

Radiance and others wanted to give chase, but Yellow Flying Tiger led them straight out of the City Gate. They soon caught up with his brothers and sons, and together they traveled toward the Western Foothills.

$$* \qquad * \qquad * \qquad *$$

Soon, the Capital City, Morning Song, was again bestirred by reports that the Grand Old Master was returning. The ministers again rushed to the Ten-Mile-Welcome Gazebo, but again, were informed that Grand Old Master would meet them at the Noon Gate.

"Why is Yellow Flying Tiger not here?" Grand Old Master asked when in the Great Hall.

. The king said, "Yellow Flying Tiger has rebelled!"

"Why?" The Grand Old Master was flabbergasted.

The king gave his shrewd version of the event, ending by saying, "I am glad you are back. You can capture him for me."

Grand Old Master listened patiently. Then with his magic eye flashing, he said, "There are too many unanswered questions, Sire. From what I can see, it was you who were responsible. Yellow Flying Tiger has an impeccable record of loyalty and nobility. I think you should pardon him, return him to his position and power. Losing Yellow Flying Tiger is like losing your right arm!"

All ministers present agreed. But there was one dissenting voice.

"What is it?" asked Grand Old Master.

The dissenter said, "The king might have done Mrs. Yellow Flying Tiger wrong. But it was also wrong for Yellow Flying Tiger to fight the king."

"You are right," said Grand Old Master. "I was thinking only of the king's fault." He called to his men, "Quick! Send out urgent alerts to all border garrisons to stop Yellow Flying Tiger. I will bring him back so we can discuss the whole matter."

▼

CHAPTER 31

GRAND OLD MASTER PURSUES FLYING TIGER

Yellow Flying Tiger led his people pushing westward. They passed Green Water District, crossed the Yellow River and arrived at the Riverpool County. Zhang Kui, the mayor of the county was known for his duplicity and greediness. To avoid trouble, Yellow Flying Tiger and his men took a roundabout way.

As they were finally heading for the White Egret Forest, they heard thundering hoofs from behind. Troops flying the Grand Old Master's banner were getting close.

Yellow Flying Tiger gasped, "Who can fight the Grand Old Master? We are done for!"

Looking at his three young sons, he sighed, "What crime have these children committed to suffer such a fate?"

In rapid succession, his scouts reported:

"Troops of Zhang Cassia of the Green Dragon Pass are coming from the left!"

"Soldiers of Zhang Phoenix of the Upon-Highwater Pass are coming up front!"

"The men of the four Diablo brothers of the Fine Dream Pass coming from the right!"

Encircled with no way out, the frustrated Flying Tiger let out a gigantic roar of anguish.

*   *   *   *

At this moment, Superiorman True Vacuum of Mount Green Top, Purple Sun Cave, happened to be in the vicinity and heard Yellow Flying Tiger. Superiorman True Vacuum understood Flying Tiger's predicament and decided to help. True Vacuum engulfed Yellow Flying Tiger and his entourage in a sleep-inducing fog and moved them to the valley outside.

Meanwhile Grand Old Master gathered all the Commanders of the three Passes to discuss how to capture Yellow Flying Tiger. But none of them had seen him or his men.

"Strange," Grand Old Master muttered to himself. "We were chasing him all the way from Capital City, Morning Song. Where could they go? You all return to your posts. I will wait for him. Sooner or later, he has to pass here."

To divert Grand Old Master's attention, True Vacuum opened his gourd and threw a little of its content in the direction of the Capital City, Morning Song.

Instantly Yellow Flying Tiger and his men appeared to be rushing back to the Capital. And Grand Old Master immediately gave chase.

At the same time Yellow Flying Tiger and his men woke up and were surprised that all the enemy troops were gone!

Flying Tiger and his men made haste toward the Upon-Highwater Pass. When they arrived, they found their way blocked by Pass Commander Zhang Phoenix in full armor on his horse.

Yellow Flying Tiger came up and saluted Zhang, "My honorable Uncle Zhang. Please help me over the Pass."

Zhang said, "Your father and I have been friends for over sixty years and you are like a son to me. But you are a damned fool! How can you forsake seven generations of good name in the service of the Son of Heaven for a mere wife? Listen to me. Let me take you back to the Capital City, Morning Song, and we may be able to talk the king into letting you redeem your crime."

Yellow Flying Tiger said, "I appreciate your lecture, Honorable Uncle. But you don't seem to realize the full extent of the king's misconduct the last fifteen years! I have tried to uphold the kingdom from all sides. But this is the last straw. Please, Honorable Uncle Zhang. Help me get away."

Old Zhang rushed up to fight Flying Tiger. But the old man hardly was Flying Tiger's match. After about thirty contacts, Zhang retreated. As Flying Tiger gave chase, Zhang reached under his armor and pulled out his One-Hundred-Crucible twin hammers which were linked by a silk cord. He threw them at Flying Tiger. Flying Tiger quickly cut the cord with his sword. The hammers fell. Flying Tiger picked them up and put them in his pocket.

Back at his post, Zhang Phoenix felt so depressed. He had hoped to talk Flying Tiger into surrender. Failing that, he had lost his cool and fought the younger and stronger man. Now he had also lost his magic twin hammers!

In his eagerness to retrieve his twin hammers, he took a long chance. He instructed his second in command, General Akin Silver, to get back at Yellow Flying Tiger. "Yellow Flying Tiger is one of the strongest warriors in the kingdom, and now he is even more so because he has captured my One-Hundred-Crucible twin Hammers. Tonight at the sound of the second gong, shoot him with your poisonous arrow and bring his head to me."

Zhang Phoenix miscalculated again. Akin Silver thought to himself, "How can I do that to Yellow Flying Tiger? He was once my mentor when I started my military career. Under his tutelage and sponsorship I

324 Tales of the Teahouse Retold

became Deputy Commander. He has always been kind and just. I would never, even in my dreams, harm him and his family!"

At dusk Akin Silver slipped out of the garrison in disguise and went directly to Flying Tiger. They met in the dark, and Akin Silver wasted no time in relating Zhang's plot. Akin Silver then quickly slipped back to his garrison, secretly opened the gate and let Yellow Flying Tiger and his entourage out of the Pass.

On hearing the report that Yellow Flying Tiger was out, Zhang came out of his office and tried to kill Akin Silver. But Zhang was killed by Akin Silver instead.

*   *   *   *

Rushing along, Yellow Flying Tiger soon covered the eighty miles to the Highwater Pass and set up camp. He was jolted into silence when he found out that General Chen Tong was in command of that Pass.

Chen had served under Yellow Flying Tiger many years before and was to be executed by Yellow Flying Tiger for a crime. But several fellow generals had begged for clemency on Chen's behalf. So Yellow Flying Tiger let him redeem himself on the battlefield. Chen had never forgiven Yellow Flying Tiger, blaming him for all his own misdeeds and harboring his hatred all these years. Yellow Flying Tiger knew the score fully.

When Chen learned that Flying Tiger was encamped nearby, he brought out his bag of magic darts he had stolen from a superiorman many years ago. Then in full armor, he came out of the garrison on his horse, calling for Yellow Flying Tiger.

Pointing his spear at Flying Tiger, Chen said sarcastically, "My honorable Prince. Why are you here without the proper passport? I have Grand Old Master's order to take you back to Capital City, Morning Song. Come, come. Please get off that ugly beast and come with me. Thank you!"

So saying, Chen came straight at Flying Tiger with his spear while furtively pulling out one of the poisonous darts and shot it at Flying Tiger. Caught unprepared, Flying Tiger was hit in the arm and fell off his magic bull.

Commence and Radiance rushed out to fight Chen while Flying Cheetah and Flying Leopard rescued Flying Tiger. By the time they reached their camp, Flying Tiger was already in a deep coma, as if dead.

Meanwhile, Chen also used his dart on Commence and sent him too into a deep coma. Quite satisfied with his handiwork, Chen returned triumphantly to his garrison compound.

*   *   *   *

The Yellow Flying Tiger camp was in shock and turmoil as the three young sons bawled piteously while the others sobbed helplessly.

At this confused moment, who would again be a savior but the Superiorman True Vacuum. True Vacuum was meditating when he suddenly became aware that Yellow Flying Tiger was again in trouble. He summoned one of his disciples, Yellow Heavenly Educated, a young man nine feet tall, strong as an ox and with eyes that shone like those of a tiger. His hair in a top knot, he wore a cotton gown with linen shah and grass shoes.

"Quick, go down the mountain. Your father is in serious difficulty."

"Who is my father?"

"No other than Lord of National Security, Prince Yellow Flying Tiger. He is in much distress at Highwater Pass. Go help him. It is also time for you to be reunited with your family."

"Why was I brought up here in the first place?"

"It has been thirteen years already. I was on my way to Mount Kun-lun when I saw your helpless soul waging a gallant fight against a deadly disease. Your body was dead but your soul refused to leave. So I dug open your grave, took you out of your coffin and brought you here to raise and educate."

True Vacuum handed a flower basket and his Non-Evil sword to Heavenly Educated and said, "Hurry back after the mission is completed. Don't go to the Western Foothills as yet," he reminded the young man.

Traveling underground, Heavenly Educated reached the Yellow Flying Tiger camp in a hurry.

CHAPTER 32

▼

THE POISONOUS DARTS

It was the fifth gong when Heavenly Educated reached Highwater-Pass. In the pre-dawn darkness, he could see a crowd gathered about a dim light and hears the sound of piteous sobs.

Someone shouted, "Who's there in the dark?"

"I am a disciple of Superiorman True Vacuum of Purple Sun Cave. I heard your master is in trouble and have come to help."

Flying Cheetah came out to investigate and found a young man in a mountain monk's attire. Strange, but to Yellow Flying Cheetah, the young monk seemed to be Yellow Flying Tiger in disguise!

Flying Cheetah invited the young man inside and asked, "May I know who you are and how you can help us?"

"Where is the Prince?"

Flying Cheetah led the young man to the rear of the tent where Flying Tiger laid, his eyes tightly shut, his face pale as paper.

"Who is lying next to the Prince?" Heavenly Educated asked.

"He is our fealty brother General Chou Commence. He too was hit by Chen's poisonous dart."

A pail of water was quickly fetched. Heavenly Educated deftly plucked some medicine from the flower basket, mixed it with water and forced it down Flying Tiger's throat. Medicine was also spread on the wound. Commence was similarly treated.

Time passed slowly. Everyone held his breath, hoping for a miracle. After about an hour, Yellow Flying Tiger screamed, "This pain is killing me!"

He opened his eyes and saw a young monk before him. Flying Tiger said, "Don't tell me that I am meeting a Heavenly lad in the realm of death!"

"Without this Heavenly person, my older brother would not have returned from death!" Flying Cheetah said.

Hearing this, Flying Tiger stood up and made a deep bow to the boy monk, saying, "My unending debt of gratitude to you for saving my life."

In tears, Heavenly Educated knelt before Flying Tiger and said, "My father. I am Heavenly Educated, your three year old son who died and was buried thirteen years ago."

"My first born! You are alive! What a miracle!" Tears rained down Flying Tiger's cheeks.

At this moment, Commence stirred to consciousness.

Heavenly Educated related the story of his rescue and training by Superiorman True Vacuum. As he spoke, he looked around and counted all his three brothers, his two uncles and four fealty uncles, but could not find his mother. His face seemed puzzled, then became red with anger. "Father, how could you do that!"

"Did what?" Flying Tiger was bewildered.

"You brought with you everyone, even family servants and treasures. But why not my mother? Once she is captured, she would not only be killed, but certainly humiliated and tortured!"

Everyone sobbed anew. Flying Tiger told the story, beginning with the New Year visit to the Palace and the murders of both his wife and sister. No amount of comforting could get Heavenly Educated to stop his bitter crying.

Then Chen Tong was outside calling for a fight.

Yellow Flying Tiger's face paled anew. Heavenly Educated assured his father that everything would be all right and urged him to go out to face Chen Tong.

On seeing Flying Tiger alive, Chen was confused. Flying Tiger yelled at Chen, "Look out, Chen Tong! You think I would let you get away with that sneaky trick?"

After a few passes with their weapons, Chen again feigned a retreat. Heavenly Educated shouted to his hesitant father to give chase.

Again and again Chen Tong shot his poisonous darts at the pursuing Flying Tiger. However, Heavenly Educated neatly intercepted each dart with his flower basket.

With no more darts, Chen turned around to fight Flying Tiger once more. But Heavenly Educated intervened.

The cocky Chen shouted, "So you stole all my magic darts! Look out! You cannot get away so easily!" Chen charged at Heavenly Educated.

Swiftly, Heavenly Educated unsheathed his master's sword and pointed it at Chen. The instant flash from the Non-evil sword knocked Chen off his horse.

The sword was the treasure of Mount Green Top, Purple Sun cave, Superiorman True Vacuum; none who had evil intent could ever survive its deadly righteousness.

With Chen Tong dead, Flying Tiger and his men easily fought their way out of the Highwater-Pass.

As they resumed their march westward, Heavenly Educated said to his father, "My father, I am sorry but I must leave you now. Please take care."

"Why aren't you going to the Western Foothills with us, my son?"

"I wish I could. But my master instructed me otherwise. Good-bye, my father. I will see you again soon."

*   *   *   *

There was more trouble ahead at the Through-Clouds-Pass where Chen Wu, the commander, a brother of Chen Tong, had received smoke signals from Chen Tong's men informing him of Chen Tong's death.

Instead of using brute force, Chen Wu decided to try his wit. As soon as Flying Tiger was within sight, Chen Wu came out to welcome him in court regalia.

Surprised at what he saw, Flying Tiger returned his salute, "I appreciate your treating me so civilly, since I am but a criminal."

Chen Wu said, "We all know how loyal you are. So there must be good reason for you to rebel. Please come in to the garrison compound, partake of our simple fare, and rest a while."

Radiance remarked in disbelief, "How strange! From the same tree grew two kinds of fruits: one bitter and sour and the other so sweet! From one mother, two sons: one so cruel while the other so kind! One would never know they are from the same mother and father. This Chen Wu is certainly better than his brother Chen Tong!"

Chen Wu entertained them lavishly with a great spread of food and wine. By evening, all were ready to retire and soon were settled and fast in dreamland.

Flying Tiger, however, was restless. He paced back and forth in his room, much troubled by the turn of events. The sound of the first gong of the night watch came, then the second and the third. A sudden breeze dimmed the light and startled Flying Tiger as a gentle voice came urgently from nowhere, "Don't be afraid. I am your late wife. I have come to warn you. Get out of this place immediately before it is too late. Take care, my dear husband."

Fully alert, Flying Tiger woke the others and told them what he had just experienced. They rushed out of their rooms and found the outside doors locked. They chopped down the doors to find high piles of firewood surrounding their sleeping quarters.

Flying Tiger and his men desperately fought their way out as the firewood was ignited.

As Flying Tiger cleared the garrison compound, Chen Wu came out in pursuit.

"Ah, my dear Commander Chen. You are certainly coarse in your hospitality!" Flying Tiger said coolly.

Seeing his plan had turned to smoke, Chen Wu shouted, "You rebel! You think you can get away free after killing my brother? I have indeed underestimated your cunning and set fire too late! But you are not going to get out of this Pass alive!"

So saying, Chen came straight at Flying Tiger. But Chen Wu was no match and he paid with his life.

✳   ✳   ✳   ✳

Dawn came as Flying Tiger and his men approached Demarcation Pass where his father Yellow Rolling was in command. Flying Tiger and his four fealty brothers knew better, but the others were looking forward to entering friendly territory and began to chatter and joke.

The father Yellow Rolling had served the late King Da Yi, King Zhou's father, personally. Now aged and full of honors, he had become an unyielding disciplinarian, putting family honor above everything.

The son, Flying Tiger, cringed at the thought of facing his father. But there was no way to by-pass the Demarcation Pass. This Pass was once on the border but had receded inland because Yellow Rolling had conquered the land which was once beyond the Pass.

CHAPTER 33

▼

DEMARCATION AND FLOOD-WATER PASSES

Yellow Radiance, Chou Commence, Dragon Ring and Wu Modesty were the first to reach Demarcation Pass. They had not expected to see three thousand men and horses blocking their way and ten prisoner carts standing on the side.

Radiance said, "Well, I can see things are worse than we had anticipated."

Then Yellow Flying Tiger caught up with them. There up front was commander Yellow Rolling!

Bending in a stiff bow, Flying Tiger said, "My father, please pardon my awkward obeisance. My armor is in the way."

Coldly, Yellow Rolling said, "Who the hell are you?"

"My father, I am your first-born son Flying Tiger. Don't you recognize me?"

"My family harbored no rebellious sons or twice married daughters!" Yellow Rolling roared. "For seven generations we have enjoyed the trust and honor of the Son of Heaven. We are the right arm of the kingdom. How then for the sake of a mere wife, you are giving up all honors and wealth! You are bringing shame to your ancestors and insults to your living father! How dare you face me and call yourself my son?"

Flying Tiger sat silently on his Sacred-Bull, not daring uttering a sound.

Abruptly the old man changed his manner, coaxed, "How would you like to be a filial son and a loyal minister at the same time?"

"Father, I don't understand."

"It is easy. Get off your beast and let me take you back to Capital Morning Song as a prisoner. The king might think kindly of me because I have done right. And you, even in death, would still be my son and a minister of the court. If you insist on rebelling, then kill me right now so that I don't have to face any pointing accusing fingers. Take your choice but don't just sit there like a dumbbell!"

"Father, please don't torture me so!" Flying Tiger cried. "Take me to Morning Song if you must!" So saying, Flying Tiger was ready to dismount.

"Don't!" Radiance interjected. "We have been loyal all our lives. But the king has turned from bad to worst, compelling us to rebel. We have come a long way, fought many battles and overcome many obstacles to get here. How can you go back? As a prisoner at that! Those who died so unjustly will ever be avenged?"

"You damned Radiance! How dare you?" roared the old man. "I know my son is loyal and filial. It's the likes of you to give him bad advice!" Waving his long knife, the old man came straight at Yellow Radiance.

Blocking with his own axe, Radiance said gently, "My lord, please listen to me. Flying Tiger and the other two are your sons, and the three young ones are your Grandsons. You can do whatever you please with them. But we four are not your sons. You think we will let you take us prisoners without a fight? Besides, even the most ferocious wild tiger does not eat its own cubs. Why, my lord. How can you do this to your own flesh and blood? If you don't think much of the death of your daughter-in-law, how about the murder of your own daughter?"

Slashing with his long knife, Yellow Rolling screamed, "Damn! You make me so mad!"

Again blocking with his axe, Radiance said urgently, "My lord! It's better to bend with the wind. Let go before the gathering storm blows you over! If I fight you, my axe has neither eyes nor ears. What if I hurt you or even kill you, how would I ever be able to live with myself?"

Even more enraged, Yellow Rolling kept on fighting. Now Commence and the rest of the quartet joined in to keep the old man from hurting himself or others.

Flying Tiger was angry, but Radiance laughed and shouted, "Dumb cluck! Get everyone out of the Pass while the old master is too busy to do anything else!"

Awakened from his mental paralysis, Flying Tiger rushed everyone out, taking the treasure carts with them. The old man was now in a fit and fell off his horse, ready to kill himself with his sword.

Radiance rushed to the old man, holding him, and said gently, "My lord. Why take it so hard?"

Opening his eyes, Yellow Rolling screamed, "You again! You let my sons go, and now you want to add insult to injury?"

"No sir," said Radiance, thinking hard to get the old man off his stubborn stand. "We have talked our faces purple, trying to keep your son from rebelling. But he threatened to kill us," Radiance lied. "So we humored him, hoping when we got to the Demarcation Pass, you would be able to take care of the matter. I have been trying to let you know by the expression in my eyes, but you kept on ignoring me. I did not dare to do it too obviously lest Flying Tiger notice. Now you blame me too. How will I ever prove my innocence?"

Yellow Rolling said, "What do you propose now?"

"My lord. Go call Flying Tiger back. Promise him you will go to the Western Foothills with him."

"So you want to entice me too?" the old man laughed.

Still lying, Radiance said, "No sir. It is only a ploy to get Flying Tiger and the others back. You wine and dine them while we four get ready to take them to the Capital City, Morning Song."

And so finally father and sons settled down to an elaborate if uneasy dinner. At the appointed time, the old man tapped his cup but Radiance never seemed to notice. In fact, while the old man was bringing his sons back, the four generals formed their own plan.

While the family was eating, Dragon Ring and Modesty packed the old man's valuables. Then in an equivalent of bridge-burning, set fire to the grain house! This was a rebellious act, for without the grain, the Garrison was without food and could not last!

Getting impatient, Rolling shouted, "Radiance, I have tapped several times, why don't you do something?"

"My lord," Radiance said with a straight face, "my friends are not all here, how dare I act?"

Just then, shouts of "FIRE!" came from everywhere. In the confusion, everyone rode out of the Pass.

Yellow Rolling realized too late that he had fallen for Radiance's ruse. There was no way out but to go to the Western Foothills with his sons.

With bitterness, Rolling hung his Demarcation Pass Seal in the Great Hall, saying, "Not that I am not loyal. I was too trusting and got tricked into this!"

He left Demarcation Pass with one thousand of his troops, joining his son's two thousand men and horses. Ahead of them, there was one more guarded mountain pass, the Flood-Water Pass, standing in the way to the Western Foothills.

*   *   *   *

The frontier Flood-Water Pass was commanded by Han Glory—cunning, pompous, but quite sharp and completely loyal to King

Zhou. Under him was General Yu Hua who possessed black magic: his Soul-Dispatching Flag could steal the soul of his opponent.

Yellow Rolling recounted all this to his son Flying Tiger. "I fear we all will be killed. There is no way to fight black magic!"

Just then his seven year old Grandson cried. The old man sighed, "Poor dear. What have we done!" Sadness gripped his old heart.

$$* \qquad * \qquad * \qquad *$$

On hearing Yellow Rolling had rebelled with his son Flying Tiger, Han Glory snickered, "Old fool! How could he let his son do this to him!"

Next morning, Han Glory sent General Yu Hua out. When Yellow Flying Tiger came to face him, he found a warrior who had a golden face with a red beard. He was wearing a leopard vest and a jade belt, riding a five-colored bull, like his own.

Yu Hua said, "Who are you?"

"I am Lord of National Security, Prince Yellow Flying Tiger. King Zhou's rule has so deteriorated we could no longer live and work under his tyranny. Please, my general, let us go to the Western Foothills."

"What makes you think you can still pull your rank? My order is to capture you and send you back to Capital City, Morning Song. You are no longer the Lord of National Security but only a common criminal!" Yu Hua replied arrogantly.

"I have surmounted four Passes, and we will do so again here!" With his long spear, Flying Tiger charged at Yu Hua. Flying Tiger's long spear was so skillfully handled it became a long silver serpent, encircling Yu Hua. Outmatched, Yu Hua waved his Soul-Dispatching Flag. A black smoke immediately enveloped Flying Tiger and he was captured.

Although a captive, Flying Tiger stood straight before Han Glory.

Han Glory said, "What had the court done that you acted so ungraciously? Have you forgotten your etiquette? You should kneel, my friend!"

Flying Tiger laughed. "Oh, indeed. A Commander of a Pass is a high position. But your authority is that of a scavenger hyena without the tiger on its side; it is really nothing. Puffing up your face does not make you anymore powerful. Now that you have captured me, do what you wish, the most is death for all I care!"

"Very well, put him in prison until we capture them all," said Han Glory.

On learning of his son's capture, Yellow Rolling sighed, "Just as I feared. My poor child, don't you wish you had listened to me? Now our fate is worse!"

Next day, in rapid succession, Yu Hua, with his Soul-Dispatching Flag, captured Commence, Radiance, Dragon Ring and Modesty, and also the young warriors Flying Cheetah and Flying Leopard.

According to the rules of combat there were only the old man and his three Grandsons to face Yu Hua. When Yu came to call for a fight, seven year old Heavenly Happy bravely volunteered to go, but he was turned down by his Grandfather. And so the fourteen year old Heavenly Portion went.

Young as he was, Heavenly Portion was mature in his training and skill. He fought valiantly and courageously. Surprised and fearing he might be defeated by a child, Yu Hua hurriedly fanned out his Soul-Dispatching Flay and Heavenly Portion too was captured.

Flying Tiger was both angered and grieved as other captives joined him in prison. Meanwhile, Yellow Rolling saw there was no way out because the opposition was not fighting on the level. In despair, Yellow Rolling gathered his men, and said to them, "I have no way to counter their black magic. I and my two Grandsons will stay here till the end. All of you have my permission to use the family treasures to buy your way out of this Pass and go to the Western Foothills. Now go as I ordered!"

No one budged. These loyal warriors would never abandon their masters in their hour of need.

Yellow Rolling decided to try a last desperate plan to save his two Grandsons. He took off his armor and jade belt, put on white mourning garment. He took his Grandsons by their hands, and went to see Han Glory.

"No use to come begging!" Han remarked when he heard that Rolling was coming to see him. He walked out and found the three kneeling at the Garrison threshold.

CHAPTER 34

▼

FLYING TIGER MEETS FLYING BEAR

Han Glory said, "My dear Commander Yellow Rolling, what can I do for you?"

"My dear sir. I fully realize I am in the wrong. But since my young grandson is only seven years old, please let him go. Even in our death, my son and I will be forever grateful to you."

"You are wrong, my General," said Han. "My order is to capture all of you and send you to the Capital City, Morning Song. If I let one of you go, that would seem I am in league with you, which certainly is not the case."

After more verbal sparring, Yellow Rolling said angrily, "Han Glory, you think you are a big shot but act like an ass! I humbly begged for your help, but you acted like you own the world! So be it! Take me to your prison!"

Kneeling before his father, Flying Tiger cried out in anguish, "My father! Forgive me for disgracing you like this!"

"My son," said the old man in despair, "it is too late to say that now."

*   *   *   *

There was no end to the celebration in Han Glory's Headquarters. They captured not only all the Yellow family members, but their treasures as well.

Next day General Yu Hua commanded three thousands troops on their way to the Capital City, Morning Song with their prisoners. As they retraced their way back to the Demarcation Pass, old Yellow Rolling agonized over the events that led to their dire straits. Tears and sadness strangled his heart as they passed his old garrison.

*   *   *   *

In his Golden Light Cave on Mount Champion, Superiorman Paragon was meditating when a sudden brainstorm hit him. Upon calculating, he found Flying Tiger and his family in trouble. He called his disciple Nezha to make haste to their rescue.

"Return after you have taken them safely over the Flood-Water Pass," Paragon said.

Quickly Nezha located them at the Through-The-Clouds Pass where he saw a long line of prisoner carts guarded by armed soldiers. At the end of the procession was General Yu Hua.

It would be more fun to provoke them into fighting than just pounce on them, thought Nezha. He stood in the middle of the road and sang loudly,

> I am ageless and powerful;
> I fear nothing and no one but my own Guru.
> A gold brick from you,
> Will get you through.

Yu Hua rode up to meet Nezha's challenge. "How dare you block our way? I am General Yu Hua of Flood-Water Pass, taking criminals

Yellow Flying Tiger and his gang to the king's Capital. Get out of my way if you treasure your life!"

Nezha said, "Ah, so you are the honorable general who captured the criminals? My congratulations. Still, if you want to pass, please hand over ten gold bricks."

Enraged, Yu Hua charged at Nezha who fought with ease. In desperation, Yu Hua pulled out his Soul-Dispatching Flag. With his bare hand, Nezha caught the flag and laughingly put it in his leopard bag.

"Any more tricks? Show them all to me, but hurry, I don't have time to waste on the likes of you!"

Nezha pulled out his own gold brick and aimed it at Yu Hua, almost knocking him off his five-colored magic bull. Yu Hua turned and fled, his right arm badly wounded.

Nezha resisted his impulse to pursue. He walked over to the prisoner carts and asked, "Who is Yellow Flying Tiger?"

"I am. May I ask who are you?"

"I am Nezha, disciple of Superiorman Paragon of Mount Champion. My master ordered me to help you over Flood-Water Pass."

He quickly released all prisoners.

$$* \qquad * \qquad * \qquad *$$

Meanwhile Yu Hua was back at Flood-Water Pass to report to Han Glory.

"What has happened? Are you injured?"

Yu Hua reported in detail.

Glory asked, "What about the Flying Tigers?"

"I don't know, sir."

"Damn! We are in trouble!" Glory pounded on the table.

All his generals speculated that Flying Tiger could not possibly escape because he was hemmed in from four directions: in the east by Through-the-Clouds Pass, in the west by Demarcation Pass and

Flood-Water Pass, in the north by Fine-Dream Pass, and in the south by Green-Dragon Pass.

As they talked, a guard reported seeing a warrior with wheels on his feet, demanding a fight.

"That's him!" Yu Hua cried with a shudder.

"Everyone! Get on your horse and catch him!" ordered Han Glory.

Ignoring all the others, Nezha demanded of Han Glory, "Where is Yu Hua?"

Angrily, Han Glory retorted, "Who are you? How dare you upset the king's order?"

"I am Nezha, disciple of Superiorman Paragon of Mount Champion under whose order I have come to rescue Yellow Flying Tiger. Yu Hua ran away from me a while ago. Now hand him over, or else!"

Quickly Han Glory and his men jumped on Nezha; Nezha held them off nicely as Chou Commence, Radiance, Dragon Ring and Modesty galloped over to help. Nezha aimed his gold brick again and sent Han Glory and Yu Hua fleeing to the northeast, badly wounded.

And so another crisis was over. The ever so practical Commence supervised not only the recovery of the Yellow family treasures, but also the confiscation of Han Glory's. Next day they left Flood-Water Pass and were soon crossing into the Western Foothills.

Nezha escorted them to the Golden Rooster Mountain before bidding them farewell. "I will see you again in the Western Foothills. Take care!"

Yellow Flying Tiger expressed his gratitude a thousand-fold.

*   *   *   *

Continuing on their westward journey, they soon passed Mount First-Sun and Mount Swallow, and soon reached Mount Singing Phoenix, a part of the Western Foothills. It was another seventy miles to the capital, Phoenix City.

"I think we better make camp here, father," Yellow Flying Tiger explained to his father. "I will first go to pay my respect to Prime Minister Baby Tooth and see how King Wu's court feels about us."

Along the way, Flying Tiger was very impressed by what he saw. "No wonder people say the Western Foothills is the oasis of the world's desert!" he said to himself.

When Yellow Flying Tiger was announced, Baby Tooth came out immediately, saying, "We were expecting you but did not know you would be here so soon. I am sorry we did not have a chance to come out to welcome you."

Flying Tiger said, "I am like a bird who has lost its forest. I came to beg King Wu to accept my service."

Excited over Flying Tiger's offer, Baby Tooth immediately went to see King Wu Ji Fa. Ji Fa received Flying Tiger with the utmost courtesy.

"I have heard so much about you. And I especially want to thank you for the assistance you gave my late father. Welcome to the Western Foothills. My Prince, tell me more about what happened."

Flying Tiger recounted the events from his wife's fateful visit on the New Year's Day to his capture by Han Glory at Flood-Water Pass and eventual rescue by Nezha near the Through-the-Clouds Pass.

"What was your rank in King Zhou's court?" Ji Fa asked.

"I was Lord of National Security."

"Very good. You will be my Lord of National Stability, with full power and responsibility for the kingdom's stability. You will command all of the Western Foothills' armies," said King Wu Ji Fa.

Then, while entertaining Flying Tiger at a banquet, King Wu ordered Baby Tooth to look for an auspicious day to start building a mansion for the new lord.

Next day, Flying Tiger returned to thank King Wu and inform him that his father and many trusted aides were at Mount Singing Phoenix, awaiting the king's order.

"Welcome," said King Wu. "Everyone will retain his former rank here."

CHAPTER 35

▼

GENERAL RICEFIELD INVADES THE WESTERN FOOTHILLS

Grand Old Master had a magic eye on his forehead, so why then was he fooled by the trick played by Superiorman True Vacuum? His own explanation was that it was the scheme of things Heaven and Earth over which he had no control. Very well, he had made a fool of himself by pursuing a phantom. But he did not really feel too bad about it, comforted by the knowledge that there were many obstacles which Yellow Flying Tiger must overcome before reaching the Western Foothills. Even if he sprouted wings, the Grand Old Master thought, Flying Tiger would never be able to get out of all the five mountain Passes to reach the Western Foothills. Sooner or later, he would be captured.

Then one after another, a series of most unexpected reports came in:

General Akin Silver killed his Commander and let Flying Tiger speed through Upon-Highwater Pass.

Flying Tiger had successively killed the Commanders of both Highwater and Through-the-Clouds Passes.

Commander Yellow Rolling gave up Demarcation Pass and joined his son.

And finally the urgent report that Flying Tiger had fought his way out of Flood-Water Pass.

His magic eye flashing anger, Grand Old Master said, "I fully know how bad King Zhou is behaving, but I promised my late king to uphold the kingdom. I will do so no matter what!" He ordered his drummer to beat a call for all his generals to attend an urgent meeting.

"Now that we have lost Flying Tiger to the Western Foothills," he said to his generals. "it behooves us to do something before the Western Foothills does it to us first! Any suggestions?"

One general said, "Floating-Soul Pass in the east has been successful for many years in keeping out the warring Grand Duke of the East. Similarly, the Three-Mountains Pass in the south has kept out the rebellious Grand Duke of the South. I think all Grand Old Master needs to do is to send out new commanders and reinforcements to the five Passes to the west.

"Besides, the empty National Treasury can hardly support our day to day operation, let alone a new campaign against the Western Foothills."

"You are right, my general," said Grand Old Master. "However, should the Western Foothills start making trouble, we must be ready; otherwise we will be sitting ducks! For they now have many men of talent: General Nimblefoot whose strength and bravery are matchless, Counselor Easy Life whose stratagem has no peer, and Prime Minister Baby Tooth whose bag of tricks is large. We must be wary. We need to dig our well before we die from thirst!"

"Grand Old Master," said a general, "if you worry about them, why not send someone out there to have a look? We can then gear our action accordingly."

Grand Old Master weighed all the pros and cons. Being a man of action, he finally decided it was better to mount an expeditionary force. So he ordered General Jade Ricefield and his twin brother Jade

Thunder to lead a thirty thousands troops for this expedition—not to fight, just to spy on the Western Foothills.

Troubles plagued them from the very beginning. The troops were not given full rations, partly because there was not enough food, and partly because the Jade brothers decided to travel light. There were many complains from the soldiers. They wanted more food and more rest.

Meanwhile their forced westward march was reported to Baby Tooth by sources friendly to the Western Foothills.

When the Jade brothers reached the Western Foothills, instead of being challenged at the border, they found the populace courteous and civil; some even offered food and wine. Finally they made camp near the Capital Phoenix City.

When Jade Ricefield called for a fight at the city walls, General Nimblefoot was there to face him. "Greetings, General Ricefield," Nimblefoot said. "Pray explain why are you here."

Ricefield said, "We have the order from the Grand Old Master to bring back Yellow Flying Tiger. Please hand him over, or else!"

"Is that so?" laughed Nimblefoot. "Don't you know how silly you sound? You are courting trouble coming here uninvited!"

They fought, but Nimblefoot easily knocked Ricefield off his mount and captured him.

Ricefield refused to kneel when he was facing Baby Tooth.

"Why, General Ricefield," Baby Tooth said, "don't you know your etiquette? You should kneel!"

"You low-born basket weaver and flour vendor! You dare to tell me to kneel? So you have captured me. Kill me if you wish but stop blowing hot air!"

"It is not an insult to be low born. It is what we do later in life that counts! Don't feel sorry for me because I came from peon stock," Baby Tooth replied soothingly. Then he ordered Ricefield's immediate execution.

Yellow Flying Tiger, the new Lord of National Stability, offered a different idea.

"Please, my dear Prime Minister. As I see it, General Ricefield follows King Zhou in his blind faith. If we can convert him to our cause, he could be a strong addition to our team. Should I give it a try?"

"Yes, please," said Baby Tooth.

Flying Tiger went straight to the detention yard where preparations were being made for Ricefield's execution.

Flying Tiger said, "My General. You don't seem to understand half the predicament you are in! Don't you know under Heaven, two thirds of the country has rallied to the banner of King Wu? King Zhou may win a battle here and there, but his mandate from Heaven has long expired. The people will no longer put up with King Zhou's wanton cruelty and endless debauchery. On the other hand, King Wu's virtues are well known. For instance, all my men have retained their rank and pay. As for me, I am now the Lord of National Stability. From this you can see what kind of person King Wu is, and the kind of administration he has. Wake up before it is too late!"

Ricefield said, "My Prince. I have insulted Baby Tooth before his men. I am afraid he will never forgive me."

"Let me worry about that," Flying Tiger assured him.

Yellow Flying Tiger led Ricefield back to see Baby Tooth.

Ricefield now knelt to ask Baby Tooth for forgiveness and to pledge his allegiance to the Western Foothills.

Baby Tooth said, "You have committed no crime for me to forgive. Since you are now a member of our team, please bring your troops into the city."

Ricefield said, "My brother Jade Thunder is out there. May I bring him in to see you first?"

*   *   *   *

Jade Thunder was relieved to see his brother. "How did you get out?" he asked.

"Oh, my brother! You just don't know how lucky I am!" Ricefield related his capture, his unexpected release, and his decision to join the ranks of King Wu. "What a break we have. Come with me to see Baby Tooth."

His twin brother was not convinced. "How could you, my brother? We are King Zhou's Palace Guards. How can you give up our wealth and position to serve an unknown king?"

"No, brother. Of all the powers under Heaven, two thirds have rallied to the banner of King Wu. We must not work against this tide. Besides, all who join King Wu retain their rank and pay. What have we to lose? Come with me now. Please."

"But have you given any thought to our family back home? What will their fate be but certain humiliation, torture and death? How can we do that to our parents?"

"What shall we do now?"

They thought and thought. Being all brawn and not much brain, they were accustomed to the lies and double-crossing in King Zhou's Court, and that was the only way they could see things.

*   *   *   *

Ricefield came back alone to see Baby Tooth. "My Prime Minister. I talked to my brother. He wonders if you could send an envoy to give him face. Otherwise, it would create unpleasantness as other Generals might look down on us."

With Baby Tooth's approval, Yellow Flying Tiger went. As soon as he left with Ricefield, the foresighted Baby Tooth sent Generals Nimblefoot, Rigorous Guard, and Rigorous Liberal together with their supporting troops to all the strategic locations to block possible escape routes.

*   *   *   *

With much fanfare, Jade Thunder came out to welcome Yellow Flying Tiger. No sooner did he enter their camp than Jade Thunder shouted, "Bind him up!" and thus took Flying Tiger prisoner by surprise.

"Ungrateful curs!" There was nothing the enraged Flying Tiger could do because he had come unarmed.

Jubilant over their easy success, the Jade twins hurriedly decamped with their prized prisoner.

They had not gone far when someone blocked their way, shouting in the dark, "General Ricefield, please release Lord Yellow Flying Tiger!"

"How dare you block my way!" Jade Thunder said, charging angrily at the voice who turned out to be General Rigorous Guard.

As they fought, Rigorous Liberal rescued Flying Tiger, and together they quickly captured Ricefield.

Meanwhile Jade Thunder realized he was not Rigorous Guard's match, and like a fish trying to jump out of a net, he ran like hell every which way. Eventually he found himself encircled and captured by General Nimblefoot.

By dawn, captors and captives all gathered before Baby Tooth who ordered that Jade brothers be executed immediately.

Jade Thunder yelled, "Injustice! Injustice!"

Smiling, Baby Tooth said, "Oh, how so, my General Jade Thunder?"

"We know King Wu has the allegiance of two thirds of the nation. We brothers do not hesitate to rally to him. But we still have our parents to worry about. How can we stay and leave them to suffer certain torture and death?"

Baby Tooth said, "You should have discussed your problem with me."

"We are only brutes. We are confused," said Ricefield as tears ran down his cheeks.

"Are you on the level now?

"How can we lie? You can ask Lord Yellow Flying Tiger about our parents."

Baby Tooth ordered the Jade brothers freed. Ricefield would stay in the Western Foothills as hostage while Jade Thunder went back to get the Jade family.

CHAPTER 36

▼

ZHANG CASSIA ON A WESTERN FOOTHILLS CAMPAIGN

Jade Thunder knew he must rehearse thoroughly as he traveled day and night. He must have it letter perfect in his head, what Baby Tooth had coached him to say when he saw the Grand Old Master. The Grand Old Master was no fool, not easily duped. When he finally faced the Grand Old Master, he told his lie very carefully and convincingly.

"How goes?" Grand Old Master asked.

"In the Western Foothills, we first fought General Nimblefoot. The next two days, we fought Rigorous Guard and Rigorous Liberal. We were not losing, but were much troubled by the low morale of our men. This is because at our last supply stop at Flood-Water Pass, we were not given enough provisions. That is why I have to rush back to ask for more back up."

Grand Old Master was much puzzled. "I have instructed all Pass commanders to help. It is strange why Han Glory refused to do so."

Nevertheless, Grand Old Master authorized additional supplies, transport, and men for Jade Thunder to take back to the Western Foothills.

Next night, under the cover of darkness, Jade Thunder rushed the men, supplies, his parents, and both his own and his brother's family out of the Capital City, Morning Song.

It was not until many days later that the Grand Old Master had time to think about this business. He felt uneasy.

"Why did Han Glory withhold supplies from Jade Thunder?" he asked himself. Casting a few gold coins, to his dismay Grand Old Master saw from the configuration that Jade Thunder had deceived him! Well, it was too late to intercept him now because Jade by this time was already out of the five mountain Passes. Grand Old Master decided to send Commander Zhang Cassia of Green Dragon Pass to the Western Foothills on a punitive campaign. He sent his urgent order by means of smoke signals first, followed by a written order.

Jade Thunder and his column went over the five Passes without incident. On arrival, he reported his success to Baby Tooth.

Baby Tooth said, "No doubt the Grand Old Master has discovered this ruse by now. We had better be prepared for his attack."

*   *   *   *

In the days of yore, the transport of supplies was difficult. And supplies for distant expeditionary army were usually scant. So, following standard military strategy, Baby Tooth didn't show much concern until it was reported to him that Zhang Cassia led a ten thousand men column, now encamped five miles outside of Phoenix City.

Baby Tooth gathered his generals to discuss stratagem.

Yellow Flying Tiger said, "Zhang Cassia and his Vanguard general are known to possess black magic. It would be tough to fight them."

"What kind of black magic?" Baby Tooth asked.

"I only heard of Cassia's magic. In the heat of battle, he would call out the name of his opponent, then without much ado, the person whose name was called would immediately fall from his mount, and then was captured and killed.

"Please inform our generals to keep their names from Zhang Cassia. Without the correct name, Cassia cannot use his black magic," Yellow Flying Tiger said.

Baby Tooth showed concern. But others thought it a big joke.

"You mean if he calls our names, we would be under his spell and die without a fight?" They laughed.

*   *   *   *

The next day, Zhang Cassia and his Vanguard, Gale Woods came to the Phoenix City walls shouting for a fight. General Ji Skye, a younger brother of King Wu, was annoyed the night before when he heard Flying Tiger tell of Zhang Cassia's black magic. A hot-tempered man, Ji Skye wanted to show the world that his military training could well handle any black magic. He volunteered to have the first fight.

Outside, Ji Skye found a general with buck teeth, a blue face and red beard, wearing golden armor with a jade buckle, and wielding two wolf-tooth clubs.

Ji Skye asked, "Are you commander Zhang Cassia?"

"No. I am Vanguard General Gale Woods. We have orders to capture the rebel Yellow Flying Tiger. Why pretend to fight us when you fully know you cannot win?"

"You come here without invitation, and you think you can bully us and get away with it? Think again, my friend! Stop bragging and bring Zhang Cassia out this minute!"

Gale woods replied, "Rebel! Look out!" and charged at Ji Skye.

They fought a big battle. It was clear that Gale Woods' skill in weaponry was no match for Ji Skye's. Skye wounded Gale Woods in the foot.

Scampering for his life with Ji Skye in pursuit, Gale Woods mumbled something and a puff of black smoke issued from his mouth. Like a slingshot, the smoke shot a bright red ball the size of a rice bowl straight at Ji Skye, knocking him off his horse. Gale Woods turned around on his horse and clobbered Ji Skye to death. Holding Skye's head, he returned triumphantly to camp.

Ji Skye's death saddened King Wu, Baby Tooth, and all of the Western Foothills.

Next day, Zhang Cassia himself led his troops to the city wall, spoiling for a fight.

Baby Tooth, with Yellow Flying Tiger's warning very much in mind, thought, "How can we corral the tiger cubs if we don't take the risk of going into the tiger's den?" He ordered preparation for a big battle.

*   *   *   *

Commander Cassia was in white armor, riding a white horse, and carrying a silvery weapon. He looked like someone made of ice. He watched intently when Baby Tooth's army came out of the city gate.

In the forefront was Baby Tooth on a black horse. He was dressed in a white cotton monk's fashion with black trigram embroidery on both front and back. His shoulder-length white hair flowed loosely under his goldfish-tail hat. He carried his twin swords.

In near-perfect precision, his generals and soldiers followed. In the rear, against huge red banners, was Yellow Flying Tiger, the Lord of National Stability, on his five-colored magic bull.

Cassia galloped up to Baby Tooth, saying, "Jiang Baby Tooth! You were once a minister in King Zhou's court. What in the world are you doing here? You not only pledged allegiance to the upstart King Wu, you are also harboring the rebel Yellow Flying Tiger! You know what crime that means? And what makes you think you can get away with it?

Be wise and see the light! Hand over Flying Tiger, and we can skip the fighting and save the innocents!"

"So that is how you think?" said Baby Tooth. "We in the Western Foothills are minding our own business and extending a helping hand to whoever requests it. What is wrong with that? On the other hand, you, without provocation, have brought ten thousand troops to invade this peaceful land. And you think you are in the right? Don't make me laugh! Take your troops back to where you belong before we annihilate you!"

"You spent some time on Mount Kunlun and should have learned something. But judging by what you just said, you are just an ignoramus!" Cassia motioned to his Vanguard General Gale Woods, "Get him!"

A flash of amber light rushed toward Baby Tooth. General Nimblefoot intercepted in time.

Meanwhile Cassia fought Yellow Flying Tiger. After a few jostles, Cassia resorted to his black magic by calling out, "Yellow Flying Tiger, get down from your beast!"

Flying Tiger fell immediately off his mount. Fortunately his brothers Flying Cheetah and Flying Leopard were able to rush to his rescue before Cassia's men could reach him.

Unthinkingly, Commence rushed out to fight Cassia, who immediately shouted Commence's name. Commence fell off his horse and was captured alive.

General Nimblefoot was giving Gale Woods a hard time. Gale Woods again resorted to black magic, shooting out a red ball and knocking Nimblefoot off his horse. He too was captured alive by Gale Woods' men.

Cassia was pleased with the outcome, and triumphantly they returned to camp.

Next morning, Cassia again came calling for a fight. But Baby Tooth declined by hanging out a "NO FIGHTING" flag.

"So just after only one little battle Baby Tooth is too scared to fight!" Cassia snickered and returned to camp.

*   *   *   *

It was again a sudden brainstorm which prompted Superiorman Paragon into sending Nezha to help with the crisis in the Western Foothills.

"Quick, go to the Western Foothills! Help all you can! Thirty-six columns of troops are about to invade there!"

*   *   *   *

Nezha introduced himself to Baby Tooth and asked who was fighting whom.

Yellow Flying Tiger replied, "We are fighting Commander Zhang Cassia of Green Dragon Pass. Both Cassia and his Vanguard General Gale Woods possess black magic. They killed Ji Skye and captured two of our top generals."

Nezha said, "Now that I am here, I will help all I can. Don't be discouraged."

The "NO FIGHTING" flag was removed.

By the order of Cassia, Gale Woods came face to face with Nezha and asked, "Who are you?"

"I am Nezha, Baby Tooth's new helper. Are you Commander Zhang Cassia? I heard you can make a warrior fall off his mount by simply calling his name. Right?"

"No, I am not Cassia. I am Vanguard General Gale Woods."

"I will let you go this time. Get me Cassia, and fast. I have no time to waste on you!"

Furious at being taken so lightly, Gale Woods came at Nezha with his black magic.

Pointing a finger at Gale Woods' black magic smoke which disappeared instantly without a trace, Nezha laughed. "So that was what they were talking about! Ha! Ha!"

Seeing his magic broken, Gale Woods charged at Nezha with his twin wolf-tooth clubs. Nezha fought back with his Omnipresent Ring, breaking Gale's right arm. Gale ran back to camp.

When Cassia came out, he saw a pompous young warrior prancing around on his wind-fire wheels, showing off. Cassia demanded, "Are you Nezha?"

"Yep!"

"Are you the one who wounded my Vanguard General Gale Woods?"

"Right again! By the way, I heard you can get a warrior off his mount by simply calling his name. Here I am on my wind-fire wheels. Why not try your mean trick and see!"

Without hesitation, Cassia shouted with all his might, "Nezha, get off your wheels!"

Nezha was startled by a jerk, but instantly regained his composure and steadied himself on his wheels.

Frightened to see his magic not working, Cassia tried again and again, but to no avail. After three times, Nezha said sarcastically, "What's the matter with you? Why do you keep calling my name? Don't you see I am right here in front of you?" So saying, Nezha threw his Omnipresent Ring at Cassia, breaking his arm and sending him fleeing to his camp.

Triumphantly Nezha returned and reported to Baby Tooth.

"Did he call your name?" Baby Tooth was very concerned.

"Yes, he did it three times. But I simply ignored him."

Baby Tooth and others marveled at Nezha's ability to ignore Cassia's calls. Little did they know that Nezha was not made of flesh and blood and therefore not subject to Cassia's black magic.

*   *   *   *

Anticipating the Grand Old Master would soon retaliate with an even mightier army, Baby Tooth secured King Wu's consent for a quick trip to Mount Kunlun for advice.

CHAPTER 37

▼

BABY TOOTH RETURNS
TO MOUNT KUNLUN

When Baby Tooth appeared at Mount Kunlun, his master Superiorman Primordial Supreme said, "I am so glad you are here. Well, the God of South Pole has the Register of the Investiture of Gods for you to take to the Western Foothills. This is the most important responsibility. No one should know about it. You have my full trust in this task and I am sure you know what is expected of you."

Baby Tooth replied, "Yes, my Master. I will do my best." Then timidly he said, "I came for advice. So far we have the help of Nezha, a disciple of Superiorman Paragon of Mount Champion. But Grand Old Master will soon send many more men to invade us. What should we do?"

"You are the Prime Minister, enjoying all the material wealth and power the Red Dust has to offer. You should know what to do. Why ask me? But from what I can foresee, when situations get too difficult, there will be help from unexpected quarters. I have full confidence in the luck of King Wu. Go now. Do the best you can."

As Baby Tooth walked out, a servant ran after him, saying, "The master wants to see you again."

Hurriedly, Baby Tooth retraced his steps and knelt before his master.

The master said, "Oh, yes, a more immediate threat. Someone is going to call you by name. Ignore him no matter what. If you answer him, thirty-six columns of enemy troops will be zeroing on you! One more thing, in the East Sea, someone will be waiting for you. Be extra careful. Go now."

When Baby Tooth walked out, the God of South Pole was waiting for him. Baby Tooth said, "I could not get my master to give me any specific advice."

The God of South Pole, handing Baby Tooth the Register of the Investiture of Gods, said, "Don't worry. When the going gets too tough, there will be help from unexpected sources."

"That's exactly what my master said to me." Baby Tooth put the Register securely inside his gown, and was ready to take the underground route to the Western Foothills when he heard someone calling, "Baby Tooth!"

Remembering his master's warning, Baby Tooth ignored the call. Again and again, the call came but Baby Tooth ignored them all.

"Baby Tooth, now that you are a giddy prime minister, you turn your back to an old friend! Don't you remember the forty years we were students together at Mount Kunlun?"

His curiosity now fully aroused, Baby Tooth turned his head! He recognized the man in a scholar's attire with a gourd and a sword hanging from each shoulder. It was Aggrandizing Bobcat, a schoolmate under Superiorman Primordial Supreme.

Aggrandizing Bobcat was later expelled from Mount Kunlun, unknown to Baby Tooth and other students.

"I am sorry. I did not know it was you. My master told me not to answer any call. How are you?"

"What have you under your gown?"

"The Register of the Investiture of Gods."

"Where are you going with it?"

"To the Western Foothills," Baby Tooth said truthfully.

"Whom are you supporting anyway?"

"I am supporting King Wu of the Western Foothills, of course. We must move with the scheme of things Heaven and Earth. Don't you see the die has been cast? Two thirds of the nation has rallied to King Wu."

Aggrandizing Bobcat said, "This is what you think. I am going to support King Zhou. Burn that Register and join me. Or else you better look out!"

"Don't be angry with me," Baby tooth said. "I am doing what master wants me to do. That's all."

"Tell you what," Aggrandizing Bobcat said amiably. "Let us both support King Zhou and I will share with you all the glories and wealth. Why bother with the unknown and uncertain? King Zhou has ready-made positions and wealth to offer. What do you say?"

"No, I am sorry." Baby Tooth said without guile. "I must not do anything against my master's wish."

Very disappointed, Aggrandizing Bobcat said, "So you refuse to join me? You have but forty years of training. What makes you think you can do anything meaningful? Besides, don't ever think you can fight me!"

Baby Tooth said, "Our ability does not depend solely on training. Sincerity is just as important."

"That is just wishful thinking. I have tricks you have never even dreamt of. For instance, I can cut off my head, cast it into the air, and then put it back where it belongs. Want to see?"

Unbelieving, Baby Tooth said, "My goodness, if you can do that, I may join you."

"No backing down?"

"Of course not. I mean what I say."

With a flourish, Aggrandizing Bobcat cut off his head with the sword in his right hand, and threw the head into the air with his left. While the head was hovering in the sky, Bobcat's body stood erect and a stream of black smoke issued from the hole where the head was connected to the neck. Baby Tooth watched, his mouth wide open in amazement.

Witnessing what was transpiring, God of South Pole quickly called one of his disciples to change into an egret, which snatched Aggrandizing Bobcat's head away.

God of South Pole then went over to lecture Baby Tooth: "My poor, honest Baby Tooth. It is good to be honest, but dangerous to be so gullible! You excel in affairs of state and military stratagem, but you are too trusting in the day-to-day dealings with this kind of people like Aggrandizing Bobcat! Your master had warned you not to answer any call. Now thirty-six columns of enemy troops will be waiting for your head! Don't you know how unethical Aggrandizing Bobcat is? After he was expelled from Mount Kunlun, he learned black magic. He wants to steal the Register of the Investiture of Gods from you! That's why I ordered White Egret boy to snatch his head away. Without his head, he will die within thirty minutes. We must get rid of him!"

Baby Tooth thought otherwise. He begged, "Please, have mercy. I don't think we should kill him. Now that I know, I will not let him fool me again. Please don't kill him."

"Then thirty-six columns of enemy troops will be coming after you!"

"Yes, I know. He did not try to kill me. I don't think we should kill first. Let him go, please."

Reluctantly, the God of South Pole gave orders to bring back the head. White Egret did so, but put it on backward. Aggrandizing Bobcat turned it around.

God of South Pole looked him in the eye and scolded, "Better get out of here before your old master sees you!"

Instead of being grateful to Baby Tooth, Aggrandizing Bobcat said with venom, "So you refused to join me. Mark my words, I am going to make a sea of blood and a mountain of white bones out of the Western Foothills!" He left without a backward glance.

*   *   *   *

Traveling underground, Baby Tooth soon arrived at East Sea where his master has said someone would be waiting for him.

East Sea was a beautiful place of green mountains, exotic colorful flowers, white sand beaches full of birds, and fish jumping among the waves.

"What I would give to leave the Red Dust and to retire here to enjoy the sea breeze and the bird songs!" Baby Tooth was startled by a sudden shout. He looked around but saw only the tumbling sea.

As the waves got higher and the sea roared, the shout became louder and more persistent. Now Baby Tooth could hear the shouts more clearly.

"Master! Master! I have been here for generations, waiting for someone to guide my soul to a better place! I beg you to rescue my soul out of this miserable sea!"

Bravely, Baby Tooth asked, "Who are you? Why the roaring sea? What kept your soul down?"

"I am Cedar Precept, the Chief Commander under the Yellow Emperor. Chief Ignoramus Chiyou threw me into the sea as he fled from our advancing army. My rotten body has kept me down here since. Help me please."

"If you truly are Cedar Precept, certainly I will do what I can."

Pointing at the sea from where the voice came, Baby Tooth summoned up his triple true whammy fire. As thunder clapped and lightning flashed, out jumped Cedar Precept.

Looking at the kneeling Cedar Precept, Baby Tooth said, "Go to the Western Foothills to build an altar for the investiture of gods."

In a flash, the grateful Cedar Precept was gone.

Baby Tooth took the underground way back to the Western Foothills. As he surfaced, waiting for him were the five colored-face wind-fire demons. They had been waiting for Baby Tooth's order since he pacified them in Soong Spectacular's garden.

Baby Tooth said, "Go help Cedar Precept."

*   *   *   *

"How was the trip to Mount Kunlun?" King Wu asked.

"My master said luck is with us. When we are in dire difficulty, help will come from an unknown source," Baby Tooth said. Of course, he did not mention the Register of the Investiture of Gods, because this matter was not for ordinary earthlings to know.

Next day, Baby Tooth ordered the attack of Cassia's camp and successfully rescued both Generals Nimblefoot and Commence. Cassia and Vanguard Gale Woods were badly wounded; however, they managed to escape from Baby Tooth's army.

*   *   *   *

The Grand Old Master was surprised and furious when he learned of Cassia's defeat. "This means that I must go there myself! However, if I leave the capital, who will protect the king? The campaigns on both the east and south are still raging on, how can I leave? But if I don't go, who can do the job?"

One of his generals said, "My lord. Why not invite some of your friends from the mountains to help? All of them possess magic, and certainly will be able to defeat whatever Baby Tooth has."

"Why not, indeed," said Grand Old Master.

CHAPTER 38

▼

BABY TOOTH TACKLES
FOUR SUPERIORMEN

To sort out his options, Grand Old Master ordered his mansion be closed for three days from business and visitors. He then got on his black qilin and flew to visit his four best friends in the West Sea.

*   *   *   *

Superiormen were a breed apart. In their long, long years of discipline, their goals were to seek the auspicious conjunctions of spiritual and physical forces. Those successful could cajole or even direct the spirits of the physical world to do their bidding. Equally important were their spiritual attainments. They had grown above temptation, both flesh and material, and could contemplate the scheme of things on Heaven and Earth without prejudice. But they could still have their blind spots. For instance, a strong inclination toward favoring old friends and ties, whether the cause argued was just or not.

*   *   *   *

Four superiormen stopped their game of chess to welcome their friend the Grand Old Master.

"What wind has blown you here?"

"This is special. I am here to ask for your help."

"Don't be funny. We have retired to this remote island for so long, we don't care what is going on in the Red Dust. What can we do that you can't?"

"Well, I am indeed in charge of the administration of King Zhou's court, and I can do much to help. However, I am now so alone in holding up the kingdom. All the loyal and able ministers were either killed by King Zhou or have rebelled. The national treasury is empty and the populace is restless. But I must keep my promise to my late King Da Yi to do my best to the very end.

"Right this moment, there is a man named Baby Tooth, a disciple of Superiorman Primordial Supreme of Mount Kunlun who is helping the upstart King Wu of the Western Foothills. King Wu is the son of the late Grand Duke of the West Ji Chang. After Ji Chang died, his son Ji Fa crowned himself King Wu and rebelled against King Zhou. I have sent my best generals and thirty thousand soldiers to fight him but my men were defeated by Nezha, a disciple of Superiorman Paragon of Mount Champion who is helping Baby Tooth.

"I would like to quell the rebellion in the Western Foothills myself. But at this time, the sons of the Grand Dukes of both East and South are fighting us. If I go to the Western Foothills, there is no one to uphold King Zhou and defend his capital. Please give me a helping hand, my friends."

"Well, in that case, I would be more than glad to help," one of the four superiormen said.

"No, if we go, the four of us will go together," said the others. They turned to Grand Old Master. "You go on home. We will come by to map out our strategy."

When the foursome showed up at the Capital City, Morning Song, the people were frightened by their strange mounts and unusual appearance. The Grand Old Master introduced them to King Zhou. They were:

1. Wang Magus. He was in blue scholarly attire, had a peaches-and-cream complexion, and was handsome as a full moon.

2. Yang Forest. In a monk-style white gown, his face was charcoal black ringed by bushy blond hair and beard.

3. High Amiable. His complexion was indigo blue, had two protruding buck teeth, bright red hair in a top knot fashion, and wore a bright red robe.

4. Li Resounding. His face was a deep plum red color, framed by long floating black hair and beard. He was in a pale yellow gown.

Grand Old Master gave the foursome a briefing on General Cassia's plight. The four went directly to the Western Foothills.

* * * *

Cassia and Gale Woods showed their wounds to Wang Magus who quickly cured them. The foursome then encouraged Cassia to encamp his army just outside of King Wu's Capital, Phoenix City.

"Tomorrow, you call Baby Tooth for a fight," they instructed Cassia. "We will hide under your battle banners until the right moment to come out."

Holding his twin swords, the unsuspecting Baby Tooth came out on his green chestnut horse. "A defeated general, how shameful to show your face again!" Baby Tooth said as he confronted Cassia.

"Winning and losing a battle is common in a war. What is there to be ashamed of?" Cassia retorted.

Then on the sound of a sudden drum roll, out rushed the foursome from the Nine Dragon Island: four strange looking persons on four fearsome animals, streaking out from behind the banners. They frightened all the mounts on Baby tooth's side; even Baby Tooth and Yellow Flying Tiger were tossed about. Nezha was the only one firmly on his wheels.

Watching the disarray, the foursome broke into uproarious laughter and teased, "Now, now. Get up slowly. Sit straight on your mount. Don't be afraid."

Baby Tooth nodded in a polite salute, and said, "My honorable sirs. May we know your names and your abode? And what can we do for you?"

"Baby Tooth! We are the foursome of the Nine Dragon Island. We are here at the request of the Grand Old Master to help you out of your trouble. Will you accept our three conditions?" Wang Magus said.

"Don't say three, thirty conditions would not be too many if they can get us out of our difficulties. Please name them," Baby Tooth replied amiably.

"Number one. Your King Wu must again become a minister to the Court of King Zhou."

"My honorable sirs. My master and his family have been loyal ministers in King Zhou's Court for generations. No problem there."

"Number two. Open up all your granaries to feast Cassia's army. And Number three. Hand over Yellow Flying Tiger and let Cassia take him to King Zhou."

Stalling for time, Baby Tooth said, "I understand your conditions. Let me discuss the matter with my people and we will let you know in three days."

They saluted each other and Baby Tooth took his men back to the City.

*   *   *   *

Back in their Headquarters, Yellow Flying Tiger knelt before Baby Tooth and said, "My Prime Minister. Please hand me over to them. It is not right that I should be causing King Wu trouble."

"Don't be absurd, my dear Prince. I was merely trying to buy time."

Again, with King Wu's consent, Baby Tooth went to Mount Kunlun to seek help.

*   *   *   *

"The foursome of Nine Dragon Island and their strange mount animals created chaos for you because you were not prepared," Superiorman Primordial Supreme said. "Take my animal with you to face them."

Primordial Supreme called a disciple to bring out his favorite four-not-alike and handed it over to Baby Tooth.

What was a four-not-alike? It was an animal with a head like a deer, a body like a dragon, legs like those of a cheetah, and hoofs like those of a qilin. In all, it did not look like any of the animals but possessed the outstanding traits of all four. Indeed, a most remarkable being.

"Baby Tooth. Your forty years with me have been good. I have entrusted you with the task of the Investiture of Gods," Primordial Supreme continued. "Now take this four-not-alike back to the Western Foothills. It will help you when you meet other strange creatures in the days to come."

He then handed Baby Tooth a wooden whip which was three feet, five and half inches long, with twenty-six notches. On each notch were four jujus, a total of one hundred and four. This was the Devil Beating Whip.

"Here, also take my XYZ Flag. Go back to the Western Foothills by way of the North Sea where someone is waiting for you. Be cautious. In an emergency, open the Flag for instructions."

The four-not-alike lifted Baby Tooth into the air and soon landed on a beautiful island in the North Sea.

The sea echoed a monster yelling, "Baby Tooth, I am going to eat you!"

Turning his head toward the sound, Baby Tooth saw a huge red being coming at him. The strange fifteen foot tall creature had the appearance of a gargantuan lobster: two huge eyes rolling like swinging lanterns, and giant snapping claws that could crush anything.

Baby Tooth braced himself and said, "I have never done you any harm. Why do you want to eat me?"

"Don't even try to talk your way out!"

Quickly Baby Tooth read the instructions inside the XYZ Flag, and shouted, "Damn you! I will let you eat me if you can pull up my flag. If you can't, then it is your tough luck!"

So saying, Baby Tooth drove the flag into the sand with all his might.

With his two powerful claws, the monster began to pull the flag. But the flag appeared to be endlessly long as he added more and more legs to the task.

Meanwhile, with a wave of his hand, Baby Tooth called for thunder and lightning, which so frightened the monster it was ready to flee; but to his dismay, his limbs had become part of the flag!

Baby Tooth shouted, "Look out! Have a taste of my sword!"

The monster cried out, "Have mercy on me! It was all Aggrandizing Bobcat's doing!"

Hearing the name of his former schoolmate, Baby Tooth asked, "You wanted to eat me. Why bring up Aggrandizing Bobcat's name?"

Crying now, the monster sobbed, "You see, I am Good Lob the Lobster. I have lived here for thousands of years, minding my own business. I practice the arts of meditation and train for longevity, hoping someday I will have a chance to become a superior being. I have never done harm to either a human or animal. The other day, Aggrandizing Bobcat passed by. He told me if I ate you, my wish would come true. I am so sorry to be so gullible. Please, for the sake of Heaven, have mercy on me."

"All right. But you must be willing to be my disciple and follow my orders."

Baby Tooth freed the lobster. In gratitude, Good Lob the Lobster knelt and kissed Baby Tooth's feet.

"What special skills do you have?"

"I can gather a swirling dust storm, or start a thundering rock slide. I can send a single grain of sand to blind a person, or control the speed of a crushing boulder," Good Lob said proudly.

Baby Tooth took Lobster back to the Western Foothills and ordered preparations for a big battle.

*   *   *   *

In the other camp, Cassia and his generals, and the foursome from the Nine Dragon Island waited patiently for Baby Tooth to open the granaries. After the appointed three days, nothing happened and they realized their plans had gone awry. So they came out in force calling for a fight.

With Yellow Flying Tiger, Nezha and Lobster, Baby Tooth came out on his four-not-alike to meet the enemy.

"Baby Tooth! You feigned acceptance in order to go to Mount Kunlun, to borrow the four-not-alike. I will let you know who is the boss here!" So saying, Wang Magus charged at Baby Tooth.

Nezha ran out to meet Wang Magus. Oh, how these two fought! When Nezha was beginning to gain the upper hand, Yang Forest pulled out his Sky Opening Pearl and shot at Nezha, knocking him off his wheels.

Yellow Flying Tiger rushed over on his five-colored magic bull, blocking Yang Forest as Yang went for Nezha's head.

Yang shot another Sky Opening Pearl at Flying Tiger and knocked him to the ground as well.

Now Lobster joined in, shouting, "Don't you dare hurt my generals!"

Yang Forest was startled by the monster but gave a good fight while High Amiable shot his Coalesce Pearl and knocked Lobster's head askew.

Now Li Resounding joined Wang Magus, charging at Baby Tooth. Baby Tooth fought valiantly but was soon forced to flee toward the North Sea.

Gravely wounded but aware that Wang Magus was on his heels, Baby Tooth gently rubbed the horn of his four-not-alike and they were airborne.

"So you think you are the only one that can fly?" snickered Wang. Patting his own animal, Wang was airborne also. In the chase, Wang shot out his Earth Slashing Pearl, knocking Baby Tooth off the four-not-alike and sending him down to the valley below. The four-not-alike landed and stood silently at Baby Tooth's side.

As Wang got off his animal to go for Baby Tooth's head, he heard someone singing,

> Gentle breeze skimming over the fields;
> Blazing flowers swaying with good cheer.
> Home is where deep cloud appears;
> Home is where I please.

It was Superiorman Broad Altruist of Mount Five Dragons. Wang Magus saluted and asked, "My friend. What brought you here?"

"My brother-in-learning. Baby Tooth should not be harmed! I have a request from Primordial Supreme to rescue him. Let him go. I thought you had retired to the Nine Dragon Island with your buddies and were quite content there. Why are you suddenly involved in the

Red Dust? Why do you have blood on your hands? As you must know, Primordial Supreme has delegated a most important task of the Investiture of Gods to Baby Tooth. If you kill him, you will never hear the end of it. If I were you, I would return to the Nine Dragon Island right away."

"Broad Altruist! Don't you dare to be cock-a-hoop in front of me! You think you are the only one who has powerful support?"

The enraged Wang Magus now charged at Broad Altruist with his sword.

"Stop! You bully! I am his disciple Jinzha!" A young monk, with his own sword, darted out from behind Broad Altruist to meet Wang Magus.

As the two fought, Broad Altruist took out his Seven-trick Lotus and threw it at Wang. At once three gold rings immobilized Wang at his neck, waist, and feet.

Holding Wang's hair with his left hand, Jinzha raised his sword.

CHAPTER 39

▼

BABY TOOTH FREEZES MOUNT WESTERN FOOTHILLS

Wang Magus, one of the Nine-Dragon Island Foursome, had studied for thousands of years. And like most of his peers, he had hoped to live forever as a superiorman. However, failing that for whatever reason, he hoped to be nominated by his fellow superiormen to that ultimate list. Nominees on that list, upon approval by the Jade Emperor of Heaven, would be invested as gods at the Altar of the Investiture of Gods. So when Wang Magus lost his head to Jinzha's sword, his soul unerringly flew to the Altar, hoping for the best.

*   *   *   *

With medicine from his gourd, Superiorman Broad Altruist revived Baby Tooth. He then ordered Jinzha to accompany Baby Tooth back to King Wu's Capital, Phoenix City.

All the Western Foothills rejoiced when Baby Tooth showed up on his four-not-alike with a new monk. Nezha was especially happy to see his older brother Jinzha again.

Meanwhile when Wang Magus failed to return, Yang Forest correctly calculated Wang's death and exclaimed in anguish, "Oh! They have killed him! Pity his thousands of years of study for nothing!"

The other two of the Foursome joined in the mourning of their friend. They vowed to avenge him.

Next morning, they came shouted for Baby Tooth.

Although still recuperating, Baby Tooth led the brothers Jinzha and Nezha to face them.

While Nezha and Jinzha were engaging the three superiormen, Baby Tooth raised his newly acquired Devil Beating Whip and hit High Amiable, killing him instantly. High's soul too went to the Altar of the Investiture of Gods, also hoping to be nominated on the register.

The two surviving Foursome, now boiling over with hatred, charged at Baby Tooth. But Nezha threw his Omnipresent Ring in time to block the attack, while Jinzha threw his Seven-Treasure Golden Lotus to immobilize Yang. With his sword, Jinzha dispatched Yang Forest, whose soul too went to the Altar.

Alone now, Li Resounding fought Jinzha and Nezha with demonic fervor. Cassia and Gale Woods had been watching on the side, now they came to Li's assistance.

In a counter-move, to the sound of a cannon boom, a seven year old boy on a white horse, in silver armor and carrying a silver spear, rushed out of the city gate. This young warrior was Yellow Flying Tiger's youngest son Yellow Heavenly Happiness. He might be young but his skill with his silver spear was so outstanding that he quickly speared Gale Woods off his horse and killed him.

Seeing the situation, Li Amiable and Cassia retreated. They sent an urgent message to the Grand Old Master.

Pressing his victory the next morning, Baby Tooth sent Yellow Heavenly Happiness to Cassia's camp, demanding Cassia.

"I have been in the army for all my life and have never been so humiliated, and by a seven year old puppy!" the furious Cassia thought to himself. He came out with his men to face Yellow Heavenly Happiness.

Baby Tooth's men, including the Jade twins, encircled Cassia.

Jade twins shouted at Cassia, "Why not bend with the wind and join our ranks to fight King Zhou?"

Cassia shouted back, "To hell with you traitors! I am a loyal minister and will forever be so!"

Seeing there was no way out, Cassia killed himself with his own sword. His soul too went to the Altar. But his head fell into his enemy's hands.

Meanwhile, Nezha and Jinzha fought Li Resounding. Baby Tooth again lashed out with his Devil Beating Whip. Lucky for Li, his mount suddenly became airborne, escaping the deadly whip.

Baby Tooth and his men triumphantly returned to the city.

$$* \qquad * \qquad * \qquad *$$

Running for his life, Li Resounding flew on his animal to a hide-out deep in a mountain, there to contemplate his next move.

"How can I possibly face my other friends on the Nine Dragon Island now that the four of us have become just a little me! We each had more than a thousand years of training and study. How could we ever be so stupid as to get involved in such a senseless fight? I think I'd better go to see the Grand Old Master who, after all, involved us in this mess!"

As he stood up, he was surprised to hear a young monk greeting him "Good Morning."

Li returned his greeting. The young monk asked, "May I know your honorable name and mountain?"

"I am Li Resounding of Nine Dragon Island. Where are you from and where are you going?"

The young monk exclaimed, "What a wonderful coincidence! When I left my cave a while ago, my master reminded me that if I saw Li Resounding, I should take him to Baby Tooth. And you are here waiting for me!"

"By the way, I am Muzha, a disciple of Superiorman Universal Converter of Mount Nine Courts. I am on my way to help King Wu of the Western Foothills," Muzha continued.

"How dare you!" Li Resounding charged at Muzha with his sword. But Muzha easily killed him. Li's soul too flew to the Altar.

Traveling underground, Muzha reached the Western Foothills in no time. He went directly to Baby Tooth.

Baby Tooth remarked, "You three brothers all rally to the Banner of King Wu. How fortunate for the Western Foothills."

*   *   *   *

The Grand Old Master was saddened by the deaths of his three superiorman friends, as the news of the fourth had not yet reached him. He mourned, "My dear friends! It was all my fault to get you involved in this death business! How am I going to live with myself? All your thousand years of training and study has gone down the drain. I am sorry! Forgive me! Oh, my dear friends, please forgive me!"

He summoned his generals for an emergency meeting. "I invited four of my friends from the Nine Dragon Island to help Cassia. Unfortunately three of them were killed. Who will go to help Cassia?"

General Honest Hero stood up and said, "My Lord. I will."

Looking at the aged general, Grand Old Master said, "I am afraid you are too old for such an assignment, my General Honest Hero. I do appreciate your volunteering."

"Sir! You are wrong! In age, I could be a bit older than most. But to fight a war such as this, brawn alone is not all! I have experience and brains, and I am in good health. I don't think I should be discriminated against because of my age and denied this mission. Look at Cassia, he is young and brave. But he has not been able to win! I know how to use my intellect to deal with Baby Tooth. Let me have a chance to prove myself. Please."

Honest Hero had spoken so convincingly that Grand Old Master decided to take a chance. But he still felt Honest Hero should be aided by some young generals and counselors to help map his strategy.

Grand Old Master ordered Higher Counselors Fei Zhong and You Hun to go along with Honest Hero.

Scared to death, Fei Zhong and You Hun protested, "We are civil personnel, not fighters. We cannot be sent to war!"

"Yes, I realize that. But both of you have quick wits which will enhance our capability. Yes, you will go and that is that!"

No one ever dared to say NO to the Grand Old Master, not even the king himself!

*   *   *   *

Honest Hero and his troops rushed westward and soon were approaching the Western Foothills. They learned that Cassia's head was hanging at the East Gate outside Phoenix City. Honest Hero ordered his troops to make camp deep in the forest at the foot of the Western Foothills of Mount Singing Phoenix.

He said, "Since Cassia is dead, we had better not advance before we find out more of the situation."

When Baby Tooth's scouts reported troops concentrated at the foot of the Western Foothills but without banners, he knew immediately who they were.

At the same time, Baby Tooth also received report that the altar for the display of the register of future gods was now completed. He felt it was urgent that he attend to its official dedication without delay.

Baby Tooth ordered General Nimblefoot and General Wu Ji to take an army of five thousand to investigate and to block any advance from the foot of the Western Foothills by these unknown troops.

On making doubly sure that the invading troops were King Zhou's, Nimblefoot ordered his own force to make camp in the open space of the Western Foothills, directly facing the forest so that their every move would be observed by the enemy.

It was midsummer, the sun mercilessly beating down with not a tree around. Why did Nimblefoot select such a spot to make camp? His men grumbled but did as ordered.

Next morning, Baby Tooth ordered Nimblefoot to move camp to the even more exposed top of the Western Foothills! The soldiers were most unhappy. Not only was the daytime heat more intense up there, fetching water for daily use became a miserable task.

Encamped deep in the forest, King Zhou's troops saw all the movement on top of the sun-baked mountain and nearly laughed themselves to death. "With heat of the sun," they thought, "in three days all will die without our lifting a finger!"

Next day, Baby Tooth led three thousand more men to join the five thousands already on top of the Mount Western Foothills. He ordered Wu Ji to build an earth mount three feet tall with a canopy. "Get it done before night fall."

Meanwhile, Baby Tooth ordered the contents of the supply carts spread out for all to see. To everyone's dismay they saw, among other useless things, heavy winter garb!"

Each soldier was given a rain hat and a winter coat. They were puzzled and some thought it a joke. No matter how ludicrous the situation might appear, the soldiers of Western Foothills had full faith in their leaders.

When the earth mount was completed, Baby Tooth let down his hair, and holding his sword, stood on the mount facing Mount Kunlun and knelt. After some incantation, he sprinkled water from a bowl in the direction of the forest where the enemy had encamped.

*   *   *   *

General Honest Hero was among the first of King Zhou's men to feel a breeze rustling through the trees. He thought the weather had changed for the better. But the breeze soon became a frigid gale. After three day it had turned into a blizzard!

With no provisions for the frigid weather, Old Honest Hero was the first to become sick. From then on, soldiers by the score died every minute from the cold.

Meanwhile in Baby Tooth's camp, everyone put on his rain hat and winter coat and thanked Baby Tooth for his foresight.

"How deep is the snow now?" Baby Tooth asked.

"About two feet up here and five feet down there."

"Good," said Baby Tooth as he got on the earth mount to do his thing again.

The snow stopped suddenly as a brilliant sun reappeared. The melting snow soon became a torrent rushing down the steep hills and drowning the remains of King Zhou's army.

Baby Tooth ordered Nimblefoot to take twenty soldiers into the enemy camp and bring back their leaders heads.

It was no problem for Nimblefoot and his men to capture Honest Hero and the two Higher Counselors. These three were shivering on some table tops, wearing many layers of soldier garments, semi-unconscious.

CHAPTER 40

▼

THE FOUR DIABLO
BROTHERS

General Nimblefoot brought prisoners Honest Hero and the two Counselors uphill to Baby Tooth. While Honest Hero stood defiant, the two counselors knelt, trembling like autumn leaves.

Addressing Honest Hero, Baby Tooth said, "My dear General. We need to know not only the condition of our world, but also the will of the people and the mandate of Heaven. There are also rights and wrongs. As you know, two thirds under Heaven have rallied to King Wu of Western Foothills. Why should you sacrifice yourself for an evil cause?"

"To hell with you, Baby Tooth! You were once a minister in the Court of King Zhou yourself. How could you behave like such an ingrate! So I am captured. Will I give up my principles to join you? Don't make me laugh!"

Baby Tooth sent the prisoners away. Then kneeling on the mound and facing Mount Kunlun again he called for a change in the weather. Now the sun burned bright and hot; the melting snow soon became a torrent drowning almost everyone who had survived the freezing cold.

*   *   *   *

The next day Baby Tooth sent Nimblefoot to invite and escort King Wu to his camp on top of the mountain.

"Why did you bring me here?" the king asked.

"To consecrate Mount Western Foothills," Baby Tooth said.

It was, actually, to consecrate the Altar of the Investiture of Gods. But Baby Tooth could not divulge the scheme of things Heaven and Earth even to a king.

As the ritual proceeded, Baby Tooth ordered the sacrifice of two prisoners.

King Wu was surprised. "But we are only consecrating Mount Western Foothills."

"These prisoners are King Zhou's Higher Counselors Fei Zhong and You Hun."

"They deserve to die!" King Wu agreed, and after the rite he led all the troops back to his Capital, Phoenix City.

*   *   *   *

On the other side of the mountains and passes, Grand Old Master was reading reports from the war fronts. He was pleased over the victory in the South, but the news from other fronts was dismal, and the urgent report from Han Glory of Flood-Water Pass in the west was especially bad. After reviewing the talents of his generals, Grand Old Master decided this was time to send the Diablo brothers of the Pleasant-Dream Pass to face Baby Tooth.

When they received their orders, the brothers laughed. "The Grand Old Master must be getting senile. Why would he need a butcher knife for oxen to kill chickens?"

Immediately they gathered ten thousand troops and left for Western Foothills.

*　　*　　*　　*

Ever since the battle of the "Freezing of Mount Western Foothills," Baby Tooth's reputation was never more grand. The morale of both troops and populace could not be higher.

After receiving reports that the four Diablo brothers were only five miles outside of the Phoenix City walls, Baby Tooth discussed the new situation with Yellow Flying Tiger. When Yellow Flying Tiger was the Lord of National Security at King Zhou's Court, the Diablo brothers were under his command.

Yellow Flying Tiger said, "The Diablos of the Pleasant-Dream Pass are four brothers, all over twenty-four feet tall. They do not ride but walk on foot. All had instructions in black magic from strange masters.

"Diablo Green, the oldest, has a face like a crab and a beard like a forest of copper wires. His weapon is a long spear. His magic is a Green-Fire Sword given to him by his master. Four words, EARTH, WATER, FIRE, WIND are carved on the sword. His Wind is black and holds countless knives and daggers that kill whatever is in their way. His Earth crawls with poisonous snakes that bite and kill. His Fire destroys what the snakes leave behind and his Water inundates everything.

"Diablo Red, the second brother, uses a lance. He owns a magic Havoc-Umbrella made of many kinds of pearls, such as the Granny-Green pearls, the Granny-Blue pearls, the Night-Radiant pearls, Water-Dust-Fire-Repellent pearls, Fever-Quash pearls, Nine-Curve-Turn pearls, Youthful-Complexion-Enduring pearls, Wind-Calming pearls and many more. On the umbrella are the words, ENCOMPASSING THE UNIVERSE. The umbrella is extremely powerful. When opened, the sky turns dark as night and people fall down and die. It also will suck up whatever its owner wants it to.

"The third brother Diablo Sea uses a long spear and carries a Fat-Belly Guitar Pipa on his back. The Pipa has four strings, each representing EARTH, WATER, FIRE, and WIND. When the strings are plucked, Fire and Wind come in great force, as devastating as his elder brother's Green-Fire Sword. The earth would be full of snakes and water would inundate the world.

Diablo Long life, the youngest, uses two long whips. He has a leopard skin bag that holds a Flying Mink. When let out, the mink turns into a flying elephant, swallows whatever is in its path, or devours anything its master wants him to.

"If the four Diablo brothers are indeed here, we are done for!"

Anxiety was clearly shown on Baby Tooth's face.

*   *   *   *

Elder brother Diablo Green boasted to his siblings, "Tomorrow we will fight Baby Tooth together, and win a quick victory."

They drank until dawn.

*   *   *   *

Worried over the Diablo brothers, Baby Tooth laid awake all night. In the morning he was so sluggish, he made no response when the Diablo brothers called for a fight.

Brothers Jinzha, Muzha and Nezha called out, "Our Uncle-in-learning! What is the matter with you? Yellow Flying Tiger may be right, but we are not intimidated! If King Wu is to have the mandate of Heaven, Heaven would not abandon us now! All we have to do is to do our best!"

Fully awake now, Baby Tooth gave the order for battle.

*   *   *   *

On his four-not-alike in his white monk's attire, Baby Tooth bowed slightly and said, "Are you the famous Brothers Diablo?"

Diablo Green said, "Baby Tooth! You left your job at King Zhou's Court, and came here to make trouble for everyone. Aren't you ashamed of yourself?"

Baby Tooth said, "My dear sir, what do you mean? We in Western Foothills are law-abiding subjects. My master's family was invested by King Zhou's ancestors as the Lord of Western Foothills. We have not even set foot in the direction of the five Passes. On the other hand, without provocation, you invaded our land with thousands of troops. And you said we are making trouble?"

"No sense arguing with you, Baby Tooth! Don't you know you are on the verge of being annihilated?"

So saying, he stepped toward Baby Tooth with his long spear.

General Nimblefoot rushed out on the left and blocked the spear with his big knife. Diablo Red now came with his lance from the right and was blocked by General Rigorous Armor. Diablo Sea charged with his silver spear but found Nezha in his way, and Diablo Long life had to contend with General Wu Ji. What a battle! Back and forth they traded blows.

Diablo Red caught sight of Nezha about to throw his Omnipresent Ring. Sidestepping his opponent, General Rigorous Armor, Diablo Red opened his Havoc Umbrella and sucked up Nezha's Ring. Seeing his brother's treasure disappear, Jinzha immediately threw his own treasure, the Seven-Trick-Golden-Lotus at Diablo Red. Unfortunately, that too was sucked up by the Havoc Umbrella!

Baby Tooth quickly threw out his Devil Beating Whip. Alas! This whip could beat any devils but not mortals. And the Diablos brothers were mortals, not devils, Diablo being only their surname. The whip was absolutely useless on them. And to add insult to injury, that whip too was sucked up by the Havoc Umbrella!

Baby Tooth was shocked beyond belief. Meanwhile, seeing their brother Diablo Red so successful with his magic, the other brothers also unleashed theirs.

Diablo Red twirled his Havoc Umbrella around and around, turning day into night. Diablo Green brandished his Green Sword, hurling smoke and fire at Nimblefoot. Diablo Sea plucked the strings of his fat belly guitar, sending out fire dragons to burn all in their paths. And Diablo Long Life let go of his Flying Mink which immediately turned into a flying elephant, roaring and stomping.

Baby Tooth's battle formation was in total disarray. Baby Tooth fled on his airborne four-not-alike, Nezha on his wind-fire wheels. Muzha and Jinzha got away by traveling underground, and Red Lobster by using his water trick.

All in all, Western Foothills lost over ten thousand horses and men, including nine generals. Of these, three were King Wu's brothers. Sorrow and grief shrouded King Wu and the whole Western Foothills.

The next morning, Baby Tooth raised the "No Fighting" flag when the Diablos came to the city walls.

But Diablo Green was in no mood to honor the flag. He ordered scaling ladders, and soon his soldiers were climbing up the city wall. Baby Tooth retaliated with fire arrows. The skirmish went on for three futile days and nights until the brothers abruptly called it off but kept the city under siege.

After two months, Baby Tooth gave no sign of surrendering. The four Diablo brothers were getting restless. If they could not get this war over soon, their reputations would be lost! They decided to pool all their magic weapons, inundate Phoenix City with an ocean and wipe it off the face of the earth.

*   *   *   *

Inside Phoenix City, Baby Tooth was in the Great Hall mapping strategy with his generals when a sudden gust of wind toppled the imperial flag and broke the staff! Pale with shock, Baby Tooth immediately knelt and cast a few gold coins to see what the omen might foretell.

He frowned at the configuration. Hurriedly he took a bath and changed into his ceremonial clothes. Then with his hair loose, sword in hand, he knelt facing Mt. Kunlun and mumbled his incantation.

Baby Tooth was to borrow the North Sea to save Western Foothills from the calamity he saw coming.

The four Diablo brothers came flaunting their magic. Fire, water, flying mink and fire dragons attacked mercilessly. In the hellish darkness, one could see the fire burning, feel the sky falling, the earth quaking; and hear the crying and moaning of the victims. The world was coming to an end!

The four brothers were so pleased. After two hours, they called off their magic and returned to camp.

"Tomorrow morning we will see what more needs to be done to wipe them off the face of the earth!"

Its work done, Baby Tooth returned the North Sea water after the Diablo brothers left.

In the early morning sun, Phoenix City stood as it always had: majestic, beautiful, and peaceful. Not even a single blade of grass was out of order!

The four Diablo brothers saw the incredible outcome of their handiwork and realized that their only option was to continue the siege of the city.

$$*\qquad*\qquad*\qquad*$$

Days turned into months as the siege continued. One day, Quartermaster reported to Baby Tooth that the supplies in the army Depots would be enough for only ten more days.

Baby Tooth remarked, "The siege of the city is a small matter when compared to food shortages for our troops. What are we to do?"

Yellow Flying Tiger said, "The Western Foothills people are wealthy and patriotic. Why not borrow from them? When the siege is over, the government can repay them with interest."

"Oh, no. It would never do. If I ask the people to bring in grain, they would be alarmed and might panic. The morale of our populace and soldiers will be undermined. Well, anyway, there is still food for ten more days. Things may change." Baby Tooth was unshaken.

However as days went by, Baby Tooth's worry deepened. Now there was food for only two more days.

Two young monks came to see Baby Tooth.

"Our Uncle-in-learning." The visitors knelt before Baby Tooth and saluted.

Baby Tooth asked, "What are your names? Where have you come from? And what can you do to help us?"

"We are disciples of Superiorman Circumspect of Jade Cave, Gold Mountain. I am Han Lethal Dragon and my companion is Xue Bad-Tempered Tiger. We have brought food supplies."

So saying, Han handed his Master's letter to Baby Tooth.

After reading the letter, Baby Tooth asked, "Where is the food?"

"I have it here," said Han and took out a pinch of rice from his sleeve. Baby Tooth sent the two to deliver the rice personally to the quartermaster.

Yellow Flying Tiger and the others could hardly suppress their guffaws. A pinch of rice? No kidding! But to everyone's amazement, reports soon came that the granaries were now bursting their seams with rice!

With the supply depots full, the army healthy, ministers and generals and the populace loyal, there was no problem whatsoever in Western Foothills. But the siege of the city was still a strain.

It was now a year since the siege began, and to the dismay of the Diablo brothers, Western Foothills seemed even to be thriving. The problem of feeding a big idling army was bad enough, but the losing of face at the Court of King Zhou would simply be unbearable. They wrote to Grand Old Master, trying to explain, blaming Baby Tooth for everything.

*   *   *   *

Then another visitor, Yang Bliss of Mount Jade Spring, Golden Cloud Cave, came to see Baby Tooth and asked what he could do to help.

Baby Tooth briefed him and ended with, "…and that is why we hang out the NO FIGHTING flag."

"Please take down the flag. I'll see what I can do," said Bliss. If we don't face them, how do we know what strategy will crush them?"

After the No Fighting flag was down, the Diablo brothers came immediately to the city walls, taunting. Yang Bliss and Nezha went out to face them.

The four Diablo brothers saw beside Nezha a young man on a white horse. He was wearing a hat with cloud-design, a cotton garment with silk sash, linen shoes, and was holding a long spear.

"Such an ordinary person, looking neither like a lady nor a monk, dares to face us?" the brothers said to themselves.

"Who are you?" they asked.

"I am Yang Bliss, a Nephew-in-learning of Baby Tooth. Why are you behaving so obnoxiously?" So saying, Yang Bliss came at the Diablo brothers.

The brothers fought Bliss together, encircling him. As the fighting raged, Ma Dragon, a Quartermaster from the Duke of Chu Region, chanced to pass by with his supplies. He did not like the way the four giants were bullying one little guy.

He pulled out his twin long knives and shouted, "Look out! Here I come!" and plunged in to help Yang Bliss.

Diablo Long Life was so annoyed he let out his Flying Mink which immediately swallowed Ma Dragon.

From the corner of his eye, Yang Bliss saw what happened and said to himself, "Ha, so that is how they do it!" Bliss deliberately put himself in the path of the Flying Mink and was unceremoniously gobbled up.

Nezha saw everything and rushed back to report to Baby Tooth. The news saddened Baby Tooth, and the feeling of helplessness was overwhelming.

*   *   *   *

The Diablo brothers returned to their camp to celebrate. During their drinking, Diablo Green said, "Why not send the Flying Mink out to eat up Baby Tooth and King Wu? Then we can go home. I am so tired of this siege business."

They all agreed to the plan but regretted they could not bring home with them the heads of Baby Tooth and King Wu. "This is only a minor detail," they comforted each other.

Diablo Long Life went to his leopard skin bag, took out the Flying Mink and said, "My precious, go and devour Baby Tooth and King Wu. When your mission is accomplished, you will be the most appreciated hero! Now go!"

Poor Flying Mink! How could he know that swallowing Yang Bliss was, for himself, the most ruinous thing ever in his entire life! How could he know that damnable Yang Bliss was not only alive, but also able to change into seventy-two shapes inside his stomach!

Yes, safely tucked inside the Flying Mink's stomach, Yang Bliss heard all the intrigue. As the Flying Mink flew over the city wall that night, Yang Bliss killed the mink from its inside and emerged, returning to his own shape to knock on Baby Tooth's door.

Baby Tooth was at that moment discussing strategy with Nezha when the guard reported that someone claiming to be Yang Bliss wished to see him.

Nezha went out to see. Yes, he had seen with his own eyes what had happened to Yang Bliss. How could there be another Yang Bliss? But here stood this man, yes, Yang Bliss in the flesh! Could this be his ghost?

Nezha said, "Brother Yang! You were swallowed this morning. How could you be here now?"

Yang said, "Don't be silly. Do I look like a dead man? Hurry and open the door. I have important things to tell Baby Tooth."

Baby Tooth could not contain his surprise. "You were killed this morning!"

"Oh, let's forget about that! I was inside the mink's stomach and heard the Diablo brothers sending it to eat you and King Wu. So I killed the mink just outside the door and here I am!"

"With this kind of magic, our fear is over!" Baby Tooth exclaimed, so delighted was he.

"I will go back there now. There is much more to learn and do."

"How are you going?" Nezha asked.

Yang Bliss smiled, "We all have our special tricks. Don't worry about me."

Baby Tooth said, "You seem to have a lot of magical tricks, why not show us one or two?"

Without replying, Yang Bliss turned around and became the flying mink, rolling and laughing on the floor. "Here I go!"

Baby Tooth said, "Wait a second, Yang Bliss my Nephew-in-learning. Why not bring all the Diablo brothers' magic tricks here? That would render them useless and we might also recover our lost treasures."

"Why not indeed!" So saying, Yang Bliss was gone.

$$*\qquad*\qquad*\qquad*$$

Diablo Long Life was delighted to see his Flying Mink back, but discovered to his surprise that it did not eat anyone. Well, there must be a reason, he thought. He was too drunk to think about it now. He put the Flying Mink into his leopard skin bag and, along with his brothers, soon fell asleep.

Yang Bliss, in his flying mink form, escaped from the leopard skin bag and began to look for the treasures. He headed for the Havoc Umbrella on the wall but accidentally knocked it down. The noise stirred Diablo Red who jumped up sleepily, found the umbrella, and automatically put it back on the hook and returned to his slumber.

Yang carefully took the umbrella off the hook and hurriedly took it to Baby Tooth, then returned to the leopard skin bag.

Next morning, when the umbrella was discovered missing, all the guards were questioned. They protested, saying the security of the inner camp was so tight not even a grain of sand could have made its way in or out. How could there possibly be a thief?

Diablo Red lamented, "All my prowess depends on this umbrella. What will I do? What will I do?"

The brothers sat woodenly, utterly helpless and lost!

*   *   *   *

On Mount Pure Light, Purple Sun Cave, Superiorman True Vacuum called his disciple Yellow Heavenly Educated, handed him the Twin Hammers, and taught him how to use them. With little practice, Heavenly Educated quickly mastered the Twin Hammers as if they had been his all his life. His master then said, "I will let you use my jade qilin, and my Fire-Dragon shafts. Go down to the Red Dust and hurry to Western Foothills to help your father. But don't ever for a moment forget your roots here!"

Mounting the jade qilin, Yellow Heavenly Educated gently touched its horn. Instantly they were airborne, and soon reached Phoenix City. Baby Tooth was with his generals in the Great Hall when Heavenly Educated showed up.

Kneeling before Baby Tooth, the young man saluted, "My Uncle-in-learning. My master has sent me to be at your service."

Yellow Flying Tiger said, "My Lord. This is my eldest son Yellow Heavenly Educated. He has lived all his life with Superiorman True Vacuum in Purple Sun Cave, Mount Pure Wind."

Heavenly Educated returned home with his father and to reunite with his other brothers and relatives. Rather absentmindedly he changed into a regular warrior's attire, sporting a red robe, gold armor and gold hair ornaments.

Next day, Baby Tooth chided him, "Even I, as Prime Minister, do not dare to forget my relation with Mount Kunlun. Put your silk sash back!"

Obediently, Heavenly Educated tied the silk sash around his waist.

"Sir, I have come to help defeat the four Diablo brothers, that is why I changed my costume. After victory, I will return to my Master. I would not dare for a moment to forget my roots with Mount Pure Wind," Heavenly Educated said.

"That is all right," said Baby Tooth. "Now you must be very wary of the Diablo brothers. They are trained in black magic."

"Yes, I know. I will be very careful." So saying, Heavenly Educated mounted his jade qilin and, holding his Twin Hammers, led his troops out of the city toward the Diablo camp, calling for a fight.

CHAPTER 41

▼

LORDS OF MOUNT YELLOW BLOSSOMS

The four Diablo brothers were lamenting the missing umbrella when a report came that someone was outside calling for a fight. They hurriedly put on their armor.

Outside they saw a young man on a jade qilin, wearing a red robe with a silk sash and gold hair ornament. He was holding Twin Hammers.

"Who are you to dare to come here?" they shouted at him.

"I am Yellow Heavenly Educated, son of Lord of the National Stability, Yellow Flying Tiger. I have orders from my Prime Minister Baby Tooth to capture all of you."

"Is that so?" The four brothers stepped out together toward Yellow Heavenly Educated.

The fight was fierce. Within minutes, Heavenly Educated was knocked off his jade qilin and killed by Diablo Green's jade bracelet, a rather minor treasure as compared to his Green-Fire Sword.

As Diablo Green was about to chop off his victim's head, Nezha rushed over with his spear. So Diablo Green threw his jade bracelet at

Nezha who retaliated with his Omnipresent Ring. Yes, Nezha's Omnipresent Ring had been sucked away by Diablo Red's Umbrella, but Yang Bliss had brought the Umbrella, as well as all their lost treasures, back to Baby Tooth. Lucky too at this particular moment! The outcome was predictable when the gold Omnipresent Ring, hit the jade bracelet. The bracelet shattered!

The Diablo brothers screamed in unison, "Get him!"

But Nezha had already taken Heavenly Educated's body and was now inside the city walls. Sullenly the brothers returned to their camp.

Yellow Flying Tiger was beside himself to see his first born dead so soon after the reunion.

As Western Foothills mourned, a visitor came to see Baby Tooth. "My Uncle-in-learning," said the young monk. "My master, the Superiorman True Vacuum has sent me to bring Heavenly Educated's body back to Mount True Wind."

*   *   *   *

Superiorman True Vacuum surveyed Heavenly Educated's ashen face, tight-closed eyes, and limp body. He ordered the administration of a magic potion through the mouth. In less than an hour, Heavenly Educated opened his eyes and saw his master before him.

"You ingrate!" the master scolded. "You seemed to have a very short memory! The minute you are in the Red Dust, you changed into a red robe and started eating animal flesh! That's reason enough for me to abandon you! For the sake of Baby Tooth, I am giving you a second chance. Now go back quickly to Western Foothills to finish your mission. I too will be there soon."

Traveling underground, Heavenly Educated returned to Baby Tooth. Yellow Flying Tiger was overjoyed to see his son alive and well.

Next day, Heavenly Educated again went to the Diablo camp.

The Diablo brothers swore to kill Heavenly Educated and to end the war once and for all. After a short fight, Heavenly Educated feigned retreat. As Diablo Green followed in hot pursuit, Heavenly Educated let go a Fire-Dragon Shaft from the bag his master had given him. The shaft pierced Diablo Green's heart, killing him instantly. His soul flew to the Altar of the Investiture of Gods. The shaft magically returned to the bag.

Now Diablo Red rushed at the young Heavenly Educated with his lance. He too was hit by a Fire-Dragon Shaft, and died. His soul too flew to the Altar of the Investiture of Gods.

Enraged, Diablo Sea started to pluck his Pipa. But before his fingers could reach the strings, he too was killed by the Fire-Dragon Shaft.

At the same time, brother Diablo Long Life reached into his leopard skin bag for his Flying Mink. What he got was Yang Bliss in the guise of the mink which promptly bit off his hand. He screamed with pain as he pulled out his blood-dripping handless arm. Heavenly Educated's Fire-Dragon Shaft also pieced Diablo Long Life's heart, finishing off the last of the Diablo brothers. His soul flew to The Altar to join his older brothers.

As Heavenly Educated reached to cut off Diablo Long Life's head, the mink turned into a young warrior. It was Yang Bliss. Nezha rushed over to introduce them. The three then went together to report to Baby Tooth, profusely congratulating each other.

Baby Tooth ordered the display of the Diablo brothers' heads on the city wall, to console the populace and soldiers of Western Foothills who had suffered so much in the long year of siege.

The survivors of Diablo camp fled to Flood-Water Pass and reported to Commander Han Glory, who immediately sent an urgent report to the Grand Old Master.

✳   ✳   ✳   ✳

Early one morning, Grand Old Master was rather pleased that Jade Cicada, daughter of the Commander of the Three-Mountains Pass, had defeated the son of the Grand Duke of the South, and Commander Restrained Glory of Floating-Souls Pass had won many battles over the son of the Grand Duke of the East.

Then Han Glory's report reached the Grand Old Master whose anger and dismay was boundless. He banged on the desk and screamed, "How dare you, Baby Tooth?" His wizard eye flashed red, while smoke spewed from his nostrils and ears!

He thought it over. "Well then, now that the South and the East are under control, it behooves me to take a trip to Western Foothills to give Baby Tooth what's coming to him!"

Next morning, Grand Old Master informed King Zhou of the situation and his decision.

The king whined, "Who will take care of me when you go to Western Foothills?"

"Fear not, Your Majesty. There are many able ministers and generals in the Court. I will be gone no more than a few months."

The king gave Grand Old Master his Imperial Battle Axe. On an auspicious day, the Grand Old Master began his Western Foothills Campaign.

When he got on his black qilin, the animal let out a piercing scream and threw his master off its back. The shaken ministers and officials on hand hurriedly helped Grand Old Master back on his mount.

Counselor Wang Jing said timidly, "My lord, may I say something?"

"What is it?" the annoyed old man snapped.

"It was a bad omen when your black qilin threw you off. May I suggest that you send someone in your stead?"

"I do appreciate your concern, my Counselor Wang," Grand Old Master said gently, sorry he had barked at him. "But being the servant of the king, we must not shirk our duty in the face of danger. We may die or be wounded in battle but we cannot let fear dominate our action. I think my black qilin is getting soft because I have not been in battle for so long. Fear not. We will be all right."

And so, with loyalty for his king and love for his country, Grand Old Master was again on his way to war.

*   *   *   *

Leading three hundred thousand troops, Grand Old Master left the Capital City, Morning Song. They crossed the Yellow River, and one day reached Riverpool County. Anxious to get to Western Foothills as quickly as they could, Grand Old Master asked a local official for the shortest route.

"The shortest way is through Green-Dragon Pass. You will save about two hundred miles. But the road is very rough."

Grand Old Master ordered his men to take the Green-Dragon Pass route, which soon became narrow and rough. So much so that Grand Old Master regretted his decision. The Five-Pass Route, though two hundred miles longer, now seemed to be a much better choice. But they trudged on.

They headed toward Mount Yellow Blossoms. One peak after another, pines and cedars so thick in places you could not even see the sky, let alone the trail. Grand Old Master ordered his men and their mounts to rest while he himself went up a tall peak for a better look around.

To his utter amazement, he was standing on the plateau. Below was a clearing with yellow flowers blooming everywhere, sending out their heavenly fragrance. All was quiet except for the gentle winds and the sweet singing of birds in the bamboo groves.

"What would I give to retire here!" Grand Old Master sighed.

The sudden sound of a gong from behind broke Grand Old Master's reverie. Turning his head, he discovered he was surrounded by a group of strangers in a Snake-Battle-Formation. At the head of the formation was a warrior sitting on a chestnut horse, and holding a huge axe. He was wearing a red robe, gold armor and a gold belt. He had an indigo blue face, fearful buckteeth and red hair. "Who are you dare to intrude into our territory?" he shouted.

"I am admiring this peaceful paradise and contemplating how wonderful it would be to build a hut and retire here. But I wonder if you would welcome me."

"Scoundrel!" The blue-faced man waved his axe and charged at Grand Old Master. Grand Old Master was an old hand in combat; his gold whips could conquer any enemy. But he saw how well this blue-faced man used his axe, and thought to induce him into the king's service. Grand Old Master feigned defeat and fled.

Blue Face gave chase. Grand Old Master turned around, pointing his gold whips at Blue Face. Instantly a gold wall appeared, pinning him down and encircling his men.

As if nothing had happened, Grand Old Master got off his qilin, sat at the foot of a pine tree, and softly hummed a song.

Now two bandit chiefs rushed up to see what had happened.

Hearing their noisy approach, Grand Old Master slowly got on his qilin, shouting, "Halt!" while pointing at them with his whips.

The two chiefs were startled to see an old man with three eyes! They shouted back, "Who are you to make trouble here? What have you done to our brother?"

"You mean that blue-faced brute? Well, really, he tried to harm me so I killed him. I merely wanted to build a little hut here and meditate, but he tried to kill me."

Grand Old Master's off-hand manner angered them. One came at him with his lance and the other with his Twin Hammers.

Again, Grand Old Master feigned defeat and fled. As they followed in pursuit, Grand Old Master turned around, pointing his gold whips at them. He immobilized one in a frozen sea and the other in a dense impenetrable jungle.

Again, Grand Old Master got off his qilin and sat leisurely against a pine tree. A sudden noise from the sky alerted him to look up. What he saw was a purple face man who was flapping his wings, waving a menacing club, and about to pounce on him.

Grand Old Master blocked the club with his gold whips. Then waving the whips at a huge boulder, he mumbled, "Put that man under!"

At once the huge boulder pinned down the purple-faced monster. Grand Old Master's twin whips came down on him with full force.

"Mercy!" cried the monster. "Don't kill me! I will do what-ever you wish!"

Grand Old Master rested his whips on the monster's head, saying, "Of course. You don't know who I am. I am THE Grand Old Master of King Zhou's court. I am on my way to quash the rebellion in Western Foothills. I chanced passing here and that blue-faced brute tried to kill me. Two other monsters also tried. So I killed them all. Now you too! Well, do you want to live or die?"

"Be kind. I want to live."

"In that case, you will have to serve me in this campaign."

"I will do anything to serve you."

Grand Old Master freed the purple-faced monster. It took quite a few moments before the monster recovered enough to stand up.

Grand Old Master said, "Tell me all about yourself and your men, and your set-up here."

"We are four sworn brothers. We called ourselves lords because, after all, we are lords of this mountain. Blue Face is the oldest, he is Lord Deng; I am number two, Lord Xin; the other two are Lord Zhong and Lord Tao. This mountain is sixty miles in radius. We have over ten thousand followers and plenty of food. We have been here for over fifteen years. Please, Grand Old Master, revive my brothers and we will be forever grateful and loyal to you."

"But they are not really your brothers."

"True. Our names are different, but we love each other no less than real brothers."

His sincerity prompted the Grand Old Master to clap his hands, making a loud noise. Oh, what happened? At separate locations, Lord Deng found himself freed from his golden prison, Lord Zhong from his frozen sea and Lord Tao from the dense jungle.

They got on their horses to return to the clearing. When they saw their brother Lord Xin talking to that damnable red robed old man, Lord Deng shouted, "Get him!" and the three charged at Grand Old Master.

CHAPTER 42

▼

GRAND OLD MASTER'S CAMPAIGN IN THE WESTERN FOOTHILLS

As his brothers charged at Grand Old Master, Lord Xin quickly stepped in front of them and said, "Why, my brothers! Come quickly to pay your respects to the Grand Old Master!"

On hearing the name, the three bandits immediately rolled off their horses and knelt before the old man. In unison, they said, "Pardon us for having eyes and not seeing Mount Tai! Now that Your Lordship is here at our humble mountain, let us know what can we do to make your stay more pleasurable."

They invited Grand Old Master to their hideout.

Lord Deng said, "We four sworn brothers have been here sixteen years. My name is Deng Loyal. Number two brother is Xin Circle, Number three is Zhong Aspiration and the youngest is Tao Exalt. We came here because we were so unjustly treated at King Zhou's court. We hope good times will return so that we need not continue being outlaws."

Grand Old Master said, "Then why not join me on my Western Foothills campaign? You are morally wrong in being highwaymen, as you are fully aware. I will be more than glad to help you come back to the right path again."

"If Grand Old Master will pardon us for our past misdeeds, we will be grateful and loyal to you for life."

"No problem in that. How big is your army?"

"We are ten thousand strong. And we have plenty of supplies."

"Wonderful," said the old man. "Tell your men that they can choose either to follow you in the king's service or return to their farms and be good subjects. For those who wish to return to their farms, give them enough money and supplies so that they can start a new life. For those wishing to follow you into the king's service, they will be treated like the regular army. Either way, all of them will be granted amnesty by the king."

Over seven thousand men pledged to follow their lords. And so Grand Old Master's army was now seven thousand men stronger and its supply considerably richer. The four mountain lords, now invested as generals, were also an unexpected bonus. Yes, Grand Old Master should be pleased indeed. But most important, now that the highwaymen were gone, the populace of Mount Yellow Blossoms could live in peace!

Grand Old Master's army marched on. One day, they came to a very steep mountain where a stone sign read, THE DRAGON PEAK.

On reading the sign, Grand Old Master became pensive and came to a full stop on his qilin.

"My lord, is something wrong?" General Deng rode up to ask.

The old man said, "I studied military science and marshal arts under my mistress the Superiorwoman Golden Soul for fifty years. She then sent me down to the Red Dust to help the kings of the Shang Dynasty. King Zhou is the third generation I have served. On parting that day, my mistress cautioned me to avoid the word PEAK. Right here is this dreaded word, standing like a sword, piercing my very soul!"

The four new generals smiled, "Dear Grand Old Master, how can you be so superstitious? It is only a word on a stone; it cannot have any bearing on our Western Foothills campaign."

The old man did not answer, and silently moved on. One day, they crossed into Western Foothills territory, and a few days later made camp five miles outside King Wu's Capital, Phoenix City.

*   *   *   *

The arrival of Grand Old Master and his three hundred thousand troops was reported to Baby Tooth long before they came near Phoenix City. As soon as they made camp, Baby Tooth led his generals up the city wall rampart, to see what challenge the Grand Old Master presented.

Baby Tooth shared his appraisal with his generals. "When I was at King Zhou's capital, I heard of Grand Old Master's reputation. Now, seeing how the camp is set up, I would say his military ability surpasses his reputation!"

They returned to the Great Hall to map out their strategy on how to engage this formidable foe.

Yellow Flying Tiger said confidently, "Why worry? We defeated the Diablo brothers. King Wu has the mandate of Heaven, therefore Western Foothills will prevail!"

"Even so," said Baby Tooth. "It still is not good to let the populace suffer and soldiers die in battle."

As they talked, a messenger brought in a letter from Grand Old Master. Baby Tooth opened and read it aloud to all: "The Grand Old Master Wen Zhong of the Court of Cheng Tang sends greetings to Baby Tooth, the Prime Minister of Western Foothills.

"Now that we have our King Zhou, why should Western Foothills want to set up their own King Wu? That is definitely against the law. You are well versed in the classics and should know the penalty for rebellion.

"On top of this, you dared to kill the king's men when they came on the king's personal order! No punishment is severe enough for your misdeeds.

"I have come to warn you: Surrender immediately or your whole nation will be mercilessly annihilated! Think of the innocent people! Do not delay in your reply!"

Baby Tooth asked, "Who is the messenger?"

"I am, sir. My name is General Deng Loyal."

"My dear General Deng Loyal," said Baby Tooth, "please take this letter back to Grand Old Master and tell him we will meet him in battle in three days."

Three days passed quickly. At the crack of dawn on the fourth day, Grand Old Master's men were already shouting for battle.

Troop formation in a battle is critical, and military science in those days was largely the study and development of battle formations [1]. One such theory was based on the Trigram (the Eight Diagrams) of the permutation of three series of horizontal lines, symbolizing the changing balance of forces. The Trigram was also much used in divination.

For his first battle against Grand Old Master, Baby Tooth decided on the use of the Five-Standpoints Battle Formation.

On the first sound of the cannon, streaming out of the city gate came four generals on green steeds, all garbed in green robes and golden armor, and flanked by four fluttering green banners. They were followed by soldiers in green uniforms, carrying green shields and broad knives. They quickly formed their battle formations.

At the sound of the second cannon, came a procession in red, with four more generals on red steeds flying four red banners. Their soldiers followed, carrying bows and arrows. In a practiced movement they rapidly formed into their battle formations.

In succession, three more cannon shots heralded three more processions in white, black and apricot yellow. The generals on steeds, and soldiers carrying spears, axes and lances now formed into battle formation.

With his troop formations in place, Baby Tooth now made his appearance on his four-not-alike, flanked on both side by Yellow Flying Tiger on his Five-Colored Magic Bull, and Nezha, Jinzha, Yang Bliss, Bad Tempered Tiger, Lethal Dragon, Yellow Heavenly Educated, Nimblefoot and Wu Ji.

On the other side was Grand Old Master on his black qilin his long beard and hair flying, his face shining like pale gold and his wizard eye flashing red. Most ominous were his Gold Whips now poised in the air.

Baby Tooth bent his body and saluted, "I am Baby Tooth, the humble Prime Minster of Western Foothills."

Grand Old Master said, "Baby Tooth. I heard you came from Mount Kunlun. What excuse do you have for not knowing the proper civil behavior?"

"My dear Grand Old Master," Baby Tooth replied, "I am doing all the right things I have been taught to do. I respect the orders of the king, I follow the will of the populace, I treat all civil matters according to the laws of our land, and educate the people according to their ability. We in Western Foothills work hard and enjoy the blessings of Heaven in prosperity and peace. I don't understand your accusation."

"Your rhetoric is impressive but your logic is bad. You don't seem to understand the real meaning of being a loyal subject. First, when we have a King Zhou in the court, healthy and hale, why do you set up a King Wu in Western Foothills? Don't you know that is outright rebellion? Second, you knowingly harbor the rebel Yellow Flying Tiger, what is the meaning of that? Moreover, you killed the generals who came on the order of the king. And here I am and you still try to justify your actions with flowery language," Grand Old Master said.

Baby Tooth smiled. "My dear Grand Old Master, you seem to have forgotten. When Grand Duke of the West of Western Foothills was released after seven years of imprisonment, your King Zhou invested him as King Wen. It is a matter of lawful right that his oldest surviving son, now King Wu, should inherit his father's title.

"Now two thirds of the nobles in your kingdom have disavowed their ties to King Zhou. But we in Western Foothills have not sent a single grain of rice to aid them. Yet you talk about righteousness. Do you mean that evil King Zhou who knows only his own lust, who lets people suffer untold hardship, who killed his loyal ministers because they dared to point out his folly, should be supported and loved? We all know, a tree has to rot from within before it is attacked from without. If a king is virtuous and upright, just and benevolent, he would not have to worry about lacking loyal supporters.

"We in Western Foothills have not sent a single soldier across the five Passes. Why do you call us rebels and want to annihilate us? Do you think we will submit to all that?

"Yes, we realize fighting you would be a folly; but we do not mean to take our undeserved treatment lying down. Please, my dear Grand Old Master, return to your capital and leave us alone. Even a crippled dog can jump over the tallest wall if his life is threatened! We can do better. We will fight you to our last drop of blood. And we will win because we have the support of our people and we are fighting for justice and righteousness."

As he heard Baby Tooth out, Grand Old Master's face turned red with shame. Then he saw Yellow Flying Tiger under the banner and his mood shifted. He shouted, "Come out here, Yellow Flying Tiger!"

As if hypnotized, Yellow Flying Tiger rode out on his Five-Colored Magic Bull and bowed to Grand Old Master.

"How are you, my Grand Old Master? It has been quite some time since we last saw each other. I hope I can explain all the wrongs I am accused of."

Grand Old Master roared, "With all the glories and honors King Zhou bestowed on you and your family, you turn around to help the rebels fight the king! And you dare to use flowery language to justify yourself!" Grand Old Master then ordered his generals to tie Flying Tiger up.

In response, General Deng charged out with his spear toward Flying Tiger who fenced with his own spear. Zhong Aspiration came out to aid Deng, but General Nimblefoot blocked him with his long handled knife. General Tao Exalt came out with his lance but was stopped by General Wu Ji.

In this free-for-all, no one seemed able to outfight the other. From the side Xin Circle raised his wings, took to the air, and came down on Baby Tooth with his Twin Hammers.

On his black qilin, Grand Old Master saw Heavenly Educated was riding a jade qilin, and knew instantly the rider was trained by a superiorman and given superior powers. Quickly Grand Old Master came straight at Baby Tooth with his Gold Whips.

These two Gold Whips were in reality two serpents, a Yin and a Yang force. They knocked Baby Tooth off his mount. Nezha rushed over before Grand Old Master could cut off Baby Tooth's head.

The Grand Old Master now raised his whips at Nezha. Concentrating on rescuing Baby Tooth, Nezha was unaware of his own danger, and he too was knocked off his Wind-Fire Wheels.

Muzha and Jinzha tried to help. They too were knocked off their mounts by the Gold Whips.

From the sideline, Yang Bliss saw everything. He raced out on his silver steed and raised his silver spear and charged at Grand Old Master. As Grand old Master lashed Yang Bliss with his Gold Whips, sparks flew when the whips landed on Yang Bliss's head. But the young man did not seem to mind. Surprised and shocked, Grand Old Master lashed out again and again but Yang Bliss behaved as if nothing touched him.

Seeing the stalemate, General Tao Exalt unfurled his magic Wind-Gathering Flag to engulf the whole battleground in flying sands and tumbling rocks, sending Baby Tooth and his troops in full retreat.

Grand Old Master triumphantly returned to camp to receive the congratulations of his men. This was the first battle in a long while that

Grand Old Master had personally participated in. They foresaw a short and easy campaign.

Meanwhile Baby Tooth gathered his generals for more discussion. Yang Bliss related his encounter with Grand Old Master, and his observations. "I think the key strategy should be to destroy the Gold Whips that Grand Old Master depends on," he said. "Then, I am certain we can win with no more than a follow-up attack at night to finish them off."

Baby Tooth said, "Good."

*   *   *   *

After three days of rest, Baby Tooth sent his troops out again. When Grand Old Master confronted Baby Tooth, Baby Tooth said, "Today we will fight to the end!"

Grand Old Master didn't reply but lashed out his Gold Whips. This time, forewarned by Yang Bliss, Baby Tooth fought gamely with his Devil Beating Whip. Baby Tooth's whip could not hurt Grand Old Master himself because Grand Old Master was merely a mortal. But the Devil-Beating Whip could cut his Gold Whips into bits and that was exactly what happened!

"How dare you!" Grand Old Master screamed with shock. Lashing out again with what was left of his whip, Baby Tooth sent Grand Old Master off his black qilin. Luckily Grand Old Master knew how to disappear underground and escaped.

The forces of the Western Foothills planned a surprise attack that night.

*   *   *   *

Grand Old Master was unhappy. Losing a battle was a small matter compared to losing face. And the damage of his Gold Whips was a great blow. His generals comforted him the best they could.

Then a sudden brain wave brought disquietude to Grand Old Master. He immediately ordered incense burned and cast a few gold coins to see what was to be foretold.

He smiled and said to himself, "So they are coming to surprise us tonight!"

He put his men on battle-ready alert, his generals all at strategic positions. He himself manned the main entrance.

At a prearranged signal that night, Baby Tooth's men rushed to Grand Old Master's camp: Heavenly Educated and Nezha went directly at the main entrance, while Flying Tiger and his other sons went in from the right, and general Nimblefoot and others from the left and the rear.

Notes

1. The inevitable escalation of war casualties had led ancient philosophers and statesmen to fashion substitutes for actual battlefield combat between armies. One such substitute, which originated with the superiormen, was in the category of battle formations. Battle formations were a stalking contest where opposing leaders matched wits and murderous magic with their honor and lives at stake

CHAPTER 43

▼

TEN CRUCIBLE BATTLE
FORMATIONS

Far from surprised, Grand Old Master was quite ready to meet Baby Tooth's "surprise attack" head on. Stubbornly wielding his damaged Gold Whips, he fought off Nezha and Heavenly Educated from the front, Jinzha and Muzha from the left, Lethal Dragon and Bad-Tempered Tiger from the right and even Yellow Flying Tiger and Nimblefoot when they came from the rear.

Seeing Grand Old Master's obstinate stand, Yang Bliss went for the supply compounds, fought off the guards and set the supplies on fire, brightening up the whole camp.

Greatly alarmed, especially when he saw Baby Tooth advance waving his Devil Beating Whip, Grand Old Master now fought to retreat. His generals followed, and Flying Tiger led others in hot pursuit.

Spreading his wings covering Grand Old Master, Xin Circle escorted him toward Mount Western Foothills near the border. The attackers abandoned their chase and returned to Phoenix City.

"We will finish them tomorrow," the warriors of King Wu crowed over their victory, not realizing many hurdles still lay ahead.

*   *   *   *

In far-off Mount South End, Superiorman Cloud Dweller said to Thunder Quaker, "My boy. Your brother King Wu is facing many difficult obstacles trying to establish the Chou Dynasty. Do all you can to assist Prime Minister Baby Tooth. Don't let me down."

Thunder Quaker spread his wings and flew to Western Foothills. As he approached Mount Western Foothills, he saw Grand Old Master fleeing with his men. Thunder Quaker decided to have some fun.

He dived, waving his Gold Stick, shouting, "Look out! Here I come!" and came directly at Grand Old Master.

"Xin Circle, beware!" the old man shouted.

Xin Circle, himself also a winged monster, blocked Thunder Quaker with his own Hammers. Oh, how the two fought! Dawn was coming but the sky was darker than ever.

Xin Circle was not Thunder Quaker's match. He fled, abandoning Grand Old Master! Luckily Thunder Quaker did not pursue because he knew he should report to Baby Tooth immediately.

*   *   *   *

Baby Tooth received the blue-faced monster in the Great Hall.

"My Uncle-in-learning," the monster saluted. "I am Thunder Quaker from Mount South End, the disciple of Superiorman Cloud Dweller. My Master sent me to reunite with my brother the king."

"What king are you talking about?"

"King Wu, of course," Thunder Quaker said.

"Any of you recognize him?" Baby Tooth asked everyone with caution. No one did.

Thunder Quaker explained, "When I was seven years old, I helped my Royal father King Wen, the former Grand Duke of the West, over the five Passes. I am Thunder Quaker of Mount Swallow."

"Ah, of course," said Baby Tooth. "I recall now the Grand Duke mentioned how he was rescued by his youngest son. Welcome, my prince. What an auspicious addition to Western Foothills."

Baby Tooth took Thunder Quaker to see King Wu, explaining the circumstances. King Wu welcomed his youngest brother with warmth and appreciation, but he did not take him to meet the rest of the family because he was afraid the females might be frightened.

King Wu said to Baby Tooth, "My Prime Minister. Will you kindly entertain my brother for me?"

Baby Tooth said, "Thunder Quaker is a vegetarian. He would be more at home with me." And so Thunder Quaker lived with Baby Tooth.

$$* \qquad * \qquad * \qquad *$$

Grand Old Master retreated to Mount Western Foothills, seventy miles from Phoenix City. He surveyed his troops and found no more than twenty thousand survivors, and among these were many badly wounded. Numbed by his loss, he sat quietly, giving long and repeated sighs.

His generals stood helplessly by. As a last resort, they suggested that Grand Old Master invite his old buddies-in-learning from the mountains to help.

"Yes, that is the only way out," Grand Old Master agreed.

On his black qilin, Grand Old Master flew to the Isle of the Giant Golden Crabs. He dismounted and walked around but everyone seemed to be away. He got on his qilin again and was about to take off when he heard someone calling, "Where are you going?" It was Lucky Fungus.

"Why, I am here to see you. I thought the whole island was deserted. Where is everyone?"

"Oh, yes. We anticipated your coming. So we are getting ready to come to your assistance. We have designed ten crucible battle formations that not even Baby Tooth can break. Everyone is on White Deer Island waiting for you. Why don't you go there now? I will join you shortly after I get my things out of the furnace."

Grand Old Master left Lucky Fungus for White Deer Island where eight of the Welkin Lords greeted him.

"Only eight of you here?" Grand Old Master asked.

"Yes, Luminous Glo of Golden Light Cave has gone to the White Cloud Island to finish her Golden Light Battle Formation."

"Are your designs all finished?"

"Yes, quite. I think we should go first. Luminous Glo can join us later in Western Foothills," Welkin Lord Qin said.

"I cannot thank you enough," Grand Old Master said, very moved.

After the nine Welkin Lords left, Grand Old Master sat under a pine tree to wait for Luminous Glo.

She soon appeared, flying from the southern sky on a spotted leopard. She wore fancy fish-tail headgear, a red robe with Trigram design, silk sash, and silk cloud-shoes. A backpack and twin swords were on her back.

They greeted each other warmly. Grand Old Master said, "The others have gone ahead to Mount Western Foothills. I am waiting to accompany you there."

When they had all arrived, Welkin Lord Qin said, "Why aren't we at Phoenix City?"

"We were there. But they chased us out here," Grand Old Master said.

"Then let's move right back," the Welkin Lords said.

*   *   *   *

Informed of the troop movements outside Phoenix City, Baby Tooth said, "I see Grand Old Master has gotten help."

Yang Bliss said, "Grand Old Master was trained by the men of the Incisive Cult. What help he got must be from them. We had better be very careful."

Baby Tooth led his generals up the city wall to see what kind of camp Grand Old Master was setting up. From ten black bolts of lightning (invisible to the ordinary eye), a murderous atmosphere emanated from the camp. Baby Tooth shuddered.

*　　　*　　　*　　　*

In Grand Old Master's camp, Welkin Lord Qin said, "Baby Tooth was trained at Mount Kunlun, and we at the Incisive Cult. We have our differences, but still we should be above the dirty business of the Red Dust. I think it best that we fight Baby Tooth with our wits rather than our brawn. After all, it is our intellect that put us above mere brawn. I have no interest in fighting a bloody Red Dust war. We have designed ten crucible battle formations which should tax Baby Tooth to the last drop of blood!"

All agreed. Next day, Grand Old Master went to the City gate on his black qilin and asked for Baby Tooth by name.

Promptly Baby Tooth came out on his four-not-alike, accompanied by his troops led by Nezha, Yang Bliss, Thunder Quaker and Yellow Heavenly Educated.

Mounted on their animal behind Grand Old Master were ten Welkin Lords with red, white, blue, green, black and other startlingly colored faces.

Welkin Lord Qin came out to face Baby Tooth who returned the salute.

"We are the ten Welkin Lords from the Giant Golden Crab Isle. I am Welkin Lord Qin."

"Glad to meet you, Welkin Lord Qin. What have you to teach us at Western Foothills?"

"Now tell me, Baby Tooth. You are from Mount Kunlun and we are from the Incisive Cult. What makes you think you are superior? Why did you bully us?"

"Sir, I don't understand. We respect your Incisive Cult as much as you respect us of the Elucidation Cult."

"Don't try to confuse the issue. Why did you kill the four Diablo brothers? We are all buddies-in-learning, not ordinary people of the Red Dust. We should not kill our own kind, right? When you killed our Incisive buddies, you were bullying us."

Baby Tooth said, "Oh, that! You should know that in the end, righteousness always wins over unrighteousness, and light always chases away darkness. Tyrant King Zhou has brought on a calamity to all under Heaven. And King Wu, like a beacon, has shown the populace and the nobles of our land the light of the right path. This is the mandate of Heaven, and whoever works against it will be destroyed. You are learned, you should understand the scheme of things Heaven and Earth."

"Why, Baby Tooth! You mean the four Diablo brothers, who came to Western Foothills on the order of the king, were wrong? How could they be wrong when they were loyal to their king? Aren't you twisting the issue? No matter, here we have ten crucible battle formations. We would like you to break them without resorting to the battlefield. Think of the lost humanity and the suffering of the people. Care to have a look?"

"How can I refuse such a charming invitation? Of course I will accept your offer," said Baby Tooth.

The ten Welkin Lords led the way. Baby Tooth followed on his four-not-alike, with Nezha on his wind-fire wheels, Heavenly Educated on his jade qilin, Thunder Quaker on foot and Yang Bliss on his steed.

Yang Bliss caught up with Welkin Lord Qin, "We come on your invitation," he said, "You better not try any funny business!"

"Of course not. When we want you to die in the morning, we will not let you stay until noon. When we invite you to solve the battle formations by wit, that is exactly our intention," Welkin Lord Qin assured Yang Bliss.

Nezha said, "Better keep your word!"

Acting as bodyguards to Baby Tooth, the four young generals also went in to view the battle formations.

Over the entrance of each battle formation, they read the following names:

1. Heaven-Extinguishing Battle Formation.

2. Earth-Quaking Battle Formation.

3. Howling-Gale Battle Formation.

4. Frozen-Glacial Battle Formation.

5. Golden-Light Battle Formation.

6. Blood-Curdling Battle Formation.

7. Blazing-Flame Battle Formation.

8. Plunging-Souls Battle Formation.

9. Crimson-Water Battle Formation.

10. Scarlet-Sands Battle Formation.

After the tour, Welkin Lord Qin asked Baby Tooth, "Think you can break them?"

"We will certainly try," Baby Tooth replied calmly. They bade their hosts good-day and returned to Phoenix City.

*   *   *   *

Yang Bliss said, "My Uncle-in-learning, is it true you know how to break the battle formations?"

Baby Tooth said, "These are the Incisive Cult's designs. So far, I am totally baffled. I cannot even perceive the configuration of any of the designs, much less understand how to break them." Worry and concern clearly showed on Baby Tooth's face.

CHAPTER 44

▼

BABY TOOTH'S SOUL FLOATS TO MOUNT KUNLUN

At his banquet for the ten Welkin Lords, Grand Old Master could not wait to ask them about their battle formations.

"How much chance will Baby Tooth have of breaking them?"

"None," said Welkin Lord Qin. "We are certain Baby Tooth will never break any of these. Let me tell you about my *Heaven Extinguishing Battle Formation.*

"After having studied the divinations for thousands of years, I perceived in the universe three main forces: the Heaven, the Earth, and man. Inter-playing the pure and the straight with the foul and the squalid, I combined these forces to design the Heaven Extinguishing Battle Formation. An ordinary mortal entering this formation will have his body instantly turned into ash in a thunderous flash. A cult trained person will not fare any better, for his bones will turn into powder."

Welkin Lord Zhou was just as eager to brag about his. "My *Earth Quaking Battle Formation* is based on the laws of geomancy and geophysics. The fires and winds of the universe are all invested on a single flag. When the flag waves, wind and fire reign, and quietude and turbulence alternate. Anyone entering, even one with cult trained skills, can't save himself from death."

"And your *Howling-Gales Battle Formation*, Lord Teng?" asked Grand Old Master.

"In my Howling Gale-Battle Formation, the wind howls with millions of knives and daggers, penetrating even thick armor to cut all to ribbons," said Welkin Lord Teng.

"*My Frozen-Glacier Battle Formation*," chimed in Welkin Lord Yuan, "was not formed in a day or even a year. It took thousands of years for the ice to become glacial. Yes, indeed, it is called glacial, but actually it is mountains of knives and swords guided by thousands of lightning bolts. All in all, no one would ever be able to come out there alive!"

"On my *Golden-Light Battle Formation*," said Welkin Lady Luminous Glo, "I harnessed the beams of the sun on the surface of twenty-one mirrors fashioned on poles. By turning the angles of the poles, I control the intensity of the killing beam. Not even wings can help Baby Tooth escape from this certain death."

"As for my *Blood-Curdling Battle Formation*," said Welkin Lord Sun. "I use the fierce wind of black sands to blast anyone who comes in, instantly curdling his blood."

"The *Blazing-Flame Battle Formation*?" asked Grand Old Master.

"My Battle Formation," said Welkin Lord White, "contains three kinds of fire, namely the Triple Whammy Fire, the Thunder Fire and the Rock Fire. I joined them together in the Blazing-Flame. Even the most accomplished will not survive the killing radiation and the heat."

"My *Plummeting-Soul Battle Formation*," Welkin Lord Yao said, "does its work by stealing the soul and strangling the spirit. Yes, there is no exception, my friend. It means certain death for all!"

"And the *Crimson-Water Battle Formation*, Lord Zhong?" Grand Old Master was getting more excited as he learned about these invincible battle formations.

"My Battle Formation is a Trigram Platform with three hanging magic gourds, each containing a different deadly fluid that can turn flesh into blood and kill instantly on contact."

"Now tell me the last one, the *Scarlet-Sand Battle Formation*." Grand Old Master could hardly contain himself.

Welkin Lord Wang said, "The last but by no means the least, mind you. My Scarlet-Sand are not really sands but millions of tiny knives in red color. They recognize neither Heaven nor Earth, nor anything in between. They very easily make mincemeat of anyone entering the formation!"

The knowledgeable Grand Old Master knew these very brief descriptions of the different battle formations were but the visible part of the iceberg. Satisfied, he said to the Welkin Lords, "Now that you are here, we really have nothing to worry about."

Then Welkin Lord Yao said, "Baby Tooth is a very shallow person. As I see it, I don't think we need to waste any of our battle formations on him. Let me try my hand on him first. I can promise you in twenty-one days Baby Tooth will be dead and Western Foothills, without him, will certainly be finished. As you well know, a snake can't do much without its head! And an army without its leader will disintegrate in no time!"

Grand Old Master said, "If you really can do Baby Tooth in without moving a knife or an arrow, I am all for it!"

*   *   *   *

Welkin Lord Yao went into his Soul Plummeting Battle Formation and built a platform. On it he set up a straw effigy of Baby Tooth. Suspended over the head of the effigy were three Soul-Chasing Lamps. At the foot were six Spirit-Strangling Lamps together with an incense urn.

With his hair down and his sword in hand, Welkin Lord Yao bowed to the effigy three times a day, mumbling an incantation each time.

*   *   *   *

Yang Bliss was the first to notice the change in Baby Tooth, who sat mute and listless when he was supposedly mapping strategy with his generals on how to break those ten crucible battle formations.

"I know the battle formations are very difficult, but how can a man with Baby Tooth's training be so devastated by them?" Yang Bliss was troubled.

Ten days passed and Baby Tooth was now in a stupor as Welkin Lord Yao continued his bowing and mumbling.

The generals of Western Foothills were bewildered. Some thought Baby Tooth was deep in meditation while others thought he was physically illness.

By the fifteenth day, Baby Tooth was practically in a coma. Yang Bliss finally broke the solemn silence.

"I don't see Baby Tooth behaving as if he had ordinary illness. More likely someone is doing some trick to his soul," Yang Bliss said to the generals.

They all went to Baby Tooth's sleeping quarters for a closer look.

"Please wake up the Prime Minister," they told the servants. "We have very urgent business to discuss with him."

The servant got Baby Tooth out to a chair where he sat silently, looked at his generals without recognition, and appeared indifferent and bored.

Nezha asked, "My Uncle-in-learning, what is the meaning of this sudden gust of wind?"

Hardly himself, Baby Tooth said, "What meaning? What wind?"

With his bowing and mumbling before Baby Tooth's effigy, Welkin Lord Yao had succeeded in removing two souls and five spirits from

Baby Tooth's body. Only one more soul and one more spirit remained. That was why he was so lethargic and uncomprehending.

*   *   *   *

My dear readers, you do remember that the Chinese think that each person is made up of three souls, six spirits and one body. Missing any part would make a person not whole.

*   *   *   *

Next day, Baby Tooth was nothing but a wilted vegetable! The ministers informed King Wu of the situation. King Wu came, and on seeing Baby Tooth's motionless body, thought he was already dead. King Wu howled with anguish. Ministers and officials stood on the side, weeping openly without shame.

It seemed Yang Bliss was the only one who kept his presence of mind. He felt Baby Tooth's body and, sensing a faint heartbeat, he said to the king, "The Prime Minister is not yet dead. There must be some way and someone we can turn to for help. Let us think!"

*   *   *   *

At this moment Baby Tooth was very near death, for his only remaining soul and spirit had left his body and floated into the Altar of Investiture of Gods. There, Usher Cedar Precept recognized the soul and spirit; he also knew Baby Tooth was not supposed to be there. So he gave Baby Tooth's soul and spirit a big push and shoved them away from the altar.

Baby Tooth's spirit and soul took the next most natural course and went to Mount Kunlun, the only real home he had ever had.

As they approached Mount Kunlun, they bumped into the God of South Pole who quickly clenched the floating soul and spirit and put them into his gourd and tightly sealed it. He then hurriedly went to see Superiorman Primordial Supreme.

"South Pole, old pal, please don't go away!" someone was calling from behind.

South Pole turned and saw Superiorman Red Nudist of Mount Grandiflora.

"See who's here!" South Pole remarked, surprised.

"Well, I don't have anything better to do today. I wonder if you would like to play a game of chess with me?" Red Nudist asked.

"I am busy," South Pole said curtly.

"Don't be funny. What do you mean you have no time to play chess with me? We have all the time in the world."

"I am really busy today. Sorry." So saying, South Pole turned to leave.

"What is the matter? Is it because of Baby Tooth, yes?"

Startled, South Pole asked, "How did you know?"

"I was merely teasing you. I happened to pass by the Altar of the Investiture of Gods and Cedar Precept told me about Baby Tooth's soul and spirit. That is why I am here. Did you see them?"

"I certainly did. And I am on my way to discuss this with Superiorman Primordial Supreme."

"Where are the spirit and the soul?"

"In my gourd here."

"Such a small thing. Why bother the master? Let me take care of it," Red Nudist said.

Taking the gourd from South Pole, Red Nudist rushed to Western Foothills by traveling underground.

Yang Bliss was at the entrance and saw Red Nudist coming. The young man knelt and asked, "My Uncle-in-learning. Are you here to save Baby Tooth?"

"Yes, but hurry!"

King Wu rushed to meet Red Nudist, who nodded his head in salute, but the king saluted fully as to a superior and offered him the guest-of-honor chair.

"Where is Baby Tooth?"

King Wu and his ministers and generals took Red Nudist directly to Baby Tooth's chamber.

"Don't you worry, Your Majesty," Red Nudist said. "The trouble is Baby Tooth's souls and spirits could not find their way back to him."

"Is there some medicine for that?" King Wu asked anxiously.

"No need for medicine. I have my own way. Call me at the third bell tonight," Red Nudist said.

Everyone felt relieved but remained concerned. When Yang Bliss came to call at the third bell, Red Nudist was ready. He strode directly from Phoenix City straight toward the enemy camp. As he surveyed the battle formations from afar, Red Nudist could see them shrouded in a dark and murderous atmosphere and hear the crying and howling of the dead. Pointing a finger, he called up from his store of magic two floating lotus flowers which afforded him both transportation and protection.

As he flew over the Plummeting Soul Battle Formation, he spotted Welkin Lord Yao, hair down, sword in hand, bowing to an effigy of Baby Tooth. Instantly he realized that the Welkin Lord Yao was trying to extinguish the two flattering lights, one each at the head and foot of the effigy. The two lights represented the one soul and one spirit remaining with Baby Tooth.

Now, fortunately for Baby Tooth, his one remaining soul and spirit were safely inside South Pole's gourd. No matter how hard Lord Yao tried, he could not extinguish the two remaining lights. So Baby Tooth remained comatose but alive.

As Lord Yao bowed and bowed, Red Nudist lowered himself to snatch away the effigy.

But Lord Yao raised his eyes just then and swiftly countered by throwing a handful of what looked like black sand at Red Nudist. Red

Nudist knew the sand was actually tiny poisoned darts. Red Nudist beat a fast retreat but dropped his lotus flowers. He rushed back to Phoenix City by traveling underground.

*   *   *   *

"My Uncle-in-learning, have you brought back Baby Tooth's soul and spirit?" Yang Bliss met him at the entrance.

"The Plummeting Soul Battle Formation is nothing to sneeze at. I lost my lotus flowers and almost lost my life!" Red Nudist said.

King Wu wailed, "You mean Baby Tooth is now dead for sure?"

"Certainly not," comforted Red Nudist. "Baby Tooth must still undergo further tribulations. But don't you worry, we will prevail and Baby Tooth will be as good as new." So saying, Red Nudist turned to leave.

"Where are you going?" King Wu was very distraught.

"Take good care of Baby Tooth. I will be back soon." Red Nudist went directly to Mount Kunlun. He met South Pole. Red Nudist related his encounter with Welkin Lord Yao, then asked, "What should I do now?"

"I think I'd better consult the master." South Pole went to see Superiorman Primordial Supreme.

The master said, "I would not be able to handle this. Better direct Red Nudist to Mount Multifarious to see the Old One himself."

Red Nudist stepped on a pink cloud and went to see the Old One. The Old One said, "Baby Tooth is predestined to go through this trial of the Plummeting Soul Battle Formation. I am powerless on that. But take my Diagram of Cosmological Scheme, it may help. But be careful."

Red Nudist returned directly to Western Foothills with the Diagram.

Again at the third bell, Red Nudist flew over the Plummeting Soul Battle Formation and found Lord Yao still bowing to the effigy.

Carefully Red Nudist opened the Diagram of Cosmological Scheme and a golden bridge materialized, leading directly into the Plummeting Soul Battle Formation. Holding the Diagram in his left hand, Red Nudist slid down the golden bridge and snatched up the effigy with his right. Lord Yao threw his black poisoned sand at Red Nudist who again beat a fast retreat. But trying to grasp the railing of the golden bridge, he let slip the Diagram, and the golden bridge vanished under his feet! He made one last lunge and escaped with the effigy.

Back at Phoenix City, Red Nudist put down the effigy and opened the gourd. With the effigy now in friendly hands, Red Nudist was able to corral the lost souls and spirits into his gourd. After collecting them all, he went to Baby Tooth's bedside and mumbled an incantation which returned all the souls and spirits to Baby Tooth's body!

Baby Tooth turned and yawned. "What a nap!" he said. He opened his eyes and was surprised to see King Wu and others watching over him.

King Wu said, "If it were not for this master, how could my Honorable Uncle be alive today!"

Now fully awake, Baby Tooth immediately knelt at Red Nudist's feet, saying, "How fortunate I am to earn your succor."

Just then Yang Bliss reported the arrival of Superiorman Yellow Dragon of Mount Twin Fairies. Baby Tooth immediately invited him to the Great Hall.

"I came to help break the crucible battle formations," Yellow Dragon said. "Soon many comrades-in-learning of our Elucidation Cult will be here to help. It would not be appropriate for us to dwell within the palace. Please build a camp for us in the open field."

Baby Tooth ordered Nimblefoot and Wu Ji to take care of the matter. When the camp was finished, Baby Tooth accompanied Red Nudist and Yellow Dragon to inspect the new facility.

The structure was a large building with many rooms. The roof was thatched with reeds and the floor was covered by thick carpets. Flowers, draperies and lanterns were everywhere. It was a festive place.

CHAPTER 45

▼

SUPERIORMAN LAMP LIGHTER TAKES CHARGE

Soon after the special tent was finished, many Superiormen from the four corners and eight directions of the universe came one after another. They were:

NAME	CAVE	MOUNTAIN
Alert Minded	Flying Cloud	Mount Thin Dragon
Altruist	Cloud Top	Mount Five Dragons
Anima Merit	Morning Sun	Mount Baldy
Broad Achiever	Peach Stream	Mount Nine Elves
Circumspect	Jade House	Mount Jade Creek
Jade Vessel	Golden Cloud	Mount Golden
Mercy Voyager	Setting Sun	Mount Puta
Paragon	Golden Light	Mount Champion
Red Nudist	Colorful Cloud	Mount Grandiflora

NAME	CAVE	MOUNTAIN
True Vacuum	Purple Sun	Mount Pure Wind
Universal Converter	White Egret	Mount Nine Courts
Yellow Dragon	Mushroom	Mount Twin Fairies

Broad Achiever said, "My dear comrades-in-learning. We are here today to investigate the trouble besieging Western Foothills. We should be able to discern the true and the false and act accordingly. My dear brother-in-learning Baby Tooth, please tell us what you know of these ten Battle Formations."

Baby Tooth was uneasy in front of this group of the most learned persons. He said timidly, "My honorable Elders-in-learning, I have only forty years of training, I am overwhelmed and totally bewildered by the ten Crucible Battle Formations! Have pity on us. Help us out of this crisis! King Wu and Western Foothills, and all under Heaven will forever be grateful to you all!"

Broad Achiever said, "It will be difficult to deal with the black magic of the Incisive Cult!"

No one wanted to assume leadership.

At this moment, a sudden breeze brought in a heavenly fragrance and the sound of a deer song, heralding the arrival of Superiorman Lamp Lighter of Intuition Cave, Mount Condor. They all went out to welcome him.

After all were seated, Lamp Lighter said, "My friends, please excuse me for coming late. The ten Crucible Battle Formations are the most vicious I have ever seen. But it is our moral duty to take up this challenge. Have you decided who will be in charge of this affair?"

Baby Tooth said, "We are waiting for you to decide."

Lamp Lighter said, "Well, in that case, I am honored and I certainly will do my utmost. My intention for coming is twofold: first, to take charge, and second, to warn you of danger."

He explained the Scheme of things Heaven and Earth, predicting ten deaths among his comrades-in-learning. Finally he asked Baby Tooth for the Commander's seal.

To everyone's relief, Baby Tooth handed over the seal without hesitation.

*   *   *   *

In the Shang Camp (represented by Grand Old Master), at the urging of the ten Welkin Lords, Grand Old Master sent a formal letter inviting Baby Tooth to break the ten Crucible Battle Formations.

Baby Tooth wrote on the invitation itself "We will be there in three days." and sent it back via the same messenger.

On the eve of the deadline, the Welkin Lords perceived a strange glow radiating from the Chou Camp (represented by Baby Tooth.)

Welkin Lord Qin remarked, "Oh, the people of Mount Kunlun are here. We had better be careful." All Welkin Lords went into their Battle Formations to wait for the assault.

Early next morning, Grand Old Master was on his black qilin, flanked on his left by the four mountain lords and on his right by ten other generals.

From the Chou Camp of Western Foothills, blazing with confidence as masters and disciples prepared to fight for justice and righteousness they stood two abreast, in two lines, facing each other. In one line were:

> Nezha and Heavenly Educated,
> Yang Bliss and Thunder Quaker,
> Lethal Dragon and Bad Tempered Tiger,
> Jinzha and Muzha.

On the opposite line were:

> Red Nudist paired with Broad Achiever,
> Paragon with Anima Merit,

True Vacuum with Yellow Dragon,
Jade Vessel with Circumspect,
Mercy Voyager with Alert Minded,
Altruist with Universal Converter.

All in all twelve generations of superiormen stood there.

Broad Achiever struck a golden bell and Red Nudist a jade disk when Lamp Lighter emerged on his deer.

As expected, the entrance of the Heaven-Extinguishing Battle Formation opened, showing fluttering flags, behind which stood the blue-faced Welkin Lord Qin.

Lamp Lighter looked about him and found himself in a dilemma because no one on his side was destined to die in this particular battle formation. While pondering his next step, he heard the sound of someone landing from the air.

Holding a long rod, the new arrival knelt before Lamp Lighter and said, "I am Deng Hua. My master of Vacuous Palace has sent me to help break this battle formation."

Lamp Lighter said to himself, "Well, he is destined by the scheme of things Heaven and Earth to die in this battle formation. Pity we cannot help him avoid it."

At this moment, Welkin Lord Qin shouted, "What is the delay? No one dares to come?"

Deng Hua stepped out and said, "Don't be such a bully!"

"Who are you to dare contradict me?" Welkin Lord Qin did not like Deng's manner.

"You mean you don't know me? I am Deng Hua, the fifth rank disciple of Superiorman Primordial Supreme of Mount Kunlun."

"Big deal! Dare to try my battle formation?"

"What is so special about it? My master sent me to break it, so why not?" Raising his long rod, Deng Hua charged at Welkin Lord Qin.

After a few contacts, Welkin Lord Qin feigned retreat and ran back to his Heaven Extinguishing Battle Formation. Not knowing any better, Deng Hua followed.

Inside the battle formation, Welkin Lord Qin jumped on a platform and started waving two flags, knocking Deng Hua down quickly. He chopped off Deng's head and took it outside to show to the Chou Camp. Pity Deng Hua, his thousand years of training came to naught! His soul floated to the Altar of the Investiture of Gods.

"Well, Lamp Lighter, anyone else you want to send to his death?" Welkin Lord Qin boasted.

Lamp Lighter sent Altruist who sang as he walked out to meet Welkin Lord Qin.

"Brother Qin," Altruist said. "I thought you were happy and free on your island. What possesses you to set up such an inhuman battle formation? I am afraid I have to kill you to save humanity!"

"Ha! Don't you claim you are holier than thou! I thought you were happy and free on your mountain. What possesses you to get mixed up in this? Don't blame me, I didn't invite you. You came of your own accord."

Altruist laughed, "Look who is talking!"

Qin's Four-Edged Rod came on like a wind. Altruist blocked it with his sword. Again Qin feigned defeat and ran back into his battle formation. Altruist ran after him but hesitated at the entrance. The signal drum in the Chou Camp sounded the call for advance. Altruist had no choice but to follow orders. He gestured with his left hand, and two white lotus flowers sprang out of the ground to float him into the battle formation.

Qin shouted, "Ten times more lotus flowers would make no difference! You will never get out of here alive!"

Altruist smiled and said, "Is that so?" He blew hard, and from his mouth came a huge white lotus flower which held five brightly lit candles illuminating the Heaven Extinguishing Battle Formation.

Qin waved his three banners frantically but to no avail. Altruist stood steadily as before on his lotus flowers, and the burning candles shone brightly.

"I am awfully sorry but I have to kill you now!" So saying, Altruist threw his Seven-Trick-Golden-Lotus on Qin. Qin was immobilized immediately by three gold rings. After bowing toward Mount Kunlun, Altruist cut off Qin's head and walked out with it.

On his black qilin, Grand Old Master was beside himself when he saw that Qin was dead. He shouted, "Altruist! Freeze! I am coming!" Kicking his qilin, he charged at Altruist like a ball of black smoke. Altruist ignored him and continued walking toward the Chou Camp.

Superiorman Yellow Dragon flew overhead and said to Grand Old Master, "Don't be a pill! Why get so excited? Qin killed Deng Hua and has now paid with his life. Fair and square. Besides, all these battle formations are battles of wits. This is but the first one. Go back to where you belong!"

At this very moment, amidst a loud report, Welkin Lord Zhou charged out of his Earth-Quaking Battle Formation on his white deer. "Forget the first battle formation," he shouted. "Who dares to try mine?"

On orders from Lamp Lighter, Lethal Dragon rushed toward Welkin Lord Zhou, shouting, "Stop!"

"Who are you but a nuisance! I hate to be bothered by a little peanut!" So saying, Welkin Lord Zhou slashed out at Lethal Dragon with his sword.

After a few thrusts, Lethal Dragon imprudently followed Lord Zhou into the Earth-Quaking Battle Formation.

Zhou waved his banners and instantly, thunder and lightning ground Lethal Dragon into powder. Poor Lethal Dragon! His soul flew to the Altar of the Investiture of Gods.

Welkin Lord Zhou came out again on his white deer, snickering, "Come on, don't bother me with another good-for-nothing green pea!"

Lamp Lighter ordered Alert Minded to face Zhou. Alert Minded said to Zhou, "My friend, what is the matter with you? I thought you people of Incisive Cult claim to be peace loving. Why set up such vicious battle formations? I am afraid you have no choice but to report to the Altar of the Investiture of Gods today! Who knows, you may even be on the register!"

Again, after sparring with their weapons briefly, Zhou led the way into his battle formation. Alert Minded did not follow. But goaded by the drum signaling advance, Alert Minded entered cautiously. Zhou was already on a platform, waving his banners and making thunder and lightning. Alert Minded spread his arms and was instantly enveloped by a protective cloud. From his pocket, Alert Minded took a skein of silk and threw it at Zhou. Zhou was so intent on flag waving, and so confident of his battle formation, he did not pay enough attention to guarding himself from attack. When he realized what was going on, he was already bound tightly by the silk into a neat bundle.

Alert Minded ordered his Yellow-Kerchiefed genie to drop the bundle from the air, killing Zhou and his Earth Quaking Battle Formation.

Again, Grand Old Master rushed out on his black qilin to fight Alert Minded. Grand Old Master was stopped by Superiorman Jade Vessel.

Jade Vessel said, "My friend. Don't you have any sporting manners at all? We are here to compete. There are eight more battle formations and you behave as if the world had already come to an end! Shame on you!"

Grand Old Master's face turned bright red. He withdrew and called his men for a meeting. He told them how sorry he was now that two of the ten Welkin Lords were dead.

Welkin Lord Deng said, "That is fate. The scheme of things Heaven and Earth is set, we cannot do anything about it. But wait until they try my Howling Gale Battle Formation!"

Lamp Lighter ordered that Welkin Lord Zhou's remain be hung outside of the Chou Camp to show the populace. "Will we be able to break the Howling Gale Battle Formation?" someone asked Lamp Lighter.

"Not easy. These are not the ordinary winds we are familiar with. They are full of Black Magic and are called Earth, Fire and Water Winds. When they howl, they carry millions of knives. We must have the Wind Calming Pearl to deal with this battle formation."

"Where will we find the pearl?"

Superiorman Anima Merit volunteered that his friend Superiorman Danger Skipper of Mount Nine Vessel had such a pearl.

"Let me write him a letter. I am certain he will lend it to us. However, there is one drawback: the person who will fetch the pearl must travel by ordinary means, and cannot be a cult-trained person. Otherwise the pearl will lose its power."

Seeing no other way out, Baby Tooth sent Counselor Easy Life and General Jade Ricefield to deliver the letter.

After many days of travel by horse, the two reached their destination. "Please inform your master that Easy Life of Western Foothills wishes to see him," Easy Life implored the disciple of Danger Skipper.

Informed of the situation, Danger Skipper handed over the pearl to Easy Life, and said, "I realize how important it is to break the ten Crucible Battle Formations. I am glad to help but you must take the utmost care of the pearl."

Easy Life thanked the superiorman, then, with Jade Ricefield, retraced his steps. When they again came to the Yellow River, they found no boatman to ferry them across. There were so many ferries when they first came by, why were there none around now?

A passerby said, "Dear sirs, misfortune has befallen our district. Ten days ago, there came two powerful strangers. They confiscated all our boats. Now only they can ferry people across and they charge a large fee."

Then Easy Life spotted the two men effortlessly pulling a boat from one shore to the other; passengers paid their fee and left hurriedly without a murmur.

On closer inspection, Jade Ricefield recognized them as the Fong Brothers of Morning Song, Capital of King Zhou.

*   *   *   *

My dear readers, don't you remember the two low ranking palace guards who rescued the two young princes from King Zhou in Chapter Eight? After they left the princes at the three-forked road, they had tried to find a master to serve but no one dared to hire them. So to make a living, they finally strong-armed the boat people.

*   *   *   *

Jade Ricefield introduced Easy Life to the Fong brothers. Fong Da said, "You are high-ranking officers of King Zhou's Court. Why are you with the Counselor of Western Foothills?"

Jade Ricefield said, "King Zhou is so bad. My twin brother and I were forced to leave Morning Song and join Western Foothills." Jade then related the Wind Calming Pearl story to the Fong Brothers as they were crossing the river.

The Fong brothers asked Easy Life, "Counselor, may we have a look at the magic pearl? We have never seen such wonder and don't quite believe it."

Since they had ferried them across, and were friends of Jade Ricefield, Easy Life showed them the pearl.

Fong Da put the pearl in his pocket, walked away in big steps, saying, "Thanks. This will cover the ferry charge."

Jade Ricefield dared not fight the Fong brothers, knowing how strong they were. Poor Easy Life, all his life he had been cautious and calculating on all matters before acting. Why did he now so casually hand over the pearl? Realizing his folly, he cried, "What shall we do? How are we to face Danger Skipper and Baby Tooth? What will the fate of Western Foothills be?"

Easy Life was ready to jump in the river. Jade Ricefield held him back, saying, "Counselor. I am sure we should kill ourselves here and now. But if we do so, who will tell Baby Tooth? They are waiting for us!"

So they rushed homeward. On their way they unexpectedly caught up with a supply train under the command of Lord of National Stability, Prince Yellow Flying Tiger.

Easy Life and Jade Ricefield knelt before Yellow Flying Tiger and sobbed out their story.

Yellow Flying Tiger asked, "When did this happen?"

"No more than an hour or so ago," Easy Life said.

"Don't worry. Wait here for me." Yellow Flying Tiger turned his beast in the direction the Fong brothers had taken. Soon he saw the brothers walking down the road. He roared, "Fong brothers, stop!"

Turning their heads, they recognized Yellow Flying Tiger and knelt. They had not seen each other since the two young princes left King Zhou's Court.

Yellow Flying Tiger asked angrily, "Why did you rob Easy Life of his pearl?"

"We did not, my lord. It was payment for ferrying them across the river."

"Give it to me!"

So scared were they of him, without hesitation they handed over the pearl.

Yellow Flying Tiger said, "I have left King Zhou and joined the Western Foothills. Two thirds of the country has rallied to King Wu's Western Foothills. If you don't have other plans, why not come with me? I am sure you will be properly invested."

"Why not indeed? We will be forever grateful if you will help us." the Fong brothers said.

Easy Life and Jade Ricefield were frightened when the Fong brothers showed up. But Yellow Flying Tiger handed over the Wind Calming pearl to Easy Life, and said, "You two rush home first. We will come soon. Be extra careful!"

Easy Life delivered the pearl to Baby Tooth. Baby Tooth became very angry when he learned of the mishap.

He said to Easy Life, "How could you be so careless! You may go now and wait for your proper punishment!"

CHAPTER 46

▼

MORE CRUCIBLE BATTLE FORMATIONS BROKEN

Early next morning, amid the musical sounds of gold bells and jade disks, Lamp Lighter led all his comrades-in-learning out of the Chou Camp to face the new day's challenge.

Meanwhile, at the sound of a cannon in the opposition Shang Camp, Grand Old Master came out with Welkin Lord Deng, designer of the Howling-Gale Battle Formation.

Strutting on his Eight-Branched Deer and waving his Twin Swords, Deng shouted, "Hey, any of you dare to break the Howling-Gale?"

As the overall Commander in this phase of the battle, Lamp Lighter was in a predicament. Even though the Chou Camp now had the Wind-Calming Pearl, the rule of the contest for each of the battle formations required at least one trial of ordinary weapons before the use of such unusual means as the Pearl was allowed. As Lamp Lighter looked about him, he could not decide which of his comrades-in-learning should be the trial balloon. Given the deadliness of the battle formation, it was certain death to whoever it was.

At this very moment, Yellow Flying Tiger was leading the Fang brothers to see Baby Tooth. Lamenting fate, Lamp Lighter sent the older Fang brother into battle.

Poor Fang, with his pea brain, what did he know about fighting with wits? All he ever had was his courage and his outstanding physique. Rushing forward with his spear and shouting "Look out!" Fang startled Deng. Fang's fresh-plum-look face, charcoal beard and roaring campfire eyes carried on a muscular thirty foot tall body was something to be reckoned with. Deng ran immediately into his Howling-Gale Battle Formation. Not knowing any better, Fang followed without hesitation.

Deng mounted a platform and waved his black flags with all his might. Instantly, Fang's body was chopped up by the howling winds. As he fell, his soul flew to the Altar of the Investiture of Gods.

Deng emerged from the battle formation on his Eight-Branched Deer, taunting, "Well, Lamp Lighter! Why are you so cruel to send such a useless simpleton to his death? Even your best would only be like a common stone to my jade!"

Lamp Lighter sent Mercy Voyager forth with the Wind Calming Pearl to confront Deng.

"I say, my friend," Mercy Voyager said. "Are we breaking the no-kill taboo? You have enjoyed a carefree life, why design such an inhuman battle formation to court your own demise? Remember when we were signing the Manifesto to the Register of the Investiture of Gods? Your Incisive Cult Leader pointed to the words on the entrance of his cave:

"Keep door closed and study your sutra;
Annihilation if involved in the Red Dust World."

Deng said, "So what! You Elucidation Cult people have always looked down on us with your holier-than-thou attitude. Or we would not have come down our mountains. I know you are a goody-goody. So you better return to where you belong lest I become powerless to save you!"

"Why worry about me? You cannot even save yourself!" Mercy Voyager said.

As Deng started to run back to his battle formation, Mercy Voyager followed cautiously. Waving his black flags, Deng sent the howling winds of millions of knives toward Mercy Voyager. The Wind Calming Pearl protected her by causing the black winds to swirl harmlessly around her. Meanwhile Mercy Voyager opened her crystal vase. Black smoke accompanied by rolling thunder sucked Deng and all his trappings into the vase. She recapped the vase, walked out, and informed Grand Old Master that she had broken the Howling-Gale Battle Formation. She then opened her crystal vase and Deng's soul flew to the Altar of the Investiture of Gods.

Grand Old Master wanted to fight Mercy Voyager. But just then Welkin Lord Yuan, the designer of Frozen-Glacier Battle Formation shouted, "Grand Old Master! I am coming!" Turning toward the Chou Camp, Yuan shouted, "Any of you Elucidation Cult dare come to my Frozen-Glacier?"

Lamp Lighter sent Bad-Tempered Tiger. Yuan looked at the youngster and said, "A baby! Still wet behind the ears! Get your master here instead!"

Bad-Tempered Tiger said angrily, "How dare you belittle me!"

Yuan led Bad Tempered Tiger into his battle formation. By moving some switches Yuan let loose two huge icebergs, crushing Bad-Tempered Tiger to death. Poor Bad-Tempered Tiger, his young soul flew to the Altar of the Investiture of Gods.

Now Lamp Lighter sent out Universal Converter. Universal Converter said, "Old Yuan, what made you so malicious? To begin with, I hate to break my vow not to kill. But what you are doing leaves me no choice, old chap."

Shouting "How dare you!" Yuan charged at Converter and led him into his battle formation. Huge icebergs started rumbling toward Converter, who calmly drew a circle above his head with his forefinger. Immediately a huge cloud appeared, with golden lights burning on the top side and golden tassels waving below. The lights melted the icebergs and the waving tassels spread the heat.

Yuan quickened his magic by sending more and larger icebergs toward Converter but to no avail. Finally Yuan realized it was hopeless and tried to sneak out of the formation, but he was swiftly dispatched by Converter. Yuan's soul too went to the Altar of the Investiture of Gods.

Universal Converter put away his lighted clouds and waltzed out of the battle formation.

In a flash, Welkin Lady Luminous Glo charged out on her white flowered leopard, waving her twin swords and screaming, "You Elucidation fellows! Who dares to try my Golden-Light Battle Formation?"

At this moment, a young and handsome lad arrived by air and knelt before Lamp Lighter, saying, "I am Xiao Qin. My master the Superiorman Primordial Supreme of Mount Kunlun sent me to help break the Golden Light Battle Formation."

Luminous Glo did not recognize Xiao, she snickered, "Who are you dare try my battle formation?" With her swords she charged at Xiao.

After a few weapon contacts, Luminous Glo retreated into her battle formation.

Xiao shouted, "Don't go away!" and followed.

Luminous Glo quickly activated her twenty-one prisms, radiating fire everywhere, and burning Xiao's body to a cinder before he knew what had hit him! Poor fellow, his soul flew to the Altar of the Investiture of Gods.

Luminous Glo came out of her battle formation on her leopard and said quietly, "Well, who's next?"

Lamp Lighter sent Broad Achiever. Luminous Glo said, "Ha, Broad Achiever. So it is you!"

"Don't be so conceited, Glo. No one is invincible!" Broad Achiever smirked.

Again Luminous Glo retreated into her battle formation. Broad Achiever followed on her heels. Luminous Glo immediately turned on her prisms. In the same instant, Broad Achiever got under his purple Trigram cape, saving himself from the deadly beams. The harder Luminous Glo worked on the prisms, the more fire and light was reflected back to herself. In the stalemate, Broad Achiever threw a Wonder Pebble, breaking nineteen of the twenty-one prisms.

Alarmed, Luminous Glo tried to maneuver her two hand-held prisms, but Broad Achiever hit her on the head with another pebble, killing her instantly. Her soul too flew to the Altar of the Investiture of Gods.

When Broad Achiever came out, Grand Old Master shouted and charged at him, "I will avenge Luminous Glo's death!"

But Welkin Lord Sun intercepted, "Please, Grand Old Master. I will take care of them all!" Welkin Lord Sun had a face like a double prune, purple, wrinkled but fat, surrounded by a stubby white beard.

Just then a new arrival came to see Lamp Lighter, saying he was Qiu Kun, of Mount Five Barbarians, White Cloud Cave. He said he was allied to neither the rival Incisive nor the Elucidation Cults, but would like to help Baby Tooth break the Blood-Curdling Battle Formation.

When Welkin Lord Sun shouted for a fight, Qiu stepped out smartly and said, "I thought you two cults were friends. What is your quarrel? I don't think it is nice to set up such a cannibalistic battle formation!"

"Bah! What do you know!" So saying, Sun ran into his Blood-Curdling Battle Formation. Unsuspecting, Qiu followed. Instantly a handful of red sand reduced Qiu into bloody shreds! His soul flew to the Altar of the Investiture of Gods.

Sun came out of the battle formation and shouted, "Lamp Lighter! Stop sending these nobodies to their death! Send someone who knows how to fight!"

Superiorman Paragon stepped out to confront Sun. Sun said, "My friend. I don't think you should be the one to come here! You will never get away alive!"

"Don't brag! Let me have a look at your Blood-Curdling Battle Formation." Paragon smiled, pointing a finger downward. A pink cloud appeared to float him into the Blood-Curdling Battle Formation. He also pointed a finger upward and another cloud appeared, circling him in a protective shield when Sun started throwing red sand at him. The red sands melted away as if they were snow flakes meeting live coal.

Sun continued his red sand storm and finally tried to escape after realizing his sands were useless. But when Paragon clapped his hands, nine fire dragons emerged to engulf Lord Sun. Sun's soul too flew to the Altar of the Investiture of Gods.

Grand Old Master again tried to fight Paragon, but Yellow Dragon, on his flying crane, stopped the old man, saying, "My friend, shame on you to behave like a barbarian! We are here to challenge your ten Crucible Battle Formations. Six are now broken. Four more to go. We will come back tomorrow morning to continue."

*   *   *   *

With his magic third eye flashing rage, Grand Old Master retreated to his Shang Camp. He called the four remaining Welkin Lords to his tent and said, "My friends. I am so sorry to have gotten you involved in this deadly business. Now that six of our friends have been sacrificed, I think you four better return to your island to enjoy your good life. The Red Dust is not for you!" So saying, tears rained down his old cheeks.

"Take it easy, old friend. What happened would have happened, that is the scheme of things Heaven and Earth. We know what we have to do tomorrow. We will never abandon you," comforted the Welkin Lords.

Grand Old Master pondered his next move. His old friend Zhou Magnanimous, an Incisive Cult Superiorman, of Mount E Mei, Floating World Cave, came to his mind.

"Everything will be all right if only I can get him to help. However, should I get him involved?" The Grand Old Master thought and thought. So many of his friends of the Incisive Cult had been killed because of his invitation to help the Shang Camp. Should he involve one more?

"There is no way out for us unless I get Magnanimous to help!" Grand Old Master made up his mind.

A decision made, Grand Old Master got on his black qilin and flew directly to Mount E Mei.

Magnanimous was delighted to see his old friend. Grand Old Master related his distress and worry. "Why didn't you come earlier? I would have stopped the slaughter! Very well, you go back, I will be there soon," Magnanimous promised.

Magnanimous invited Chen Nine and Yao Young, two fellow Incisive Cult buddies who were also close neighbors, to go to Western Foothills with him. They rode their tigers with the wind and arrived at the Shang Camp in short order. They were welcomed with a banquet by Grand Old Master and the surviving Welkin Lords.

Magnanimous asked, "Whose body is hanging at the Chou Camp?"

"The body of Zhou River, designer of the Earth-Quaking Battle Formation."

"How dare they do that to us! The different cults are all equals. Yet they are insulting us. We must hang one of theirs and see how they feel!"

So saying, Magnanimous got on his tiger, rushed out, and demanded to see Baby Tooth.

The war would continue.

EPILOGUE

▼

The war between King Zhou of the Shang Dynasty and King Wu of the Chou continued for some time. King Zhou's representative, Grand Old Master Wen Zhong, and King Wu's representative, Baby Tooth, dueled in many battle formations set up by the superiormen who came to the aid of the Shang, each formation more intricate, more sophisticated, and more cruel than the previous. These formations, veritable crucibles, included pestilence, conflagration, and flood, all of which were visited upon the Western Foothills. Yellow Flying Tiger, after a distinguished career as the highest military chief under King Zhou, died in battle fighting on the side of King Wu. Grand Old Master Wen Zhong, despite the power of his magic and his cunning in battle, was ultimately killed in battle by Superiorman Cloud Dweller. Seeing the war had been won by King Wu's forces, King Zhou finally saw the inevitable. On his last day, he went up to the Star-Picking Belvedere in his full royal fineries but without his Daji, and ordered his last, lone, faithful eunuch to set fire to the building. The eunuch died with him in the fire. Baby Tooth's men captured Daji, the Thousand-year-old Fox Specter, and her two specter cronies, the fat belly guitar Jade Pipa and the Nine-headed pheasant specter Splendor, with the help of Snail Goddess Nu Wa Niang Niang. At their execution, the cronies were beheaded, but Daji, beautiful and wicked to the end, bewitched her executioners such that none were able to lift their weapons to strike her. Finally, it was Baby Tooth, using the magic gourd, who beheaded Daji, the evil of evils.

Baby Tooth was entrusted by the Supreme Jade Emperor of Heaven with the task of investing the deserving men and women of the conflict as gods, in accordance with the Register of the Investiture of Gods that Baby Tooth had been given by the God of South Pole. Bi Gan, who had died when King Zhou ordered that he give up a slice of his heart for a soup to cure Daji's "illness" was invested as a god, as were many other brave victims of King Zhou's cruelty. Yellow Flying Tiger, Grand Old Master, Ji Chang, and many of the other generals from both sides of the conflict were also invested as gods. Nezha survived the war and returned to his mountain. His final task completed, Baby Tooth retired to his native state of Lu. Baby Tooth himself was not invested as a god, but he was revered as one, even today. The Chou Dynasty lasted for 800 years (circa 1122-249 BC).

0-595-25419-5